THE
BALEFIRE
EXPRESS

Book One

DONOVAN LEWIS

Visit our website at **www.StillwaterPress.com** for more information.

First Stillwater River Publications Edition

ISBN: 978-1-960505-49-1

Library of Congress Control Number: 2023912641

1 2 3 4 5 6 7 8 9 10

Names: Lewis, Donovan, 1991- author.
Title: The Balefire Express. Book one / Donovan Lewis.
Description: First Stillwater River Publications edition. | Pawtucket, RI, USA :
    Stillwater River Publications, [2023]
Identifiers: ISBN: 978-1-960505-49-1 (paperback) | LCCN: 2023912641
Subjects: LCSH: Zombies--Fiction. | Messengers--Fiction. | Delivery of goods-
    -Fiction. | Dogsledding--Fiction. | LCGFT: Dystopian fiction. | Thrillers
    (Fiction) | Fantasy fiction. | Action and adventure fiction.
Classification: LCC: PS3612.E9627 B35 2023 | DDC: 813/.6--dc23

Written by Donovan Lewis.
Cover and interior design by Elisha Gillette.
Published by Stillwater River Publications, Pawtucket, RI, USA.

For Momo,
I made you a promise.

A promise that when we met again on
the other side of that grey rain curtain,
I would have some damn good stories to tell.

So, here's to honoring old scars,
embracing new adventures,
and keeping the promises
that matter most.

PART ONE

THE BALEFIRE EXPRESS

I

—

"Three hundred suns."

I pushed myself up from the bar. "Thanks for the drink, Ronny."

"OK, OK, OK. Five hundred suns."

"Six hundred suns, plus a hundred bonus for on-time delivery. The storms have been vicious this season. We might already have lost a crew, though I'm hoping they're just late," I replied.

"The package needs to be on time; it's worthless if you're late. It's a special case; it needs to get up to Skyroost and stay warm during the whole ride. My people will rig a battery to heat the package, but that'll only give you five days, maximum. After that, it will be as cold as ice and useless. You'll need to stop at a military outpost I know about to get the battery replaced, they already know to expect a courier."

I settled back down onto my stool and gestured to get the attention of Pietro, the bartender.

"Skinny Mule, with lime, please," I told him, knowing that a single slice of fresh fruit would double the price. But if everything worked out, I would soon have a fat payday coming in. Seven hundred suns was quite the windfall, easily two months' wages for your average soldier. If I were lucky, I could find cargo in Skyroost to bring back south on the return trip, but it was still a tidy sum even if I traveled empty on the return leg.

"You have my curiosity piqued, at least. But first, I need to know what I'm transporting. That's non-negotiable. And second, I don't think you've done the math on this. You would need a battery the size of my sled to run the heat for that long."

It was only in the last year or so that electricity had become commonplace this far north, and it was still more a novelty than anything else. The Duke's manor had a few strings of electrical lights, but it was mostly a status symbol. Wood and oil could do the same job and were far more dependable, especially when the weather rolled in.

Ronny gave me a genuine smile, the first I had seen from him tonight, then beckoned me to lean in closer.

"I have a contact, Boyd; he makes expeditions into one of the western exclusion zones, been dredging up all sorts of old-world technology." He said in a low voice, then held up a hand as I began to argue. "I know, don't worry, he's not exporting it, just pulling it apart to see how it all works. We don't have the metallurgy to completely recreate the machines anyway, but what we've cobbled together is still far more advanced than anything else you'll see in the Empire."

I leaned back and enjoyed a long sip of my drink, letting that ginger burn spread warmth through my chest. That lime looked like it had seen better days though, these storms were playing hell with food shipments, but it still tasted lovely.

"That's quite a tale. Though you seem to be forgetting that the church has outlawed any exploration of the exclusion zones, so I should just report you. Plus, you have already implied that you've given this tech to the military as well, which I imagine makes you an apostate twice over . . . .The inquisitors don't take kindly to that sort of behavior, and they pay informants well . . . ."

Ronny blanched, then let out a giant sigh when he caught me grinning.

"You're a terrible person Winona."

"Hey, I'm technically a deacon! You're lucky you didn't drop that information with a different courier, some would see you strung up for that offense. Thankfully for you, I take a more pragmatic view, though if anyone finds that battery on my sled, I'll swear I didn't know a thing about it. So, what are you trying to transport?"

"Weather equipment," Ronny said after taking a long drink to steady himself again. "Barometers, anemometers, and some other glasswork that can't withstand the cold."

"Fragile cargo too? Lovely." I gave a friendly wave to another courier coming in from the cold and contemplated how to proceed. "Why me? Everyone else turn you down?"

"It's because you're the best," he told me, even managing a straight face.

"Bullshit." I let out a boisterous laugh, which lapsed into a wet cough halfway through. I swear I caught a cold every time I was back in town; too many damn people. "Mildred is the best in town, and she just finished a run, though you'd have to pay her double what I'm asking. Gerald has an armored cab and more bandit kills than the next three sleds combined; I swear he rides through bandit territory on purpose. I even heard Old Muldoon is coming out of retirement. His team is twice the size of anyone else's, and he doesn't stop. Somehow keeps 'em running even when he sleeps."

"Oh, now who's full of it?" Ronny barked a laugh, waving his hand as if to disperse the lie. "Nobody can keep a team on course without a courier guiding them."

"Hand to my heart! Wouldn't have believed it if I hadn't seen it myself. His team rolled into the Yard, but nobody came out of the cab. We peeked in, and there he was, snoring!" I declared, enjoying the banter. Ronny was a decent guy, even when he was trying to underpay me.

"Regardless, I need you on this one, Winona. I've already sent two shipments to Skyroost. The first never arrived, and the second courier stumbled back out of the wilderness days later on foot. He was half dead, no balefire, and raving about green fire and talking ghouls. There's something on that road, maybe bandits, maybe worse, but nobody is getting to Skyroost by the conventional route, and this is the last battery I have available for the trip. You know how hard winter can hit when you live that far north; this equipment could make an enormous difference," he sighed, shaking his head.

"So, you came to the one sled that can take the unconventional route. That costs extra, you know. So, let's see . . . six hundred for the trip, another hundred for on-time delivery. Then you've got a fragile package, a contraband battery, and unconventional routing . . . I'll do it for a thousand fifty." Ronny began to argue, but I interrupted. "I know the price is steep, way more than I'd charge for a standard run up to Skyroost, but you've added some extra risk here, and I can't ignore that or budge on the price. You can take my offer or try walking the crate there yourself."

And then that glorious pause, there's no better feeling in bartering. You know you've got them, and they know that you know you've got them, and all that's left is the shaking of hands.

"Deal, you drive a hard bargain," Ronny admitted, extending his hand.

"I'm worth every sun, I assure you. I need to check on the team and my sled tonight, but I can head out tomorrow at first light when the gates open. Send a runner with the weight and dimensions of your package as soon as you can so I can plan accordingly. I'll write up the contract and send it back with him." I told Ronny, shaking his hand. I rose to depart, taking a moment to drain my drink before slamming the copper mug on the counter.

"Pietro put it on my tab!" I yelled as I pulled my overcoat from a peg on the wall.

"Hey *mu'dak*, you can't pay that tab if you're dead!" He laughed, throwing his hands up in mock anger.

Pietro was good people. He had the only bar in town that would open a tab for a courier; the mortality rate was high enough that a handful of those tabs were never closed by their original owners. But another courier would always pick up the bill; we took care of our own. I braced myself for the wind as I shouldered the door open and pressed out into the cold streets of Ozero.

And it was a windy one, dammit, though the true chill of winter was still weeks off. Every courier I knew would take a windless day at negative temperatures over a howler at ten degrees above every single time. This wind had nothing on its fiercer cousin beyond the wall, but that's not to say it was pleasant. Though you would always see one courier striding around bare-chested, proclaiming that it felt like a summer breeze to him. In my opinion, the meekest dogs barked the loudest, but to each their own. Hood up, I pressed on towards the Yard.

The Spine was the main road in town, starting from the Duke's manor at the north end of the settlement and stretching all the way to the Yard at the south. Or as the locals liked to say, from the brain of the town to the ass. And right where the kidneys would be on this body was Oleg's House of Curiosities. His store served the same purpose as kidneys too, since it seemed like all the weird or dangerous stuff that came into this town filtered through his place at one time or another.

The heavy door creaked open, setting a windchime arrangement of animal jawbones clattering.

"Normal people use bells, Oleg!" I hollered, shrugging out of my coat. I shook out my chin-length brown curls, trying to dispel the chill that had seeped in during the walk.

"*Devushka*! I have missed you! One moment!" A voice boomed from the doorway behind the counter.

I took a moment to browse his wares, an eclectic mix of occult material and the various bits and bobs people came in to sell or pawn. Drawings of the balefire brazier were common, the twisted iron of the holy container represented in miniature, supposedly offering the same protection as the genuine article. Alongside it was a smattering of lesser protective symbols from pre-cataclysm days. I don't know why people would trust in a god that didn't survive the end of the old world, but Oleg boasted that he did a thriving trade in little pentacles, hammers, and crosses. The rest of his shop displayed more practical wares of dubious quality, each with a little handwritten sign cheerily extolling their virtues; a barrel of rusty shovels (only slightly used!), bottles of murky lamp oil (100 percent pure guaranteed!) and frayed courier coats (ignore the stains!).

"Ah, Miss Winona, my favorite customer! It has been too long. You don't stop in, you don't write, it hurts my feelings!" Oleg laughed as he emerged from the curtained doorway with an armful of junk, spilling it on the counter in front of him.

"Oh, come off it, you old charmer. I've heard your new favorite is the Duke's wife, since you can pawn all this pentacle and incense crap off on her."

He stepped from behind the pile, a man of extremes. A rounded gut overhung his belt, though his thick arms still bulged with strength. Oleg may have indulged a bit too much in quality food and drink since retiring from his courier days, but the layers of fat could not fully disguise the dense muscle that could still snap a ghoul's spine in two. Multiple chins fought for dominance on his face, and he had started to bald in the past few years, though the hair that remained fanned out in a greying starburst on either side of his skull.

"The Duchess merely wishes to pursue . . . alternate means of protection in these trying times. I am merely a humble purveyor of such curios for those interested." Oleg shrugged.

"Uh-huh . . . Well, would this humble purveyor still be involved in certain . . . curios of a more practical application?" I asked, knowing the answer but enjoying the familiar exchange.

"Ahh, HAHA!" Oleg barked a laugh, tapping a finger against his nose. He strutted to his door, turning the lock and switching the sign to "CLOSED."

"This, this is why I like you, *Devushka*, nobody understands quality anymore! Come, let us see what Oleg has for you today," he chortled, leading the way behind the counter and holding back the curtain with a theatrical bow. "I assume you have a job you're shopping for?"

"To Skyroost, yes. Something time sensitive, so I'll be pulling long days. Gotta keep the weight down, though."

"Yes, yes, I know of your team, have no fear. Light, light, always light! Like you, eh? You must eat more, Winona; you are too skinny for this weather. A courier must have insulation to survive!" he laughed, slapping his bulging belly for emphasis.

Where Oleg's front room was a sprawling mess, the backroom was organizational brilliance. Every wall was lined with cabinets, each meticulously labeled in Oleg's cramped handwriting. There were large boxes that could have held a human body and tiny pigeonholes that stretched from floor to ceiling. A long table dominated the center of the room, holding the half-disassembled carcass of a pre-cataclysm machine that Oleg swept into an open drawer before I could get a good look. He then skipped around the room with surprising grace, opening and closing various containers while humming an old folk tune. In a moment, he had returned, delicately placing three items on the table. All three were intriguing, though I worked to keep my expression neutral. Oleg was a decent guy but a shrewd negotiator, and showing overt interest would increase the asking price.

I gave Oleg a "may I?" hand gesture, then picked up the first item at his nod.

"Now these, beautiful goggles, pre-cataclysm, exceedingly rare. Look at the golden hue of the lens, barely scratched! It is said that they cut out sun glare, increase your visual acuity, so useful in a courier's life, right? These would be a steal at one hundred suns, but for you, my dear friend, I would part with it for a mere seventy."

I picked the goggles up, turning them over in my hands. They seemed to be in decent shape, with only a few small scratches across the reflective surface. The original strap was missing, but the contemporary replacement looked well made, and after a moment adjusting it, I eagerly slipped them on.

Wow, the first thing I noticed wasn't even the view; it was the comfort. My own goggles hung on a thin leather strap that cut into the skin and gave me a pounding headache. The broad leather band of these goggles was well padded with sheepskin, as was the inside edge of the goggles where they pressed against my skin. It felt like the goggles were floating on my face, casting the room in a warm, amber hue. It was hard to judge exactly how effective it would be without using them in the light of day, but I had enough experience with various shades of crudely colored eyewear to appreciate the superior make and visibility.

"If these are so amazing, how'd you get someone to part with them? I can't imagine a courier giving these up."

"It was among the effects of a courier who owed me some outstanding debts upon his passing," Oleg shrugged. "Man spent years beyond the wall and died of a heart attack in his bed, oh the irony. Nobody you would know, though; he only came this way recently, was based further south."

"You know, Oleg . . . you still haven't paid me back for the gold mine job six months ago."

"Uhm, well, you know . . . these are grim times, money is tight . . . ," he protested weakly.

"That they are, but I'm sure we can come to an arrangement. I do believe I was working for you during that job, so maybe an . . . employee discount is an order? At least until you can come up with the money."

Oleg's smile became wooden as his eyes narrowed. "Of course . . . it is only . . . fair, after all."

"Oh, lighten up, you big bear. You need at least one shrewd customer to keep you on your toes," I laughed. We bartered down to fifty suns and moved on to the next item.

I did not need an introduction for these as, while uncommon, they were far from unique. It was a box of flares, though of a newer design, fresh from the capital's alchemists. Oleg extolled their virtues, explaining the improvements that had been made in the construction and composition. Typical flares had come a long way in recent years, but they were still horribly smokey and unreliable if you ever let them get wet. I waffled for a moment, hyper-aware of the payday I hadn't yet earned. Oleg clearly wanted me to take the box, but I restrained myself to a single flare, mainly because I knew how the world worked.

If I passed up on these, the fates would do their damnedest to see me soaked to the bone and stranded in the dark just to prove that I should have made the purchase. There was a multitude of scary things beyond the wall, but finding yourself soaking wet in below-freezing temperatures was one of the most terrifying propositions a courier could face.

And lastly, the mystery item, a long shape bound in burgundy fabric. Oleg had a predatory grin now, that salesman smile when they know they have something you would pay anything for. He slowly untucked the edges of the wrapping, letting the tension build, then whisked the fabric away with a flourish.

I took in the sight of the item, looked back up at Oleg, then down at the item again.

Then I punched him in the arm.

"You're going to get us excommunicated!" I barked, scanning the room in a panic, scarcely able to breathe until I verified that all the windows were covered.

"Only if the church hears of it!" Oleg shrugged, "And I do not think you are the type of person to be ratting me out. Many would be angry to hear that dear Oleg has had to close shop."

I looked down at the item again, taking in the details now—a short club of vibrant-red wood polished to a beautiful, lacquered sheen. The top of the club widened like a rowing oar, and shards of polished black stone jutted from the sides of the oar. The whole ensemble was carved with the elaborate curling metal iconography of the Balefire Church.

"Where . . . I don't even know where to start, Oleg. Why do you have a coalblade? How did you get your hands on this?" I gestured for his permission to touch it, and he nodded.

Oleg looked anything but cheerful now as he regarded the weapon. "You remember hearing about Glenhearth, a few months back?"

"Of course, their balefire went out somehow, ghouls tore apart the whole town. I met the courier that came across it, he said it looked like a slaughterhouse. The church declared it cursed ground, no salvage on penalty of excommunication," I answered.

"Mhmm, this is true. Unless you know a cadre of foreigners from across the ice fields that are in town to do a bit of trading, and you convince them that the anger of a church they do not believe in is worth far less than a fat bag of suns. I was expecting the usual knickknacks, hidden savings under the floorboards, etcetera. But what the church will not tell you is that they banned salvage because a cardinal and his retinue were passing through that town. They were torn apart with all the rest, and my ice fielders stripped the party of everything that was not nailed down. I've been burning church robes in my fireplace for a week to get rid of the things."

"Wow, a real coalblade, I've only seen them in ceremonies. But Oleg, let us say I did want one, and I'm not saying I do because if the church found out, they would cut me open and leave me tied to a tree for the ghouls. But even if I did, you know I don't have enough money to afford this. Hell, I don't know if the Duke could afford it." I picked up the weapon with reverential care. The handle was wrapped in a rough white leather I didn't recognize, but it provided a fantastic grip. Hefting it and giving it a few experimental swings, I found the balance to be perfect—top heavy, like an axe, with just enough weight to add a vicious heft to a strike.

"The Duke is the problem, actually. Or rather, his wife is. The Duchess does love my wares...a bit too much. I have two artisans in town making more baubles to sell off to her every week. But the Duke is concerned about security, and every week she stops by with more guards in tow. Eventually, he is going to take an interest in his wife's new obsession, and I worry what he will find if he sends his men sniffing around my shop. This...This is too hot for me to hold onto."

I set the weapon back on the table, handling it as if it were a holy relic. "Soooooo, what you're saying is that I'd be doing you a favor by taking it off your hands."

"Not so fast, *Devushka*. We'd be doing each other a favor. So, I give you this, and we wipe the slate clean from the gold mine. And if anybody catches you with it, you did not get it from me."

I thought about it for a moment, but the choice wasn't hard. I would take the Balefire Church's ire over death in the icy wastes any day. "You've got yourself a deal, Oleg. Though I'll need a bag if you please, I can't exactly stroll through town with this in hand."

II

—

Evening was well underway by the time I left Oleg's shop. He had a "family tradition" of celebrating a big sale with a shot of his cousin's rotgut vodka. One shot had a habit of becoming three, and I forced myself to leave before I ruined any chance of an early start tomorrow. Oleg had found a cloth bag large enough to conceal the coalblade and also given me the sheath in which the weapon had been found. The brown leather of the sheath had a bit of water damage but seemed overall intact, and anyway, it wasn't like I could stroll through town with a coalblade strapped to my back.

There wasn't much natural beauty to be had in the frozen hellscape I called home, but the sunsets were an exception. Blue sky to orange and red, shifting and blurring together from moment to moment. It always reminded me of my dad. Whenever he returned from a trip, it was always just before dark, the last rays of sunlight silhouetting him as he opened the door.

The Spine was still congested at this hour but emptied out quickly as I made my way further south. The external gates of Ozero would be closed for the night, so there was little business going on amongst the warehouses that crowded the southern quarter of the city. I could still feel the warmth of alcohol in my chest by the time I reached my destination, but the fierce cold was a potent remedy for the lingering effects of the drink. At least it meant I wouldn't embarrass myself in front of the guards . . . again. The Yard functioned like its own miniature town, with separate walls enclosing it and an internal gate separating it from the rest of the settlement. I didn't recognize the guards on duty today, so I figured I would make things easy by fishing out my holy symbol, a pendant shaped like a stylized brazier pressed flat with a chip of amethyst at the center. All couriers were tangentially members of the clergy by law, and some guards were sticklers about proving your credentials prior to entry. Of course, Ronny would have no such symbol, but the contract detailing our deal would identify him as a client.

I stepped in front of the guards, bowed stiffly, then held the tiny brazier up by the chain, letting the amethyst twinkle in the firelight, a pale imitation of balefire's purple flame.

"Courier requesting entry," I intoned.

One guard stepped forward, clad in the traditional garb; layers of thick fabric and leather covered him from head to toe, with not a single loose buckle or strap you could grab onto. It would do little against a battle-axe, but that was not what this guard was protecting the populace from. In his hand was a long staff, topped with a circular brazier, smoldering with purple flame. All balefire braziers were open-topped, as the magic would sputter out if completely enclosed, though only the upper echelon of the clergy was rumored to know why that was. The brazier sat in an elaborate gimbal to counter this, allowing it to stay upright regardless of the direction the staff was moving.

"What be your purpose?" The guard intoned.

"Deacon Winona, checking sled and team for a morning departure to Skyroost. The patron of the trip is a local merchant, Ronald. He will be delivering the package tomorrow morning. Oh- and a boy will be here later tonight to deliver the dimensions of the parcel for planning purposes."

The guard nodded to his compatriot, who fished out a key and unlocked the wicket door, a smaller door set into the wood of the heavy main gate.

I squeezed through and entered the Yard, letting its unique ambiance wash over me. The first thing you notice is the light. Ozero had two grand braziers, one atop the church in the affluent part of town and the other in the Yard. The edifice here was a massive construction—a metal cage large enough to hold a horse—mounted on a forty-foot-high scaffold. The brazier blazed with purple fire, casting the entirety of the walled space in its holy light.

The next thing you notice is the smell. One might think the late autumn chill would dull the scent, but I don't think there's a place in the world with temperatures cold enough to completely banish the smell of rotting corpses. Tall corpses, short corpses, bloated and emaciated corpses, the Yard accepted all types. Some were so fresh that you might mistake them for a living person at a glance. Others were merely bone and magic, nothing left of them but a skeleton and the ethereal purple glow in their eye sockets that signified the balefire's influence. I quickstepped down the path, making way for a sled hauling pallets of wood that crossed behind me. At the front of the sled were a trio of skellies—slang for ghouls that had rotted away until nothing but bare bone remained. Good laborers, skellies were the strongest ghouls we used. It was a prevailing belief among the uninitiated that a ghoul was strongest when it was freshly turned, but most people didn't realize that ghouls were animated by magic, not muscle, so those kilograms of frozen meat were just slowing them down. Contributing to this myth was the fact that wandering ghouls usually befell some misfortune long before their flesh rotted away entirely, so encountering a skelly in the wild was rare. No, the magic that infused them only seemed to intensify with age, granting them strength far beyond that of the living people they had once been. The downside was that skellies had lost so much of themselves that they could only obey the simplest of commands: *run, stop, lift, pull.* They also had lost all but the most ingrained skills and talents that made the fresher undead so useful.

Well, useful when they weren't tearing the flesh from helpless people. But that's where the Balefire Church and its miraculous flame came in. There were the obvious theological benefits of uniting the masses and such, but my job relied on the more practical aspect of the fire. Any ghoul that wandered into the light of the balefire was . . . calmed. I guess that was the best word. They would still attack if you gave them a chance, but in the same way that an aggressive dog would lash out. And like a dog, you could train them to follow all manner of simple tasks. Like, pull a sled.

I stopped in at the general store and put in an order for the trip. Like most couriers, I bought all my specialty gear, favorite rations, and such in town, but all the basic needs could be supplied in the Yard at a price kept low by church decree. The next stop was my sled, sitting in one of the covered berths set along the wall. I had inspected every centimeter of her after my last run, but complacent couriers soon became dead ones. Anyway, the *Ridgerunner* was practically a relative at this point. She had been in my family since before I was born and hadn't let me down yet; I'd be dead and buried before I let her fall into disrepair.

Measuring just four and a half meters long and a hair under two meters wide, she was one of the smallest sleds I knew of making multi-day runs. A small sled could make the short hops between towns with ease, but spending night after night in the wild dark added layers of complexity to the job. You needed the right amount of food for the trip, and the same balance had to be struck for tools, replacement parts, and everything else. Pack too much, and you wouldn't be able to haul enough cargo to make a living. Pack too little, and . . . you died.

I knew the *Ridgerunner* inside and out. She had solid bones, but even I had to admit her appearance was patchwork. My girl had so many upgrades, refurbishments, and slapdash repairs that I wondered if there was a single original part remaining from the day my dad had built her. The sled had three primary sections: cab, sleeping compartment, and cargo bay. My inspection started at the front, where I searched for any sign of damage. Most of the sled was constructed from treated pine and scavenged aluminum to keep the weight down, but no material could withstand the rigors of the north indefinitely, though thankfully, any scratches or gouges I found looked superficial. Glass was sold at exorbitant prices, so my windshield was composed of six separate panes arranged in a two-by-three panel rectangle. It could be a nuisance at times since the wooden frame between planes could create blind spots, but the upsides were well worth it; the wilds were not kind to fragile materials, and this setup meant I could replace a single broken pane instead of having the entire sheet shattered by some mishap. The current windshield glass was pitted and cracked with age and hard use, but I figured I could get a few more runs in before needing a replacement.

The cab itself was quite austere, though I would double-check all the stored charts and navigational equipment tomorrow morning when I had more light to work by. I also pulled a blank contract from a drawer and tucked it into my coat for later.

Once that was done, I ducked inside the living area, which appeared at first to be a bare, meter-wide corridor that stretched the width of the sled behind my cab. Any courier worth their salt was a master at utilizing every centimeter of usable space, and this room held far more than a glance could tell. Almost every available surface was taken up by a drawer or cubbyhole, and even the ceiling was festooned with loops and hooks that one could hang items from. A small table could fold out from one wall while my cramped cot folded down from the opposite side to settle in the gap between the two walls. The wooden board my cot sat on was just slightly thicker than it needed to be, and a secret latch split the top from the bottom to reveal a hidden space. No courier I could think of would risk the punishment of stealing from a sled, but with something like a coalblade, I wasn't just going to hazard leaving it out for anyone to find. After hiding my newfound contraband, I sorted through my cargo bay, running through a written checklist I kept of various supplies needed for the journey. Lastly, I crawled underneath the sled, checking for rot on her underbelly while making sure the metal runners that the sled would slide on were free of damage.

Once I'd given the *Ridgerunner* a clean bill of health, I made a quick detour to the Yard's base of operations, a squat stone building manned by a bored looking aspirant. Contracts were copied from a standard template, so it was a simple task to scribble in the details and complete the form. I left this with the worker with orders to give it to Ronny's messenger if the kid stopped by. Most civilians never stepped foot in the Yard, and those that did were in and out as fast as possible. The messenger was more likely to head towards the well-lit building than to go wandering off into the half-light in search of a courier.

With that done, I set off toward the abattoir to check on my team.

They could be felt before they were seen. That was how the magic of the balefire worked: when both a person and a ghoul were bathed in that purple light, a connection was formed between them, a bond. This bond strengthened with proximity to the flame, and I began to feel it now like soft music slowly growing in volume. The first ghoul I felt was Tybalt, as always. My oldest and strongest skelly, his mind was barely present, just a discordant drum beat of repressed violence. He was the brawler on my team, the ghoul I set loose when bandits attacked and bloodshed was the sole recourse. Curved metal claws had been affixed to his fingertips to add to his already potent lethality, the additions making his hands look like the talons of a bird of prey. His bones were bleached white and mottled in places with smears of grey paint, an effective camouflage in snowy conditions.

The rest of my team's melodies rose into my consciousness soon after, adding their sound to Tybalt's. The oldest of them were drum-beats, loud but simple, while the youngest had the essence of a violin or guitar, soft and complex. Every courier I knew ran their team in the same order. The newest, freshest, smartest ghouls in the front to lead and the oldest in the back, dumber now but far stronger workhorses. I had eight ghouls on my sled team now, and I sent a pulse of welcoming thought to them as I reached their cage.

From youngest to oldest, they were: King, Bonk, Grah, Craven, Heist, Scramble, Champ, and Tybalt.

A key had been given to me when I housed my ghouls, and I unlocked the door, giving it a quick glance for any signs of obvious damage. The balefire light kept the ghouls in a more docile state than their wild counterparts, but if that fire went out . . . well, we would have nearly a hundred wild ghouls clamoring for our flesh. Hence why the Yard had its own walls separating it from the town proper; it was both a defensive bastion and a prison for the walking dead. With that macabre thought in mind, I opened the cage and stepped inside, checking over the team with the same care I had given my sled.

I started with King, of course. He was the leader, the top dog who ran at the front and led the team; only after I had looked him over did I move to check the others. None of them could speak, of course, but they all showed their quirks in subtle ways. Craven, for example, pressed himself into a corner, constantly on guard, while Scramble had somehow climbed up and threaded his legs through the top of the cage, and was now dangling upside down like a child on a playground. Despite their various physical and sartorial differences, each wore the same pulling harness that would connect them to the sled through the main gangline. These harnesses were constructed from a series of leather loops that helped to distribute the pulling strain evenly across the ghoul's body. I had added sheepskin padding in certain areas, especially across the shoulders, to reduce the wear and tear damage that the shifting leather could deal to ghoul flesh; even bare bone could be worn down by friction over time. The necromantic power that animated them did help to some extent, the magic binding the bones together so that joints could flex long after the associated ligaments had rotted away. Even the flesh was affected, desiccating to the texture of leather instead of immediately going to rot. It was one reason why ghouls could be so damned loud; their lungs held on far longer than most would expect.

Those thoughts of decay brought my attention back to the hole in my team; I kept reaching my mind out to find the missing ghoul, like when your tongue happens across a hole where a lost tooth should be. We had lost Wizard on the last run. He'd been an old man with a long white beard before he was a ghoul, and the strain of pulling had added stress to some preexisting bone damage, building bit by bit until he literally snapped in half mid-run.

It was a surreal moment, the crunch of breaking bone, his spine cracking in half, lower body bouncing down the line until the bones were pulverized under the runners of my still-moving sled. By the time I had the sled stopped, his flailing top half was so tangled in the harness that I'd had to cut the thing off him.

Couriers were split on what to do with a lame ghoul. Many would just hack them to pieces so they couldn't hurt anyone and leave them on the side of the road, but that never sat right with me. Cut a ghoul in half, and the legs would run off on their own. Even bashing their skull in would not stop the random clawing spasms as they searched for prey. It was obvious to any courier that ghouls retained some part of their past life, even if they were just distant echoes, and abandoning one that had served me well never felt right.

So, I packed his shattered bits up in my sled and brought him home. The priests had a weekly ceremony where they would commit the bodies of ghouls to the purple flame. The fire that helped us control them was also the single force we knew of that could truly "kill" a ghoul. I hoped that the cremation had brought Wizard some small measure of peace.

"Let's go, King," I called; my mood soured by the memory. Technically, King responded to my thoughts, not my voice, but vocalizing my orders always helped me get the message across.

Not that King needed prompting; he was sharp as a tack, alarmingly so sometimes. He was also the first ghoul I had ever made a dedicated attempt to preserve, given how useful his skillset was. All ghouls we put into service went through basic preservation, removal of organs, and such, but there were ways to go further if you had the coin. I won't go into the gory details, but there are plenty of back-alley ghoul morticians with procedures that could delay rot. He was also my only ghoul that wore a full set of clothes, with a mask and tight-fitting coat and pants to prevent the damage done by running through underbrush naked for days on end. I had cut holes in the fabric at specific intervals to reveal the dead skin beneath so that the balefire light could always reach him regardless of how he moved. King also had boots wrapped up to the top of his calf. All my ghouls wore them, though there were a fair number of the old guard couriers who would judge me for it. They believed that ghouls were animals and should be treated as such. I believed it was idiotic to let your prime ghouls wear their bare feet down to bony nubs.

I flagged down a worker and ordered a full meal for my team since we would not have time to hunt on the way, then continued with King to the cartographer's building. The line already had two couriers with their lead ghouls in tow, also planning for early departures tomorrow, but it was a good opportunity to catch up with friends, and the line moved quick enough anyway.

"Here to Skyroost, quickest route available," I told an aide making their way down the line, and they had my order ready when I made it to the front.

"You're up, King. Watch the pictures . . . Waaattttcccchhhh," I ordered, then nodded to the cartographer on duty. She held up the first image, a realistic painting of the front gate we would depart through tomorrow. King grunted, a chuffing exhalation through his dead lips, then jerked his hand to the side in a clumsy wave. The next was a rarity, an actual photograph; the colors faded. It depicted the crossroads just outside of town. And on and on from there, flicking through a variety of photos, paintings, and drawings that represented the various waypoints between here and our destination. King had run this route before, but giving him a refresher would keep me from having to micromanage him every step of the way. Gods only knew how ghouls continued to see a picture long after their eyes had rotted out, but that was a mystery I would leave to the scholars.

After that, it was back to the cages, just in time for feeding. The ghouls technically didn't need to feed; the magic that animated the creatures would sustain them indefinitely. But the life force they drained from their prey tonight would energize the creatures for a time, and that strength would give us a boost of speed on the first leg of our journey. As for me, I would stick to coffee.

Pig was on the menu, and I put King back in the cage just before the meal arrived. Hypothetically, I should have been able to mentally hold back my team while the workers put the pig in, but ghouls were notoriously unpredictable around a meal. Instead, the back of the cage had a layered system where the pig could be secured into a partitioned portion of the cage. The partition was then removed, and the ghouls were free to feast. The frenzy that followed painted the cage floor red and made it abundantly clear why the abattoir had its name. I watched, though, every time they fed. I had to. It was easy to think of them like pets after a while; smart, dependable, loyal. Right up until you made a mistake, and you became their next meal.

III

———

Ronny was late, the bastard. I had no idea what the problem was, I'd already gotten word that his payment had been submitted and was sitting in the Yard's coffers, so it wasn't like he was trying to stiff me. My team was hitched up and ready to go, though Craven was giving me problems. Bonk and Wizard used to run behind King, but with Wizard's destruction, Bonk and King now had to run side by side. Craven was now directly behind the leader, and the gutless bastard kept trying to back away from him, pulling the sled off center as I steered it into position by the outer gates. My team was excited, though, energized by the meal last night and straining at their harnesses. Ready to move, ready to run, I had to drop the snow hook brakes on the ground just to keep them from yanking the sled forward.

"Sorry, I'm so sorry! Packing took longer than we expected!" Ronny burst into view, two assistants maneuvering a skelly-drawn cart with a suspiciously large package on it.

"Daylight is wasting. The sun doesn't give a damn about your excuses . . . And neither do I." I barked at him as he brought the cart alongside, which confirmed that the size of the parcel was off.

Ronny went to unbuckle the straps securing his crate, but I put a hand over the buckle to stop him. "That's not the package we agreed upon, Ronny. I got the dimensions you sent, and that thing is at least two meters square, nearly double what you told me."

"Well, yes . . . ," he mumbled, looking guilty, glancing between the crate and my sled. "I gave you the dimensions of the package . . . I sent a runner last night. We needed to secure the cargo inside a larger crate that held the battery and heating elements this morning, which added to the bulk. The battery barely adds any weight, though, I promise."

There was a moment where I imagined the sound Ronny would make if hurled over the wall into the wilderness beyond, and Tybalt perked up nearby, picking up on my violent thoughts.

Then I took a long, calming breath before speaking. "I need to know the weight to judge how fast I can move. I need the dimensions to know what else I can bring along. Why would I care about the dimensions of a package . . . if you were just going to put it INSIDE ANOTHER CRATE!?"

Then I turned away, pulling up the snow hooks that anchored the sled.

"What are you doing?" Ronny asked as I began to lead my team back toward the abattoir.

"Putting my team back in their cage, go find a courier who has a higher tolerance for bullshit!" I called over my shoulder.

I heard him let out a nervous laugh, then pause, then scramble after me as he realized I was serious.

"But you can't! This needs to get to Skyroost! We had an agreement!" he began to shout, flapping the contract out in front of him. He also happened to get too close to Tybalt, who took the opportunity to throw his arms around Ronny, pulling the struggling man into a bony embrace.

I sent out a spike of thought, overpowering Tybalt's instinct to take a bite out of his next meal, but it was a close thing. I took my time walking back to the restrained man, picking the contract up off the ground where it had fallen.

"Yes, we had an agreement, an agreement to transport a package of a certain size to a location. You change the package; you change the deal. If I can't trust you to be honest about this, I can't trust that this crate isn't a dozen liters of nitroglycerin ready to blow me sky-high when I hit the first bump in the road. Your payment will be returned to you, minus a penalty for late cancellation."

Ronny was starting to turn quite an alarming shade of purple as Tybalt's grip tightened. "Medicine! It's medicine!" he gasped.

I signaled Tybalt, who released the man to fall to his knees in the mud. "Skyroost..." He gaped like a fish, trying to get his breath back, "They reported a few sick people on a supply run, then a dozen confirmed cases of cholera on the next run. We haven't been able to get word from them since then, no idea how far it has spread. Please... I'm sorry I lied, but you were my last hope. I have family up there. I had to try."

This job had more red flags than I cared to count. A time-sensitive run, on a team missing a ghoul, to a location that could be shaping up to be the next plague town. But cholera was a bad way to go, a real bad way. If Ronny was right about the normal routes being blocked, I had the only sled with a chance of making it, of saving those people. The fact that he lied about the package was an annoyance, though not necessarily the deal breaker I made it out to be. I always planned a bit of leeway for my packages, and the trip should still work, assuming Ronny wasn't transporting a cube of solid lead or some such. Worst case, I could always drop my nonessential gear during the trip and retrieve it later.

Sometimes I cursed the sense of morality my dad had instilled in me. It was far safer to be a cold-hearted bastard, someone who wouldn't let their heart tug them into a dangerous situation. It was often a more lucrative attitude as well, but in this case, I decided that my heart of gold should come with an equally high price tag.

"Damn me for a fool! Fine, thirteen hundred suns, call it hazard pay. Deal?" I extended a hand to the kneeling figure.

"Yes, please, I'm sorry I lied, but I have family there. Please help them," he took my hand and shook it.

I leaned back and pulled him to his feet, then launched into action now that the deal was struck. First, I ran to the other side of my sled, unhooking Champ from the gangline.

"Crate, now!" I ordered, sending him lumbering down towards the crate, still sitting on its cart.

Then I clambered up onto my sled, hurriedly unclipping gear to create a space in the back of the cargo bay wide enough to accommodate the larger package. While this was going on, I sent a mental pulse, and King responded, tugging against his harness until the others caught on, pulling together to lead the sled back toward the gate. There was a horrific crunching noise nearby as Champ tangled himself in the packing straps of the cart, panicked like a cat with a string tied to his tail, and reduced the cart to kindling to get free. He was smart enough to keep the crate safe at least and returned with it held aloft over his head.

"Here, here!" I directed him to the open spot I had cleared, and he placed it down with surprising delicacy. Ronny gave me the new weight and dimensions, which I scrawled onto the side of the crate with a stick of charcoal, wincing at the increase. That "light" battery tipped the scale to the limit of what I was comfortable hauling, and that was assuming Ronny was telling the truth this time. Any scrap of guilt I might have felt about charging Ronny such a premium faded in an instant, and I made a mental note to get the crate weighed if I could find a cargo scale at one of my pitstops.

By the time I had the crate buckled down and Champ untangled and back in line, the priest was there for the most important part. Thank the gods, it was Rosco, an aged, perpetually smiling priest that was far more concerned with his expensive cigars than the various scriptures and intonations required by the ceremony of the Passing of the Flame.

"Here we gather to gift Deacon Winona a portion of our sacred balefire so that she may brave the wicked wastes beyond our walls. Godspeed and give 'em hell!" he cackled, which quickly turned into a hacking cough. With a wave of his hand, two acolytes came forward bearing a small container with a half dozen smoldering coals. They mounted either side of my sled, then dumped the coals into the brazier mounted on top of my cab. There was a flare of purple light, and my own miniature balefire roared to life on top of my sled. It was a flame I could take with me out into the wilderness, one that would allow me to maintain that magical bond with my team beyond the confines of the Yard. I bowed to Father Rosco, then turned to accept a sizable bag of coins from Ronny.

"Don't worry, that crate is as good as there already, courier's promise," I told him, winking.

With every preparation done, I climbed into the cab of my sled, settling against the padded rear wall and gripping the handles just under the windshield. There was a small ledge I could lean on but no place to sit. My dad always explained the construction choice by saying that sitting couriers became sleeping couriers, and sleeping couriers became dead ones. The guards ahead cracked open the outer gates, pulling them wide and letting in a chill wind from the frozen wasteland beyond. The purple light of the brazier poured in from a skylight above, binding the ghouls to my will.

And there it was, the adrenaline rush, right on time. That high that comes from challenging the unknown and knowing you might just be clever enough to make it back alive. I could feel my team pulsing in my head, almost begging for the command they knew was coming.

"OK. Balefire Express, next stop Skyroost . . . Let's run!"

King responded first, his mind a deep base thrum, like plucking the lowest string of a guitar in slow repetition, a metronome the other ghouls tuned to. Tybalt and Champ answered his call, gripping their chest harnesses with skeletal hands and leaning forward, taking the weight of the sled and pulling it forward, decimeter by decimeter, then faster, their minds a pair of steady timpani drumbeats. It almost looked like they would trample the pair in front of them before Scramble and Heist caught on. I saw Heist tuck something into a hole in her abdomen, likely another of the shiny trinkets she seemed to accumulate out of thin air. But the pair finally understood the message, taking up the slack of the gangline and adding their energetic snare drum noises to the building song. Lastly were my three fawns, the fresh ghouls who were still a bit clumsy but held on to that useful spark of individuality. Grah, Bonk, and Craven all stumbled for a moment, then synchronized and pulled with the team, adding their music and completing the mental melody. The sled moved to a walking pace, then a jog, then a full run as we slid out into the wilderness beyond the wall.

IV

——

The light was dazzling at first, as it always was when the sun shone on the snowy plains surrounding Ozero. I sighed, steeling myself for a day of squinting against the glare, then laughed aloud as I remembered yesterday; I had made a purchase for exactly this occasion. With near-giddy excitement, I leaned over to the small fixed table that covered the third of the cab opposite the door. From one of the many cubbyholes, I pulled out my new goggles and eagerly slid them on. Immediately my eyes relaxed, the wondrous amber lenses dulling the harsh brightness of the snow. They were also far clearer than my old, scratched goggles, and the color brought out further details in the scenery that I would have missed otherwise. It was one of those wondrous moments (like the first time you try coffee) where afterward, you wonder how you had ever made it through life without it.

The sled cruised down the gentle slope outside the city, holding speed as my team found a steady rhythm after their initial acceleration. As we reached the bottom of the short hill, the road curved to follow the tree line, paralleling the walls of the city. The main gate of Ozero was already open wide, revealing a host of workers whose vocations could not be practiced in the city. In front of them were the soldiers, moving ahead of the crowd and dressed in close-fitting leather armor like those of the Yard guards, though these men and women carried poleaxes instead of staffs of holy balefire. A handful of ghouls had wandered near the city during the night, but the soldiers set about their clearing duties with gusto. Their weapons were the perfect tool for the job—a five-foot length of hardwood tipped with a long, leaf-bladed spear point. Just below the spear, a half-moon axe blade jutted out, with a thick hammerhead mirroring it on the opposite side. The warriors moved in squads of three, and I had a front-row seat to the nearest squad executing a textbook takedown. The first member (usually the rookie) charged a ghoul, spearing it in the ribcage and driving the creature to the ground. He held the ghoul there, leaning his weight on the haft of his weapon while his companions closed in from either side, reducing the ghoul to a pulp of bone shards and rotten flesh with long swings of axe and hammer. After they had broken the arms and legs enough to render the creatures immobile, chain gangs of prisoners would come out to scoop the ghoul giblets into carts for burning in the grand brazier. A prisoner could earn a reduced sentence with the work, but the job was so foul that most convicts chose to remain in their cells. Once the all-clear was given, the mass of workers waiting by the gates dispersed, moving to their various tasks. The snowy track I was on ringed the entirety of the city, and the woodsmen came out every morning to keep the space between the road and the walls clear of any trees or brush that tried to take root. No force, alive or undead, would have any natural cover to hide behind if they tried to attack Ozero. Most vital of the emerging workers were the food producers. Farmers went to their greenhouses to coax their plants to life, while fishermen moved towards the lake, where they would break the ice at various points, retrieving traps and dropping fishing lures. Almost all the city's food was stockpiled during the harvest, but fresh fish or a few berries could be sold at a premium to those suffering from culinary boredom. Herds of sheep and cows were last, driven out to pasture by their shepherds because, well, nobody wanted to walk *behind* two hundred farm animals.

The scene of the countryside coming to life was so distracting that I almost missed the speed stripes on the road ahead. I dug out my father's lovingly maintained pocket watch and noted the time as we passed the first marker, a tall tree with horizontal stripes of red paint up the trunk. The tint of my new goggles distorted the color somewhat, another reason I had almost missed my mark. I noted the time again as we passed the second marker. Then it was time for the hidden killer, the monster that haunted the dreams of even the staunchest courier—Math.

From another cabinet of my table, I pulled out my whiz wheel, a little marvel of mathematics comprised of three interconnected wooden wheels that rotated in a stack, each with an array of numbers around the edge. Before I tried to slay the math monster, I sent a mental pulse to remind King of the intersection ahead. *Take the turn,* I ordered, *but plan for a stop at the Farmhouse.* King gave me the mental equivalent of a sarcastic salute and began the turn, angling us off the loop road and onto a wide track leading away from Ozero. With our course set, I returned my focus to inside the cab. The speed stripes had given me time over a set distance, and I spun the disks of the whiz wheel to align the two numbers and give me a speed, which I noted in my courier's log. That speed was vital for two reasons, it would let me calculate how long it would take me to get to Skyroost, and it would let me gauge how much the loss of Wizard was hampering my team. The results were mixed: The good news was that even running an incomplete team, I should be able to reach that halfway outpost by late morning of the fifth day without pushing too hard. The bad news was that Wizard's absence had reduced our speed noticeably. It wasn't a backbreaking loss, but it was an annoyance. It was possible I could have found a spare ghoul in the Yard before I left (they kept replacements on hand for just such situations), but I was loath to add a random ghoul to my team. Breaking a new team member in was an arduous, time-consuming process and not something I would risk during a time-sensitive run unless it was a ghoul I could get some real utility out of. My main concern was that if I suffered another team loss on this trip, I might end up severely short on the necessary ghoul-power to pull the sled. I had a possible solution in mind, though, and it involved my first stop of the trip: The Farmhouse.

No person in living memory had ever seen the Farmhouse host any farm animals or crops. The running joke was that it had been a dilapidated wreck when the first humans had walked the earth, and things had only gone downhill for the establishment since then. It did serve a valuable purpose, though, as a meeting house/bar/roadside inn. Its main customers were late couriers who were going to arrive at Ozero's closed gates after dark, but it also served as a stopping point for those on longer trips who, for whatever reason, preferred to stay outside the city walls. Lucky for me, it should still be packed at this time of day, and I would arrive before most of the overnighting couriers started to depart, leaving one by one. The Farmhouse was a well-guarded secret, and if all the sleds arrived together at the gates every morning, those in charge would start to wonder where their couriers were spending their nights.

King knew the route, thankfully, turning off the track to skirt a refuse pile so pungent that even the frigid cold could not mask it. It was effective at deterring passersby from discovering the hidden path, at least. We had to slow our pace as the forest path narrowed, though at least it gave me time to finish my log entry. Bolted to the outside of the cab was a quadruple pack of weather instruments: thermometer (temperature), barometer (air pressure), hygrometer (humidity), and anemometer (wind speed). The anemometer was next to useless while on the move, but the others might give me a heads-up on upcoming changes in weather. In a world of zero visibility whiteouts and torrential freezing rain, even a vague prediction could be a lifesaver. I had a bit more paperwork to do, but the Farmhouse was drawing near, and I wasn't about to leave my valuable navigational tools strewn about the cab. The same laws against thievery didn't apply out in the wild. Most couriers still held to them, but "most" was not something I was going to put my trust in.

The Farmhouse's lot was still packed at this hour, though the early risers were already at their sleds, preparing for departure. The vast majority were skimmers, smaller sleds almost identical to pre-cataclysm dog sleds. Most skimmers ran teams of four tough skellies with one bright fawn to lead. Light and fragile, they were limited to day trips but made up for it with a top speed far above any a long hauler sled like mine could manage; I was banking on that fact to help me out on my own trip now. The sleds were arrayed in a wide circle around the aged structure, their balefire light creating a protective shield of violet light. The Farmhouse had no brazier of its own, but the ghoul population was thin enough this close to a major settlement that it was almost never an issue. I pulled into the lot and found an open slot around the perimeter; the snow and earth churned to thick mud by the passage of innumerable sleds. Hopping down, I winced as my boots sank into the muck, and there was a moment of panic where I thought I might trip face-first into the filth. Putting a hand on my cab to stabilize myself, I squelched over to Scramble and Champ, detaching their harnesses from the gangline. Together, we drew a heavy tarp over the cargo bay; it wasn't much, but it would keep the weather and prying eyes off my cargo. Unwilling to risk getting stuck in the mud, I decided to have Scramble ferry me across. I ordered him to turn around and stepped down onto him from the raised sled. My feet fit comfortably on top of his hip bones while my hands used his clavicles as handles. It wasn't a dignified sight, but it beat a face full of mud. I ordered my noble steed across the expanse, ignoring the stares of other couriers; clearly, they were just jealous of my ingenuity. Scramble deposited me at the door with a gentleness that belied his massive strength, then wandered back, clambering on top of the *Ridgerunner* alongside Champ to assume guard duty. They'd keep anyone from getting too close while using more discretion than I could expect from Tybalt.

I walked to the door, nodded to a bemused old man sitting on a bench, then pushed my way into the dim interior of the Farmhouse. The first thing that hit me was the acrid scent of pyreweed, a useful but mildly addictive plant. Drying and smoking it like tobacco gave you a warm toasty feeling and could help stave off frostbite for a bit. That made it a godsend to couriers if they found themselves stranded without shelter; even I had a pouch of the stuff tucked away for emergencies. The problem was that overuse could leave you with nasty shivers, which you then self-medicated by smoking...more pyreweed. Given that effect, smoking the substance had been banned in all public places in Ozero, and stops like this became a haven for those getting their last fix in before returning to civilization.

The smoke formed a thin miasma that drifted over the interior, casting warped haloes around the oil lamps that tried and failed to chase off the gloom. The wind took the heavy door and slammed it behind me, subjecting me to the same experience you would get walking into any townie bar. All noise ceased, every head turned to take in the newcomer, and there was a pause for a moment until it was confirmed by unspoken consensus that I was, in fact, "one of them." With the test passed, normalcy resumed, and the hushed burble of conversation returned. In the corner, a man with a battered acoustic guitar strummed a soft, foreign tune. I picked my way through the gloom to the makeshift bar, a thick plank of scavenged wood laid over a pair of upright barrels. Behind it, Julianne worked feverishly at a wood-burning stove, shifting various pans across the hot surfaces with the agility of a concert pianist.

"Julianne! How's business?" I asked, settling into one of the mismatched stools.

"Oh, booming, sugar! Can I get you something? Got some grits, eggs, and biscuits coming out in half a jiff."

Oooohhh, that was tempting. Julianne's cooking was legendary in that glorious, homecooked, heart-attack-inducing sort of way.

"No can do, sadly, just stopping in for business. Any skimmer crews around?" I asked.

"Over in the corner there, dear, though do be careful; they ain't the most personable sort," she warned.

I made my way over to the group, sticking a hand in my pouch to double-check what money I had on me. For safety, most of my cash was kept banked in town, but it was always useful to have coins on hand for ... problem-solving. One interesting quirk of the imperial coin system was that it was a byproduct of the apocalyptic shit show that was the world immediately after the scourge of ghouls emerged. It was a catastrophe on a global scale, and not a time when you wanted to display how much money you were carrying. Because of that, our denominations were eventually standardized so that each value had a unique shape, so you could tell a gold sun from a silver moon or copper star without having to bring all your cash out.

"Hello, gentlemen!" I declared, gathering their attention. "Would any of you happen to be crossing near Zeb's ghoul ranch? I'm looking to make a quick stop there, but he won't have time to arrange my order if I don't get word to him prior."

The group laughed uproariously like I had stumbled on some private joke.

"Maybe, little one, but this isn't a charity," a heavyset man with a bushy brown beard growled.

"Oh, I wouldn't dream of it," I grinned, drawing a handful of round golden suns from my pouch. "A fair tip if it's not too out of your way."

One man, a skinny blond, raised a hand to draw my attention, but Bushy Beard pulled his arm down.

"And now you think you can just buy our services?" he asked.

"Yes, I think I can pay a courier to deliver a message because that is ... our job ... ," I looked at him, genuinely perplexed. I was used to a bit of friction, being a woman with a nice sled could draw the ire of the terminally obtuse, but this guy was getting all sorts of worked up.

"This is what we get, guys. Another long hauler thinking they're better than us. And worse, this girl's young enough to still be hiding behind her mother's skirts!"

Ah, that cleared it up. Skimmers and long haulers had a rivalry as old as the profession itself. Skimmer crews hated the better pay and more comfortable sleds of the long haulers, while we derided the skimmers for never having to spend a night outside in the wilderness. Add on the fact that I was maybe twenty years younger than the instigator, and it was a recipe for conflict. It almost never escalated above good-natured name-calling, but there were exceptions.

"Hey, if you don't want my money, that's fine. But don't deny your buddies the opportunity to make a buck," I argued.

He looked like he was planning to argue more, but his friends overruled him, razzing the man into silence. Blondie there was happy to take my money and hastily scrawled letter, informing me that he planned to rest at Zeb's tonight before continuing his route. With my speed, I could hope to reach old Zebadiah's place by noon tomorrow, so he should have plenty of time to prepare, if the old bastard was in a helpful mood, that is.

Task finished, I made my way back to the exit, hoping that the benefit of getting my message to Zeb would make up for the time I'd spent on the detour.

Julianne intercepted me right as I reached the door, pressing a small, paper-wrapped package into my hand.

"Take this with ya, sugar, and let me know what you think next time you're back. I've been looking into making my meals a bit more portable since y'all are always running out of here in a hurry," she explained.

Julianne refused any attempt to pay her and gave me a quick embrace before she ushered me out the door. She had become a sort of surrogate mother for the couriers based in Ozero, and I was happy to get one last moment with a friendly face before the tougher legs of my journey began. Reinvigorated, I tucked the package into my coat, mentally calling Scramble back to me as I reentered the violet light. He didn't respond for a moment, but I picked up on Champ's focus, realizing that for the first time in recent memory, someone had been stupid enough to poke around my sled while Champ was on guard. I took in the scene as I rounded the corner of the house, my eyes confirming what Champ's mental music had hinted at. My guard ghoul was still on top of the sled, but he now had a man with him, one who was currently dangling upside down from an ankle clenched in the skeleton's iron grip. Champ looked over to me and gave the man a slight shake of emphasis, very much like a cat playing with his food and broadcasting, "Hey, look what I caught." The poor man's green-dyed long johns were showing, and that, paired with the layers of colorful fabric that had fallen around his face, gave him the look of a vibrant tulip. Scramble, true to his nature, had climbed a low-hanging branch overhead and was hanging upside down and attempting to pull one of the man's shoes off for reasons I could not fathom. Various personal items had fallen from the man's clothing, forming a small pile beneath him that Heist was picking through with obvious glee.

I squelched through the mud, shaking my head at the stupidity of strangers.

"Hello, friend. You seem to have found yourself in a bit of a bind," I joked, leaning casually against my sled chassis next to him.

"Ahhh . . . yes," a young, cloth-muffled voice responded from below. "I was admiring your fine northern stock and was . . . apprehended. He's quite strong."

"And you're quite lucky. The last time we caught a thief, I had Tybalt on duty. He had the poor man strung up by his intestines, was bouncing him up and down like a giant meat yo-yo. Truly horrific, was cleaning gore off his harness for days . . . ," I went on.

"Please, please! I'm not a thief! I came here for research!" he wailed.

I squatted down to examine the items at his feet, smacking away Heist's wandering fingers. The ghoul had lost her lower jaw before I'd found her, and the wooden replacement tended to hang open, giving her a look of permanent excitement that matched her curious nature.

Instead of a coin pouch, there was a flat leather booklet filled with colorful paper money. Alongside it was a beaded necklace with a rotating cylinder of foreign script hanging from it.

"You're not from around here, are you?" I asked, recognizing the items.

"No! My name is Coda, I am from Bolero. I am a Song Islander!

Please . . . I don't feel so—" His words started to slur as the blood rushed to his head.

"Hmm, if you were actually a thief, I imagine you would have been smarter about it. Put him down, Champ."

Thud! Champ dropped him onto his head in the muck.

"Not like that! Get back in line, you big lummox," I shook my head. That was the problem with skellies. King or Craven could have sensed my intention and lowered him to the earth, but Champ's duller mind simplified the order to *Drop it!*

"Sorry about that," I apologized, helping the man rise on shaky legs and pulling his layers of robes down from around his head. "There we go, good as new!"

The flustered mass of cloth revealed a far younger face than I expected, with a pale complexion and a bald head shaved smooth.

"It's rare to see your people this far north. How'd you get way out here?" I asked.

"I'm on a research grant from the University of Bolero to study temperature influences on ghoul behavior." He enthused as his nausea faded.

"And that brought you to this little shack in the middle of nowhere?"

"Yes . . . Well, I heard about this place from a bar in Ozero. I had hoped to interview couriers before they dispersed into the city. Do you have time for an interview, perhaps? I would love to learn more about your team."

"Can't help you little man, I'm on a timeline, gotta get moving. Best of luck to you, though; I'd be happy to give you the tour next time I have a few days in Ozero," I offered.

The little guy had seemed crestfallen at first but brightened considerably when he heard my offer. "I won't be around here long, I'm supposed to return to your capital soon, but you can visit me at the embassy there!" He handed me a card of thick, cream-colored paper with two lines of text written in a swirling golden script. One was an address in the city of Drand, the capital, written in standard imperial, and below was an unreadable line in what I assumed to be the language of his homeland.

"I look forward to our meeting! May the Melody guide you!" he declared, folding his fingers in a complicated pattern and bowing deeply, then stepping away from the sled.

"Yup, this is going to be a weird trip," I groused, hooking Champ and Scramble back up to the line, then climbing into the cab. Song Islanders were isolationist by nature, even going so far as to limit all foreign trade to a single port on their largest island. But maybe they were opening up foreign relations at long last and letting their citizens wander farther afield. That kid still seemed a bit young to be out on his own, but he must have had some amount of fortitude to make it all this way.

Coda started waving with such genuine enthusiasm that I felt compelled to return the gesture, and he kept at it till my sled pulled out of sight.

V

—

I was eager to get on my way and even more eager to taste whatever delight Julianne had packed for me. But I had to backtrack past the refuse pile before getting back on the road, and I could not imagine a scent that would be more effective at killing my appetite. While I waited for us to pass the pungent landmark, I did a bit more trip planning, reaching into the storage space beneath my table to retrieve a chart depicting the northmost reaches of the Empire. It showed all the major cities along the northern border, Ozero chief among them, as well as most of the towns large enough to have built protective walls. A web of roadways connected these points of civilization, meandering to follow the local geography. Pondering to myself for a moment, I reached into the map compartment again and drew out a second map case, pulling my scarf over my nose as we passed the refuse pile again. There were already a handful of ghouls crawling over the pile, pursuing the carrion birds and rats in a fruitless hunt, scavengers chasing scavengers. From the second case, I withdrew a delicate item, a thin, translucent scroll of paper painstakingly etched with soft pencil lines. The drawing was useless on its own, but when I overlaid it on top of the Empire map, they lined up to reveal a host of new routes connecting through the empty space. These were our courier paths, one of the most well-kept secrets among our order. Some were discovered by accident, others were blazed by couriers and concealed from the casual observer.

Either way, they allowed us a far greater freedom of movement than the average traveler, letting us beat deadlines and confound the bandits that tried to track our movements. These shortcuts also helped keep way stations like the Farmhouse in business. Let's say you were paid for a five-day run that you knew you could cut down to four with shortcuts. Well, you didn't want to give that secret away to your employer. Much safer and more enjoyable to just spend your last night drinking with friends at the Farmhouse, then ride into town just before sunset as if you had spent the whole trip at a full sprint.

Lost in my reverie, I almost forgot Julianne's gift, and my stomach rumbled now that the refuse pile was far behind us. I dropped my coin pouch on the maps to weigh them in place, then drew the still-warm package from the depths of my coat. Peeling back the layers of wrapping, I was presented with a wonder of culinary engineering, a paradigm shift that definitively stated, "Breakfast will never be the same." Now, I had experienced breakfast in many forms, from campfire to restaurant kitchen, but the staples remained the same—the holy trinity of bacon, egg, and biscuit. Julianne, that angel, had brought this combination to its ultimate conclusion. She had taken the biscuit and cut it in half, placing between the two pieces an egg over-easy, three strips of crispy bacon, and a circle of cheese, melted to gooey perfection by the heat. I bit into the sandwich with slow reverence, and the intense flavor left me speechless. King turned to look back at me while running, noticing the waves of contentment radiating off me.

"Hey! If you would eat anything besides live pig, you could enjoy it too! Keep your eyes on the road," I grumbled through the crumbs.

Finishing that fantastic meal, I wiped my greasy hands on the front of my coat, resolving to stop by on the return trip to praise Julianne and get seconds. To stave off the food coma, I returned to planning, examining the courier paths for any shortcut. Tracing the path, I didn't see any way to shave off time, but there was a less traveled route that should have a good spot to camp for the night, marked by a little stylized tent symbol. It would also join back up with our planned route with only a minor deviation. The bandits knew all the main roads but were becoming increasingly adept at sniffing out courier paths as well, planning ambushes in the hunt for the expensive goods we carried. I hoped they hadn't found this one yet.

Reaching out with my thoughts, I sent the new route to King. I couldn't send him an image of the path as we hadn't ridden it before, but I conveyed enough that he knew where to slow down and look for it. All my tasks completed for the moment, I allowed myself to relax and enjoy the scenery. Other travelers had begun to emerge on the trail; small squads of soldiers on patrol, merchants bringing their wares into Ozero, even a whole family packed into a horse-drawn cart, traveling between two of the smaller settlements that dotted the landscape. None of those had the protection of balefire, but the soldiers kept ghoul numbers low this close to a large city. The only other courier I saw was Blondie, carrying my note and his own cargo. He drew up alongside me, perched on the end of his old-style sled and bundled up in heavy layers to withstand the frigid wind that curled around him. A short pole stretched up from the back of his sled, holding a small brazier of purple flame aloft. Blondie pulled down his mask to flash me a brilliant smile, waved his hand, then shouted something to his team, though I couldn't make it out over the howling wind. His ghouls picked up the pace, going from matching my jog to a full-out sprint in the space of a few heartbeats. I can't lie, the sight of his team charging through the fresh powder at speed was a damn impressive sight, but all it took was looking at the poor man exposed to the cold to remind me how nice it was to have a cab to stand in that shielded me from the elements.

Clouds rolled in during the afternoon, though I was happy to note that it was just a thin layer of stratus that did not portend any adverse weather. I checked my watch again, then glanced at the calculations I had scribbled out earlier. Given our speed, that shortcut should be somewhere nearby. I stripped off my overcoat as I ordered the team to slow, then hopped out the door and jogged alongside. Partially, this was to get a closer look and have a better chance at identifying the turnoff, but it was also just for the exercise. Courier work was both stressful and sedentary, and I refused to be one of those couriers you hear about that was eaten by ghouls because they had let their cardio slip.

The snowy road we walked was quite wide, covered in a mess of footprints and sled tracks. But if you knew what to look for, these tracks could tell stories. It was one such story that clued me in to our goal. At a slight bend in the road, one set of sled tracks swung wide, clipping the pine trees and knocking the snow free before merging back into the mess of churned mud and snow. Maybe the sled driver had gotten spooked by something, maybe they had needed to swerve to avoid an obstacle, or maybe they were covering their tracks. My suspicion was confirmed as I lifted a pine bough that drooped to the ground, revealing a thin but well-defined path behind it. I had to give this person credit; there was no way they would be able to get their sled under the branches without knocking the fresh snow from this tree, so they had concocted a cover scene that justified it. Taking a page from their book, I decided to repeat the deception. I had a spare runner in the back for repairs, which I used to hold the bough up as my team made their way under it. Then I walked along the false path, dragging the long metal runner like a giant pencil to imitate the path of a second sled veering and returning to the road. To complete the ruse, I walked backward to keep the footstep direction consistent and ducked back along the hidden track. It wasn't perfect, but it didn't need to be. I had only spotted the deception because I knew where to look for it. A bandit hunting party moving at full speed would have almost no chance.

As I replaced my equipment, I took a last look at the new set of tracks. Judging the age of a track in the snow was an educated guess at best, but if I was right, it looked like we might have company for dinner.

"OK, boys! Let's get moving!" I ordered. "Bonk, stop trying to eat the birds." The idiot had stretched to the end of his tether to try to pluck a robin off a nearby branch, though I had a better shot at becoming a duchess than he did of catching that bird.

We made good speed after that, though the path was thin and low branches scraped along the sides of the sled from time to time. I wolfed down a light lunch of nuts and cheese as we moved, foregoing the retrieval of more hearty food in the back so we wouldn't have to stop.

It was hard not to space out on these longer sections of the journey, and it was easy to catch yourself drifting. It was during one such lull that we hit the first minor setback in our journey.

Drifting in my reverie, I failed to notice a long branch, maybe the thickness of my thigh, that had fallen across the path at head height. King, the saint that he was, pulsed a warning in my head as we drew near, but by then, it was nearly too late. I lunged for the brake lever, deploying a pair of claw brakes under the sled that began digging into the snow. Annoyance and embarrassment flashed hot in me as I tried to hold the delicate balance necessary to stop the sled short. Stop too slow, and I would slam the sled into the branch; it wouldn't total my sled, but it could've wreaked heavy damage and slowed me down. Brake too fast, and I ran the risk of snapping the gangline of my whole team, yanking them backward, and damaging both their harnesses and their bones. It was a close thing, and King had to duck into a low slide to avoid contact. Bonk was not so quick thinking. He slammed into the branch, his head snapping back as he tumbled to the ground, tangling with the ghoul behind him as Grah stepped on his fallen comrade.

"Dammit, dammit, dammit!" I growled, hopping out of the sled and racing forward as Bonk and Grah began to fight, their struggle further tangling the pair as Grah bellowed. I extended my mind to calm them, but it was like restoring rhythm to an orchestra when the brass and string sections were having a bar fight. Thankfully, the fight resolved itself almost as soon as it had begun; Bonk crawled over his teammate like a spider, using the scraps of shredded harness around them to hogtie Grah and leave him trussed up on the ground, struggling in vain to free himself.

"OK, OK, one thing at a time." I paced back to the sled, scrambling around in the back until I found the hand saw. I tossed it to King and ordered him to start working on the branch while I dealt with the other two. First, I checked Bonk for any damage, focusing on his head and neck. Thankfully, Bonk had earned his name by forgetting to duck and slamming into low-hung objects with alarming regularity, so I had decided to invest in a padded leather helmet for him a few months back. It seemed to have paid for itself today, as Bonk had come through unharmed.

King cut through the section of branch with little effort, and I ordered him and Bonk to drag it off the path while I dealt with Grah.

"GrahGragGrah . . . GRAH!" the ghoul moaned as he struggled.

"Oh, hush now," I admonished, working to untangle him without having to cut any of the valuable leather. It didn't help that Grah wore a quilted gambeson and a shield slung over his back that further tangled with the harness in some places.

"Grah! Gahlahmahdah!" Grah continued to grumble. Most ghouls had a hole pierced in their throat before they were put to work that muted their voices entirely, but Grah was an exception. Ghouls didn't need to breathe, but those with intact lungs could still make a racket if they were inclined to. In general, all that noise was dangerous in the wilderness, but a loud ghoul had its uses if you could teach him to shut up when it mattered. Grah had worn a muzzle for the first three weeks I'd had him before he learned to quiet down.

I did the best I could, but Grah's harness was a mess of bent buckles and torn leather. I could patch it with a bit of time, but I wouldn't trust those ad hoc repairs to hold up to the rigors of our journey ahead. I would have to pull a spare from the back and get him refitted when we stopped for the night. In the meantime, I looped the harness around his shoulders and ordered him to hold it in place as we moved. It wasn't perfect, but this way, he could still help pull till nightfall. King and Bonk hauled the heavy branch clear, and I reboarded, wondering to myself if this alternate path had been a good idea after all.

VI

——

Determined not to lose focus again, I settled into a comfortable position and dug out a pack of conte crayons and my sketchbook. Every courier had their own way of staving off that dull mental haze that set in after kilometers on the same snowy path, staring at the skeletal trees. You needed something to keep busy; it was less about being observant and more about anchoring yourself in the "now" instead of spacing out. My father had his mandolin that he would pluck at for hours; I also had a friend who whittled wood into little animals that he would give to his kids. I would be the first to admit that I was no talented artist, but I had seen too much in my years beyond the walls to trust those images to memory alone. My little apartment in Ozero had a whole corner plastered with drawings of the things I had seen, memories both fantastic and terrifying. An aurora borealis that lit up the whole sky in blues and greens, soldiers doing battle with a thousand-strong ghoul horde under a purple flame, a village burning orange and red as people fled from bandits. Those images became lodged in my head, especially the bad ones, and it sometimes felt like the only way to get them out was to transfer them to paper. It was an expensive habit; conte sticks and fresh paper were both scarce commodities, and the pigments necessary for the more vibrant hues even more so. But hey, courier pay was good, and there wasn't much point in dying rich.

The path we traveled was gifting me with a breathtaking subject today. The trees around us leaned close on either side, their trunks like columns of an old-world temple, the branches curling up overhead to form a natural arch. As the sun set, rays of orange filtered through, casting the whole forest in fire and shadow. It was views like this that reminded me of why I loved this job, even with all the hardship it entailed. It certainly beat eking out a living behind city walls, that was for sure. I finished sketching out the scene, then checked my calculations again, seeing that we should be coming up on our planned rest stop soon.

"Do your thing, Craven!" I yelled, slowing the team to a walk and hopping out, remembering to grab my own poleaxe from its rack on the back wall of the cab.

Most couriers wondered why I kept Craven around. He was twitchy, unreliable, and useless in a fight, but he also had a pedigree, which meant that I knew who he was before he had been a ghoul. Those known histories were a rarity, and it made Craven worth his desiccated weight in gold. It was the difference between knowing what a ghoul was capable of and having to figure it out by trial and error. Tybalt was the perfect example of that trial and error. He was a violent bastard with the killer instincts of an alley cat. But I also spent every day wondering if he was going to disembowel the next fisherman he saw because the ghoul that killed him had smelled like halibut or something equally absurd. Ghouls had all sorts of weird quirks they carried over from life; the more you knew, the more you could plan for.

Craven, during his living days, was known as "The Late" Arthur Cullen, a moniker he earned for being the slowest damn courier to ever grace the northern wastes. Commission him for a four-day trip; you would see him in a week. Urgent and time sensitive were not words that entered his lexicon. But he always made it. In thirty years, he never lost a shipment, never even had an injury, from what I had heard.

Well, except for the injury that killed him, of course.

Cullen had pulled this off by having extensive knowledge of every hidden stop, hidey-hole, and natural piece of shelter that dotted the landscape. That knowledge was still there, locked up in his rotted skull, and I could use it.

Craven perked up, glancing around as I brought my mental focus to him. Even if Craven hadn't been to this particular rest site before, he knew what to look for.

He peered left, then right, then put a hand on King's shoulder, pointing to a nondescript portion of the path up ahead. I led the team up to the point Craven had directed us to, noticing that, once again, the tracks in that area seemed muddled. Between that clue and Craven's guidance, we found the turnoff easily enough, cunningly disguised behind tied bundles of brush made to look like an impassible wall of shrubs. Tossing those aside, we slid down a steep embankment, finding ourselves in a clearing backed against a sheer cliff face, maybe twenty meters tall. Set into one side of the cliff was a relic of a bygone age, the tall stone arch of a tunnel entrance, maybe for a train. Nature had long since reclaimed the metal tracks, so my guess was little more than speculation.

I also found the person we had been following; another sled was already tucked into the tunnel, with a small campfire blazing away with merry light. Gods, it seemed so inviting, a little island of warmth as the sun continued to set and the outside temperature plummeted.

Maybe too inviting . . . The line between caution and paranoia was a tightrope that every courier walked. I saw a cozy place to stay the night, but I also saw a tempting piece of bait that might trap me in that tunnel as soon as I entered. So, I approached with caution, unhooking Champ in case sudden violence became necessary.

"Deacon Winona, seeking a hearth far from home!" I called out, shifting the grip on my poleaxe.

A figure emerged from the cab, then immediately tripped and tumbled head over heel onto the earthen floor. He stumbled upright a moment later, peering out into the darkening landscape with a dazed expression.

"Oh . . . Deacon Billy! Yeah, come on in!" He called out, gesturing with an awkward wave to the open space against the opposite wall.

I looked at Champ, who shrugged. Champ shrugged at everything he didn't understand, though, so it was his go-to reaction for most things. The figure looked like a young boy, so there was a chance he was just a newbie.

"Listen, kid, that's not the correct response. You can tell me what you're supposed to say, or I can get my other ghoul to turn you into a flesh yo-yo. Your call!"

"Oh . . . oh gods, oh gods." He pulled out a folded piece of paper, hurriedly scanning the contents.

"Deacon Billy, offering a safe hearth. We are cooking . . . bacon?" he read off the sheet, looking confused.

That settled it. Maybe the bandits had somehow obtained this season's phrases, but I had been a new courier once and could sense that nervous newbie tension from here. We switched the greeting every few months, a simple way for couriers to confirm identities in the wild. It wasn't perfect, but every little bit of extra caution helped.

"OK, you pass, relax!" I yelled, leading my team to the open space to which he had pointed. The tunnel stretched away deeper into the rock, leaving an alarming pool of darkness hanging at the edge of the firelight.

"You take a look down that way?" I asked.

"Yes, ma'am, there's a cave-in maybe fifty meters down, no way through," he answered, poking at something he had roasting on a spit over the fire.

"Please, please don't call me ma'am . . . Hey Billy, your dinner is on fire," I mentioned casually, unhooking Grah from the line.

"My rabbit!" he cried, pulling the spit from the flames. The carcass continued to smolder until he was forced to drop the creature and stamp out the flames in the dirt.

"Did you . . . did you leave the fur on that rabbit?" I asked, shocked at the wasted meat.

"You're supposed to take it off? I thought you just . . . stuck a stick through it," he answered, staring at the remains of his meal, still nonplussed at the outcome.

"How did you graduate without knowing how to field dress a kill?" I questioned.

"My teacher was a skimmer courier. He always told me that if I found myself stuck outside overnight, I was dead meat anyway. Then my aunt passed on, and my family didn't want to sell her long-haul sled, so . . . here I am," he shrugged self-consciously. "I still have the grouse I shot earlier; maybe I can do better on a bird, no fur, at least."

I thought for a moment about letting the boy desecrate another animal cadaver but figured he could use the help. We had all been newbies at some point, after all.

"Listen, I'll make you a deal. I've got some fresh-ish veggies from town to add; if you let me have half that bird, I'll show you how to clean and cook it."

Billy eagerly accepted, and I walked him through the process step by step. He turned a bit green in the face as I yanked out the organs, but a few months of hanging out with rotting undead every day would cure his squeamishness quick enough. Or he would watch a new ghoul void its bowels along with a rope of intestine and would quit the career the next day. We lost a lot of prospective couriers that way; they prepared for everything in the profession on paper, but no book could cure squeamishness. Luckily, we soon had the grouse rotating on the spit, and the delicious scent of sizzling game bird chased away the less savory thoughts.

"Now you just need to keep it rotating so it cooks even, and you're all set." I finished, my own mouth beginning to water.

"Wow, thank you, Winona! I wish I could pay you back."

"Ha, you can make me dinner next time we run into each other . . . Or you can get my ghoul's harness situation figured out," I joked, gesturing to the pile of leather straps and buckles that I had retrieved from my sled. Fitting a new harness on a ghoul was a time-consuming process.

Everything had to be secured exactly right, and the ghouls were rarely helpful participants. It was a task new couriers usually struggled with, but maybe I could use the chance to teach Billy a bit more.

"Oh, that's easy; I'll get him suited up after dinner. Just pull him out of line and get him muzzled for me," he answered absently, still intently focused on the bird.

"Huh, you can fit a ghoul harness, but you can't cook a rabbit. You're a weird kid," I laughed, sliding the cooked grouse onto two waiting plates.

"My dad was a leather worker, he had tons of business fixing and fitting courier harnesses, so I saw a bunch of them come and go. You grow up on those stories for long enough, and you catch the bug for adventure," he explained.

We ate in silence after that, just enjoying the unexpected proximity of another living human out in the wild. Afterward, I retrieved a muzzle for Grah, though he fussed like a toddler as I covered his mouth. I would order him to hold still while Billy worked, but nobody in their right mind would get close to a ghoul not under their control unless they were muzzled, and for a good reason.

Ghoul bites were terminal. The necromantic magic that animated them was deadly to the living, and a single bite would send that fetid power spreading through your body. It would move through you like a poison, and no known medicine or treatment could reverse the spread. If you were quick and lucky, amputation could save your life, severing the source of the corruption before it could reach your vitals. But get bitten somewhere that couldn't be cut off, and you were done for—the magical infection would slowly consume you, converting life to undeath until only a ghoul remained.

Some couriers kept their ghouls muzzled for the entirety of a run to avoid mishaps, an understandable caution given the danger. Though I always thought of that behavior like you were muzzling an attack dog. Yeah, it couldn't bite me anymore, but I also couldn't sic it on the bandit trying to kill me. I was relieved to see that, while he was a terrible cook, Billy seemed to know this craft well. He stripped the old harness away with practiced ease, using deliberate, careful movements that were unlikely to antagonize the ghoul. I cleaned the dishes as he went to work, keeping a careful eye on Billy, partially to make sure Grah behaved and partially to see if I could learn any tricks from this new kid; the world was always changing, and the people who thought they had seen it all generally found themselves eaten by something they hadn't seen before.

After we were done removing the old harness, I packed it away, then brewed a pot of tea while he fitted the replacement.

"So, what are you carrying?" I asked, glancing at the pyramid of nine barrels strapped onto the bed of his cart.

"Oh, no idea. Some fancy goop they pulled out of an old-world ruin, apparently. But it was all hush-hush, so I didn't ask," he explained, not taking his eyes off the task.

"Well, you might want to ask next time since it's leaking green fluid, and we're sitting around an open flame."

Billy nearly fell over in his panic to jump up and check his cargo, and I nearly fell over from laughter after he found out that there had been no leak. Grah started raising a fuss over the movement, but I calmed him with a thought.

"Sorry, newbie, that joke is a bit of a rite of passage. But really, you should know what you're carrying. For the smaller stuff, you'll likely be fine, but when you are transporting in bulk, it's worth finding out," I explained.

"Sounds like you learned from experience," Billy said ruefully, sitting back down.

"Oh yes. I was naive and inexperienced once too. Camped out in a random cave I came across, I had a cargo just like yours. Some alchemists in Drand were trying to recreate old-world chemicals and needed a courier to deliver their experiment to colleagues. Turns out there was a bear already taking up residence in that cave, and he did not take kindly to my intrusion. He smashed up a barrel trying to get at me, and these gods awful fumes started gushing out. Killed the bear, almost killed me. That was a lesson learned ... Speaking of. ..."

I hopped up into my cargo bay and gave the crate a quick once over; all the straps were still tight, and I didn't see any cracks or holes that might let that precious heat escape. After a moment of searching, I found the catch for the lid and lifted the top of the crate up on oiled hinges. I would have felt rather foolish if I discovered that Ronny had duped me right after I scolded Billy for not knowing his cargo, but everything seemed to be in order, as far as I could tell. The inside of the crate was heavily padded with quilted fabric, and lifting the top layer revealed a slightly smaller crate within. This one had a series of latches instead of a hinge, and I pulled the top off and set it inside. The interior of this crate was separated into two sections. One side held a large ceramic vessel, which I assumed was the battery. Wires spiraled off it, through the partition, to the other side, where they coiled around a metal box. I was *not* going to touch that thing for equal fear of breaking it and electrocuting myself, but I could feel that it was a few degrees warmer inside the box than outside, so I assumed the battery was doing its job.

With my worries set to rest, I spent the rest of the night helping Billy out, examining his sled, and passing on the same pearls of wisdom that my mentors had passed on to me. Before I knew it, the hour was late, and it was time to get to bed. I wished Billy luck and said my goodbyes; I'd be leaving at sunrise tomorrow and would eat breakfast on the road. I left most of my team hitched in place but pulled Grah, Craven, and Champ out for guard duty, setting them up on short tethers around the sled. Champ was the obvious choice, ready to intercept any threat with violence. Grah and Craven were tethered together as my alarm system. Craven would try to bolt at the first sign of danger, yanking on Grah and making him holler belligerently. Stepping outside, I used chunks of snow to clean the worst of the day's dirt off myself, then climbed into the tiny living quarters of my cabin, locking the door behind me. The various layers

I wore came off one after another, and I organized them around the cramped space so that they could be donned swiftly in an emergency. Then I indulged in a small luxury, pulling on the soft flannel sleepwear my mother had given me on my own graduation day. Sliding under the quilted blanket of my short cot, I let the rigors of the day pull me into a deep, dreamless sleep.

VII

―――

Morning came all too soon, and I was nearly overwhelmed with the urge to snuggle under the covers and drift—No! I had to get up, start the day. The darkness of the tunnel around my sled was so deep and close . . . and comfortable—No!

I pulled myself out of the cot with a herculean effort, stretching my arms to the extent that the small sleeping compartment would allow. I had worked hard to insulate the space, but nothing could completely keep the chill at bay. The sole source of illumination came from a small window set into the ceiling, positioned so that the purple balefire light would fall on my pillow. It allowed me to project my mind and check in with my ghouls without leaving my room, a trick I had learned from an old courier who had modified his sled extensively over the years. Yawning, I pulled on my various layers of outerwear and opened the door, bracing myself for the drop in temperature. Grah and Craven were sitting calmly, staring off into the middle distance with no sign of alarm. A quick glance at the tunnel entrance confirmed that the weak glow of dawn was beginning to brighten, which was a relief. My internal clock was solid, but oversleeping was a real danger on the job. The water clocks that most people used at home were far too unreliable to have any use beyond the walls, and clockwork was prohibitively expensive, whether it was a pre-cataclysm relic or a new creation from the capital.

A fire still blazed in the circle of stones between the two sleds, which stood out as strange to me. The fire we lit last night should have burnt down to cold coals by now, and I couldn't imagine that Billy was up as early as I. The mystery was solved when a ghoul on Billy's team rose and placed another log on the flame, the blackened bones on one hand attesting to its carelessness.

"Huh, a fire starter ghoul. That's useful, though a bit terrifying if you don't keep an eye on it. I wonder where Billy found you?" I wondered aloud.

There wasn't time for a full breakfast, but the fire was too tempting to ignore, and I took a few minutes to warm up a bit of bread and brew a cup of black coffee. Putting milk or sugar in your coffee was grounds for a beating in some courier circles, the common reasoning being that a good courier shouldn't be wasting the weight and space on their sled to carry such extra comforts. Though a few will brag that couriers simply had more refined tastes than the average person and that genuinely good coffee needed no additives. My guess was that we just did it because drinking black coffee had been synonymous with tough, no-nonsense bastards since time immemorial.

It didn't take long to get the team hitched up and turned around, but I took one last look at Billy's sled before departing. The kid was likely still asleep, and the thought of leaving him alone and exposed out here put a minor twist in my stomach. As soon as the feelings surfaced, I shook them away. Billy was one of us now. Either he'd be smart enough to survive on his own, or he wouldn't; coddling him wouldn't do him any favors.

"Let's get a move on, boys, don't want to be late for Zeb. Yah!" I called.

The ghouls leaned against their harness and pulled, lurching the sled into motion. We gained speed at a steady rate, retracing our steps through the morning light. I stopped for a moment, long enough to replace the bundles of brush hiding the tunnel path, then we were off again, cutting through new snow. I busied myself with the various calculations of the day, adding extra notes about the tunnel itself. Knowing where to find shelter was always good, but the devil was in the details; knowing if you were riding towards a shallow outcropping or a deep, insulated tunnel could be the difference between life and death when a bad storm hit. Come to think of it, that's what most of this job was, skirting that thin line between another day breathing and catastrophic disaster. You had to be smart and methodical true enough, but you also had to be lucky. The smartest courier I knew had died when an ice bridge he had crossed a hundred times before collapsed, spilling him into the frigid water below with no warning. There was no abnormally warm weather, no sign of weakness, no way to see it coming, just a loud *crack!* And he was gone. No matter how good you were, eventually, the gods would come to collect, and you needed that little spark of luck to give them the slip for another day.

But it didn't seem like I would need to test my luck today. It was gorgeous out, with only a few wispy clouds to break up the endless blue. We made good time back to the main path, running through kilometer after kilometer of clear track. It went so smoothly that I could even get some work done in the cargo bay, checking and repairing various bits of gear as the ghouls continued their way. This . . . this was one of those precious moments. Good team, good route, good weather. You needed to enjoy those because when it was two in the morning, and you were chipping ice from a ghoul's rotting chest cavity, you would need those nice memories to keep from going crazy.

Before I knew it, we were closing in on Zeb's place. Unlike most people in the Empire who survived by crowding into walled settlements, Zeb had near unlimited land to do with as he wished. This manifested in several ways, most notably in a vast zoo of larger-than-life animal sculptures erected at various points around his compound. The first thing I saw leading up to the turnoff was a giant sea creature he had modeled after a squid. Zeb had erected a small silo dragged from who knows where, painted cartoonish eyes on the sides, and placed bundles of cable at its base to serve as a sprawling mass of tentacles.

After that, there was a giant dog with an ancient vehicle perched on top as an oversize head, its bulk supported by wires extending up to the nearby trees. As we made the turn down the winding path to his property, I spied a new construction, something along the lines of a metallic horse.

These sculptures, though fanciful, went a long way to establishing Zeb as a man of near-terrifying power. The size and scope of them hinted that he had a massive workforce at his disposal. Rumor had it that they were made of old-world metal, which, even rusted, sold at a price so high that Zeb had more wealth than most ever saw in a lifetime just sitting in his front yard. Though he had once confided that the vast majority were well-crafted replicas, as centuries' worth of exposure had broken down most pre-cataclysm materials.

One might think this display would attract thieves, but Zeb was merciless in protecting what was his and would be happy to spend a fortune hunting down a man who had robbed him of a few copper stars. Plenty still tried, though, and the giant cat sculpture we passed next had a mangled corpse of the most recent thief perched in its jaws. Yeah, don't fuck with Zeb.

Even if there hadn't been a well-maintained path, I could've followed my nose. The light wind at my back did little to dispel the impermeable aura of stank that surrounded the compound. As we drew closer, the ground fell away on both sides, shaping the path into a thin earthen ramp that rose to a new gate of stout hardwood. I hopped out as we stopped, raising my hands above my head to be on the safe side. Zeb recruited his guards from sturdy, experienced folk for the most part, but the last thing I needed on this trip was a twitchy greenhorn pointing a crossbow at me.

"I am Deacon Winona! I have a meeting with Zebadiah! Please don't shoot me . . . " I called out, holding my holy symbol up where it could be seen. There was a smaller door set in the gates, with a sliding panel that clacked open at eye level. I stepped up to it as a pair of sapphire blue eyes rose into view.

"Deacon Winona?"

"Yep, in the flesh," I answered.

"One moment." The panel slammed back, and there was a creaking of wood and rope as the gates retracted inward. The guard who awaited was far shorter than the eyes I had seen through the panel, and I spied the small stool he had stood on, partially hidden around the corner of the guard shack.

"The gate is new; you been having bandit problems?" I asked, leading my team inside.

"Eh, nay problems as much as interest," he sighed, indicating for me to follow as he hollered for another guard to take his place. "Been sniffing around like scavengers waiting for an animal to die. I'm sure you saw the last one we caught, strung him up for the rest to see. Me name's Duncan. You come out here just for Zeb or stopping by on a trip?"

"Oh, just a pit stop on my way to Skyroost. I didn't want to risk the journey without a full team," I answered as the path flattened out.

"I get you. Did some mercenary work up that way years ago, it's some tough country."

Zeb's compound had once sat atop a low hill, but ghoul teams had spent months excavating the hillside, transforming the innocuous mound into a flat plateau with slanting sides all around. It now looked like an island if the sea around it were composed solely of ghoul flesh. Hundreds of them, maybe over a thousand in total, housed in six massive pens that surrounded the plateau. The raised path we traversed fell away to a pen on either side, and Zeb did not waste money on railings. If you slipped, you would be the main course for the hungering masses below. Soon we reached the plateau proper, the border of which was lined with defensive hedgehogs; giant wooden caltrops with lengths of rope strung between. They would be an annoyance to any bandit that managed to scale them, but they were more to hold back a rushing tide of undead if the ghouls turned nasty.

To combat that danger, Zeb had not one but two grand braziers casting their purple light from high scaffolds to keep the ghouls sedate.

Entering that purple light with such a mass of ghouls was always a disorienting experience. With my own team, it was like entering a room with nine musicians quietly playing their instruments. Here, it was like standing in the center of the capital arena while thousands of spectators cheered. The mental noise was like a physical wave, and it took me a moment to steady myself against its pressure.

"Jarring, isn't it?" The guard asked, noticing my discomfort. "Feel like my ears are always ringing, gotta take a walk on patrol every now and then just to remember what silence sounds like." He shivered all over.

"Yeah, no wonder Zeb's so eccentric. I guess you need to be crazy to run a place like this," I replied.

"Ain't that the truth. He is the best, though. You can park your team here. I'll get Zebadiah." He pointed to a section of the plateau to our right, divided into a series of rectangular bays, then headed off to the two-story chalet at the rear of the plateau. Roofless, the bays would let the purple glow in while still giving couriers a bit of privacy to care for their teams. Only one other bay was occupied, a skimmer by the looks of it, but of a different design than Blondie's.

Pulling my team into one of the open bays, I let myself enjoy a long sigh of relief. Zeb's was the last true bastion of humanity till Skyroost, not counting that shady military outpost hidden somewhere ahead, and I would enjoy having sturdy walls around me for the brief time it lasted. While I waited for him, I busied myself checking over my team after our run, paying special attention to their boots. Ghouls wouldn't notice a stick piercing straight through their foot, but objects like that could still snag on some bit of terrain and cause a sudden stumble at the worst possible time. It was a minor thing, but I would take any advantage I could against the wilderness to come.

"Winona!? Well shit, you were knee-high to a sparrow last time I saw you!"

I turned to see a tall, thin, elderly man. Despite his age, his eyes remained bright behind a pair of Drand-made eyeglasses, and his sun-browned arms remained strong with sinewy muscle. He had been balding before I was born, the wispy remains of his hair pulled into a grey braid that lay coiled against the back of his skull. Despite the rough terrain, he was decked out in a three-piece suit of white and burgundy, and he leaned on a cane of bloodwood topped with silver. He looked like a man who had been born at seventy and wouldn't see eighty until the moon fell from the sky.

"Zeb, you old goat, I was here a few months back!" I rushed over, giving him a playful punch on the arm before embracing him.

"Eh, couldn't resist. You'll always be the little girl bouncing on your dad's knee when he visited. No fear of ghouls, even then! Leaning over the drop, almost was ate half a dozen times, though we'd never tell your mum." He gave a sly wink.

"Uh-huh. Glad you got my letter. Blondie make it OK?" I asked.

"Blondie? Oh, do you mean Haakon? Heh! Yeah, he's good people, headed out this morning." He gestured for me to follow, then hobbled off, leaning a bit more heavily on his cane than the last time I had seen him.

"You doing OK there, old timer?" I caught up to him as we made our way to the last structure on the plateau, a heavily reinforced single-story building squatting opposite the sled bays.

"Yeah, yeah. Ghoul took a chunk out of my leg . . . Scratch, not a bite!" he corrected quickly as I gasped and stopped short. "Hehe, it'll be a few years yet before a ghoul takes me down, don't you worry."

"Glad to hear it, don't know what we'd do without you. Hey, I could use a favor, two, actually. First, do you mind throwing my crate on your cargo scale? I didn't have the chance to weigh it myself, and I don't completely trust my client's numbers. Also, my fawn with the helmet took a run into a tree yesterday, mind getting a doc to give him a once over?" I asked.

He waved to another guard, then passed the messages along. "It's my pleasure, Winona, we try to be a full-service ranch here, and I'm training up a new doc that could use the practice anyway."

Ghouls could not feel pain, but they could absolutely get injured. While they no longer needed muscles to move, they did still need skeletons for structure. Tiny fractures could build up over time, and with no sensation of pain, you wouldn't know a ghoul was damaged until it fell to pieces. The image of my old ghoul Wizard snapping apart was still fresh on my mind, and I did not want Bonk suffering the same fate. Since ranchers like Zeb sold ghouls, they also kept skilled help on hand to spot such damage and repair it early.

Zebadiah held the door open, and we stepped into the warm semi-darkness beyond. Inside was a small viewing area lit with oil lanterns and studded with a row of thick metal bars partitioning the space from a larger pen beyond. There were sturdy doors spaced at even intervals around the area.

"Not gonna lie, I was surprised that you called in that marker after all this time, thought you'd be using it to replace King when his skills faded," Zeb laughed, though there was a question in his tone.

"Eh, desperate times call for desperate measures. This run could get tough, and I don't want to risk it without a full team. You know me, I hate to waste the effort breaking in a new ghoul if it's not a keeper."

Any courier under the auspices of the church could withdraw a certain number of ghouls from ranches like Zeb's to fill out their team, the same as we could in the Yard in Ozero. Problem was, it was a bit of a crap shoot on what you would get. A courier might find a fawn or skelly to replace one they had lost but would have no idea if that ghoul had some hidden talent or crippling deficiency that could crop up at an inopportune moment.

That's where the wilderness economy kicked in. Zeb had to provide you with basic ghouls but could be convinced to part with his "special stock" for a price. It could be an old-world artifact, art from a distant land, or a ghoul with a peculiar skill. I had earned a marker with him when I'd brought in a ghoul a few months back that obsessively collected berries, which was a unique one even for me.

"So, Zeb, what do you have for me today? I know it's short notice, but you've got a reputation to uphold." I playfully elbowed him in the ribs as we moved to stand near the bars.

"Listen here, little one; I was breaking in the undead with my bare hands before you were born, and I'll be doing it long after you've passed on," he growled, tone light but with a dangerous edge to it. Men like that you could tease in jest, but if they thought for a second you were disrespecting them, there would be consequences.

"That's why I come to you, Zebadiah, you're the best in the business," I backpedaled, assuaging his ego. "I'd love to see what you have for me, please."

"Mhmm, that's what I thought," he chuckled, letting the tense moment pass. "Well, I picked out three solid choices for you, plus an extra special one that you might like, though she has a mean streak a mile wide."

"All with pedigrees, I assume?"

"Of course! What kinda two-bit dead peddler do you take me for? First one up is Lars, a weapon fighter about midway decayed. Was a town guard before he was bitten and still remembers a thing or two. Pull up door one!" he shouted into the darkness beyond.

One of the heavy doors slid upward, and a muscular ghoul shambled into view, a heavy wooden cudgel clenched in one hand.

"Can he fight with anything other than that?" I asked, gesturing to the crude weapon.

"Of course, he can use a poleaxe too, but the first time we gave him one, he came within a centimeter of spearing a buyer through the bars, real bad for business," he explained.

Inside this covered building, the purple light could not reach the ghouls. In its absence, they would revert to their normal behavior and try to consume anything with a pulse. Since trying to reach through the bars and eat us wouldn't be helpful for assessment, another door opened to release a wild grouse into the pen, which the ghoul immediately focused on.

The poor bird noticed the attention and scurried to the far side of the pen. Ghouls could be quite clumsy, though they did have a natural stealth to them and could remain stone still since they didn't need to breathe. The wildlife of the Empire had adapted to the undead long ago, likely due to the ghouls culling the stupid or slow animals early on. Observing a ghoul hunting a crafty bird was the best way we had come up with to judge their talents and drawbacks.

Lars came over to us first and tried to fit his beefy arm through the bars before giving up and closing in on the grouse, who gave a quick half-flying hop to the far side of the pen. He chased after the bird again, and again it evaded. Lars changed tactics, rearing back and throwing the cudgel with considerable strength. The club collided with the bird, leaving it twitching and stunned long enough for Lars to close the distance and raise the creature to his rotting jaws. I grimaced as the sounds of wet crunching echoed out. As always, ghouls were . . . messy eaters.

A worker with a handheld brazier torch came in after, lighting up the area and leading Lars back into storage.

"What do you think?" Zebadiah asked.

"Not bad. I didn't see any weird movement you'd see from broken bones. He switched tactics quick enough as well; that throw isn't something he would have practiced too much while breathing. What else do we have?"

The next two were more competent and far more interesting. First up was a heavyset woman with lightning-quick hands named Astra. She plucked the bird from the air with ease as it fluttered by and snapped its neck with a practiced motion. She peered at the bird for a second more, then bit into it halfheartedly, her prey now devoid of the life she wanted to feed on. The ghoul had just deprived itself of a meal, but this type of behavior was common. Every ghoul "echoed" the skills and habits they had while living, and sometimes these echoes ran counter to their own hunger. Our girl Astra had worked in a remote logging camp and knew a decent amount of survival and carpentry skills to go along with her talents in bird execution. If I weren't so pressed for time, I would've loved to examine her further: having a ghoul that could help with sled repairs was a dream scenario for any courier.

Next up was a tough-looking piece of work, a forty-ish-year-old bounty hunter by the name of Gorm, also known as Gorm the Devil Claw. Surprisingly, I knew of him. He was a minor celebrity in Ozero but had disappeared a few months back. That wasn't too odd, as we'd just assumed that he'd headed off south after a target. Apparently not. At the moment, he was stripped down to just his pants but still had his signature weapon. The devil claw was a polearm over two meters in length, topped with short, barbed spikes that curved forward and back. Decimeter-long spines studded the last half meter of its length. It was a tool commonly employed by law enforcement in larger cities. The barbs could snag a fleeing man's clothing, the length kept you out of striking range, and the spines deterred the fugitive from grabbing the pole to free himself.

"Damn, Gorm's dead," I whispered. "Never met him in person, but heard he was honest enough."

"Just wasn't fast enough," Zeb remarked, then gave a shrill whistle.

The ceiling rumbled, and a portion slid back, allowing the grand brazier's light in.

"That's new, a bit excessive, though," I laughed. "You could just bring some torches in."

"Selling a product is half about the goods, half about presentation. Big capital types have been stopping by recently, buying up all my fighting ghouls. Had to hide my special stock to keep them from going after it. I like to keep something good for the couriers, and those idiots would just use them all as dumb bruisers anyway. Care to take him for a ride?"

"Oh, it would be my pleasure," I answered, letting my mind reach out to Gorm.

Interacting with a new ghoul was always a bit strange, especially with a fawn as fresh as Gorm. He was still so full of personality and intellect that trying to force my will on him was like trying to throw a harness on a wild horse; tiring and dangerous. As I examined Gorm's mind, another door retracted and released a club-wielding ghoul, though this one was far smaller and more worn down than Lars. Zeb must have taken control as the ghoul perked up and let out a rasping growl, shambling over to attack Gorm. Gorm's mind pulsed with the echoes of his life experience; he wanted to track, to disable, to restrain. The urge was engraved in him, and it only took a flicker of thought to set Gorm against his attacker. The ghoul moved fluidly, sidestepping the charge and tangling the barbs of his weapon in the ghoul's pants. Using the pole like a lever, Gorm rotated and knocked the ghoul off his feet. The creature lashed out again, but Gorm blocked the strike with contemptuous ease, hooking the creature's sleeve and yanking the limb behind his back. The ghoul was pinned, and Gorm was unscathed, easily keeping his quarry restrained and helpless.

"Damn, that was impressive, I won't lie. Consider me interested," I admitted.

"Your family always did have an eye for talent," he replied as the ghouls were led out and the balefire light cut off again.

"And you're saying that wasn't the extra special one you mentioned? Damn, Zeb, you pulled out all the stops for me. I appreciate that."

"Well, despite the fancy clothes, I haven't forgotten my courier days. You look after your own. Out here in the cold, each other is all we got." He raised his voice as if calling out to someone else in the room. "To me, there's no cardinal sin greater than betrayal. We are a family out here, and there are hard choices that come with that. Sometimes you gotta leave a man behind; it happens. Sometimes you need to put a ghoul-bit friend out of their misery; fair play. But when you SELL OUT YOUR FAMILY TO BANDITS, THERE ARE FUCKING CONSEQUENCES!"

A door opened, and Duncan, now beaten and bloodied, was tossed into the pen.

VIII

———

My immediate reaction was to ask Zebadiah what the actual fuck was happening, but the violence of his outburst stopped me cold. At the end of the day, this was his little kingdom, and I was just a visitor. I considered Zeb a friend, but directly challenging his authority was dangerous, especially since I knew so little about what was happening. I remained silent.

Duncan, the guard who had let me in earlier, coughed and heaved himself up into a sitting position, blinking myopically into the gloom. "Zebadiah, Gunther and his boys just beat me half to death; what gives!?"

"Playing dumb won't help you, Duncan! Might as well come clean and die an honest man." Zeb hollered in response.

The guard crawled to his feet and stumbled over to the bars. One eye was already swelling shut, and he spoke with the thickness of someone who had bit their tongue in a scuffle. "Please, let me out. Deacon Winona, you can't let him do this. Help me."

"Oh, she won't be helping you once she hears about what you've done." Zebadiah turned to me, careful to stay out of reach should Duncan try to lunge at him.

"Duncan here has been selling us out to some fools in a town not too far off. Convinced them that there was a more lucrative career in stealing than in dirt farming or whatever it is they do. Then he told them about our patrol schedule and where we keep payments and pedigrees. Damn amateurs, I guessed we had a rat after the second time they knew just where to strike. Planted a little trap for them next time, changed the patrol times to leave an extra big gap, then laid an ambush with a few of my workers I knew I could trust. We put down three, and the last one we caught sang like a canary to save himself," he summarized.

Duncan had given up on the bars at this point, going over to attempt to lift one of the doors open. Those gates were built to withstand skelly strength, though, and didn't even budge. "I'm surprised you let a bandit walk away," I admitted. "You've never seemed like the merciful sort when it comes to thievery."

"It's just learning good business, improving my technique, if you will. If half a bandit crew goes missing without a word, the other half will come sniffing around looking for 'em. If I send a survivor back with his hand lopped off, they learn real quick to avoid my neck of the woods. Now all that's left is to tidy up this loose end. Thanks to you, I can get a demonstration out of it too," he whistled shrilly, and a door on the far side of the pen slid up.

An icy feeling slid down my spine as the meaning of his words became clear. Even in the cities known to execute their prisoners, death by ghoul was considered inhumane. An axe or a noose was quick and impersonal, but ghouls were just hungry animals. This was . . . catastrophically fucked up. But Duncan had endangered the lives of his community with his betrayal, and I was not going to stick my neck out to save the bastard.

The creature in the cell moved with such fluidity that I almost missed its entrance. Instead of the expected shamble, the ghoul swung out from the top of the doorway, twisting its body and slithering up into the rafters above. In seconds, it had disappeared into the gloom that shrouded the ceiling.

"Good gods Zebadiah, what kind of devil did you find?" I asked, trying to spot it in the darkness. Duncan was having the same problem, scrambling into a corner as his wide eyes darted around the space.

"Amelia Davies. Parents were from the Song Islands, but she grew up around here. Some sickness took 'em when she was young, and she started running messages for local gangs to buy food and the like."

Duncan was edging around the perimeter of the room now, trying to reach the open door from which Amelia had emerged. I doubted it held any escape, but it wasn't like he had anywhere else to go.

Zeb carried on, "Became a skilled runner, delivering elicit messages and such. But she ended up transporting something a bit too hot, and a competitor tipped off the guards. She slipped out of the city jail, so they tossed her in some mountainside prison. Apparently, she scaled a vertical cliff in a full blizzard to get out of that one. I spent a fair bit of suns tracking down her story, but I swear it was worth it for just the entertainment value; this girl had some grit."

Duncan was closing in on the door, crawling with his back to the wall, watching the rafters for any sign of movement.

"She managed well enough for a few more months, but then her luck ran out. She got bit, though I don't know the specifics there," he continued.

"That's a shame; she seemed like quite the character," I remarked.

"Ha! Then you'll love this. She survived; guards only caught up to her when she went to a sawbones to get the infected arm lopped off. She slipped away, then led them on a merry chase for months, brandishing this nasty hook where her hand used to be. Don't know what took her down in the end, but one of my contacts reached out to me; he recognized her when a courier brought in a ghoul with a hook for a hand."

With a flurry of movement, Duncan made a break for it, scrambling to his feet and bolting for the exit. There was a flash of movement in the lamplight as a hooked blade swung down from the darkness above, slamming into Duncan just below his collarbone. Duncan tried vainly to pull himself off the blade, but his legs soon gave out, and the ghoul in the rafters came down with him, twisting in the air to land squarely on his chest. I turned away as the sounds of feeding began, stumbling to the exit and just managing to see daylight before my stomach jettisoned breakfast all over the muddy ground. Every time I thought I had it under control, another image of that ghoul falling onto Duncan's chest pulsed through my mind, sending a twist through my stomach. I felt a gaunt hand patting me between the shoulder blades, Zeb making an awkward attempt at comforting me.

"Sorry about that, Winona. He had to be dealt with, but I could have warned you or handled it in private. I just got my blood up, those bandits hurt folk when they attacked. Don't worry, we'll burn his body in balefire; nobody will ever accuse Zebadiah of adding another ghoul to the world," he told me, dropping his voice to a reassuring tone.

"It's . . . it's OK." I rose unsteadily, then spat in a vain attempt to clear the taste from my mouth. "Yeah, a warning would have been great, and using a ghoul doesn't sit right with me, but I understand putting him down. Like you were saying, when they mess with family, you gotta send a message."

The silence stretched on for an awkward moment before Zeb cleared his throat. "Well . . . See anything you liked?" Zebadiah asked sheepishly.

I barked a quick laugh at that. "Yeah, I'll take the girl, Amelia. I've already got a solid ghoul for wrangling, but if I ever need a replacement, I'll happily take Gorm off you another time."

"If someone else doesn't beat you to it, that is, he's a rare find. But for what it's worth, I think you made the right call. Word of warning, though, she's slippery. Amelia's the docile type when you have your focus up, so I don't think she'll be any trouble on a sled team, but she tends to wander if you don't have your eye on her. We found her on the roof the first time she went missing, in a tree the next. Had to make a new solitary cell just for her after that."

"Oh boy, can't wait to take an escape artist out past the Wilderness Arch. Do you have a place where I can get to know her and get her harnessed?" I asked.

Zebadiah flashed me a gap-toothed smile. "Ya know, luckily for you, some old bastard figured you'd choose Amelia and had a harness made up for her just in case. The holding cell is out back, and I'll have her and the harness brought out."

I gave the man a quick hug before heading off in the direction he indicated. His methods were still a bit . . . brutal, but he had always looked out for me. If a man was cruel to his enemies but loyal to his friends, well, that was still a good man in my book.

The cell was a short distance behind the testing pen, with a guard standing by to unlock it. The purple flame above cast a lattice of shadows across the space, seeming to cut the ghoul inside with long lines of darkness. The guard handed me the harness, then swung the door open for me, shutting it again the moment I entered. A canvas duffel bag lay in the corner near the door. Amelia was crouched in the far corner, squatting down to rest on the balls of her feet, ready to move in an instant. I extended my mind out to her, sending out a rhythm of calm and safety that should keep her from lashing out. Any courier developed an eye for gauging a ghoul's age, and it was clear that Amelia had been recently turned. Her skin was an ashen grey, with a gaunt look around her cheekbones. There was a small cut in the skin near the corner of her mouth as well, but that was to be expected. That sort of damage was exceedingly common in even the newest ghouls; the creatures chomped their teeth endlessly, and the constant movement deteriorated the flesh.

"What's in the bag?" I asked the guard, nudging it with a toe.

"Her personal effects," he answered gruffly.

Now that was unexpected. When a ghoul came in, a rancher would strip them of anything valuable if the person who'd found the ghoul didn't get to it first. The exception was if the item were useful to the ghoul's skillset, like Gorm's weapon, and might up the resale value. I knelt to explore the bag, careful to stay facing Amelia. She should remain passive if my focus didn't slip, but I still wasn't turning my back on her until we were better acquainted. The bag was . . . full of arms? It took me a moment to put together that they seemed to be a variety of prosthetics, which I guess counted as personal effects. I would examine those on the road, but it did remind me of a more immediate concern.

"Stick your arm out, Amelia," I commanded, gesturing for her to show me her hook.

Amelia stood, strode over, and stuck out her skin-and-bone arm.

"Oh, a smartass ghoul, fantastic, you'll fit right in. The *other* arm, please."

Her reaction itself was interesting, maybe slightly concerning. Contrary to widely held belief, ghouls didn't actually hear orders. How could they? Their ears were as rotted as the rest of them. What they responded to was the mental connection we shared through the balefire. This meant that the intent of a command mattered more than the wording. Amelia could feel my intent and still deliberately chose to screw with me by offering up her other arm instead of the prosthesis. New fawns like her were strong-willed, but finding one so . . . nonverbally sarcastic was rare. I would have to keep an eye on her.

With amputation being the sole cure for a ghoul bite, prosthetics of varying quality were a common sight in the Empire. Most that lost a hand had to settle for an unmoving facsimile of a hand carved from a block of wood or maybe a simple metal hook. I had taken Amelia's arm to be a basic hook design as well, but further examination revealed an item of refined, efficient beauty. It resembled the head of an ice axe, the tip of the tool ending in a sharp pick, like the beak of a bird. The body of the tool was canted forward to help the tip pierce into an icy wall, though the slight red stain that adhered to it was a reminder that it was also adept at piercing flesh. From the quality of the build, I'd guess it was a custom piece.

"Let's get that off you," I told her. "I'll give it back when you need it, but I'm not letting you carry that around after seeing what you did to Duncan with it."

She removed the item with a series of deft, practiced movements, undoing the straps along her forearm, but a flash of metal under her sleeve gave me pause. Examining further, I found a metal brace that ran up her arm, hinged at her elbow, then stretched up further to a small metal spaulder that encased her shoulder. Underneath her oversized coat more straps extended out, firmly securing the whole apparatus to her body.

"I've never seen something like this . . . Show me. Show me what this does, Amelia."

The ghoul paused, and I swore she rolled her eyes, but she dutifully set to the task, holding her climbing tool steady between her thighs as she lined up the ends and buckled it back on. In a single fluid motion, Amelia leapt up to the side of the cage and hooked her climbing tool through the bars. Pulling herself close to the wall, she leapt again, threading the tool into the ceiling and allowing herself to hang there, all her weight suspended on her prosthetic.

"Ah, clever," I told her as she descended back to the ground. "You know, I had a drinking buddy try to shake a guy's hand once, accidentally pulled the man's fake arm off. Reeeaallyy embarrassing. But with that fancy harness, that hook isn't coming off you unless you want it to. You were damned smart when you were breathing, or you knew someone who was."

The rest of the process went smoothly, and she was outfitted in the new harness without too much difficulty, though I had to add a bit of padding to keep it from chafing against her prosthetic rig. Her pale dead eyes followed me the whole time, the balefire giving them the slightest purple tinge. On closer inspection, I realized that her hair had likely been cut post-mortem. The jet-black locks had been roughly hacked off, leaving her with a brutal case of undead bedhead that was the standard for working ghouls; long hair would just get in the way, and the ghoul doctors weren't concerned about what hairstyles were in fashion.

While I strapped her in, I kept a strong mental connection, listening to the discordant tones of her mind as they spilled back to me. There was a craving for wide open spaces, to feel the wind underneath you as you ran. That was exactly what I wanted to hear from a new team member, and I wondered if being confined was contributing to her mood. That suspicion was confirmed when I led her out of confinement, and her tense demeanor settled somewhat.

"Ha! Don't you worry; you'll have your fill of open spaces by the time we're done. Let's introduce you to the team," I told her, leading my new acquisition back to the *Ridgerunner*.

"Hey, kids, say hi to your new sister!" I called out to the group as I led Amelia back. Zeb had once again been good on his word, and a young man with an apron full of tools was finishing his examination of Bonk.

"What's the verdict, doctor? Is the patient going to pull through?" I asked, tossing Amelia's duffel bag into the cab of my sled.

"I'm sorry to tell you this . . . But we couldn't bring him back . . . He's dead." The doctor replied, straight-faced.

"You know, I've met dozens of ghoul docs, but they all have the same jokes."

"It's part of our training," he reasoned. "Your ghoul is good to go. There's a small fracture on his skull, but it's old. If he takes another hard knock, it might spread, though, so I'd get a stop hole drilled next time you're in town."

"Thanks, doc, have a drink on me." I smiled, tossing him a few silver moons for his troubles.

After he departed, I reorganized the team, allowing King to take his rightful place at the head of the pack, with Amelia replacing him alongside Bonk. I buckled her harness into the gangline, allowing her to pull against it and explore the small range of movement her position allowed. Before I left her, I made sure to remove her prosthetic, which garnered a dry chuff of discontentment from her. Most ghouls could make some sort of noise if their lungs were intact, but with their human intellect gone, they were largely limited to dog-like chuffs, barks, and howls.

"Yeah, yeah, yeah. Amelia, I watched you put this thing through a man's chest; you're not getting it back till I can trust you a bit more."

Amelia chuffed again, turned, and punched Craven in the face with her intact hand.

"Oh, come on!" I chided as Craven went down in a pile. "At least punch Bonk! He's wearing a helmet!"

Amelia went to act up again, but I sent a quick mental pulse to another ghoul. When she reared back to strike, she found her wrist encased in King's steel grip.

"I'll only do this once, Amelia," I told her. I knew she could not understand my words, but the emotions behind them would ring clear. "Everyone earns a nickname here. King earned his by being the absolute boss. I am sure you saw tough times while you were breathing, but I promise you that King saw twice as much when he was alive and twice as much again leading this team. This pack lives or dies together, and neither King nor I care for that lone wolf shit. So, you can run with us, or we can tie you up and dump you in the next lake we pass. Make sense?"

Amelia gargled a bit but fell in line sedately after that. It was my will that cowed her, but King was a capable instrument to get the point across. After that was settled, I led my team to the gates, where Zeb was waiting with a different guard. He handed me a scrap of paper and a small cloth sack.

"Here, Winona, that's the weight of the cargo, my workers saw to it while we were inside. A few mushrooms from our new grow house as well, to liven up your rations a bit," he explained, handing me a small bag.

"Mushrooms? Look at you, Zeb, picking up a hobby in your old age? I hope these are edible." I laughed, giving him a wink. Then I took a quick glance at the cargo weight they had written and sighed with relief. Ronny had been honest when he gave me the larger cargo's weight, and that was one less unknown I'd have to worry about on this trip.

"Hey, every mushroom is edible; some are just only edible once. We thought we'd got the good stuff the first time around, but poor Geoffrey was stuck in the outhouse for days...." He grinned back at me slyly.

"Ha! Well, I'm off." I gave him a quick hug goodbye, then climbed aboard my sled. "You stay safe, Zeb, and thank you again for the rush order; you're a lifesaver."

"My pleasure, young'un. Now get out there and make your dad proud!"

I waved to him once more, then stirred my team into motion, already feeling the slight increase in power through the tugging on the gangline. A big grin crept unbidden onto my face, and I didn't try to suppress it. A team with a missing member was like a hand with a missing finger. Now that my team was complete, I felt confident that we could punch out any obstacle ahead.

Zebadiah had the equivalent of speed stripes on his property, though, in true Zeb fashion, he had embellished the markers with his trademark flair. Instead of paint on trees, I passed the first of two large lion sculptures, sitting proudly with jaws open mid-roar. Once again, the timer started, and we cruised along until we passed the second lion. Jotting the time down, I was happy to see that my feeling was confirmed, and we were indeed moving at an increased pace. Admittedly the increase was small, Amelia was only a fawn and petite as well, but I had the feeling that her addition might have benefits beyond her ability to pull a sled.

With that in mind, I dug into the bag at my side, wanting to give Amelia's equipment a closer look as we cruised along. First off was the climbing tool she had brandished before. Someone had wiped off most of the grime, but I couldn't ignore the spots of red hiding in the corners. Duncan's blood was a grisly reminder of what happened, and I went to work cleaning the tool with an old rag and oil, both to prevent rust and to quiet the memory of his final moments. The chance to take a closer look confirmed the quality I'd noticed earlier. Amelia certainly had connections during her life. It was a shame she couldn't tell me her sources; I'd love to commission some of my own gear from such a skilled craftsman.

The next object was thinner, a flattened length of metal enclosed in a triangular leather sheath. I loosened the sheath and drew the item out, revealing the sheen of sharpened steel in the sunlight.

"Daaammmnnn girl. Shame you weren't wearing this when the ghouls found you; bet you could have cut your way clear of a dozen of the bastards with this thing," I murmured.

The blade in my hands was reminiscent of a sickle, but instead of a smooth curve, there was a series of straight double-bladed segments. The tip tapered to a point, then doubled back on itself to create a backward-facing barb. It was a vicious weapon and would have been impossible to conceal if worn. I couldn't recall ever seeing a weapon with a design like that, and certainly not one mounted to a prosthetic.

"This isn't something you build overnight, and I can't imagine this is a weapon you can just pick up and use without practice. Weird . . . "

How long had Amelia been surviving with one arm? There were so many jagged edges on this, the blade would be more of a danger to you than to anyone else unless you had trained with it extensively. Nothing in her pedigree implied that she was a warrior, but I also found it hard to believe that she had just stumbled across something this unique. A few spots of rust were evident on the blade, and it was clear that it had not been seen to since Amelia's death. Thankfully, I already had my cleaning supplies out and took care of the weapon as well. There was no way I was trusting Amelia with it for the foreseeable future, but I would much rather have it ready on the off chance I needed it.

Lastly, there was a piece I recognized, which was a relief after all the weirdness I'd pulled from the bag. It was a false hand, or to be more exact, a false arm. The prosthetic started where a person's bicep would be, then continued to an elbow joint, then down to a false hand. The hand was obscured by a long leather glove while a length of dirty, cream-colored fabric wrapped around the arm.

The proportions were lifelike as well, though maybe more suited to an average-sized man than a petite woman. Something felt off though . . . .

"Hey! Amelia! Raise your arm!" I prodded her through the bond, glad to see she was keeping pace with the others. After a stubborn pause, she raised her arm, holding the stump high for a moment before dropping it and falling back into rhythm with the team.

"You lost your arm below the elbow, so this wasn't made for you. Huh...You were a thief; maybe you stole it? Even then, how would you even know where to find something like this?" I mused aloud, unwrapping the fabric covering.

I had expected to find wood, maybe a bit of iron at the joints, but as the sunlight fell upon the prize in my hands, I saw the glimmer of gold instead. This prosthetic was a far cry from the utilitarian examples I'd seen other ghoul-bite survivors wear...It was art. There was a framework of metal, yes, but polished to a brilliant luster. Curved pieces of ceramic were inset at the bicep and forearm, mimicking the natural curve of muscles a real arm would have. Two solid bands of metal circled the arm, one at the top of the bicep, one midway along the forearm. They each protruded a few centimeters out, breaking from the natural lines of the prosthetic, but I couldn't even begin to divine what their purpose might be. Gold filagree swirled in delicate patterns across the entirety, forming letters that seemed vaguely familiar. I wracked my brain for a moment, frustrated with that tip-of-the-tongue sensation.

"Song Islands! That kid from the farmhouse, his stuff had the same designs! Amelia, you were a Song Islander too, right? Gods, you're a long way from home," I wondered aloud, hefting the arm in both hands. "Barely ever see your kind up this far north, and now I've come across two of you in as many days."

Instead of finding answers, further inspection just created more questions. The entire apparatus was hollow, and I soon found the hidden clasps that held each section closed. Maybe it wasn't a prosthetic after all; maybe it was...armor? I tried buckling it on, but it had been made for someone of a larger stature, and my elbow and wrist couldn't reach far enough to fit in where they should have.

"Who were you, Amelia? What were you up to before the ghouls got you?"

Regardless, it was a beautiful piece with the quality of an heirloom and begged to be put to paper. With that in mind, I propped the device against my windshield and took to sketching, doing my best to capture its elegant lines and strange runes. I let the hobby whittle away the afternoon, looking up briefly to confirm the waypoints on our route or to check in on how Amelia was faring. I was happy to see that she was holding her own for now, her course only showing slight deviations as she loped along with the rest of the crew. Amelia's placement had worked out well; Craven ran behind her but was so terrified of the newcomer that he drifted back slightly, giving her more space to run in. If she had been behind Tybalt, he might have simply trampled her if she began to lag. King also helped, pulling the gangline hard to keep it taut; it was common for new ghouls to get tangled in the gangline if there was too much slack. Fortunately, running a team was a simple task on a flat path in fair weather, so I was happy to build her experience now before things became tougher. The route to Skyroost led through harsh country, and Amelia was going to get a crash course in wilderness survival before the trip was done.

The rest of the day was uneventful, and we pulled into a deserted courier stop as the sun set. It was a bare-bones affair, one of many scattered across the wilds to provide small bits of comfort to a courier overnighting. There was an open-air shelter with a slanted roof, some-thing that I was grateful for as a flurry of snow began to fall. There was also a fire pit and a wooden outhouse reinforced with bands of iron, a common sight at these stops and a running joke among long-haul couriers. Due to the sparse construction of their sleds, skimmer couriers would be hard-pressed to survive a night outside, and more than one had been forced to spend the dark hours holed up inside one of these outhouses to shelter from wild ghouls or predators. Rolling into a courier yard smelling like sewage was a fantastic way to get your friends to laugh at you for weeks to come.

Heist wandered the ground just outside the shelter's coverage, digging in the snow and pulling up a rock she found buried, then dropping it and drifting off again. I left her to it as I attended to the various camp chores but called her back as I began to settle in for the night. When I had first acquired Heist, she had shown a talent for finding hidden caches; it wasn't uncommon for a courier to find something on their journey, then bury it near a courier stop to retrieve later. I always made Heist put her discoveries back, but the activity seemed to entertain her. She had lost the talent eventually, though, as all ghouls did. Time always eroded the echoes of a ghoul's past, turning them from clever fawns into strong but simple skellies, and you needed a good mix on your team to be successful as a courier.

Dinner was simple but filling, garnished with Zeb's dubious mushrooms. I glanced over at the outhouse again, now imagining spending my own night in the cramped space. Luckily, the mushrooms stayed settled, and after completing the standard array of chores, I slipped off into an easy sleep.

IX

——

Morning came, as it usually did, far too early. Even worse, I no longer had Billy's miracle ghoul to get a fire started. The ticking clock was always on my mind, conjuring images of that package losing heat with every passing minute. That was just my anxiety digging its claws in, though. I had done the calculations, and I knew that we should make it to that military outpost with time to spare. To reinforce that fact, I made sure to take a few minutes to build up a small fire from the dry kindling stacked nearby for hot breakfast and coffee. Fixating on time ticking away could be dangerous in this business, leading a courier to take more and more risks to chase the deadline. I would get my package where it needed to go on time, but I wouldn't let the stress of it all make me sloppy.

The snow was still coming down lightly, muffling all the sounds around us in that unique insulating way that new snow had. I took a step outside the shelter, savoring that first *crunch* of boots on virgin snow. I loved blazing new trails, seeing things that a scant few had laid eyes on, and living to tell the tale, all the stuff you read about in swashbuckler stories. But for today, I would be content with being the first person to carve some lines in this fresh powder.

"OK, team, if all goes well, we'll hit the Wilderness Arch this afternoon; then it's wild territory from there to Skyroost," I exposited. They couldn't understand the words, but you spend enough days alone and you start talking to all sorts of things for company.

"Let's pull hard, and . . . where's Amelia?" I stopped short, noticing her empty place in line. Even King looked nonplussed, which was an impressive emotion for the masked ghoul to convey. I looked closer and noticed that the harness had not been torn; it had been deliberately unbuckled. Heist and King were the only ghouls on the team with the mind and dexterity to pull that off, and Amelia had managed it literally single-handedly.

But, despite all her cleverness, Amelia suffered the same drawback every other ghoul did. She was incredibly stupid. Don't get me wrong, ghouls could be shockingly good problem solvers, even creative at times, but their ability to take in and process new information was severely limited. King was so useful because he had seen most of these routes in his living days, but if I took the team somewhere completely new, I would need to walk him through every turn. Ghouls could learn new skills and habits, but it took far more repetition than even a young child would need before the behavior caught on. In the same way, the ghoul that was Amelia Davies could surprise me with her skills, but was inherently predictable once you knew her quirks. I reached out with my mind to confirm, then slowly looked up to spot where Amelia nestled in the rafters. Gods only knew how she had scurried up there with one hand, but I ordered her down and back in line, then hopped up into the cargo bay, digging around for a small wooden trunk filled with various odds and ends that were specific to my ghouls. There were blinders to keep Craven from panicking in a crowd, a coiled spring that Scramble liked to play with, and a thick pair of mittens that I had bought soon after acquiring Heist. I carried one back to the line and slipped it over Amelia's intact hand with a satisfied smile. There were a few lengths of leather cord hanging off the end of the mitten, and I wrapped them around her arm several times before tying them tightly.

"You know, when I found Heist, she was an insatiable pickpocket, would pull the whole team off course to chase after a noblewoman with a pretty necklace. I swear, she must have been one hell of a thief in her living days. But I had to curb that behavior, so we strapped these mittens on. Just like that, she couldn't pick up a single thing, drove her crazy. But it stayed that way until she learned that the team came first. Now, I let her grab most anything she can reach, but only if she stays in line. You want your hand back; earn it. You want your fake hand back? You can earn that too. But only if you fall in line."

Amelia growled and stepped up to me. She had a slight advantage in height, but I didn't back down. She'd be able to sense my fear through the balefire bond, and it would only embolden her rebellious nature. But there was no fear to find, not today at least. As long as we both stayed in that purple light, I had all the power. Amelia chuffed and stepped back in line, pointedly staring forward.

"That's a good ghoul; we'll make a runner out of you yet! And hey, Mittens isn't the worst nickname a ghoul can have." I laughed, pushed aside the reminder that I was once again just talking to myself, and spurred the team into the swirling snow.

The gentle snowfall continued throughout the morning, limiting visibility somewhat but not enough to impede our progress. The light flakes merely blanketed the horizon, giving the world a close, quiet feeling as if we were running through a shaken snow globe. An hour or so later, we slid out onto the shore of a frozen lake, the clear shoreline offering a respite from the winding forest path. I winced as the sled bumped over a rock hidden by snowfall and glanced longingly out at the frozen lake to our right. It was so, so tempting to steer us out onto the ice and enjoy the smooth ride it offered, but I knew that a decision like that could turn deadly in an instant. There were a handful of ice paths commonly monitored and used by couriers, but for anything else, you were rolling the dice on if the ice could support your weight. It was especially dangerous in these conditions, with the recent snow obscuring any cracks or wet spots that might hint at thin ice. For now, I would take my bumps and stick to the shore.

But, another bump nearly sent my head to the ceiling, and I decided to pull out my chart and see if we could plot out an alternate path. It felt petty to change course just to avoid a few bumps, but I reminded myself that bending a metal runner or smashing a ghoul's foot would slow us down more in the long run. I bent over to retrieve the first chart when a sudden jerk pulled the sled to one side, paired with a cacophony of panicked feedback through the mental bond.

"What the hell are you guys playing at!?" I barked, hauling myself back up. Peering ahead, I could see three mounds, probably boulders covered in snow, except that the first boulder had sprouted some sort of mast, maybe two meters high, by my guess. Another moment passed, and two more masts sprouted up. People clad in leather and fur appeared at the bases of the masts and were laboring to lock them in place, their white and grey cloaks rendering them almost invisible until now.

The pure absurdity of the sight left me stunned for a moment, but I snapped out of it as my training took over. I followed a hunch and cracked my door open to glance behind us. Two mounted horsemen had burst from the trees behind, churning through the powder with long strides. A dog sled followed a second later, with two more people crouched on it.

I closed the door, took a deep breath, and then enjoyed a long slurp of coffee from my flask. The next few minutes would be life or death, but panic was just as deadly as my assailants; I wouldn't let fear kill me even before these bastards had their chance.

"OK, bandits ahead and bandits behind. Let's go to work," I snarled.

My assailants had bungled the ambush, fortunately. Though I had never seen this sort of trap in person, I had heard stories from other couriers. There would be rope or barbed wire strung in between the poles to entangle my team and bring the *Ridgerunner* to a halt, easy pickings for these brigands. But they'd sprung their trap prematurely, giving me time to react. I retrieved an unstrung recurve bow from the wall behind me, lodging one end in a corner of the cab and compressing it until I could slip the string around both ends. I retrieved the quiver as well, slinging it over my back and wincing at how light it felt. These arrows were meant to take down small critters for dinner, not kill bandits. If I survived this trip, it might be time to upgrade to a bow with a heavier draw weight or even a firearm. Those were expensive and temperamental, but it was better than shooting at bandits with a bow I used to hunt hare and grouse. As this was happening, I was also reaching out to King, feeding him new orders. A steep hill had risen beside us, preventing escape into the forest and pinning us between the two bandit parties.

"King! I want you to give us a last-minute turn, take us out over the ice, and loop around the trap!" I called out, pushing the door open and steeling myself to crawl out, the baying of sled dogs growing louder. But before I did, I had my own trap to spring.

"Let's show these assholes exactly what they've caught," I growled, yanking down on a yellow-handled lever on the console. There was a click of hidden clockwork, and three spring-loaded latches opened, releasing Grah, Champ, and Tybalt from the gangline. The sled began to slow with the departure of the two strongest members, but I lashed at the remaining ghouls with my mind, forcing them to pull in a frenzy to keep our speed from dropping. With that task done, I swung outside and sidled around the edge of my sled until I could step into the cargo bay. As I performed that tightrope act, my three fighting ghouls snapped into motion, released to their tasks with only the barest motivation from me.

Grah was first to react, his newfound freedom causing him to shout with unrestrained joy.

grahgrahgrahgrAHGRAHGRAHGRAH!!!

Despite his usual clumsiness, he was quick to slide his shield into place, affixing it over one arm as the first projectiles fell around him. Grah was a screaming ghoul with a bright red shield, and every bandit along the ambush line took a shot at him as he thundered toward the trap. Various arrows thudded into the shield or slipped by to slam into his padded gambeson, sending the ghoul reeling drunkenly. It wasn't enough to take him down, though, and Grah regained his feet, running headlong into the trap's embrace. The hidden wires slapped into his chest, ensnaring him even as he tried to push through to the bandits on the other side. His momentum flipped him over, slamming him back-first into the snow with a final indignant *Graahhh*.

While the bandits had spent an armory's worth of ammunition trying to bring Grah down, they had failed to notice the greater threat. Tybalt had disappeared moments after release, fading into the white around him like a dissipating ghost. Between Grah's display and Tybalt's mottled camouflage, not a single bandit noticed the killer until it was far, far too late. Tybalt dove through the gap Grah had forced in the trap, landing bodily on a hapless man who had been moving in to finish Grah off. Tybalt cradled the man's head with almost tender care, then jabbed both his iron-clad thumbs down, pressing them through his prey's eye sockets with agonizing slowness. One of the man's compatriots rushed to his friend's defense, swinging a hammer down at Tybalt's skull. Without even seeming to notice the man, Tybalt lashed out with a foot, snapping the bandit's knee backward in the joint and sending him sprawling into the snow.

"No . . . NO PLEASE!" the bandit cried in terror as Tybalt scuttled over to his next victim. The pitch of his screams seemed to enrage Tybalt, and the ghoul silenced the noise violently. Iron claws were forced into the man's mouth, then down his throat before emerging in a spray of red at the base of his neck. Tybalt flexed his arm almost casually, tearing the bandit's jaw out in a spray of gore that speckled the ghoul in crimson.

The massacre was stomach-churningly savage, but it was that exact brutality that led me to keep such a violent creature around. Almost all ghouls were single-minded hunters, and if they pinned down prey they would tear into their target until long after the creature was dead. Tybalt, on the other hand, was like a feral cat, with a hunting tendency that bordered on sadistic. He would leap from kill to kill, taking down his fifth target while a normal ghoul would still be chewing on the first. Letting him off the leash always meant buckets of blood, but better theirs than mine.

While Tybalt played offense, Champ took defense, drifting to the back of the sled just as I knocked an arrow. Our pursuers were still closing the gap, so Champ put his hands on the back of the sled and pushed, pouring his considerable strength back into the sled's speed. Leaning into the back wall of the sled to steady myself, I fired an arrow, swearing as it went wide. Our pursuers fired back in kind, and I dove for cover behind the crate, curling into a ball as arrows started thudding into the sled around me. Damn, they were good shots if they were managing to hit the sled while firing from horseback. The dog sled pulled alongside, and the woman who crouched in front leapt across the gap, an impressive feat with both sleds careening across the uneven ground. She flashed me a feral smile of broken teeth, eyes flashing in madness or desperation, then raised an axe to strike. Champ let go of the *Ridgerunner* with one hand and grabbed her ankle with frightening speed; as swiftly as she had landed, the woman was airborne again. Champ snapped his arm forward as if he were cracking a whip, and the woman was slammed back onto the sled, her scream of terror cut short as her head hit the lip of the sturdy crate. With the casual violence of a child abusing a toy, Champ lifted her again and used the limp woman like a club to swing at the other man, still clinging to his dogsled. Both went down in a tumble of cascading snow, and the dogs took off, still doing their best for a musher who was no longer present.

With one foe foiled, Champ latched back onto the sled just in time for King to initiate the turn, steering the team out onto the ice to avoid the trap. I grabbed my brazier's mounting as we slid across the ice, looking forward to gauge our progress as we skirted around the main group of bandits, drawing jeers and arrows in equal measure. One enterprising individual stepped out on the ice as if to pursue us; he only made it a meter further before Tybalt materialized from the snow behind him. The ghoul stretched his massive arm span, grasped the man by skull and ankle, then folded him in half with a horrific muffled crunch of bone, killing him as casually as I might snap a twig.

Averting my eyes from the massacre, I caught a strange pattern ahead—footprints on the lake snow—stomped in circles. The circles were dark in the middle, wet patches where water had seeped through.

"King! Take us out farther, now!" I ordered.

Clever bastards, they had hidden a second trap for anyone who dodged the first, and I'd run us right into it. The ice began to crack under the snow, hidden fractures spiderwebbing out between holes that had been dug in the ice. King had turned quickly, but in this case, quickly was not fast enough. The ghouls were too light to get proper traction on the ice, and they scrabbled desperately for traction as the *Ridgerunner's* momentum carried it forward: With a sudden resonant crack, the ice gave way. The back of the sled dropped, and Champ went with it, nearly disappearing into the muddy water that swirled up around us. The front of the sled seesawed upwards in response, and I was cast down onto my bags, scrambling for purchase in the cargo bay to avoid tumbling into the icy water myself. Luckily, our precious box of medicine halted my slide, giving me something firm to anchor myself with. The sled made forward progress, and it looked like we would pull back onto thicker ice, but then the next section gave way, tilting us back into the water again. Freezing water splashed up around me, and my balefire flickered as a few drops hit the fire with a low hiss. My mental connection to the ghouls grew fuzzy for a moment, then strengthened again as the flame recovered. If that fire went out, the bandits would be the least of my problems.

"Champ, buddy, I need you!" I cheered the ghoul on, only his head above the water now. Champ had a protective streak a kilometer wide, and I poured my will into it through the balefire bond. "Lift us up! C'mon, lift!"

In the end, it was the shallow lakebed that saved us. We had not ventured far onto the lake, and the silty bottom couldn't have been more than a meter and a half below the churning surface. With a bit of careful coaching, Champ was able to get his feet under him and lift the rear of the sled upward, tilting us back to a level footing. Now that the other ghouls were no longer fighting the weight of the sled slipping back, they began to regain traction, pulling clear of the broken ice. It happened so fast that the sled slipped free of Champ's hands, and we almost left the floundering ghoul behind. With a lunge, I managed to reach down and grab his hand, pulling him along behind us until he could get to his feet and run again. It was always surprising to remember how light the skellies were. Despite the massive strength they were gifted with, they had no mass besides bare bone, and even the smallest courier could probably shoulder a pair of them in a pinch.

Free of the ice, we pushed on, rounding a nearby outcropping before skidding to a halt. I stepped clear of the sled and hopped to the ground, then nearly fell face-first into the snow as my legs buckled. Adrenaline still pulsed through me, gripping my heart like a vice, begging me to run, to hide, anything but stand here. The whole encounter, from first contact to this moment now, might not have lasted more than two minutes, but I swore that I had lived entire days that felt shorter, and this day was still far from over.

X

—

We approached the ambush point from the opposite side, treading carefully, ready to retreat or fight again at a moment's notice. The first movement I saw was the two horsemen, now in full retreat, one riding double with another survivor on board. It looked like we had won the fight, though I had to admit luck had factored into the victory as much as skill. A more experienced group would have raised the posts at the last minute, then the unavoidable impact would have snared or outright dismembered a substantial portion of my team. After that, they would attack the balefire, covering it or upending it into the snow. No balefire meant no bond, and my team would be reduced to wild ghouls that would be far easier to dispatch.

This trap was indicative of a larger arms race, the bandits inventing new ways to catch us as fast as we found new ways to fight back. The harness release I had utilized was a good example of that, a recent innovation to help us better protect ourselves. The latches were still prone to freezing shut when you needed them, but overall, the system was well worth the price. Being able to free up a portion of your team to engage the enemy while continuing your escape was a godsend, and I promised myself that I'd preach the virtues of the system to any courier I came across who had yet to adopt it.

The biggest drawback was that once you set the ghouls free, you now had to capture them again. The balefire's influence faded with distance, and I'd have to drag Tybalt right underneath it to get the wily ghoul back under my control.

The danger of trying to recapture him was made even more evident as we entered the killing field where Tybalt had done his grisly work. You could fight a ghoul like Tybalt; of course, a war hammer strike could shatter bone and leave the ghoul crippled. But landing such a heavy blow on a creature so preternaturally fast took a level of skill that these bandits clearly did not possess. The people that tried to fight had been taken out with surgical precision, metal claws or gnashing teeth delivering wounds that killed in an instant. Those that tried to run, or those that failed to see him coming, were given executions so creatively sadistic that it made me glad that Tybalt was a ghoul now instead of a living person who could pursue their own agenda.

Grah, on the other hand, was where we had left him, ensnared and struggling pitifully in the trap. I left him in place for the moment and found Tybalt not too far away, tracking him by the swathes of red blood that stood stark against the white snow. Unsurprisingly, he was doing something horrendously cruel. One last bandit was trying to crawl away, a hand pressing against her fatal stomach wound. That sort of injury would kill slowly, and Tybalt showed no interest in hastening the process. He squatted on his haunches behind her, reaching out a claw to drag her back to him every time she tried to get away. Another bandit lay dead nearby; his intestines pulled out in long loops that had been wrapped around his neck and used to throttle him.

I moved to draw my bow, planning to put the woman out of her misery, but found my hand shaking. The limb seemed fine—no injuries to speak of—but the white snow around me was turning grey at the edges, my vision tightening to a dim tunnel. The blood, the viscera, it was too much; oh gods, the bodies were steaming in the cold, broken open like rotting fruit. The last of that adrenaline-fueled energy bled away, and black horror spilled in to fill the gap, squeezing the air from my lungs.

With a groan, I fell to one knee, the panic hitting me like a suffocating wave.

"C'mon... Come on... get up," I grunted, trying and failing to stand on shaky legs.

In those moments of violence, there wasn't time to think. When the metal hit the meat, you either acted or you died; there was no third option. You took that fear and revulsion and panic, and you locked it away long enough to do what was needed, but those feelings never stayed buried for long. I lifted my head and almost vomited, the carnage around me overwhelming. There wasn't much that could shake the constitution of a courier—we dealt with the dead too much to be squeamish—but hearing the sobbing cries of the dying, smelling vital organs now exposed to the light of day... fuck. Some days I wished I were numb to it all; other days, I wondered what kind of monster that would make me.

I forced my lungs to work, pulling in deep breaths that steadied my vision and slowed my pounding heart. I would handle this later, maybe do some journaling, maybe have a good cry. I'd let those ugly emotions have me, but not right now. Besides recapturing Tybalt, there were other pressing concerns. Ghoul bites were usually a slow death, but there were exceptions. If you were bitten, then died of other causes before the bite killed you, the magic would flare up and overtake your body in moments. Tybalt had killed every other bandit in sight, but I was sure he had taken a bite out of more than one before executing them. Which meant we didn't have long before these bandits reanimated and went looking for a meal.

Punishing myself to stand, I turned and dug into the back of my sled, never taking my eyes off Tybalt. Navigating by touch, I retrieved a long stake and a small hammer that Champ then used to drive the stake deep into the frozen earth. The stake had a hook that I hung a small pulley wheel from, and then I finished the assembly by threading a long length of rope through it. Now that my fishing rod was built, I just needed the bait.

"C'mon, Bonky boy, time to get some exercise," I sighed, shrugging off the fatigue for a bit longer. I unhooked Bonk from the line and handed him the end of the rope. "Make it quick. I want to put this place behind me."

Bonk stalked towards Tybalt, the difference in physicality almost comical. Tybalt was two meters of distilled violence, camouflaged bone now splattered crimson with fresh blood. Bonk was a stocky fellow with a beer belly, a fawn who was only just beginning to show the more severe effects of decay. The five o'clock shadow he'd died with and his padded leather helmet gave him the air of a star athlete now well past his prime. Tybalt sensed the new intruder and spun around, his mouth dripping red as he sank into a defensive crouch. Bonk merely regarded him calmly, knotting the rope into a looped lasso. Tybalt put one foot on the woman, then reached down and snapped her neck with a quick twist. The grotesque sound of the execution nearly had me retching again, but I forced it down. Show that sort of weakness now, and Tybalt might try to make me his next meal.

To the surprise of absolutely no one, Tybalt attacked first, exploding out of his crouch in a leaping strike toward Bonk's head. Bonk responded by swaying to one side and throwing the loop up in Tybalt's path. As Tybalt's momentum carried him past, Bonk tightened the loop, lassoing Tybalt's wrist. The taller skelly flailed around in a backhanded swing, but Bonk was already gone, sliding between his opponent's legs and taking the rope with him. Every strike Tybalt threw met with nothing but air, and every movement entangled him further. The larger ghoul was death incarnate to any human target I had set him against, but now Bonk was making him look like a drunken brawler, swinging at thin air. Bonk withdrew moments later, leaving Tybalt a tangled mass of rope and frustration that ineffectually hobbled after his opponent.

"OK, Champ, reel in our catch," I commanded. Champ pulled on the far end of the rope, dragging Tybalt back towards the light. With each meter, the murderous drum beat of his rage grew stronger, pulsing in my head like a migraine, resisting any attempt at control. But the balefire bolstered me as well, giving me greater strength to exert my will as we reeled him in. He lashed out, both physically and mentally, but it was a battle I had won before, and I wasn't losing the fight for dominance today. Tybalt was a mountain of hatred and aggression, but I was the ocean, and I would pound into him with waves of mental strength until he fell to rubble at my feet. Every courier had their own approach, but I found out that the tried-and-true carrot-and-stick method worked best. For the carrot, I sent images of our past adventures. The battles we had fought, the people he'd slain in my employ, and most importantly, the rivers of blood I could lead him to if he fell in line. I followed it with an image of Tybalt chained up and tossed in the lake, sinking into the inky blackness forever, never tasting a fight or wielding his sadistic artistry again. The mental battle raged for a few moments longer, but the victor was never in doubt. Tybalt knew it as well as I did but still put up token resistance to avoid complete submission. Once I had him back under control, I put him to work, helping me collect the corpses that had been slain. We'd hobble the lot of them, then tear that trap down and use it to bind them to one of the posts so that neither the trap nor the ghouls could pose a threat to travelers. Taking down the trap also freed Grah, who had accumulated a handful of deep cuts from the wire, along with a grouping of arrows that stuck out of his shoulder and thigh. The flesh wounds were superficial, but it also looked like he had snapped a bone in his left forearm, judging from the malformed shape jutting out. Grah couldn't feel it, obviously, but a break like that would soon push through the skin, snag on things, and eventually rip the limb clean off.

I unhooked Heist so she could strip the bodies of any valuables, though two were already twitching as they finished the transformation from person to corpse to ghoul. I could feel them through the balefire, though the sensation of two ghouls coming into existence from nothingness was always unsettling. The connection confirmed that these were the only two bandits that had been bitten, and again I was glad that Tybalt's urge to kill had been greater than his urge to feed.

As we worked, the sled dog team wandered over, shy of the new presence and tense from the spilled blood but unsure of what else to do. I approached the dogs with caution, keeping a close eye on their body language. The sled dogs I had encountered before were intelligent, energetic animals, but of all the ways to die, torn apart by bandit dogs was quite low on my list. I knelt and let the lead dog sniff at my hand until he butted his head against me, searching for head scratches. Once I had won over the leader, the others piled on. Between a flurry of dog licks, I managed to cut each of their harnesses off, freeing them to chase each other in the snow. It was a shame; if I'd had the time, I'd love to bring them with me, strong dogs like this would fetch a high price. But with wilderness ahead and no feed for the animals, I was not willing to deal with that added responsibility. Looking at these half-wild hounds, I had little concern about their survival. They would be hunting on their own by the end of the day, if they didn't decide to feast on the corpses of their previous owners first.

After freeing the dogs, I searched around, discovering the bandit's impromptu camp just inside the tree line. My bet was that they had a more permanent base nearby, but this would give them some comfort while waiting in ambush, as well as a place to store their ill-gotten gains. There were small crates filled with canned food, a pile of dried lumber, and at the back, a long shape hidden by a tarp. I pulled the covering away; I figured that since these bastards had nearly gotten me killed, I was going to steal anything that looked vaguely useful.

All thought of salvage disappeared when the tarp slid away, revealing the skeletal shape of a skimmer sled. A nagging familiarity pulled at my mind. The sled tugged at the edge of my memory ... every sled was unique, and I had seen the sleek lines of this one before, and recently ... Damn it.

The bandits had jumped Blondie.

It was, without a doubt, Blondie's sled. The young man who had taken my message to Zeb's place had departed early this morning, but it looked like he'd never reach his destination.

It felt like I had been punched in the gut. Losing a courier to the dangers of the wild wasn't an uncommon occurrence, but the suddenness of it all . . . It had barely been a day since the last time I'd seen Blondie, and now he was just . . . gone. He would never laugh again or hold his loved ones. He would never again lend a hand to a courier in need . . . .

Some, you knew it was coming; the drunks, the addicts, the ones who refused to retire as their health faltered, those were the ones you knew would push their luck too far. But the young ones, the bright sparks like Blondie and Billy, seeing one of those sparks go out before they could grow to their full potential always cut deep. Blondie had gone down fighting, though, as evidenced by the fact that the tiny balefire brazier on the back of his sled had been extinguished. The bandits would have had to extinguish my fire to take me down, or else I would just have my ghouls cut them to pieces while I hid in my cab. But for a skimmer, the ambushers would have done everything they could to capture a lit brazier. One well-placed arrow to down the exposed courier and they would have their own flame, allowing them to command ghouls for their own ends.

No courier would allow such a powerful tool to fall into bandit hands if they could prevent it, and Blondie had likely cast the coals into the snow seconds before they cut him down. The bandits could collect the brazier and the extinguished coals, but they would have no way to light it and gain control over their own ghoul minions. I would need to alert local guards to this place at some point; they would retrieve and safeguard the sled until it could be returned to church service. There would also be a decent sum in commission for returning the sled, which would be split between me and whatever living family Blondie might have. I made a mental note to check up on who Blondie's next of kin was once I was back in Ozero. He might have been the sole breadwinner for his family, and I could spare the coin from my share if they needed it. He had helped me out, after all; the least I could do was pay the kindness forward.

Returning to the team, I ordered Bonk to tie up the two bandit ghouls that had started to shamble towards me; then, I performed a bit of quick field repair on Grah. I splinted the arm with thin strips of wood, bound it tight, then strapped it to his chest so it wouldn't bounce around. There was a kit in the back for a more permanent fix, but that would have to wait until we stopped tonight. With all that taken care of, I turned to Heist and the little pile of goodies she had gathered at her feet.

"What do we have here, girl? Anything good?" I asked, squatting down next to her.

The pile was typical for a bandit clan of this size, a mix of home-made items and trinkets stolen from their victims. You couldn't eat gold, so anything of real value was traded for more practical items. Most of it wasn't worth taking, though there were a few pieces I could pawn for drinking money. Of these items, I tossed a handful of colorful pebbles to Heist, along with a thin necklace of fake gold, all of which she eagerly slipped into a leather bag hidden inside her semi-skeletal body. Previously, Heist would try to steal from the pile before I could notice, but the restricting mittens and having Champ grab her by the feet and shake the valuables loose soon taught her that she would keep more trinkets by playing along. There were two items of note, the first being a bone-handled knife of knapped obsidian in a brown leather sheath. Knives like that were devilishly sharp but also inconsistent and prone to breaking. The volcanic glass actually bore more than a passing resemblance to the stone edges of the coalblade. I wondered if those stones were as brittle as obsidian; it would help explain why coalblades were designed as a sort of bladed club since a sword made of obsidian would have shattered the first time you hit something with it. Regardless, the knife was a beautiful piece and would be a nice addition to the shelf of oddities in my tiny apartment back in Ozero.

The other prize was a pouch of golden coins, though they were a coinage unlike any I had seen before. The Balefire Express was a network of couriers that spanned the entire Osgil Empire, and working out of the port cities exposed you to a variety of distinct cultures, along with their respective currencies. In my time I had seen a half dozen forms of money, but this was new even for me. There was only one denomination present, a thick golden coin stamped with the image of a skull, its jaw hanging open in a silent scream as flames enveloped it. Many of the coins had irregular edges, though I couldn't discern if that was from poor manufacturing or due to enterprising conmen clipping the coins for the gold shavings. Either way, the few coins in the bag should have been more than the bandits would make in half a year's dishonest work if they were limiting themselves to ambushing the occasional traveler. This discovery brought up multiple possibilities, all worrying in their own ways. It could be that there was a group of rich travelers with a currency I didn't recognize plying Empire roads, and they had been caught in the bandit trap, or there might be a new player in the area that was paying off the bandits. It might be that they had bribed the bandits for safe passage, or worse, they could be financing them to set up shop here and jump any poor traveler that came this way. It wasn't unheard of, and more than one trade guild had used bandits as a sort of dry land privateer force to hinder their competitors.

"Stranger and stranger," I muttered, rubbing a thumb over the stamped image. "OK, everyone, we've lost enough time here. Get in line and let's hit the road."

Bonk had secured the two ghouls to a nearby tree, and I debated what to do with them. Hypothetically, I could have commanded them to climb my sled and stick their heads in the brazier, letting the magic flame burn them to ash. But freshly turned ghouls could be capricious creatures, and I wasn't planning to let them anywhere near the sled I called home. I settled on ordering Champ to break their limbs. It was grisly, but hobbling the creatures like this would ensure that these bandits would never endanger anyone again.

I reorganized my team back in line, then did a quick walk around, looking for any damage from our encounter that I had missed before. My attackers had targeted my sled far more than my team with their arrows, and while there were a few shafts I had to twist and pull from the wood, I didn't see any damage that looked concerning. Reaching with my mind, I stirred my team to motion, and we left the slaughterhouse we'd created far behind. Once we were moving, the fatigue really set in. Cold shakes shivered down my spine, and my eyes drooped, setting me to lean heavily against the rear wall of the cab. From my snack drawer, I withdrew a small pack of chocolate-covered nuts from my favorite confectionery shop in Ozero. I was hopeful that the influx of sugar and protein would keep me alert throughout the rest of the day.

There was also the knowledge that I hadn't seen the ambush coming and that if not for King's quick reaction and the bandits' incompetence, I'd have been a goner. Admitting that came with a wave of hot shame, but I could either wallow in that feeling or do something about it. So, I took that shame, let it fill me, then let it flow back out, off into the cold wastes behind us.

Instead of wallowing in it, I endeavored to do better. The next time bandits came calling, I would see it coming, and all they would see was my sled gliding off into the distance, with me laughing all the way.

XI

——

After the excitement of the morning, I felt confident that nothing could surprise me. A mythical yeti could descend from the mountains and ask me to play cards, and I would probably just ask what the buy-in was. After we left the lakeside, the path widened out into a more established track. There was a sparse cluster of villages in this area, all trying to find that balance of being remote enough to avoid Empire control but close enough to a city to benefit from Empire protection. We made a short detour to one such settlement, the hamlet of Bale's Blessing. It was a bold name for a small group of houses, its claim to fame being an old grand brazier that had stood extinguished for longer than the eldest villager had been alive. But at least it was large enough to warrant a small guard contingent that I could alert to the bandits I had run afoul of. They had noted the decrease in travelers in the last few weeks, but it had not yet reached a level that garnered investigation. The guards would spread the word to other villages as well in case the remaining bandits went looking for new targets. I also handed over a quick sketch of the strange symbol I had seen on the coins, which the guards would send back to Ozero with the next courier. I had debated giving them an actual coin to return to my superiors but figured that if I handed over an actual gold coin to a backcountry guard, it would find its way into the local bartender's pocket instead of the intended recipient.

My civic duty complete, I left the sleepy hamlet behind and continued north, watching the road we traveled dwindle to a meandering path. Towering pine trees cropped up on either side, blanketing the path in deep shadow. There was little movement between the pines, and their thick trunks formed bare columns that led us deeper in. A power lay here, a . . . sanctity to this place that made it feel more ancient and primal than any other stretch of forest I had ridden through on the trip.

Then the forest opened into a glade; wild grass would grow here in the summer, but for now it was simply a bare circle of fresh snow. I ordered the team to a stop, then climbed into the back, withdrawing a long package wrapped in cloth from the storage under my bunk. With quick, practiced motions, I pulled the cloth away, revealing a cane of blackthorn wood. The gnarled length was textured and dark, contrasting with the golden honey brown of the polished knob that served as a handle. Every trainee was gifted a cane on their graduation day, a physical symbol of their elevation into the ranks of a full courier. Officially, the cane served as a status symbol, a way to demonstrate that these ruffians clad in fur and leather were no mere traders and had the backing of the church behind them. Couriers existed with a foot in both worlds; they should be as comfortable in the wilderness as we were in a cathedral, though in reality, that was rarely the case. Anyway, the cane was a symbol that opened many doors and made us feel a bit more civilized after long days beyond the walls.

In my experience, the canes served a secondary purpose as well. As Balefire Church officials, couriers rubbed elbows with the gentry of the Empire from time to time. There were a handful of good people among them, but in general, the upper class was as eager to take offense as couriers were to give it. The nobility also favored dueling to settle disputes, but imperial law stated that the person challenged to a duel had the honor of picking the weapons. Many a nobleman had issued a challenge, confident in his years of sword training, only to face a knife-wielding courier who'd honed their skills wading into back-alley brawls and fending off attempted muggings. That was ages back, though, when the Osgil Empire was still in its infancy. It became such a problem that someone decided to give the couriers something less lethal to carry around. This single act likely dropped the rate of stab wounds among the gentry overnight, though I imagined cases of concussions rose proportionally. Dueling had fallen out of fashion, and new couriers were taught to mind their manners around the nobles, but the tradition stuck. Cane in hand, I led my team across the glade on foot, breathing deep of the clean, pine-scented air. This was an old tradition, and a sacred one for couriers. It could not be rushed.

At the far end of the glade lay the Wilderness Arch, standing tall and proud among the pines. It had come into existence centuries ago when the borders of the Empire were still in flux. Some enterprising duke had ordered the construction of a large, sturdy, wooden trellis built to form a sort of ceremonial gateway when crossing the border of his lands into the wilderness beyond. For reasons lost to time, a courier had threaded his cane into a hole in the trellis before departing, then perished in the wastes beyond. The cane was left behind, a monument to the loss. Thus began the tradition: couriers would thread their cane into the trellis as they left, then retrieve it again when they returned. But not every person returned, and as more couriers fell, more canes stood abandoned. With time, it became a memorial for all couriers who lost their lives in the line of duty, and any canes recovered from the fallen eventually found their way here.

The arch that towered before me now had hundreds of staves threaded into it, bundled so densely that the lacquered canes supported each other long after the original trellis had rotted away. Long canes, short ones, bare wood, and vibrant paint spanning generations of styles and materials. All glittering with frost, each a memorial to the fallen long after their names had been forgotten. Carefully, I found a spot and slotted my cane firmly into the mass, adding another support to the growing archway. I hadn't found Blondie's cane, but it wasn't uncommon for skimmer couriers to leave their canes at home for convenience; I would ask his family about it when I followed up with them and would see to it that his cane made it to this final resting place. And hell, maybe one day a young courier like Billy would be looking at my cane, wondering what my story had been. But, if the fates had decided that it was my time to die, I was going to make the bastards work for it. My ghouls dug their feet into the snow, and we slid under the arch out into the wilderness. The towering pines began to dwindle soon after, to be replaced with hibernating deciduous trees, winter birds singing from their skeletal branches. It was a wonderful way to shake off the gravity of the arch, but I reminded myself that the landmark had real consequences. From here on out, there were no guard patrols to rely on, and the far-flung villages out here were wary of outsiders. One settlement might trade for goods, but the next might just as likely kill you and take whatever you were transporting. The singular light of safety in the wild darkness was a dot on the map, an alleged military outpost I had never heard of before, sitting out beyond Empire borders for no discernible reason. I just hoped I could find the place. You would think a large settlement like that would be hard to miss, but given the endless expanse of the north, it could become a needle in a haystack.

But that was a problem for another time, and there was a smorgasbord of current issues to deal with. First on the list was finding a place to sleep for the night. There were no marked courier refuges this close to the arch since outbound couriers would generally rest nearby and cross the arch in the morning, and inbound couriers would push on into the night to reach the safety of one of the local villages. Given that, I steered the team off the track as the light began to fade, paralleling the path in a search for a safe place to stop. After some searching, we stumbled across a dry gully and carefully slid down to the bottom. Come spring, this would be home to a torrent of ice-melt water. But in the dead of winter, it served as an impromptu shelter that would let us build a fire safe from prying eyes.

I set my ghouls to work as we unpacked. With a bit of prompting,

Craven gathered firewood within the confines of the balefire light while King and Heist set up a tarp to create a lean-to shelter against the side of the sled, angled so it would still let the purple light in. The cold didn't bother the ghouls, but there was still a danger in the possibility of ice buildup. With no body heat, any water that landed on the ghouls could freeze overnight, leaving the weaker ones frozen to near immobility come morning. It was a lesson I had learned the hard way on one of my first solo courier trips. Freezing rain had swept through overnight; I had slept soundly while my ghouls sat outside, getting coated with layer after layer of ice. When I woke, I could barely force my door open, then spent almost half the day chipping ice from ghoul and harness before we could get moving. We were reaching the latitudes where the cold went from biting inconvenience to lethal threat, and I would not make the same mistake twice.

Once we had a fire crackling and dinner starting to cook, I had a moment of free time to see to Grah. In a perfect world, we would keep that arm bound until we could get a ghoul doc to repair it, but I wouldn't find one of those until Skyroost and Grah would likely need both his arms well before then, so it fell to me to perform a bit of primitive surgery. We cleared a space near the firelight for Grah to lay out his broken arm, and I dug around until I found a small, lacquered box of tools for just this purpose. Pressing into the dead flesh with gloved fingers, I found the source of the break, a clean snap in one of Grah's forearm bones. I couldn't recall if it was the ulna or the radius, a slip that my father would have berated me for, but I didn't need to know the proper name of the bone to fix it. I strapped Grah's wrist down, then drew out a thin scalpel, palpating along the forearm with my thumbs to find the exact location of the break again. The malformed bulge was easy to find, and I cut into the flesh, working slowly and methodically until white bone emerged into the firelight.

"Oooohh, that's one nice break, Grah. We're gonna need some help getting this set," I told him conversationally, then turned away to holler at the others. "King! Get over here and help me yank this back in!"

King came over, and I mentally explained what I needed done. He put his weight on the prostrate ghoul, wrapping his arms around Grah's shoulder. While we set up, Grah began his soft babbling again, the rough handling leaving him feeling a bit confined.

"OK, let's try to get this in one shot. King, start pulling," I ordered.

In the end, it took us two attempts, King pulling on his arm to create space while I tried to realign the bones, but on the second try, I managed to realign the broken bone to my satisfaction. Next, I dug out a pair of flat metal rectangles studded with holes at regular intervals. With a retractor in place to hold the cut open, I pushed the metal into the wound, fitting it flush against the bone on either side of the break. Adding another assistant to my operation, I utilized Heist's small hands to hold the plate in place while I started to drill, spinning a brace drill round and round to start holes, then to drive a set of screws into the bone, anchoring the plates in place over the break. After that, it was just clean up, as I put everything back where I found it and used a curved needle to stitch the incision closed.

Overall, it went as well as I could have hoped, though I wondered if this would be Grah's last run. He had lost any ability to heal when he'd died, and the damage to his arm would crack and worsen with time, regardless of the best ministrations. A clean skelly like Champ could have its bones impregnated and lacquered with various solutions to vastly improve durability, but it was far more difficult to work on a ghoul that still had so much flesh. Even if I could extend his working life, Grah's skills in drawing bandit fire were not valuable enough to offset the cost of such a procedure. It was quite possible that I would be shopping for a replacement at Zeb's ranch again on the way back.

Speaking of ghouls with arm problems, Amelia had been watching me like a hawk through the whole procedure, keeping her eyes on me as I washed off bits of ghoul filth from my hands. Between the ghoul surgery staining my arms and the bandit attack soaking me in sweat, I made a note to melt enough snow in my pot after dinner for more thorough ablutions. The simmering stew turned out delicious, though, the experience only slightly marred by Amelia's piercing gaze. After enduring her attention a while longer, I decided to reach out with my own mind, focusing on the notes of mental noise radiating off her. The sense I picked up was one of... confusion?

That was a bit eerie. Most of my ghouls had been dead for months or years before entering my service, with the intervening time robbing their minds of all but the basest emotional tones. Interacting with a ghoul who was still so... alive... was rather disconcerting. Her confusion seemed to be focused on Grah, though parsing out her mind was more art than science. I sent her two mental images, one of Grah, broken-limbed and tangled in the bandit trap, and a second with Grah's arm repaired and him running with the team. She seemed to accept the images but still appeared nonplussed.

This reminded me of the internal battle every courier had to deal with. Were ghouls just tools, or were they people? Erring too far on either side had its dangers, and the stories of those extremes were told to young trainees as cautionary tales. There was Karl One Eye, who treated his team like the family he'd never had. A fire sparked up in the farmhouse stabling his team, and One Eye ran back into the blaze to save them. He perished in the flames. Stephan The Lesser had an alpine ghoul that could sniff out avalanche country, but he kept the creature muzzled all day to keep its cries from waking him at night. When that avalanche came thundering down, Stephan had no warning and was flattened. These ghouls were not people anymore; no soul was left in those old bones. They were just echoes of the past, carrying on long after the soul had gone silent. But dealing with a fawn like Amelia could skew that perception.

A quick bath of snow melt after dinner did wonders, wiping off both the mental and physical grime that had clung to me. There were few things better than being cold and clean all over, then sliding under thick, warm blankets. I was fast asleep as soon as my head hit the pillow.

XII

———

Despite the quick slip into slumber, my dreams were troubled. First, I floated in darkness and felt a ceaseless crowd pressing in around me, though my eyes remained blind no matter how I twisted and turned. Then I sat at a table stacked high with decadent food, though every course turned to ash in my mouth at the first bite. The dreams continued like that, scene after strange scene. A thundering waterfall of blood, flesh melting from bodies like candle wax, a green flame burning into my skin, sending searing light through my veins.

The last one woke me with a start, and I sat bolt-upright in my cot. Leaning forward, I massaged my temples gingerly, trying to rub the dreams from my head. Nightmares weren't uncommon for me, and that bandit ambush was frightening enough to pull my dreams into dark corners. But still, something was off about this one. My nightmares tended to be drawn from real events, like I would find myself back in that ambush, but this time we would fail to escape them. But that sort of sporadic, disjointed dreamscape was uncommon for me.

Peering out the skylight, I could still see a dusting of stars in a lightening sky. I would wager that I'd woken maybe an hour earlier than usual. It wasn't enough time to make going back to bed worth it, so I figured I might as well get an early start on the day. Stretching broadly, I leaned back, fingertips brushing the purple light streaming in from above.

Then I sensed it.

Ghouls . . . hundreds of them.

They were packed in around the sled, so close that I was amazed it had taken me until now to notice the rotten smell leaking into the space. I wrenched myself out of the light with an effort, severing the bond and silencing the mental cacophony pouring into my head.

"Shit! Shitshitshit. OK, take a breath, calm down, figure this out . . . It's a horde; it must be," I whispered, pulling my clothes on.

Hordes were a rarity within the Empire, and I hadn't expected to find one so soon after leaving its borders. Ghouls in proximity to each other tended to clump together like heaps of trash floating in the ocean. The growing horde would shamble off in a random direction, collecting more and more members into the mass. And if you were truly unlucky, the horde might stumble over the lip of a gully and tumble down onto the courier sleeping at the bottom. With enough time, I might be able to seize control of the horde a few ghouls at a time and feed them into my brazier, but that course of action was a last resort. The animated corpses would burn up in an instant, but any clothing, armor, or supplies they carried would remain unaffected. If enough of that detritus piled up, it could smother the fire and leave me even worse off.

On top of that, the ghouls could sense that there was something living in the area, though the walls of my sled had obfuscated my presence somewhat. If they had known my exact location, the horde would have torn the sled apart with no more effort than I used to crack open an oyster. But just because they couldn't find me didn't mean that they were leaving; they knew prey was somewhere nearby and had nothing better to do than mill around until they found a different prey to chase. Given that every wild animal with half a brain would avoid this horde by a country mile, I was on my own.

"Come on, Winona, think! What would Dad do?" I asked myself.

I was on my own, yes . . . but a courier was never truly alone. My ghouls had been under the awning last night, so they must still be out there, lost in the press of bodies; locating them had to be my first step if I was going to reestablish a measure of control over the situation. I crossed my legs on the cot, took a deep, steadying breath, then extended a hand into the light. The weight of the horde rushed into my mind like a tide, but this time I was braced for the influx. From this, I was able to sense that there weren't hundreds of ghouls outside after all; the number was closer to seventy. The exact count was immaterial, though; the important thing was that there were far too many of them to just dominate and order away through the balefire bond; their collective energy was just too much for my will to pierce.

So instead, I looked inward, methodically blocking out the mental static, observing the press without letting it consume my mind. Right now, I would give up a hand to be able to see through my ghouls' eyes, but the bond didn't work like that. I could only reach out blindly, trying to use what I knew about them to determine where they were hiding.

Easiest to find were the two ghouls perched in the branches of a tree far above, just at the edge of the balefire's light. Scramble had lived up to his name, scrambling up the nearest tree at the first sign of danger. Unsurprisingly, Amelia was perched up there next to him, though how she'd managed it with that mitten on was beyond me.

"OK, we've got our pair of climbers; let's check in a bit closer," I whispered, moving my fingers as if over piano keys. It was a bit of a crutch that could get you teased by other couriers but vocalizing and moving my hands always helped me focus.

I dove back in and crossed King and Champ off the list; they had both clambered onto the roof and were sitting above me. And if they were above, I could bet there was another below. I found Craven moments later, hiding between the runners of my sled. A situation like this would have been Craven's nightmare when he was alive, and he'd clearly bolted for cover at the first sign of trouble.

"More than halfway there," I whispered. "Let's finish this up."

The last four were far more difficult, lost somewhere in the crowd, and I had to pour over a sea of unfamiliar minds to find them, searching for a needle in a needle stack. Tybalt was the first I sensed, standing in a clear circle. The towering skeleton wasn't particularly violent to anything without a pulse, but he also wasn't particularly tolerant about being pushed around and had channeled some of his aggression into clearing out any who ventured too close. Heist hadn't been so strong or lucky, and the weight of the press had pinned her to a large stone nearby. A mental command sent Tybalt off to free her as I turned my attention to the last two. A strange knot of agitation caught my attention, and I found a struggling bundle of ghouls near the sled, with Bonk sitting triumphantly atop them. If I had to guess, I'd say he'd used that tarp to envelop and restrain a knot of ghouls when they'd first entered camp. That would have been great if he hadn't also snagged Grah, who had been wrapped up with Bonk's other victims. Convincing Bonk to release a ghoul he'd restrained went against Bonk's behavior to the core, but I eventually coerced him into letting his teammate free. Once I had everyone in my grasp, I gathered them together, back to the sled. It wasn't easy going, as the wild ghouls were prone to lashing out as my team pushed by. Tybalt and Champ could make short work of them, but they couldn't be everywhere at once, and pockets of agitation started building in the crowd.

With my team reassembled, I set them to getting us out of this mess. My bruisers parted the crowd while the others latched onto the sled, pushing and pulling it out of the horde. Through all this, I was stuck inside my bunk, trying to direct an orchestra I couldn't see. With one final push, we broke clear and began a haphazard slide downhill away from the horde. The team pushed the *Ridgerunner* for a few more minutes, long enough for me to verify that no curious ghouls were following us. Only then did I step out, taking in the scene under the strengthening sunlight.

My sled was . . . a mess. Those horde ghouls had thoroughly gone to rot and had smeared everything they'd touched with coagulated blood, excrement, and a plethora of other ungodly fluids; it'd take hours of scrubbing to get the sled clean. The team hadn't fared much better, each ghoul looking like they had been dunked in a sewer. I tried to avoid the worst of the muck while harnessing them, but some contact was unavoidable, and I doubted any amount of scrubbing would purge the scent from my gloves. But, at the end of the day, I'd rather be a living woman smelling to high heaven than a corpse that smelled like roses. Plus, I consoled myself by remembering that we should reach the military outpost by noon tomorrow. My dealings with the military were few and far between, but I had learned enough to notice the similarities between camps. If my past experiences were anything to go by, there would be a group of new recruits stuck doing the menial work. There would also be a grizzled sergeant gleefully directing them to perform the most unpleasant tasks available. . An afternoon picking ghoul guts off my sled sounded like a fantastic learning experience for the young soldiers, real character-building stuff, and I would hate to deny them that education. With that thought in my mind, we set off once again, leaving a trail of scattered ghoul bits in our wake.

After the excitement of the morning, the rest of the day was blessedly straightforward. We did have to make one stop for repairs, though; one of my sled runners must have taken a knock from the horde and developed a nasty wobble that vibrated through the left side of the sled. It was a straightforward process to use my ghouls to lift the side of the *Ridgerunner* while I scurried under to tighten the bolts. In a way, I welcomed it, letting the manual labor burn off the jittery energy I'd been holding onto since the rude awakening earlier. With a more stable sled and a more relaxed driver, we set off again. The methodical stride of my ghouls ate up the kilometers, and it was quite pleasant after I managed to block out the smell wafting off my bedraggled team ahead.

Seeing a horde so close to the border was a bit worrying, but I knew that the border towns were well-practiced in dealing with them. Those places practiced evacuations a few times a year and could easily get out of the way long before the mob of ghouls stumbled in. After that, the local guards would raise a militia to deal with the threat. Men on horseback would tempt a dozen or so ghouls to split from the horde and give chase, where they would be led into carefully laid traps. The horde would be taken apart piece by piece using this method until nothing remained. I'd taken part in one such hunt a year or so back while on a return trip from the outer settlements. The villagers had made a holiday of the hunt, putting aside petty squabbles to band together against the dead. The celebration after had lasted three days, and the memories became blurry after the locals brought out their homemade *akvavit* spirits. Sadly, those memories were distant now, and there were no festivals waiting for me in the cholera-riddled city of Skyroost. But hey, once I delivered this medicine, maybe I'd get a holiday named after me. Savior of Skyroost certainly had a ring to it.

It never ceased to amaze me, though, the true scale of the undead menace. It felt like every time we fed a hundred ghouls to the fire, another thousand rose up to take their place. According to the Balefire Church, the continent extended east for thousands of kilometers, so who knew how many of the monsters were still shambling along, migrating towards the Empire. Still, some talked of a day when the last ghoul would be slain, and civilization would rise to the technological heights of our pre-cataclysm ancestors. Personally, I found it hard to rally much enthusiasm for the idea. The hordes were endless, and all the technology imaginable hadn't protected the old world from its apocalyptic collapse.

We kept moving for the rest of the day, though I did do a bit of cleaning on the go. I was sure I could get someone to help clean the sled, but I wouldn't trust them with my various tools and equipment that had also accumulated stains from the horde. When I'd woken earlier, my plan had been to call it an early night, but now there was a creeping temptation to push on through the night until I reached the outpost, the promise of a hot meal and warm bed achingly close. I curbed that urge, though, knowing that thundering on through the darkness was a recipe for disaster.

We stopped for the night under the skeletal branches of a sprawling oak tree, sliding in just as the sun was beginning to set. My ghouls set to their tasks, but I had one adjustment to make to our nightly chores. I dug out my longest length of rope, tied one end to Grah's wrist, then coiled the rest of the length over my shoulder, paying out slack as I walked. Then I approached Amelia, removed her mitten, and handed her the climbing tool she'd worn before.

"Let's get some exercise," I told her, turning to the ancient oak. The rough bark was a welcome sensation, though these massive trees were a rarity this far north. I'd been quite the intrepid climber as a youth, but Amelia soon outpaced me, stepping from branch to branch with ease while I crawled along at a more cautious pace.

"Not gonna give me a hand?" I asked as she overtook me.

Amelia looked at me, then down at her stump, then back at me again.

"Oh . . . I didn't . . . never mind." I put my head down and worked to catch up. It had never occurred to me how often I used idioms until I had to deal with a ghoul that was so damn literal.

I caught up to her near the middle of the tree, on a thick horizontal branch that gave a stunning view of the setting sun, the balefire light highlighting us from below.

"It's beautiful, isn't it?" I asked, not expecting an answer.

Amelia chuffed at me, then stood, hooking her climbing tool to a branch above to hold herself steady.

It truly was beautiful, the yellows, oranges, and reds pooling together. But those colors would soon fade to purple and blue, so I had to get on with it.

"I know you can't understand me, but I always found talking it out better for my head than journaling. So, I admit it, I fucked up today. Guess I was a bit complacent, still being close to the border and all that. I was tired after our excitement with the bandits too, made me sloppy. We've had a blind spot on the team for a while; there's nobody to warn us when trouble is coming. Grah is a great noisemaker, but he's not exactly observant, and Craven is too unreliable. Scramble could get up high and scout, but he's way too old to maintain the focus needed for guard duty."

I pulled the rope off my shoulder, then tied the end to a loop in her harness. She tugged on it experimentally, testing the slack. With my prompting, she pulled a bit harder, and the rope tugged on Grah's arm, tipping him over from where he sat and setting him babbling.

"Grah!Grah!grahgrahgrah"

"Good. Now . . . here's the deal. If you see any trouble coming, give that rope a pull. Grah will wake me up, and we'll deal with whatever's coming. If you can manage that, I'll let you climb up high every night," I finished.

In addition to the speech, I continued to trickle in a series of images to reinforce my orders, focusing on scenes of bandits or hordes approaching and Amelia alerting Grah.

"Got it? Good. I'm still taking your climbing hook off in the morning, but maybe you can start working at earning the privilege back."

Once I was back on the ground, I used a shorter cord to leash Grah's harness to the sled, creating a long link that tethered Amelia to the *Ridgerunner*. She wouldn't leave the light of the balefire of her own volition, but there was a risk that she'd slip and fall out of the tree, land outside the firelight, then wander off. At least this precaution should keep her from wandering too far on the off chance my concern became a reality.

My ghoul alarm system wasn't a perfect fix, but it was a start. There were a lot of things that happened out here that you couldn't prevent, but getting caught with my pants down like that was inexcusable. I couldn't avoid every bad turn of luck, but I could make sure that I didn't make the same mistakes twice.

XIII

———

Breakfast was a simple affair this morning, the knowledge of a real meal in my near future serving to galvanize me through my morning chores. I held a biscuit in my mouth as I ran through my last checks, preparing for departure. Amelia descended from her perch with some reluctance as if unwilling to return to ground level until the last possible moment. She fell in line soon after that, though, even relinquishing her climbing tool without a fuss; it seemed that returning Amelia's arm and giving her a dose of purpose during the night had made her far more cooperative.

As soon as the coffee was made, I kicked dirt over the remnants of the campfire and departed, heading deeper into the wilds. Early morning was not my preferred time for complex planning, but homing in on an outpost somewhere in this vast wilderness would take a fair bit of figuring. Ronny had given me a solid idea of the camp's location, but this area was carved up with deep patterns of fjords and mountain ranges that twisted the landscape in strange and confusing ways. The path to the outpost would lead me deeper into this maze than I had ventured in the past, and the important cargo I carried made me wary of losing my way.

But damn, it was stunning to behold. The mountains towered above me as the sled clung to thin paths; to my right was sheer rock, and to my left, a short drop down to black waters below. It was frigid, desolate, and absolutely awe-inspiring. I imagined that an ancient god had trailed his massive fingers through the earth, leaving kilometer-long indentations in their wake. But, even with this austere beauty, I still loved the summer fjords more. The plants bloomed, crawling up the edges of the fjord and painting it in lively, vivid hues. A blast of icy wind surged past, rattling the sled and pulling me from my reverie. It was a stark reminder of the danger of traversing these paths and how perilous these thin passes could become if I were still navigating them come nightfall.

Luckily, my growing anxiety was soothed as the road widened into a crossroads, set in the center of a burned-out hamlet that looked to have been abandoned years ago. There was little to mark the site other than charred timbers and stone foundation, and the sad ruins were not an uncommon sight this far north. Settlements out here wanted freedom from the taxes and laws of the Osgil Empire, but gaining independence had cost them their safety. Without balefire or military support, all it would take was a few dozen ghouls to destroy a vulnerable community like this one. It made me wonder about the bandits that hunted at the fringes of the Empire. How many of those people had been decent folk until the ghouls chased them out and forced them to find other ways to survive? Morality was all well and good, but it wouldn't feed your family when times were hard.

The intersecting path was marred by a set of deep wagon tracks. I stepped out of the sled to examine the area and was heartened by what I saw. The wheels that made these tracks had sunk deep into the frozen earth, indicating that the cart had been carrying significant weight. There was also a blaze of red fabric wrapped around a low branch of a nearby tree, delineating a path along the same route those wheels had taken. There had been a weak attempt to obfuscate the markers by placing them slightly off the path, but it was amateurish at best, the equivalent of hiding a red-roofed house by laying a half dozen branches over it. The locals up here would have been traveling lighter and done a better job of disguising their trail markers. All evidence pointed to imperial military equipment moving this way, blazing a trail farther north as they went.

Feeling more confident in my directions, I turned to follow the trail, keeping a meter over to one side so that the sled's metal runners didn't slip into those deep wheel ruts. As we went, I mentally reviewed the procedures for dealing with the bigwigs I was likely to encounter. Couriers were blessed with a long leash as far as bureaucracies went, and we generally gave authority figures a wide berth unless our station demanded otherwise. The military types would hopefully be easy to work with as long as they were cut from the same cloth as other northern soldiers I'd met. Ozero was rough enough country that the military contingent was a meritocracy, for the most part. Of course, there were still the rare moments of nepotism that might give leadership to the unfit, but most were simply men and women looking to kick some ass and get their job done. I was looking to do the same, so we should get along swimmingly. Given the size of the outpost Ronny had hinted at, I could expect an officer with the rank of captain to be leading operations here. Someone of that rank would hopefully be more grounded than the higher echelons I had encountered at church functions, though I still wished that I didn't have to roll into camp smeared in ghoul crap from the horde; not the best look for first impressions.

More worrying to me than the military was the ecclesiastical attaché that would likely be attached to such a group. While most of the clergy were allowed to handle balefire, one needed to be a bishop or higher to be taught the secrets of kindling the magical flame. This meant that the outpost would contain a "Firekeeper" in charge of maintaining the camp's balefire, and it could be someone wielding significant power in the hierarchy of the Balefire Church. Us couriers had a saying, "The closer you are to Pope, the farther you are from piety." In the church, the farther you rose in the ranks, the more power you wielded, and the better the lifestyle you lived. That sort of influence could corrupt even someone who had started with the best intentions. So, by that logic, the most holy members of the church must be the ones at the bottom . . . the couriers.

Fancy that.

Regardless of my ecclesiastical musings, there would be a fair bit of bowing and scraping when I made my report, and I practiced the words out loud to avoid making a fool of myself later today. Our new track wound upwards, and the drop to one side rose again, becoming sheer and falling away into a vertigo-inducing cliff face. The fjord itself morphed shortly after, the black water giving way to snow-covered earth as the valley rose and narrowed, petering out into a dry gorge with steep sides. Piles of scree spilled out on either side, though there seemed something off about the stone that I couldn't put my finger on. Through the short, scrubby trees, I spied three large red blobs, like fat holly berries hanging from a branch. As we drew nearer, the blobs resolved themselves into three red-coated men huddled around a crackling fire, fur-lined cloaks pushed back as they enjoyed the heat. Sitting on the ground at each of their feet was a winged golden helmet.

"Holy shit, the Bloodbirds are here!" I whispered to myself in shock. "What are the royal guard doing way out in the wilds? They're a damn long way from home."

Curiosity reeled me in, and I spurred my team on, climbing the gentle rise toward them. We rounded the final corner, though the guards did not notice until we had nearly pulled alongside them. When one finally caught on, he bolted upright, scrambling for his gear, while the second panicked and fell backward over the log he was sitting on. The third guard, the one with his back to me, reacted the fastest. Noticing his compatriot's reaction, he spun around, leveling a musket at me while the others were still trying to get their helmets on.

"Step out of the sled now with your hands up!" The tall man barked, keeping the firearm trained on me.

I stepped out slowly, keeping my hands in sight. I had expected the weapons as soon as I recognized the royal guard but had never had the displeasure of having one aimed at me before. Pre-cataclysm firearms were incredibly rare and strictly regulated; they were only to be used by the military in times of war. We had lost the technology to recreate the advanced weapons or their ammunition, so every shot counted. Instead, the royal gunsmiths had done what they could with the technology they had, plying their trade to create weapons that would have been considered ancient and ineffective by pre-cataclysm standards. But the difference became immaterial when the weapon was leveled at your head.

"Easy . . . Easy now. My name is Deacon Winona, I'm a courier for the Balefire Express. I am here on a stop to restock vital supplies before continuing north. Ronald of Ozero assured me that I would be expected."

The tall guard nodded his chin to a compatriot, who ran off down the gorge, his kit still in disarray.

"My name is Corporal Larsen; this man is Private Kolstad. He will perform a thorough search of your vehicle; then we will escort you to the outpost," he barked authoritatively.

It was a strong tone meant to intimidate me into compliance. It was the wrong tone to take and raised my hackles immediately. Soon enough, I would be bowing and scraping to this man's superiors, but I wouldn't take this treatment from him.

"No, can do, boss, can't let you poke around my gear. Separation of church and state, you know how it is," I told him conversationally, failing to hide my contempt.

The corporal took a step closer, continuing to brandish his gun.

"You will stand down and submit to search, or we will take you into custody!" he shouted, though there was a note of uncertainty in his voice now, he clearly hadn't expected resistance to his orders.

"Yeeaahhh, I don't think so, treaty between the Balefire Church and Emperor . . . Bergström, I believe? Anyway, no member of the military may conduct a search of church property without a church official present of higher rank than the official whose property is being searched," I quoted.

"What . . . What does that mean?" he growled, trying and failing to cover his confusion with aggression.

"It means get my boss here to oversee the search, or I'll wrap you up in so much litigation that your grandkids will still be paying off your debt to the church."

I admit, watching the poor man pale and bluster was highly amusing. The church obviously lacked the military's firepower, but we did have our own standing army of sorts. Instead of soldiers, we had an army of bean counters, stuffy men who sat at little desks and reveled in extracting every last sun from whoever had garnered the church's ire.

"Now, you can get my superior, but he's likely sitting in a haze of cigar smoke back in Ozero, so I guess you're out of luck," I shrugged, doing my best to appear nonchalant with a gun still trained on my chest.

Now, if he were clever enough, he could hunt down the church attaché that must be here, but I was betting that a corporal wouldn't risk dragging a senior official out into the cold just to root through my sled.

Fortunately, it seemed I was right as the corporal took a step back, uncocked his flintlock, and slung it over his shoulder.

"Follow me," he growled, storming off towards the gorge entrance. His compatriot assumed a position behind my sled a moment later.

Courier-1. Royal Guards-0.

I pulled myself up onto the side of my sled, holding on with one arm so I could keep an eye on both of them. The entrance to the gorge narrowed sharply, so much so that I wasn't sure if two long-haul sleds could have passed by each other at the same time. I did spy a bit of loose stone at the base of the walls, which drew my eyes to the gouges marking the wall, evidence of strikes from picks and hammers. It seemed like the guards had made some effort to widen the gorge, probably using ghoul power to break the rock and cart the rubble away. Now that I thought about it, that would explain the strange scree piles I'd seen on the approach. The sheer walls on either side made me feel a bit penned in, and I distracted myself by aggravating my escort.

"Corporal Larsen, is it true that you wear red coats so that your enemies can't see you bleed?" I asked.

"Yes, Deacon, we are the Emperor's shield and his sword. We wear red to show that we will not hide, and yes, so the blood will not show," he expounded stoically.

"Is that the same reason you wear brown trousers?" I asked him, straight-faced.

"Hah!" The private behind me barked a quick laugh but immediately quelched it, knowing the outburst would get him chewed out later.

Courier-2. Royal Guards-0.

Once the corporal stopped responding to my jibes, I let my mind wander back to earlier, thankful that I had prevented that search. I had more than a few items that might raise eyebrows, including a very illegal coalblade that would put me in hot water with the church's representative here.

Damn, I needed to do something about that. I could stave off a search if I was near the sled, but I wouldn't put it past the soldiers to nose around once I was gone. Slipping back into my living area, I lifted my cot up and opened the compartment that held the coalblade and its sheath. Everything was how I'd left it, but I took a moment to cram a pair of old shirts into the space so that the weapon wouldn't rattle around if they moved my cot. Giving the cot a shake produced no noise, so I gave the space one last look over, then stepped outside.

Emerging back into the chilly air, I stepped to the ground as the path began to widen. It looked like the corridor was opening out to something more substantial, but a log gate blocked our way, the bark still clinging to the fresh-cut wood. A small walkway topped the gate, with two more armed guards patrolling across it.

"The fifth ghoul knocks twice at midday!" Corporal Larsen called out to them as we drew close.

"Open the gate!" The guard above hollered behind, and the gate began to creak open moments later.

The shade of the gorge was dispersed as sunlight poured back in, revealing a scene far greater than what I had expected. This was not a small outpost; the royal guard were building themselves a fortress.

XIV

———

The *tik tik tik* ring of pickaxes echoed out on all sides as we entered the complex, ghouls working tirelessly to chip away at the cliffs. The guards had endeavored to create a modified motte and bailey fortification, which made sense given our environment. It was a simple defensive construction, but formidable if done right. The guards had chosen an ideal position for it, nestled up at the far end of a fjord with a commanding view of the terrain.

The ghouls had managed a substantial excavation as well, flattening the area at the top of the fjord into a bailey courtyard. A palisade of sharpened wooden logs curved from one cliff face to the other, with an elevated walkway behind it and a long ditch that had been dug out just in front of the wall. I didn't envy anyone stupid enough to attack this place. You could choose between pushing through the kill box gorge behind the outpost or rushing uphill and climbing the wooden fortification under a withering hail of musket balls. All the dirt from their excavations had to go somewhere, and the military had chosen to pile it up on a nearby outcrop, forming a flat top earthen motte that they had topped with a stout wooden keep. The first concern that came to mind was about the cliffs above. After my own mishap, I was very wary of a horde tumbling down into the camp. But my fears were proved unnecessary as a guard leading a horse looked down from the cliff top above, clearly placed to provide advanced warning and lead an oncoming horde away from the outpost.

We pulled into the bailey proper and stopped before a small delegation awaiting our arrival. Besides the small squad of soldiers, there was a female officer a year or two older than I, along with a cassock-wearing church official. I stepped forward to stand beside the corporal, then bowed deeply at the waist, hoping that I would appear professional and uninteresting to the onlookers.

"Deacon Winona, arriving from Ozero, on official courier business bound for Skyroost. Requesting a replacement battery for my cargo as per prior arrangement and lodgings for the night," I intoned officially.

The officer stepped forward, returning my bow with a stiff nod, her dark hair braided on top and cropped close to her skull on the sides. The uniform she wore was well cared for but showed the marks and scratches accumulated through hard work, a detail that wasn't present on the immaculate outfits of her subordinates. A pepperbox pistol was holstered at her hip.

"I am Captain Calliope Deimos, serving under Lieutenant Colonel Berg. Welcome to Outpost Three-Oh-Five. You are welcome to whatever resources we can spare to aid you on your journey," she replied in a businesslike tone. The woman's olive skin and dark eyes marked her as a foreigner, a rarity this far from the capital. But, the Osgil Empire was always expanding its borders, so it made sense that some of those new citizens would enter military service.

"I greatly appreciate the assistance. You have my gratitude," I replied, then turned to the church official and bowed again. "Deacon Winona, ready to give my report at the Firekeeper's earliest convenience."

At a closer glance, I'd say the official was a vicar, judging by his vestments, though, like Oleg, he had the build of someone accustomed to large meals and hard labor. His black cassock strained around his sizable gut but also struggled to contain his thick arms, bulging with muscle. He had a head shaved bald and skin that was tanned by sun instead of by ancestry.

"My child," he began, smiling beatifically, his deep voice speaking in a slow, measured tone. "I am glad that you have found your way to us safely; we received troubling news from the road. I am Vicar Dupont, serving under Bishop Rimkus. He understands the rigors of the road and wishes that you join him for dinner tonight once you have had some time to recover."

That was a good start, at least. Meeting with superiors could be unpleasant even when you were well-rested, and I would be glad for the opportunity to clean up before making my report.

"Actually, I'm sorry, but the lieutenant colonel has asked for the deacon's presence at dinner to discuss news from the Empire," Captain Deimos interjected sheepishly.

I hated to turn down the captain; her boss was important, but my allegiance was to my own superior first. I opened my mouth to decline when the vicar interrupted. "Of course, Deacon Winona would be happy to dine with the lieutenant colonel and his officers. The bishop would have no issue rescheduling. But let us allow the deacon to attend to her team; I'm sure she's had a long day."

The vicar embraced me, then enclosed my hand in his, leaning in to kiss my still dirty knuckles. It was a lovely bit of theater, given that I could feel him press a scrap of paper into my hand right under the captain's nose. I bowed again as he stepped away, using the motion to slip the paper into a pocket.

"We will speak again soon, Deacon Winona. Please enjoy your hard-earned respite," the smiling vicar told me, then departed.

Captain Deimos watched him leave, glaring daggers at his back.

"You can follow me to the ghoul pens," she sighed, dispersing the soldiers around us with a wave.

Hmmm. There was clearly tension between the two. It could be that they had a personal disagreement, but I was willing to bet that this was more of a church vs. state friction that was trickling down through the ranks. That animosity could extend to me as well, but I hoped to win the captain over to my side before she could solidify her opinion of the newcomer.

"May I ask about the purpose of this outpost?" I ventured tentatively.

"I was given the location of this place but wasn't expecting such an established presence here."

"Fin tribes," she answered. "Usually solitary people, but we have received reports that they may be massing in large numbers. This outpost was established to provide early warning in case of an invasion."

Now that smelled a bit fishy to me. It wasn't impossible that the Fins were massing, even if it was a bit farfetched. Those tribes were typically too busy fighting each other to attack someone else, but there had been points in history where a charismatic leader had united the nomadic people together for a larger goal. What I couldn't fathom was why you'd sent royal guards up here when there were more skilled and experienced northern troops available for this kind of work.

The captain led me through the bailey, where I noted all the expected buildings: barracks, workshop tents, mess hall, etcetera. Closer to the defensive wall were the ghoul pens, placed where a bit of wind could flow in to alleviate the ever-present smell. The large pens were packed with ghouls, but there was also a small set of open bays nearby, similar to those at Zebadiah's ranch.

"Excuse me, Captain, I do hate to infringe on your hospitality any further, but as you can see, I ran into a bit of trouble on the road, and my team and sled are a bit . . . soiled . . . ."

That coaxed a smile out of her, and she turned to flag down a stocky enlisted man with a stubble beard. He hurried over, saluting the captain and removing his hat to sketch a quick bow to me.

"Sergeant Greaves, I believe you discovered a few men drinking on last night's watch, correct?" she questioned.

"Yes, ma'am! I was planning on giving them latrine duty to straighten them out."

Captain Deimos looked pointedly over at my sled, where a loop of ghoul intestine I had missed slipped off the roof and squished into the mud.

"Hmm, I do think I may have another task for them if you don't mind," she grinned.

"Of course, ma'am," the sergeant grinned back, showing a gap-toothed smile. "I'll have them sent over as soon as I can rustle them up."

"Thank you, sergeant. You're dismissed," she told him, and I gave him a respectful nod, glad that my earlier guess about a grizzled sergeant had been correct. He saluted and retreated, but I made sure to add my own instructions.

"Don't try to clean the ghouls, though!" I yelled after him. "I won't be responsible for any disemboweled privates!"

The captain gave me a perplexed stare, and I caught my own awkward wording.

"I meant like soldiers!" I corrected sheepishly, feeling my cheeks flush. "Not like ... private privates ...."

The captain paused for a second, then her composure broke, a long cackle of laughter escaping and puncturing the tension that had surrounded her since we first met.

"Oh ... oh gods, I needed that!" she exclaimed, wiping a tear of laughter away. "My apologies for my demeanor earlier. There's been a great deal of friction between our sides in the camp, but letting that turn us against each other isn't helping anything. You have just arrived, and it is not fair to judge you by the actions of your superiors. So, when the other soldiers are not present, you can call me by my first name, Calliope."

Damn, now I felt like a jerk. Calliope might have a stick so far up her butt that we could use her as a scarecrow, but at least she was trying to show some kindness.

"Thank you, Calliope; you can call me Winona," I replied, happy at the small bit of progress that had been made.

"It's my pleasure. We do not use bells for the hours to decrease the risk of detection, but I'll come to collect you here about two hours before sunset. It will be a dinner with the lieutenant colonel, myself, and three other captains. You may want to dress ... more appropriately," she told me, glancing down at my travel-stained clothing.

"Oh, I'll be all preened and proper, don't you worry!" I laughed as she departed, then turned around grimacing. My official deacon vestments hadn't seen the light of day in six months and were currently balled up in a drawer somewhere in my sled. It looked like I had some errands to do.

Despite the stuffy residents, I was still quite content to find myself back in this little pocket of civilization. The military would have a variety of specialized workers to keep the place running, and I intended to stretch Calliope's promise of aid as far as I could. But before my shopping trip could begin, I had some immediate concerns to address. To start, I ducked inside my sled and fished out the piece of paper the vicar had given me. Unrolling it, I found a short message written in a flowing script.

Be cautious in disclosing details of your journey; we are not welcome among the Bloodbirds.

Huh, the tension I'd sensed earlier might be even worse than I'd assumed. I was already hiding my coalblade, but after the message, I hid the gold coins I had discovered as well. Gods only knew what the vicar was concerned about, but I intended to appear as unremarkable as possible until I knew more.

I ripped up the paper as I stepped back outside, dropping the scraps onto the ground and grinding them into the mud with my heel. Subterfuge complete, I took care of my team, stripping them of their harnesses and outer clothing for the soldiers to clean. I would have to clean the ghouls myself later; even with the balefire's influence, I wouldn't trust them not to take a swipe at the men. In Ozero, I could trust the Yard attendants to take all precautions, but I had no idea how experienced these capital residents were at dealing with ghouls. For now, there was a cell in the back of the bay that should keep my team out of trouble for the remainder of the day.

A small party of workers arrived soon after, leading a pair of skellies that unloaded the precious cargo under my watchful eye. I hadn't dragged the crate this far just to watch a half-rotted ghoul drop it onto the hard ground. The transition went smoothly, though, and soon enough, the crate was ensconced in a small single-story warehouse purpose-built to hold other items that were susceptible to the biting chill. Other packages were nestled inside, and a large fire crackled in the stone fireplace, filling the cramped interior with dry heat.

With that task complete, I dug my wrinkled vestments out of a drawer, tossed them into a satchel along with Grah's broken harness, and set out into Outpost 305. There wasn't much need for military outposts like this in the Empire, but civilian workers set up similar camps for logging and mining all the time. Couriers could be the lifeblood of these places, delivering vital supplies or escorting the harvested materials to market. So, I considered myself to have an experienced eye for these sites, and I wasn't impressed with what I saw. The settlement had looked solid enough at first glance, but the cracks began to show under closer scrutiny. The ghoul pen was too distant from the paired balefire braziers, with buildings obstructing the light in multiple places. This created long shadows of darkness over the pens where the ghouls were immune to any control. The various buildings looked clean and well-kept but lacked the mud packing between the wooden boards that would plug holes and keep the drafts out. Even the guards seemed a bit unprepared; many of them shivered in the cold as if either not used to or not properly prepared for the conditions.

As I made my way over to the workshops, a nagging memory surfaced. My dad had taken us on vacation once, where we discovered a tiny museum full of scale models of various cities and settlements. That's what this outpost reminded me of—a perfect design out of a manual. Everything was constructed to specification, but no care had been taken for practical planning. Regardless of the other failings, I could not fault the massive balefire towers they'd hauled up here. They were the size of the grand braziers back home but were mounted on massive wooden wheels. Each could be moved while lit to bring the fire outside the walls and must have been the source of the colossal tracks I'd followed earlier. Leaving the braziers behind, I picked my way over to the workshops. The skeletons of several small buildings stood half-constructed, with a swarm of busy workers climbing over them. In the interim, a cluster of canvas tents had popped up like toadstools to shelter the craftsmen. I followed the sound of shouting until I discovered an older man berating his subordinates as they struggled to wash bundles of red cloth in long wooden tubs. The frigid water and harsh soap could do serious wear and tear on your hands, so it wasn't too difficult to find a volunteer to avoid that work and run a hot iron over my vestments, restoring them to some level of respectability. After that, I went searching for a leatherworker, following my nose to the pungent vats used to treat animal skins. There I found a heavily muscled woman stumping around on a prosthetic wooden leg, her coat replaced with a more practical apron.

"How did you get permission to shed that lovely red coat of yours?" I asked, hoping the woman had a sense of humor. She turned to take me in, noting my appearance and nodding in greeting.

"Got reprimanded for it once, then started wearing it while I worked. You know we use horse piss to treat the hides? Well, I walked into the chow hall, reeking like ghoul butt, and stank up the whole place! They granted me a uniform exemption right quick after that. Heh!"

She hobbled over, eased down onto a stool, and began to knead her hands into the place where her leg met the prosthetic.

"Haven't seen you around before, and we don't get many new faces. Name's Curtis."

"I'm Courier Winona, a pleasure to meet you. I just came in from Ozero, stopping for resupply before I continue on," I introduced myself.

"Mm, respect, that's some tough work. Had a cousin training for a skimmer, ended up getting eaten," she told me matter-of-factly.

"Uhm . . . I'm sorry to hear that. I was hoping to beg a quick bit of work from you. One of my ghouls took a fall, mangled his harness, and I had to use one of my two spares. I don't like traveling with only a single backup harness, so I was hoping you might be able to fix this one up. The repairs don't have to be pretty; I just want the spare until I can buy a new harness."

Curtis held out a broad palm, and I handed over the tangle of leather. Her hands glided across the material with practiced ease, accompanied by a series of noncommittal grunts as she examined each strap.

"Yeah, this is fucked, not worth the effort to salvage," she declared, dropping the harness into a bucket filled with other scraps.

I deflated slightly at that. "Well, thank you anyway; I'll just . . . "

"But we have plenty of spares around," she continued. "Shouldn't be a problem. I'll have one dropped off later; you're over in the sled bays, I assume?"

Relief flooded me. It was one small problem solved, but every little bit helped. "Yes! Thank you again; I really appreciate it."

Curtis waved the thanks away, then gestured to another stool across from her. She pulled out a small flask and enjoyed a quick draught before handing it over to me. "You do a lot of standing on a courier sled?" she asked.

I took a sip myself, suppressing a cough at the rough spirit even as it bloomed a welcome warmth in my chest.

"All day. My father built the sled from the ground up but thought that a sitting courier was a complacent one. He made that damn thing without a seat in the front," I reminisced.

"Heh, sounds just like my Da. I never took sitting for granted until I had to hobble around all day, damn ghouls."

"I'm sorry to hear it, Curtis, though I'm glad the leg is all those bastards took from you." I leaned back, glancing left and right to see if there were anyone else in earshot. I couldn't see much through the fabric of the tent, but I imagined that the smell of the tanning vats was an effective deterrent to random eavesdroppers.

"Level with me, Curtis. I don't want to pry, but you don't match the royal guard stereotype I've been seeing around here," I mentioned.

"You mean about how I don't look like a nobleman's third son? Walking around with a silver spoon in me mouth? You caught me," she grinned, her eyes twinkling.

"Yeah," I laughed. "Something like that."

"To be honest, I didn't give a rat's ass about the Bloodbirds until a few months ago. They tottered around the upper districts doing whatever it is they do, same as always. Then I start hearing that they're looking for new recruits, needed skilled craftsmen and were willing to be a bit more flexible on standards. No commoners, of course, but I have a widowed mum who remarried and managed to sink her claws into some geriatric nobleman, and that gave me enough fanciness to get in. Took the oath, and now I have a nice fat pension waiting for me in a few years."

"Huh, and here I'm thinking it was all just the gentry's kids playing at being a soldier. I stand corrected," I admitted, standing and stretching slowly.

"It's no problem. I think they only did it so they could come out here and hunt Fins. Knew they'd need some craftsmen once they couldn't pop down to a shop for all their needs."

"Fair enough. Thank you, Curtis. For the help, the booze, and the conversation. You have a good day," I told her, turning to leave.

"You too! Stay safe out there," she replied as I left the pungent workspace behind.

As I walked away, my mind poured over the interaction; Curtis had also mentioned the Fin tribes as the Bloodbirds' purpose for being up here. That explanation still didn't feel quite right to me, though Curtis seemed like a genuine sort. That didn't mean anything, though, since the military brass might just be withholding the true purpose from their soldiers; you couldn't catch people in a lie if they didn't know they were lying.

With that in mind, I went through the rest of my errands, using Calliope's promise of aid to gleefully replace any bit of worn equipment I could think up. Soon, the sun began to dip, signaling that I needed to start preparing for dinner. One surprise of the outpost was a robust bathing facility, complete with individual stalls and a cistern of water with a complex maze of piping stretching down into each cubicle. I had seen actual public baths in cities with less elaborate setups. As eager as I was to rinse off, I was also in an unfamiliar camp full of soldiers. With that in mind, I grabbed a fresh bar of soap and a towel, then retrieved Champ from our bay, along with the obsidian knife I had found in the bandit camp. With Champ guarding outside and the knife within reach, I felt a bit more comfortable letting my guard down and enjoying the rinse.

I turned the valve above me, and a cascade of ice-cold water poured in, eliciting a rather undignified squeak. Fortunately, the water warmed up after the initial deluge, and I wondered at the amount of engineering it took to get a hot shower out in the wilds. The hot water didn't last long, but I'd taken enough dips in frigid streams to have built up a bit of a tolerance and still enjoyed the sensation of flowing water as I scrubbed myself with the rough bar of soap. I couldn't exactly make a silk purse out of a sow's ear, but at least I wouldn't have any dirt under my nails. After some rushed but thorough ablutions, I cut the water off, then quickly dried and changed into a clean set of clothes before the cold could sink its teeth in.

"Move! Get back to the pen, you idiot!" A voice from outside my stall yelled.

Shifting the knife so I could draw it in an instant, I pulled the curtain back to see a soldier berating Champ. Opening the curtain spilled purple light over me, and I reasserted my power over my ghoul with ease, slapping away the man's attempt to control him with a thought. With me out of the balefire light, Champ would've reverted to his ingrained behavior, acting like a sort of sedate guard dog. But without my continued influence reinforcing that command, it was not too difficult for anyone else to subvert that order and gain control.

"Uhm, what are you doing to my ghoul?" I asked, ordering Champ back to my side. The man had long brown hair drawn back in a queue, though a few errant strands had escaped, giving him a slightly over-wrought look.

"Your ghoul!? I'll have you on report, soldier! Controlling a ghoul for your own personal use is an egregious breach of conduct. I hope you enjoyed that shower because it's the last you'll see for the rest of our deployment."

Again he tried to wrest control of Champ, and again I mentally slapped him away. Champ was mine; I knew every quirk of his mind. In a tug of war for control of him, I would always win. The man's failed attempt only incensed him further, and he closed his eyes for a moment, gesturing with his fingers. My guess was that this meant he was summoning ghoul backup, and I had the overwhelming urge to punch him in the face while he concentrated. But it was becoming abundantly clear that he'd mistaken me for one of his soldiers, and I was content to let him dig himself a nice, deep hole before I corrected him. The altercation had started to draw a crowd as other soldiers heard the shouting; I even saw Vicar Dupont striding towards us, his beatific smile still ever-present.

Thud Thud Thud

Heavy footfalls rumbled so loud I imagined I could feel the vibration in my bones, and a seven-foot-tall juggernaut clad in armor strode into view. The juggernaut was arguably the deadliest weapon in the imperial arsenal. Rare too; the last time I had seen one was in a military parade my dad had brought me to, back when I was still young enough to sit on his shoulders. The juggernaut was far more intimidating up close than it had been back then. While the back of the armor was opened to let the balefire light in, the front was an impenetrable carapace of overlapping metal plates. In its hands was a two-handed war hammer. You still couldn't truly destroy a ghoul with conventional weapons, but pounding their bones to kindling was an extremely effective way to disable one.

The soldiers surrounding us seemed quite confused, either because they didn't recognize me as a fellow soldier or they *did* recognize me as a courier being accosted by their superior officer.

"Given your continued noncompliance, I have no recourse but to take you into custody and escort you to the brig!"

I studiously ignored him, looking over his shoulder to meet eyes with the vicar. "Uhmmm, help?"

The vicar coughed, and the soldiers who noticed him immediately cleared a path.

"Captain Foss, what seems to be the problem here?" he asked, stepping between us.

"A military matter, vicar, none of your business. Just a bit of discipline," Foss told him dismissively.

"Ahhh. So, harassing a church official is now a military matter? I wonder if your superior would agree with that assessment?" he mused, almost to himself.

"No church officials here," Captain Foss growled. "Just a soldier out of line."

Dupont's expression turned dark, his seemingly infinite patience apparently depleted. "That is not a soldier, you halfwit; she is a courier. I understand your father was so proud that his third son took up the red coat. It would be a shame if he were to hear of your . . . inadequacy."

The captain looked at the vicar, then at me, and back to the vicar.

"Heellloooo. I'm Deacon Winona. It's a pleasure to meet you." I smiled with saccharine sweetness.

His face flushed red, and he turned his anger back on his soldiers.

"Well, back to work, all of you, no lallygagging!" he shouted to disperse the crowd, then slunk away with his head down.

"I'm sorry about that," I told Dupont sheepishly. "Didn't mean to cause a scene, just got a bit surprised having someone try to steal my ghoul when I literally had my pants down."

Dupont sighed, putting a hand to his temple in the first display of frustration I had seen from him. "I understand, but it isn't your fault; you have merely stumbled upon some preexisting confrontations."

"Well, either way, I apologize for drawing you into conflict with the captain. I know most of these soldiers are noblemen; I hope Foss's father won't cause you grief."

"Haha! Captain Foss' father still owes me fifty suns from poker night. We grew up together; otherwise, I would not have embarrassed the child so publicly. But he will either pout and sulk or learn some humility. Now, I believe you have a dinner to prepare for?"

"Oh shit! I mean, yes, yes, sir. Thank you, sir!" I turned and ran back towards my sled.

Thankfully, my vestments had been restored to order and were hanging on a peg in my bay. I ducked into my sleeping compartment, using it as a cramped changing room. There was a tentative knock on the door as I was midway through tying the last few cords.

"One minute!" I called, looking down and patting my new outfit to make sure everything was in place. Then I stepped outside, almost running headlong into Captain Calliope.

XV

——

"**O**h, sorry! I got a bit . . . held up . . . " I explained, stepping out onto the ground and pulling my only clean coat over my shoulders.

Calliope did not reply, merely taking in my ensemble with an open mouth.

"Enjoying the view?" I grinned, watching her cheeks flush red as she became aware of her own staring.

"Oh my gods, I'm so sorry. I've just never seen a courier's formal clothes so close before! It's . . . it's not what I expected."

"That's fair; it is a bit . . . nonstandard." I laughed, lifting my arms to show it off.

I couldn't blame her for the shock; the vestments were certainly a far cry from most religious attire, with good reason. Way back when the couriers had been officially absorbed into the clergy, they had been supplied with white robes that were the standard base garment for all deacons. The main problem was that these white robes were: 1. White and 2. Robes. Legend has it that it took only three days of couriers tromping through mud or tripping each other for laughs before the church decided that a wardrobe change was in order. In a moment of colossally poor decision-making, they had allowed the couriers themselves to design the new garment. As the story goes, the first version was a golden loincloth with a flask holster, based on a diagram sketched out on a bar napkin ... Oddly enough, they'd needed a few more revisions to come to something more acceptable.

What they'd ended up with was a two-layer garment. The first layer was a simple long sleeve tunic and pants combo, both made from form-fitting dark grey fabric. Over that went a long sleeveless tabard of intricate brocade that trailed down to calf length, splitting at the hips to allow for easy movement. A stylized brazier was embroidered over the heart.

"Well, what do you think?" I asked as she led me across the outpost, the purple balefire light mingling with orange torchlight.

"It's beautiful, different from anything else I've seen church officials wear. It looks rather comfortable, to be honest," she remarked with a tinge of jealousy.

"It is! It even has pockets!" I laughed, glad that Calliope had loosened up a bit around me. I had the feeling I was walking into the lion's den for this dinner, and I would be glad to have at least one of them on my side.

"If it's OK, can I ask about the color? It's hard to make it out in the light, but I remember the couriers in Drand looking different," she asked, squinting to try to parse out the colors in the purple light.

"You have good eyes. It depends on the city you are based out of. Every major city has its own color scheme and symbol. The capital is red with yellow embroidery, and their balefire brazier is wrapped in chains. Ozero's couriers wear a fetching purple with sky blue, and our symbol is wreathed in ice shards because Ozero is colder than a witch's tit."

"A what?" Calliope asked dubiously.

"Uhm ... it's just really cold," I muttered, slightly embarrassed. We reached a small gate at the base of the motte, where two soldiers waved us in, then began the steep climb up the hill.

"So, this Lieutenant Colonel Berg, anything I should know before meeting him?" I asked as we scaled the steep steps set into the hill.

"This is my first deployment with him; he has an eye for detail and a brilliant tactical mind ...."

She faded into silence, and I decided to prompt her a bit. "I'm sensing a 'but' coming. You don't have to say anything you're not comfortable with. I don't want to push you to badmouth your boss."

"No, no. It's fine; I just want to phrase it right. Berg is . . . inexperienced in practical deployment. I believe this is his first post outside the walls of the capital."

I mulled that over. It explained the outpost, at least, how everything was textbook perfect with little practical thought put in. I tried to keep my mind open, though. An inexperienced officer was not necessarily a bad one. I imagined soldiers were like couriers in that you needed a sturdy base of personality as much as you needed experience. Without that, you were just stacking experience on a rotten foundation, waiting for it to crumble.

Thus informed, I felt more comfortable going into this meeting. And that was just in time, as we had reached the reinforced doors of the wooden keep. Up close, the squat two-story structure looked formidable, a solid final defensive point if all else failed . . . Until they opened the doors at least. Instead of a defensive structure, the doors pulled back to reveal a . . . coat room?

"Huh, that's a new one." I wondered aloud, placing my coat on one of the unoccupied pegs. Then Calliope pushed the interior door open, and we stepped into the keep proper.

I had never seen a nobleman's hunting lodge, but if you'd asked me to describe the image that came to mind, it would be nearly identical to the room I'd stepped into. The bare logs of the walls had been polished to a lacquered gold shine, while the stone fireplace blazed merrily, filling the space with a comfortable heat. A staggering array of hunting trophies were arranged along the walls, many displaying animals I had never seen before. Calliope nudged me, and I snapped out of my surprise, turning my eyes to the center of the room.

An antique table sat on a plush red rug. Six high-backed chairs were set around the table, but only three were occupied. Two of these were clearly fellow captains, given their dress, but the man at the head of the table was outfitted far more opulently. His red coat was liberally embroidered with gold thread, and a brace of colorful medals was arrayed across the left breast. Clothing aside, the lieutenant colonel himself was in his mid-forties, with a high and tight haircut and the deeply tanned skin of an outdoorsman, though his complexion was stained ruddy, likely due to the half-empty wineglass beside him.

"Come in, Come in!" he waved without standing, gesturing over to the empty chair at the foot of the table. I moved to my seat, though I struggled a bit, sliding the high-backed chair in closer to the table. Calliope came to my rescue, lifting my chair and sliding me forward with surprising strength before taking her own seat.

"We welcome you to our table Courier Winona! I imagine you have missed the luxuries of civilization on the road. I am happy to be able to rectify that during your stay here!" Berg called in greeting. An enlisted soldier came over with an open wine bottle, but I politely held my hand over my glass.

"None for me, thank you, wine doesn't agree with me," I declined.

"Haha! Giving wine to a courier? My mistake; I'd be better off trying to feed salad to my hunting dogs!" he laughed, then snapped his fingers. The soldier retreated, then wheeled a small wooden cart over, stacked high with glass decanters filled with an array of colorful liquids. "Please, help yourself; I only allow the finest in my homes. We have whiskey from the Song Islands, dark rum from the southern colonies, anything you could want."

I chose the rum, allowing the man to pour just two fingers worth into my glass; this was not a night to let my composure slip.

"The dinner service will start soon; we are just waiting for one more of our party to begin. Captain Foss sometimes gets overzealous in his duties and can run late. How was the road?"

I regaled him with an abbreviated version of my journey, remembering the vicar's warning and skipping over a few details like Julianne's farmhouse and my discovery of the bandits' skull-stamped coins. Even without that detail, the officers seemed particularly interested in my near escape from my attackers, asking question after question about the bandits and their tactics, which I went over again in detail.

"Have you seen that type of trap before?" One of the officers asked. Both other captains at the table were tall and blond and had been introduced as Andersen and Petersen, though I immediately forgot which one was which.

"Not personally, but I'd heard of it. We try to disseminate that information to other couriers when we encounter something new."

"Good to hear! Those bandits have become far too bold as of late. It's about time we gave them a proper thrashing!" Berg declared, smacking the table for emphasis. I looked around the room again, taking in the animal heads. If Berg were half as good at hunting bandits as he was at hunting animals, we'd have the troublemakers eradicated in a season.

The door slammed open behind me, making me jump. I hated sitting with my back to a door, it made me feel too exposed, but the lieutenant colonel had not given me much choice in that regard. A chill wind blew through the opening, followed by an equally cold individual as Captain Foss stormed in. He snapped his fingers at the soldier holding the wine bottle before slumping into the chair across from Calliope.

"Damn those new recruits! Mark my words, allowing people with diluted noble blood to join the royal guard will be the death of this organization!" Foss groused, swirling the wine in his glass.

"Oh, relax, Foss." Andersen/Petersen admonished. "It was either that or cart a bunch of civilians out here, and hope they did their job right. Now that they've taken the red, they are sworn to the oath and are making twice as much money. I haven't had any problems with them."

"That is because you're too easy on them, Andersen. They don't respect you." Foss brushed him off.

"Or maybe they respect him more . . . " I grumbled, quietly enough that only he and Calliope could hear. Foss turned in surprise, finally noticing my presence.

"Deacon Winona." Foss hissed through gritted teeth. "I didn't see you there. So glad you could join us for dinner . . . "

Berg coughed pointedly, and Captain Foss continued.

"Also, I just wanted to . . . apologize for that case of mistaken identity earlier today."

Oh, that's all right, Fossy Boy." I laughed louder than necessary, then playfully punched him in the arm. "We're all friends here, right?"

"Yes . . . We're all . . . friends . . ." He pointedly turned away and found conversation elsewhere.

With everyone present, dinner began, and what a dinner it was. Five full courses were planned for the night, which was four more courses than I'd ever had in a meal. Given that I'd spent the last few days subjected to my own subpar cooking, I was eager to dig in. Every selection was introduced by Lieutenant Colonel Berg, detailing the dishes as if he'd cooked them himself. First was a fish soup, cooked with some haddock that Berg had caught earlier that day. I wasn't big on fish, but I tore into the appetizers that came after. Berg introduced them as "høns i asparges," but all I needed to know was that they were delicious little chicken and asparagus tartlets, the pastry having that perfect flaky consistency. I piled the glorious little things high on my plate, only stopping when the others started to stare at the small tower I had constructed. Next was salad, which I barely picked at while digesting my assault on the appetizers. I took the moment to engage Berg on something that had been on my mind.

"Excuse me, sir, I hate to bring up business during such a lovely meal, but I was hoping to ask something before it gets too late." I began.

"Of course, Deacon, whatever you need." He gestured for me to continue.

"Well, as much as I have loved the taste of civilization this outpost has brought, I did come here with a purpose. My cargo needs to be kept at a stable temperature, and I was promised by the patron of this trip that he had arranged for a replacement battery to be available upon my arrival. I'd just like to make sure that the exchange is all in order so I can depart as soon as possible."

Berg fidgeted, unwilling to meet my eyes, then sighed and turned to face me.

"Of course. Your patron Mr. Ronald was immensely helpful in arranging the supplies necessary for our trek. He also shared his remarkable technological advancements! I would never have believed I would see old-world miracles brought back to life! Devilishly difficult to produce, though, even more so than gunpowder, from what I'm told. Hard to come by the ingredients as well. Our alchemists have the materials packed away somewhere, I'm sure, but at the moment, they are quite busy with other tasks. It may take a few days for them to get around to the job, but we would be happy to keep your cargo in warm storage in the meantime, though," he waffled.

Something felt off. Berg's tone was oddly evasive, and Calliope was avoiding my gaze while the other captains watched me closely, sneaking quick glances when they thought they could hide it.

"I'm sorry, sir, but this cargo is sorely needed at its destination; I can't delay any longer than absolutely necessary," I explained.

"Ah yes, in Skyroost, I believe? I'd ask you what you were carrying that was of such importance, but I know you couriers love to claim confidentiality with your patrons. So, I'll make you a deal; if you are willing to help consult on a minor project of ours, I would be more than happy to move your battery to the top of the priority list," he offered.

Wow, if BLACKMAIL had appeared above the lieutenant colonel's head in giant flaming letters, it could not have been more obvious. I had my doubts that acceding to his offer would truly help me, but there was little else I could do right now. Agreeing would at least buy me some time to figure out what was going on.

"Absolutely!" I agreed woodenly. "You've been so kind to me; I would be happy to assist in any way I can."

"Fantastic!" Berg clapped, his relief palpable. I'll give you the details soon, but first, the main course!"

Another cart rolled out, this one bearing a massive covered platter that two chefs had to muscle onto the table. One pulled the cover back with a flourish to reveal an entire suckling pig, its dead eyes staring forlornly back at me. Berg stood with visible excitement, sharpening a large knife against a honing rod with quick, practiced motions to the cheers of his subordinates.

I used the distraction to lean over to Calliope.

"Our food is looking at me . . . " I whispered to her.

Calliope hid a grin and whispered back. "It's fine; it's just pork. You must have had pork before."

"I have! I've just never had the pig judge me while I ate it!" I replied, leaning back into my seat as Berg doled out portions, the cooks delivering a variety of sides as he worked. Once our plates had been filled, Berg continued his explanation between bites, scattering crumbs of fresh bread as he spoke through a full mouth.

"So, the royal guards are the best soldiers in the world; that fact is beyond doubt." Berg boasted. "But sadly, our duties keep us from solving all the Empire's military problems. Protecting the royal family is a noble task, but it has left our force . . . inexperienced in handling other foes of the Empire. While I am sure we will give those Fins a thorough thrashing, we have been having difficulty with . . . shall we say, less lively foes."

"So, you're having ghoul problems," I stated, already annoyed at Berg's wraparound way of getting to the point. I had already agreed to help. Just get on with it.

"Yes, the ghouls! Such disgusting creatures! They cause all sorts of problems; they were tumbling right off the cliff into camp before we posted men up there. Some were caught on the rocks up steam, their filth contaminating our water supply! We have already had two patrols attacked, and one poor lad will lose his arm from a bite! Our soldiers need experience fighting these creatures before someone gets killed," he told me, forking another piece of pork into his mouth.

"Well, I'm happy to show your men a few tricks I picked up, but most of your problem is just area clearing. A settlement of this size will attract a lot of local ghouls, but once you knock out the local population, the rest should be too far away to sense you," I explained.

"Well, thank you, we will certainly take any advice you give to heart. But I was thinking of more direct involvement. Our horsemen have been rounding up the local ghouls and compressing them into . . . I believe you call it a 'horde.' They will lead the monsters back here, and we will exterminate them in one fell swoop! With your guidance, of course."

I rubbed my temples for a moment, suppressing the first three rude comments that came to mind. It was almost worth it just to see the expression on his face, but insulting powerful men was rarely a clever idea in the long run.

"You want to form a horde and destroy it here? Well, it seems like you've built some sturdy walls; given some time, we should be able to chip a decent—"

"Nonono." Berg interrupted. "We will engage the ghouls beyond the walls, face to face. There is a field a short distance away that will work for the task. My men have begun developing an irrational fear of the creatures, and I would have them face that fear directly. If that is not satisfactory, you are welcome to wait safe behind the walls, though I cannot promise that my alchemists will have time to see to your needs in a prompt manner."

Ugh, that rat bastard. Fine, If I was going to "consult," I may as well throw my weight around.

"When will the horde arrive?" I asked.

"Our estimate is just before sunrise, the day after tomorrow. And yes, before you say anything, I understand that a night battle is not ideal. But, as the horde has grown, my men have had more trouble controlling their horses near such a gathering. I have decided to draw the horde to us in a controlled manner rather than fail at delaying tactics and bring them on our heads in less ideal conditions," he explained.

That was the first smart decision he had made all night. The horses' behavior wasn't too surprising, though. Any domesticated animal not raised around the animated dead tended to react poorly in the presence of ghouls.

"OK, we can hash out the details later, but there are a few things we will need. One of those movable braziers will have to come with us; we will need it to help manage the horde. You're also gonna need all your juggernauts present, they're the best resource you have. I'll need one of those handheld balefire torches as well, the ones I've seen your watchmen use. I'm going to be moving around during the fight and can't risk getting stuck in a shadow away from balefire light," I explained.

A handheld torch also meant that I could abandon the whole event if necessary, but they didn't need to know that I was giving myself some insurance. Berg agreed easily, though, happy that I'd signed on to his venture. He celebrated with a dessert of krumkake, a rolled waffle cookie filled with light sugary cream. As I crammed pasty into my mouth, I noticed a strange inconsistency among the captains; while their uniforms were practically identical, only Calliope had an armband of dark green fabric around her upper arm.

"Waz that?" I asked through a mouth full of crumbs, pointing at the band. "Some kinda special rank?"

This question garnered a look of embarrassment from Calliope and a bark of laughter from Foss, which was more than enough to signal that I had committed some sort of social faux pas.

"Great question, courier! As you likely know, only members of imperial nobility may stand on the royal guard. We can't trust just anyone to protect our dear Emperor Konrad and his family. But every now and then, a foreign house of noble standing finds themselves needing to take refuge within our borders," he explained as Calliope glared daggers at him. So, the Emperor allows a child of the noble family to serve in his royal guard so as to maintain . . . supervision over them, with that lovely band to help us remember who they are."

"Thank you for the . . . thorough explanation," I replied through gritted teeth.

"Oh, my pleasure," Foss grinned. "It's not every day you get to meet a genuine Mouse. They say the warriors of Mycenae are the best formation fighters in the world, or so some would have you believe."

The pleasant conversation died after that, despite Andersen/Petersen's attempts to revive it. We kept the topic to business, with Berg outlining his command structure. Andersen commanded the scouts and would be leaving tomorrow morning to oversee the soldiers guiding the horde to our position. Petersen had overseen the construction of the defensive works and would be staying behind with a small contingent to hold the outpost. Berg commanded the outpost overall and would also oversee the main contingent during the exercise. That left Foss and Calliope, who commanded the fighting ghouls and a platoon of specially trained soldiers, respectively. They would both be present during the lieutenant colonel's planned exercise as well.

With dinner ending, I gratefully took the opportunity to excuse myself, bidding the table goodnight with a promise to return to Berg's keep tomorrow to continue planning. I didn't think I'd sleep much, though; this whole situation already had me feeling out of my element. My fighting experience was generally personal, poleaxing individual ghouls or tangling with a rowdy drunk. My fights lasted only until the moment I could make a break for safety. A quick stab and a quicker retreat had kept me alive this far, and a protracted fight, especially a large-scale one, was something I avoided at all costs.

The wintry weather outside the keep cut through my vestments even with a coat, but that dinner had left me hot with frustration, and I welcomed the chill. So lost was I inside my own head that I did not hear the voice calling out behind me. I pushed on through the wind until a hand clasped onto my shoulder. Whirling around, I drew my hands up in defense but paused when I saw Calliope drawing her hand away.

"Deacon . . . I'm sorry, I called out, but you didn't seem to hear," she explained.

"No worries, captain, just lost in my own head . . . And sorry for earlier, I didn't realize what that armband meant."

"I told you to call me Calliope," she chided softly, walking alongside me. "And it's not your fault. Foss was waiting for you to say something he could jump on. He would have found a way to get under your skin no matter what; taking a jab at me was just a bonus."

I appreciated her attempts to make me feel better, but I still felt sickly hot embarrassment in my gut. I could wrangle bloodthirsty ghouls, but a bit of fine dining had left me feeling like an idiot child.

"I should have known, though. Calliope isn't exactly a common Empire name. Beautiful though. I've never met a Mouse before."

"Uhm . . . We don't like to use that term. I know we get called mice by many, but it carries a bit of a negative connotation. Mycenean is the name we prefer," she corrected, though not harshly.

"Oh . . . I didn't mean, I mean, I didn't know . . . I'm SO sorry," I floundered. Fantastic job, Winona; you finally make a friend and immediately call her a slur.

We lapsed into an awkward silence for a moment, and I racked my brain, trying to remember if there was anything else about Calliope's people that I should know about. After the world had fallen apart, humanity found itself kicked back to the dark ages. Countries, religions, economies; all cracked and shattered overnight. When faced with that, many people looked to the ways of their ancestors for guidance. Ancient ways saw a resurgence, though pre-cataclysm historical sources were so hard to come by that it was impossible to tell how closely these cultural revivals mirrored their ancient sources. Of all the ones I knew of, the Free Cities of Mycenae were the only such culture still thriving, laying claim to a large swath of territory on the northern shore of the Southern Sea.

"Anyway, I haven't encountered any others since we moved here either. Which is probably why my father moved us so far north," she reasoned.

"May I ask why you moved? Foss mentioned you being nobility, taking refuge up here." I asked, worried about further alienating her with the questioning but still curious.

"It's a reasonable question. My father was an ephor, part of a small, elected council that served under the kings. I assume you've heard the rumors of what we do to the infants that don't live up to the standards of our inspectors?"

Of course, I had. It was one of the two things everyone knew about them. They were all incredible warriors, and they killed the babies they deemed too weak to be warriors. I simply nodded to Calliope in affirmation.

"It is a rare event, and the frequency has been exaggerated to demonize us. However, the truth is no less cruel. Among the lower classes, those who cannot fight are . . . disposable. They are taken from their families and treated as slaves, forced to toil in the worst, most dangerous conditions. But for the nobility, yes, that barbaric tradition is real. My father had been a loyal citizen for years . . . until his own son was born lame. We ran before the inspectors came to our house and kept running until we landed on your Emperor's doorstep," she finished.

"Thank you for sharing. I can't imagine what that must have been like." I went to pat her on the shoulder, then flinched away as a large shape emerged from the gloom behind her.

"Hello, my children," Vicar Dupont spoke, stepping into the torch-light. "I hate to intrude, as we all know that the Balefire Church and military could use more friendships across the line. But I must spirit away Deacon Winona for the remainder of the night. Bishop Rimkus wishes to speak with her."

"Thank you for the escort, captain." I bowed to Calliope formally, unsure of how much the vicar had overheard. "I would appreciate talking more tomorrow; we have much to prepare for before the event."

Calliope nodded, bowed to us both, then turned on her heel, departing into the night. She had helped me to face her boss, but now I found myself wishing she could help me face mine.

XVI

"**M**aking allies among the officers?" The vicar asked politely as he led me across the outpost.

"Is that a problem? I had hoped that greater union between our factions would benefit both sides." I countered placidly, keeping my eyes down.

"Ah, becoming a diplomat then, I am heartened to hear it! I would hate for you to grow too close, though. Friendships over that line can be . . . fickle." The statement had a subtle hint of threat to it.

Hmmm, this wasn't working. I was terrible at subterfuge, but I figured I needed to take a shot at it or risk Calliope becoming a person of interest to the clergy and getting drawn into whatever was going on between the two factions.

"She's an outsider. A Mycenean transplant, distrusted by her fellow soldiers. She holds no loyalty to their cause beyond the refuge that the government provides her family. I believe she would be a worthy ally," I explained.

The vicar grinned widely, though I could not tell if it was because he believed my subterfuge or because he had seen right through it.

"I see that my fears were unfounded, Deacon. You clearly have some skills beyond wilderness survival. Not enough to fool me, but I do appreciate the effort. A bit of advice then: be honest with the bishop. He has spent decades digging the truth out of far better liars than yourself," he cautioned.

I nodded stiffly, and he led us up to a small chapel nestled against the cliffside. The vicar cracked the double doors open just wide enough to allow us entry, then closed them behind, sliding a heavy bar into place. The scraping sound reverberated through the dark hall, now lit solely by glimmers of moonlight peeking through locked shutters.

"Wow, this place is built like a fortress," I whispered, following his shadowed form between the pews.

"Every church is a fortress to a believer of the sacred balefire . . . and extra thick doors help too," the vicar explained though I caught a hint of laughter in his tone. He led me behind the altar to another door which he unlocked with a key pulled from a cord around his neck. He swung the door wide, and I stepped inward, entering a cave of tapestries and mint-flavored smoke.

Fabric covered every available surface of the wide living space. Bolts of cloth stretched across the ceiling, making the room appear smaller than it truly was. The walls were padded with elaborate tapestries depicting purple flames and other religious iconography. The floor space was dominated by overlapping rugs and dotted with wide pillows. Squatting in the center of the room was a low table with an elaborate hookah standing in the center. Behind it, a single figure sat cross-legged; a hooded robe masked his features, and the garment hung down to the floor, pooling around his form in a wavy pile. The ensemble gave him the appearance of a massive serpent, rearing up to strike me down with a single bite.

"Courier." A raspy voice intoned from beneath the hood. "Sit."

A bony finger emerged, pointing to a pillow opposite their own. I nervously took my place, keeping my eyes down and trying not to cough in the thick smoke that shrouded the room. Suppressing a cough was always a lesson in futility, though, and soon my eyes were watering as I tried to hold back the growing tickle in my throat.

"Oh, just get it out, girl!" the figure barked, causing my concentration to slip and a hacking cough to slip out. My first breath to recover was filled with mint-laden smoke, which further lengthened my coughing fit. The vicar took pity on me, bringing over a glass of water from a side table that helped to ease my embarrassing outburst.

"Not a smoker, then?" the figure laughed, gesturing for Vicar Dupont to sit.

"No . . . No bishop. My dad came home smelling of smoke once, and mum said that next time she caught him, she'd tan his backside . . . ," I petered off, flushing red in embarrassment. Ugghh, I preferred talking to ghouls; they never looked at me funny when I rambled like this.

"Ha . . . Hahaha! I like this girl! The other courier was scared shitless when we met. I was worried he'd leave a stain on the pillow!" the figure laughed, finally drawing his hood back to reveal the wrinkled face of a man in his early sixties.

"Apologies for the theatrics. I find that it's an effective way to judge someone's character, barring more . . . invasive means. From what our dear vicar has told me, you are an honest sort, though with a smart tongue that gets you in trouble."

"That's a . . . fair assessment," I hesitated, unsure of what he wanted me to say on the matter.

"And how is the *Ridgerunner* these days? Still as dependable as ever?" he asked.

"Absolutely, sir. She may not be the fastest sled or the heaviest hauler but give me a package, and my crew will get it there. I'd bet my life on it," I answered with confidence. There wasn't much I had pride in, but I'd put my team and sled against any I could think of, short of a few near-legendary crews like Mildred's back home.

The bishop smiled at that, nodding before taking another puff from his hookah. I took the moment to give in to my curiosity and examine the elaborate piece. I had only seen them at a distance, outside bars when the weather was nice, or being sold in various shady bazaars. It had a strange clash of styles, a combination of a Dutchess' decorative vase and an alchemist's scientific flask. Between the heat, smoke, and bubbling water, there was certainly a great deal going on with the process, though the allure had always been lost on me.

"You know, the clergy in Ozero have been keeping an eye on you. I checked in with them about their courier corps on our way north," he stated, exhaling a long stream of smoke.

"Well . . . I hope they haven't found my performance to be subpar." Nobody liked hearing that their bosses were keeping tabs on them, though I was picking up the sense that the bishop was mentioning it more to savor my discomfort than out of any real disapproval.

"Oh, don't get your hackles up. They did not say anything I couldn't already tell by meeting you. A solid courier, dependable, good at adapting to changing situations, but better at handling ghouls than she is at handling people," he grinned, seeing if he could get a reaction, but I was determined to remain politely silent. "Anyway, the scrutiny is not your doing. It is because you're a legacy courier. Church doctrine dictates that your father's sled falls to your ownership after his passing, but what we don't advertise is that we keep special tabs on those inheritors of family sleds. Those new couriers are not always as fit to serve as their relatives were, though I am heartened to see that it doesn't seem to be the case with you."

My stomach turned, and it wasn't just due to the over-rich food and sickly-sweet smoke. The *Ridgerunner* was my pride and joy; it was both my profession and my home. And I would happily burn her to the ground if it meant I could have my father back.

"I apologize, courier. My life's work has been dedicated to uncovering the truth. It is a skill I've cultivated over decades, but one that can be difficult to turn off. So let us restart; in the safety of this room, I will call you Winona, and you may call me Rimkus. Would that be acceptable?"

"Yes . . . sir—Rimkus, rather. I can do that," I answered, trying to unwind the knot of stress in my gut.

"Good . . . feel free to indulge yourself with tobacco or any other vice of your choosing. Now, to get down to business, what do you know about the Fin Tribes?"

The bishop seemed like a man who appreciated well-thought-out answers, so I took a moment to formulate my response. In the meantime, I pulled a leather pouch from my pocket, removing a piece of *mastic* gum, and slipping it into my mouth. The bitter taste gave way to pine notes as I chewed, helping to settle my stomach.

"I haven't come across them too much, just the odd trader and the like. I know they do a decent trade in forestry, floating their barges to the Empire across the Baltian sea. Up north, it's furs and such, sometimes bits of rare metals," I explained.

"Very good! A courier with a brain for more than ghouls is always nice to see. Now the real test, though. Do you think the threat they pose warrants the significant response you've witnessed here?" he asked.

"Hmmm . . . I've heard that the tribes have united for war before, so I guess it could be happening again. But the thing that keeps nagging at me is that this outpost is filled with royal guards, not northern regulars."

"Oh?" Rimkus leaned forward, steepling his fingers and leaning forward. "But the royal guards are the best soldiers in the Empire!" Rimkus boasted, mockery dripping from his voice as he unknowingly parodied the lieutenant colonel's earlier words.

I snorted in amusement but still tried to maintain a respectful tone. "Yes, and if we had to worry about assassination attempts or dispersing mobs, I'd call for them in a heartbeat. But fighting Fins in the wild dark? I'd rather have some hard northern bastards who are used to fighting in this terrain."

"I agree, which leaves us with the obvious question. What are we doing here?" Rimkus flicked his fingers, sending a golden disc rolling across the table. I watched it until it spun to a halt, revealing a thick golden coin with a flaming skull stamped on it. "That's not Empire coin, not Song Island, Fin Tribe, Mycenean, or any of the other dozens of cultures that the church has encountered or heard of. It's like it appeared out of thin air, materializing in the pockets of bandits and smugglers across the northern borderlands."

There was a tentative knock at the door, and the vicar rose to answer it while Bishop Rimkus continued.

"We didn't have time to brief you today, so Dupont wisely passed you a message to ensure your silence. Good job keeping your mouth shut if you have encountered these coins or playing dumb if you had no idea what I'm talking about. Either way, we are lucky enough to have a man here whose firsthand account may help us uncover what is happening here."

The far door opened, and in walked Blondie.

"Blondie!" I cheered, jumping to my feet. "You're not dead!"

"Blondie?" I haven't been called that since I was a kid!" he laughed ruefully, shaking my hand with a firm grip. "You're the girl from the farmhouse. I'm sorry I never asked your name. But I did drop off your message at Zeb's, as promised."

"I'm Winona." I supplied, sitting down as he sank onto the last open pillow at the table. "And you're . . . Haakon, right? Thank you for the help, by the way. You saved me a ton of time. I'm actually running with one of the ghouls I picked up from Zeb's; she's a damn firecracker, let me tell you." I laughed.

"Oh? Tell me more; what kind of ghoul were you looking into? You know, I've been looking—"

"*Eh hem.*" Rimkus cleared his throat. "I'm sure you can find time to talk about the finer points of your teams another day. We do have other things to discuss."

"Sorry, sorry!" I apologized, sinking back into silence, but only for a moment. "Oh! I found your sled! The guards at Bale's Blessing probably have it by now—Oh, sorry . . . ."

I sat back again, closing my mouth and miming that I was locking it up and throwing away the key. Rimkus gestured to Haakon, who gave me a summary of his own tale. It began quite similar to how I'd guessed from the evidence at the ambush site. The bandits had sprung their trap flawlessly that time, entangling Haakon's ghouls and sending him tumbling forward over the handrails. He had reacted with bravery, though, toppling his balefire brazier into the snow moments before the bandits tackled him to the ground. But, instead of killing him, they'd put him in chains and tossed him on one of their dog sleds. He glossed over his time in captivity, but it wasn't hard to tell that it had been rough on him. You could tell by the way he skipped over portions of his imprisonment, there were dark memories there that he didn't want to bring to mind again. At some point, he had tried to pick a fight with one of his jailers, with the hope of pickpocketing the key in his confusion; he hadn't found a key, but he did discover one of the strange gold coins.

As Haakon posted his elbows on the table, I could see white bandages around his wrists, the remnant of injury from his confinement. The bandits had taken him past the border, farther north than he had ever been. In a stroke of luck, the bandits had ventured too close to outpost 305 and been set upon by the outpost's scouts. The bandits had escaped, but Haakon managed to roll off the sled in the chaos, tumbling into the snow as his captors fled. The scouts found him shortly after, and his harrowing experience was brought to a close.

I picked up my part of the tale from there, filling in my own fight with the bandits. From a pouch, I brought out one of my own coins, an identical twin to the one on the table.

Rimkus' eyes sparkled as he listened intently to my story, asking questions now and again to clarify details.

"Have you shown this coin to anyone outside the church? Any members of the military?" he asked.

"No, not that I can think of. I gave a sketch of it to the guards in Bale's Blessing to send back to my superiors in Ozero, but I didn't trust giving them a gold coin," I explained.

"You made the right call. The Empire switched to using lesser metals years back due to scarcity, but from what we've determined, this is, in fact, solid gold. They may not be as well made as our currency, but their construction clearly takes at least a basic amount of industry, enough that we should be aware of a culture that has achieved that level of production. There is a new player making moves around our borders, and it is clear that they have taken pains to obfuscate their involvement. Which brings us to Skyroost." Rimkus finished, gesturing for Vicar Dupont to continue while he took another drag of smoke.

"We are aware of your destination and cargo, as is the lieutenant colonel. Ronald, your patron, was a valuable resource in the planning of this venture and made his goals clear. We believe that a cholera outbreak is truly ravaging the city, but we do not believe that cholera is the sole source of Skyroost's misfortune. Two experienced courier teams have been lost so far attempting to reach the city. The journey is perilous, but we do not believe that both teams were lost to common mishaps, especially given the military interest here."

"And the fact that they're all royal guards," I added.

"Exactly. Emperor Konrad must know something he has not deigned to tell the church and has sent his personal guards to keep it quiet. Our best guess? The owners of these gold coins have made a move to seize control of Skyroost, either personally or through the proxies they seem to favor."

Haakon leaned back and stretched, then withdrew a pipe from his jacket that he prepared and lit.

"It's legitimate, Winona. I know we all joke about how stuffy our bosses can be, but these two are the most competent pair of upper clergy I've ever met," he remarked, nodding respectfully to Rimkus and Dupont.

Rimkus coughed out a hacking laugh. "Well, the Balefire Church may be a majestic ship, but it can be slow to change course. In recent years, the Pope has decided, in his infinite wisdom, to pursue the training of officials with . . . nonstandard skillsets. Our dear vicar was a . . . problem solver for many unsavory individuals before the light of the balefire found him. And myself? Well, I was apprenticed to the grand inquisitor before the Pope decided that my talents were best used elsewhere."

That new information sent a feeling like ice water down my spine. The Balefire Church treated other religions like a tired mother with rambunctious children. It tolerated them to practice as they would, until the line was crossed. The extremist sects, or the terrorists who used the gods as justification, found themselves under the knife of the grand inquisitor, whose secret methods had the poor souls more than happy to convert and give up the locations of their fellow dissidents.

I moved the conversation along, now very much aware of the danger contained in the frail individual sitting across from me.

"So, why are they trying to keep us out, and what do we do about it?" I asked.

"In politics, information is power, and the throne is never as unassailable as it seems. If our Empire was blindsided by an attack from forces unknown, that would reflect poorly on the Emperor; it is advantageous for him if he understands the nature of our foe before anyone else does. And, if it is the work of bandits or a minor rebellion, the royal guard may be able to take care of it quietly before knowledge of the threat ever gets out."

My head was starting to spin, and it wasn't just from the smoke. I wanted nothing to do with this, with being just another piece on a political chessboard, but it looked like I was being pulled in regardless of my wishes.

The bishop continued. "As for what we must do, we find out what's happening in Skyroost, regardless of the military's attempts to delay us. That duty falls to Deacon Winona, though I apologize for forcing that responsibility upon you. Those alchemists will never replace your battery. They will make excuses, promise to do it soon or find other ways to delay you indefinitely. That way, you can never reach Skyroost, never uncover the truth." Rimkus stretched and groaned, a series of alarming pops emanating from his hunched frame, and the vicar again picked up the thread of conversation.

"Fortunately for us, the loosening restrictions on recruitment has allowed us to plant multiple soldiers in this outpost that are loyal to the church first. One of the alchemists reports to us and has the necessary skills to help you on your way. Doing so covertly will still take time, though, so as to not raise suspicion. So, for now, play your part and help the guards with their exercise. While they are out fighting, we will have your sled resupplied and made ready so that you can depart immediately upon your return. I understand that leaving under such conditions in wild territory is not ideal, so of course, the decision falls to you." Dupont outlined.

Dupont had the same ability that all skilled negotiators, from parents to managers, cultivated. He could give you an order and make it feel like a helpful suggestion. But I had no illusions about the instructions I was being given.

"Of course, sir. If we can make sure that the cargo's battery is replaced and that loyal men are present to open the gate, I will depart as soon as I return." I agreed. It was starting to feel like powerful forces were stirring up waves on all sides of me, and I was just a little paper boat trying to stay afloat. I'd be glad to be back in the wild; as dangerous as it was out there, politics was still scarier to me. At least the ghouls didn't pretend to be your friend before they tried to kill you.

But as scary as political intrigue was, the approaching horde was a far more pressing threat. So, we switched from strategic planning to tactical, focusing on the events of the coming exercise. I suppressed a yawn, my eyes heavy from a long and eventful day. I was eager to get to bed, as it looked like I would have some exceedingly early days coming up.

"So, I am many things, but neither the vicar nor I have had the practical experience facing the undead that our two young associates have accrued. The lieutenant colonel is a well-read man, but I doubt that he, nor any other member of the royal guard, has much knowledge on the topic either. My dear couriers, what would you have us do?" Rimkus asked.

I started, filling them in on my experience taking part in a ghoul hunt. The various traps they had employed were too complex to be built in a day, but we could take some ideas and apply them to our current dilemma. Haakon contributed even more; he was from a small border village and had regularly ridden horseback to split and guide segments of the incoming horde during the cullings. He would meet with the scouts tomorrow to pass on what advice he could.

"I think we should work with Calliope too," I added. "I mean, Captain Deimos."

Vicar Dupont snorted, crossing his arms. "Be careful, young courier. Do not let your feelings cloud your judgment. I know you seem to get along well with the woman, but she is still a royal guard. I know for certain that they chose her to greet you because they thought she had the best chance of winning you over."

That was a surprise to me, though it honestly shouldn't have been; I had been watched and manipulated since I had first set foot in this camp. But I still had to go with my gut, and my gut told me that she was trustworthy.

"I know she's royal guard, but she's also a foreigner. From what I gathered at dinner, her position makes her a prisoner as much as an officer, leverage against her family. She doesn't have that nobleman's loyalty the rest of 'em do. Plus, she's been trained under Mycenean teachers, so I'd trust the troops under her command more so than any of the rest of them," I defended.

"Well, we will need to work alongside her regardless of her loyalties but do not inform her of your plans to leave after the exercise. We cannot allow that information to get to the lieutenant colonel before you make your escape. For myself, I will make sure that the troops are well supplied with balefire, in addition to the grand brazier you will be bringing out. You will need ample flames on the ground to dispose of the ghouls, and I doubt these soldiers are very practiced in their maneuvers." He took a moment for one last pull of smoke, then rose to his feet. "The hour is getting late, though, and we all have long days tomorrow. Courier Winona, we have an extra guest room here. Please make use of it. You deserve one good night's sleep with a roof over your head before venturing back into the wild dark."

XVII

———

I slept like the dead. Though admittedly, that phrase had fallen out of popularity, given that our dead tended to wander around if left to their own devices. Regardless of phrasing, I slept better than I had all trip. On the road, you learned to sleep light, never letting yourself fall into a completely relaxed slumber. But in my safe little room, with the door locked and a chair wedged against it for good measure, I fell into a deep, restorative sleep.

It took a firm knock at the door to rouse me, and by the insistence of the noise, it was clear that the person had been at it for a while. I pulled a pillow over my head, but the noise continued, pulling me out of my bed's warm embrace. I stumbled through the darkness, pulling on clothes at random, then unjammed the door and cracked it open.

"Hello?" I asked, blinking blearily in the hallway's light.

"Good morning, Deacon," Vicar Dupont smiled, pressing a covered platter into my hands. "I hate to wake you, but it's just past seven, and we have a busy day ahead. I brought you breakfast."

"Thank you, sir. You don't know how much good this night has done for me," I told him gratefully, taking the dish from his hands.

"My pleasure. Bishop Rimkus would like to see you before you leave for the day. He also said to inform you he's making coffee, which he was confident would serve as a powerful motivator."

"Oh, well . . . Yeah, that's fair," I admitted. "I'll be quick."

"Oh, and Deacon? Maybe make sure you are properly dressed first," he instructed before departing.

I looked down, then blushed deeply. In my blind hurry, I had only managed to don my sleeveless tabard and pants; my shirt lost somewhere in the dark room. Couriers spent most of our time covered up in the harsh winter sun, so I had some legendary tan lines across my arms and face to extenuate the whole embarrassing ensemble.

"Yup, starting the day right," I muttered to myself, ducking back into my room.

Fully clothed and contentedly full, I made my way to the bishop's chamber, trying in vain to wipe the wrinkles out of the clothes I had tossed onto the floor last night. Rimkus was in his favorite spot across the table, though the hookah had been replaced with a simple platter of sliced fruit and granola.

"Good morning, Winona. Sleep well?" he smiled, picking delicately at the food with his long fingers.

"It was glorious," I laughed. "Thank you so much for the room; it means more than you know."

"My pleasure. I wasn't always a bishop, and I learned to appreciate the simple pleasures like a warm bed and a safe room many years ago," he smiled as the vicar entered, carrying a small wooden case, with Blondie in tow behind him.

"Mornin' Blondie." I greeted him, stretching languorously.

"You do know I have a real name, right?" he asked, sitting down next to me and digging into the breakfast spread.

"Uh-huh, and I will continue to ignore it in favor of the nickname I have graciously bestowed upon you," I explained.

"If I could have your attention for a moment? There is a bit of business to address before you depart. I have been thinking about how you are acting under my aegis in this venture, and that your position should reflect that. Please give me your brazier pendant," he commanded, stretching out his bony hand.

I did not like the sound of that. The pendant was a symbol of my station as a deacon, with all the benefits that position granted me. Handing it over felt as unnatural as being told to hand over my sled. But the bishop was not a man I could deny, even if I had been inclined to try. Slipping the leather cord off my neck, I sighed and pressed the pendant into his palm.

"Feels odd, doesn't it? It's amazing the things we take for granted until they are gone," he mused, handing the symbol to Dupont, who opened his little case and began picking at the metal with a small set of jeweler's tools.

I watched in horrified fascination as he pulled the pieces of the pendant apart like a jeweler dismantling a broken watch, but Rimkus' stern voice pulled me back.

"As I was saying, I was thinking about last night and the quest that we've set you on. I understand that this venture has increased in danger far beyond the parameters you originally agreed to. In addition, you have been saddled with the job of discovering what has happened to Skyroost and whether these flaming skull coins relate. The subordinates who operate under me commonly find themselves assigned to difficult tasks, but those who complete them also find themselves well compensated. So, I believe a promotion is in order. Please rise, Winona."

I stood shakily, mind in a daze. Promotion?

"Now, this ceremony is rarely performed, but I believe it is appropriate," Rimkus coughed, then continued in a deep, stately tone.

"We have gathered here to witness the ascension of Deacon Winona to the position of archdeacon. She will maintain this position until her return from Skyroost, where she may choose to relinquish it or continue under my auspice. Do you accept these terms?" he asked.

"I do," I replied, still shocked at the suddenness. Archdeacons upheld responsibilities delegated by a bishop, though I had never heard of a courier attaining the rank.

"This ascension must be ratified by a majority vote of her peers. Is there anyone who would vouch for the character of this deacon?"

"I would," Blondie stood. "I, Deacon Haakon of House Namos, would vouch for her character."

"That is one. Do we have another?" Rimkus asked.

"I would," Dupont added, though he stayed seated, still focused on his work. "I, Vicar Dupont of Goth, would vouch for her character."

"And I, Bishop Rimkus of Goth, would vouch for her character. That is a majority. Kneel, Winona."

I did so, and Rimkus took my pendant back from Dupont, rounding the table to stand before me. He slipped the cord back over my neck, then took my hands in his own, pulling me to my feet.

"Rise, Archdeacon Winona, there's work to be done," he smiled, clapping me on the back with what seemed like genuine mirth. I stood and pulled the symbol back up into view. It looked much the same as before, a tiny, flattened brazier with a circular chip of amethyst at its heart. But now that chip was encircled with a flat disk of hammered gold, imbuing the piece with a glint that had not been present before.

"I'm honored, sir. I'll do my best to live up to this," I told him as he stepped away.

"Ha! Thank you, Winona," Rimkus laughed, all sense of seriousness gone. "But it's not something I want to push on you. We can speak more about what responsibilities this offer might entail when you return from Skyroost. And negotiate your stipend, of course."

Rimkus winked, then dismissed Blondie and me with a promise to meet later to finalize plans.

"So, a single day to get these guys ready to fight ghouls. I don't like our chances... What do you want to do first?" Blondie asked as we stepped out into the morning light.

"Well, first, I need to change back into something more practical than this." I gestured to my ceremonial outfit. "Then I need to watch some training with the lieutenant colonel. It should give us a better idea of what they need to work on."

"I still need to meet with the scouts. Do you want me to round up some ghouls from the pen after, give them something to practice on?" Blondie asked as we stepped out of the chapel into the bright morning light.

"Yes, please. Pick a few that are ready to fall apart anyway; I don't want the soldiers accusing us of stealing their best workers. Then get 'em mittened and muzzled; the last thing we need is them blaming us for one of them getting a boo-boo." We shared a laugh at that, then parted ways.

I may have lacked allies in this camp, but at least my ghouls were happy to see me, though they were still covered in filth. Their clothes and my sled had been washed thoroughly, so at least the sergeant had been good to his word. Even better, Curtis had followed through, and a wrapped package revealed a pristine new ghoul harness. Judging by the angle of the rising sun, I still had a bit of time before I needed to report for training. Leaving my ghouls in such a sorry state did not feel right to me, but washing that filth off them by hand was a chore that'd eat up far too much time. What to do . . . ?

A solution dawned on me, though it was sure to turn heads. I mulled it over for a moment, unsure if I wanted to risk alienating the soldiers any more than I already had.

"Screw it," I muttered after some brief deliberation. "They're not gonna like me anyway, might as well earn it."

While most of these soldiers were green, they should have received training to adapt professionally to almost any situation. I guess that training hadn't included ghouls enjoying a public shower . . .

"Uhhm . . . What are you doing?" Foss asked when he found me a few minutes later.

"Washing off my ghouls!" I explained, reclining against a pole as I ordered Scramble under the rushing water. Most of the showers had internal cubicles, but there was an outside faucet for cleaning off animals and equipment.

"You can't do that! You're endangering the health of every soldier out here," he argued, his face growing red.

"I thought about that, but I checked, and all the water runs out beneath the wall through that culvert. Ends up in the stream, but it's downstream of where we draw water. I promise to pick up all the fleshy bits that drop off them, it's still way easier than cleaning them by hand," I told him, waving nonchalantly to the sergeant I recognized walking by.

"I'm sure this behavior violates at least a dozen rules," he threatened.

I spat a bit of *mastic* gum into the mud. "Can you name one?"

Foss had no reply to that, and I ordered the ghouls to towel off, leaving a heap of soiled fabric that would likely need to be burned. Someone would probably make me pay for it, but I'd let them track me down first. A few more minutes and my ghouls were dried, dressed, and back in their cage. I was tempted to bring one along with me for added authority, but I had my suspicions that carting a hulking skelly around might come off as more of a crutch, like an insecure man with an opulent weapon. Though I might send an acolyte back depending on how the training went, I could think of a few members of my team that might provide valuable insight for the soldiers.

Back in my usual courier garb, I set off to the training grounds. My coat remained in my sled, though, it was an unseasonably warm day, and I had reason to believe I would spend the morning working up a sweat. Remembering at the last minute, I also retrieved my own poleaxe; the courier variant was built with weight in mind and wasn't nearly as large or sturdy as those a soldier might wield, but it had never failed me before, and the familiar heft of the weapon was reassuring.

I lifted the weapon across my shoulders, stretching my body back and forth as I walked towards the open gate. The soldiers had cleared out an area just outside the walls, which provided them with long sight lines in case of attack, as well as a flat field for activities that would not fit inside the outpost proper. A small wooden pavilion had been constructed to overlook the field, and I wandered up the steps, finding Berg and Calliope observing the proceedings.

"Good morning, Deacon!" the lieutenant colonel boomed, slapping me on the back.

"Is there anything we can get you?" Calliope asked, gesturing to a nearby table of refreshments.

"Ugh, do you have coffee? I usually have quieter mornings than this." I had already enjoyed one cup today, but having access to unlimited caffeine was a privilege I would abuse until it was pried from my hands.

"Just wait until tomorrow. We'll all be up long before the sun," she laughed ruefully, moving over to the table as Berg led me to the railing.

The training area was well constructed and clearly delineated, with different portions cordoned off for varied types of training. This morning there were four contingents working. The first was a line of musketeers at a firing range, taking shots at targets set at various distances. Second was a dirt circle surrounded by men, inside of which two sweating warriors dueled with wooden straight swords. Next were spearmen, the largest group present, taking experimental stabs at cloth dummies dangling from a wooden scaffold. Lastly, there was a square of soldiers stomping around in a phalanx formation.

"Impressive, are they not?" Berg asked, gesturing to his guardsmen.

"They are . . . certainly very disciplined," I told him as Calliope brought a steaming mug over. I used the interruption as a temporary escape, eagerly accepting the warm cup. The strong coffee was pure ambrosia, filling me with heat and energy.

"Lieutenant Colonel Berg, I hope you know I mean no disrespect, but I have my concerns about your soldiers. Not of their discipline or skill, mind you." I held up a hand to forestall his argument. "Rather, I worry that their current training may be ill-suited to ghoul fighting. I understand that it is hard to hear, and I don't expect you to believe me just yet, but I've arranged a small demonstration. I hope you'll allow me to support my concerns before judging my doubts," I explained.

Berg still looked like he wanted to raise a fuss but settled down after a moment of deliberation. "I admit, I do not like hearing any ill word spoken about my men, but we did ask for your guidance after all. I will restrain myself until your demonstration," he agreed.

"Thank you. I'll get it all set up. I hope you'll allow Captain Deimos to accompany me. I'll need your men to cooperate, and they may not agree to it on my orders alone."

Berg released her from her duties, and she followed me down from the pavilion just as Blondie emerged from the outpost gates. He made quite a scene, accompanied by a pair of the bishop's acolytes leading a horse-drawn cart. Instead of cargo, the cart held a brazier two meters across at its widest point, blazing with purple flame. We wouldn't need one of the outpost's massive braziers today, and this was the largest we were able to muster for our demonstration. Behind the cart were a dozen ghouls wandering along in a line like rats behind the pied piper. Each one wore a muzzle and thick mittens, though their undead strength still made the older ones dangerous.

"What do you have planned?" Calliope asked, her tone wavering between doubt and amusement.

"I want to see how these soldiers manage when the targets fight back. Let's head over to that firing range first; I don't have much experience with firearms, so I would like to figure out exactly what they're capable of."

We caused quite a stir as our little parade rolled into the training ground, though the various officers shouted their charges back to work. Before we began, I jogged over to Blondie and pulled him aside.

"Hey, can you help me out on this? I'm not exactly in my element here."

Blondie seemed nonplussed by the request. "Well, yeah, of course. But you have way more practical experience than me, and Berg wanted your help specifically. I know a fair bit about handling a horde, but this up close stuff is all you."

"I know, I just . . . " Gods, how could I explain it? "I'm not great with people, and if I start fumbling over myself, then nobody here is going to listen to what we have to say. I'll start us off, but I'd appreciate you jumping in where you can."

"No problem, I have your back," Blondie confirmed, surveying the gathering with easy confidence. Ugh, give me a horde of ghouls over a crowd of people any day. Well, might as well just dive in.

"Hello!" I yelled, fueled by spite and caffeine. "My name is Archdeacon Winona; this is my associate Deacon Haakon, and you all know Captain Deimos. We will be conducting a quick demonstration for Lieutenant Colonel Berg, and we require your assistance. Who is leading this unit?"

A red-bearded sergeant introduced himself as "Mole," a moniker he had carried for so long that his real name had long been forgotten by everyone else present.

"OK, Sergeant Mole. What's the range of your musket?" Blondie asked, smoothly taking the reins of the demonstration. The acolytes led the cart and ghouls downfield, then moved the horse to safety.

"We have targets out to one hundred meters, but we focus on practicing volley fire at fifty and twenty-five meters. I could shoot the wings of a fly at any range inside that," he boasted.

"That's quite impressive!" Blondie slapped him on the arm good-naturedly. "How fast can you fire?"

"About twice a minute, three times if we're feeling good," he judged.

"Fantastic! Here is the scenario. A ghoul has just wandered out of the woods and caught your scent. Pick your five best soldiers to shoot it down before it can close the distance. The acolytes will set the ghoul on you from the farthest target, but I swear on my commission that we will not give it any orders that might make your job harder. Deal?"

He agreed, and soon we had Mole and four others lined up. We even gave them the advantage and allowed them to have their muskets already loaded and ready.

I looked back at the pavilion and verified that Berg was watching, then signaled to the waiting acolytes.

"Let her run!" I yelled.

The first ghoul set off from the farthest target, shambling towards the distant soldiers. She was no sprinter by any means, but fresh meat was a powerful motivator, and the ghoul would reach them in maybe half a minute. The first volley was orderly and professional, the air filling with a single combined crack of noise and a blast of white smoke as all the weapons discharged simultaneously. The ghoul staggered for a moment, reeling from at least one confirmed hit, though, at this range, I couldn't tell how many shots had landed. She recovered swiftly, though, planting her feet and building up speed again, her shamble turning to a run as the ghoul closed in on her quarry.

"She's still coming!" I cheered out, casually watching the panic that swept through the musketeers.

They immediately set to reloading, but the complex process of reloading a flintlock was made far more difficult with death bearing down on you. Only three managed to get shots off, and all seemed to pass harmlessly through the target without slowing it. I had to give Mole credit, though; the man was no coward. He stepped forward, protecting his men and attempting to bash the ghoul's brains out with the butt of a musket. Poor man misjudged the creature's speed, though, and she promptly tackled him, ineffectually battering at his huddled form with mittened hands. I gave it a moment to let the fear sink in, then exerted control over the ghoul, peeling her away from her quarry.

Mole jumped up, turning to me with murder in his eyes when a bloodcurdling howl drew him up short. The acolytes had released another half dozen ghouls, and one was a screamer. They tore through the wild grass, and the panicked response was even more pitiful. The musketeers barely managed a half volley before Blondie, myself, and the two acolytes had to throw our wills out to restrain the ghoul rush. One enterprising soldier even tried to throw his musket at them in a panic, with negligible effect. I beckoned the shaken soldiers to circle around me while Blondie and our assistants herded the ghouls together.

"Sorry to do that to you all. I know it wasn't pleasant. But I want you to imagine that same scenario, but in the dark of tomorrow morning, with flames roaring and men screaming out." I told them, feeling more comfortable now that we were on the topic of ghoul behavior.

"We hit that first one three times. It just kept coming. I knew they were dead, but I've never seen anything like that . . . ," a younger man stammered, eyes still wide with shock.

"Exactly. The fresh ones might look like people, but they aren't anymore. You probably get told to aim for a person's chest, the center of mass. Won't do anything to a ghoul unless you get lucky and shatter the spine. I'm gonna be honest, we won't have much use for your skills tomorrow; a piercing wound like a musket ball just isn't that effective against these things. If you find yourself needing to take a shot, aim for the head. Hitting it won't finish them off, but it's the biggest hunk of bone on them. Landing a shot should at least knock them off their feet and give you time to run," I explained.

The lesson seemed to set in, and I spent a bit more time chatting with them, learning more about their weapons, and giving them a few tips in return. In all likelihood, they would be folded in with the spearmen if we had enough weapons to outfit them. At Blondie's prompting, I shook hands with each person who had been part of the demonstration before we departed to find our next victims.

"See, that wasn't so bad," Blondie laughed, patting me on the shoulder.

"Yeah, yeah. Just don't expect me to give an inspiring speech." I brushed him off, though it did feel good to talk shop and pass on some training that might save lives.

We headed over towards where the spearmen were drilling, and I couldn't resist waving at Berg as I went; maybe these demonstrations might be enough to make him see sense in the end. Calliope had been quiet and peeled off to talk with the square of soldiers practicing formation maneuvers.

The poor spearmen were subjected to a similar experiment, with ghouls rushing at them from a shorter distance away. During the first charge, the soldier's spear hit flesh, momentarily halting the ghoul. The young woman behind the weapon even let out a cheer of triumph before the ghoul redoubled its attack, pushing against her weapon and sending her stumbling back into the dummy scaffold. With its meal now pinned, the ghoul pushed even harder, struggling on until the spearhead burst through its back. The creature impaled itself, sliding down the entire length of the weapon until it could reach the soldier. The exercises with the other spearmen met with similar failures. Blondie and I had predicted the result and already had a solution for this, and we brought out the prototype that had been cobbled together.

"Any of you ever been on a boar hunt?" Blondie asked the group, garnering a raised hand from a middle-aged corporal who had done some hunting down south.

I tossed him our prototype, and he took his position. Our new weapon was a simple modification of a standard issue spear, a sturdy wooden crosspiece that was attached to the spear just below the blade. When the next ghoul charged, the corporal shouted and drove the butt of his weapon into the dirt, angling the spear forward into the path of the creature. When it made contact, the ghoul impaled itself on the weapon but stopped abruptly as the crosspiece slammed into the ghoul's ribs. Try as it might, the creature could not circumvent the weapon to get at the man behind the spear, a result that was repeated as the other soldiers tried out the new modification. I could not promise them anything, but I hoped to convince Berg to make as many metal crosspieces as we could before tomorrow.

"OK, let's try one more before we stop harassing you all," Blondie chuckled, eliciting a good-natured laugh from the soldiers. They were still a nervous lot, but giving them a solid way to fight back was doing wonders to bolster their confidence.

I pointed to an older soldier with a red nose and pockmarked skin by the name of Arne, then reached out and drew on a familiar rhythm from the corralled group of ghouls.

Grah shambled forward, now muzzled, and took up position across from his target. With a balding head and jowled face, it was hard to identify him as any deadlier than the other ghouls present, which was exactly why I'd sent an acolyte to retrieve him.

"Ready? Go!" I barked, setting Grah loose.

GRRAAHHH!

To his credit, the ghoul's cry didn't rattle Arne, and he smoothly dug the butt of the spear into the dirt, angling the tip to intercept Grah's rush.

Grah slipped on his shield mid-sprint, and the strange behavior caused Arne to hesitate, rising as if to run away, then crouching back down to take charge. Grah wasn't particularly agile, but even he had no trouble batting the stationary spearpoint aside and plowing into the exposed soldier behind. Their momentum sent both tumbling across the ground, and I reasserted control before Grah could attack again.

"You need to watch out for abnormal ghoul behaviors, for echoes," I told Arne, raising my voice to address the entire group. "You had great form. It would have worked on most ghouls, just not this one."

"What should I do then?" the soldier asked, stretching their shoulder where Grah had slammed into him. "How do I know what a ghoul can do?"

"That's a great question, and the answer will never be the same twice," I explained, pulling Grah over to me. "Every ghoul has echoes, skills from their life that manifest in death, to varying degrees. Your first clue is clothing since the ghoul will be wearing whatever the person died in. Look here, he's wearing a gambeson and has a shield, so this ghoul might have been a soldier in his day. That means he may be unpredictable in a fight, acting on the echoes of old training instead of just blindly running in."

Blondie brought over a few more ghouls, pointing out various details of their clothing that might hint at who they had been while living. "Most times, you'll likely miss these tiny details, and that's OK. Just focus on always being open to those hints and always keeping an eye out for those minor differences. Most importantly, be careful about your own expectations of what you will face. Many ghouls will attack you in the same way, over and over and over, with no tactic or variation. But if you get complacent, that one outlier will be the one that gets its teeth into you."

The soldiers sobered at that. Their high spirits had been dulled somewhat, but tempering their confidence with the dangers they would face was far better than letting them feel invincible.

Calliope joined me as we closed in on the swordsmen, preparing to ruin their day next.

"What were you up to?" I asked, looking back as the soldiers she had been speaking to, now huddled in a circle.

"Oh, sorry. Berg wanted me to train a few soldiers in Mycenean tactics. Most of the old members wanted no part in it, so my squad is mostly just the craftsmen we picked up before leaving," she explained.

"You giving them a heads up for what they're in for? We're supposed to be showing how these soldiers aren't ready for the fight your boss is planning," I chided.

"I'm sorry. I don't want you to think I'm trying to interfere. But I don't know what you're planning any more than they do. I just wanted to tell them to pay attention to your other demonstrations. Any tactics they produce are their own, I promise," she explained.

I still wasn't sure how I felt about that, but I also understood that she had more to prove than most of the officers here. Anyway, the swordsmen had noticed our presence and had bunched together like cattle turning their horns out to face the wolves.

"Good morning! Now, you've already seen what happened to the other two groups. Do we need a repeat?" Blondie asked, regarding the soldiers. "I can tell you that your swords won't be as effective as polearms, but I'm not sure you'll believe me without seeing it."

"We were actually hoping for a demonstration. You've felt so comfortable embarrassing all our men, but we've yet to see you fight yourself. How can we trust your advice without knowing if you have skills of your own?" The young soldier had directed the question at me, ignoring Blondie entirely. He had a lean muscular build that certainly looked the part of a swordsman, though I couldn't stop myself from focusing on the pencil mustache that perched on his upper lip.

"Hmm, that's a good point, mister . . ."

"Wallin," he supplied. "Private First Class Wallin. My father is Duke of Strava."

"Well, I'm Archdeacon Winona, and my father is someone who taught me that people who brag about their parents are compensating." I shot back. "I'll make you a deal. Let's grab two ghouls about the same age, then you and I can take our shots at them. I'll even go first."

He agreed, and we selected two male ghouls of middling age. Shortly after that, I took my place across the ring from the creature, poleaxe held in a relaxed grip.

"Oh, one more thing, take off the muzzle and mittens," I ordered Blondie.

"You're sure?" he asked.

"Yup. If I can't handle a ghoul without a muzzle, I don't deserve this job. I can always seize control with balefire if need be. Keep his attention on me, but other than that, just cut him loose," I ordered.

Blondie removed the muzzle, and the ghoul gnashed its teeth, now restrained by his will alone. Damn, that sight sent the adrenaline pumping. I hadn't felt that fear surge since the bandit attack; those rotted teeth could end it all with a single bite.

"Time for a lesson!" I shouted, channeling enough bravado to drown out my own nerves. "Today's topic: echoes. Every ghoul thinks it's still a person, to a degree. But they also have a starving hunger for your flesh. Imagine you've been without food for days, and a giant walking steak wanders by. Nine times out of ten, he'll go for the shortest, simplest attack. The ghoul will rush you, grab your shoulders, and try to sink its teeth into your neck. Now watch closely; this will go quick, one way or the other. Let him loose!"

Blondie nodded, stepping out of the ring. The ghoul launched itself forward a split second later, crossing the distance with stunning alacrity. I shouted defiance and planted the butt of my poleaxe into the ground, aiming the spearpoint towards my target. The ghoul slammed into the point, feet leaving the ground for a moment as its charge was halted. The poleaxe's axe head acted like a crosspiece, preventing the ghoul from getting any closer to me. I rose, still hollering, and pivoted to the side, letting the ghoul run itself in a circle as it tried to get closer. Between the force of my weapon and the awkward circular path, the ghoul soon tripped, stumbling to the ground. I pulled the weapon free and raised it above my head.

"*KAAAHHHH!*" I shouted, bringing the axe head down on the ghoul's lower spine with a deep, resounding crack. The monster began to lever itself up, and I struck again, slamming the axe head down and cracking the bone. As a coup de grace, I thrust the spearpoint down between the ribs, driving through flesh and into the earth below. I placed one foot on the hammerhead and leaned down, pinning the ghoul helplessly to the earth.

"And THAT is how you do it," I growled triumphantly. "Remember, understanding echoes is the key to surviving a ghoul attack. They will generally act like people. Physically, this ghoul could dislocate both its arms, reach back, and pull my weapon out. But it isn't going to do that because a person wouldn't. And if I do this—" I pulled the weapon out, froze the ghoul with a thought, then slammed the axe down again in a series of chops, leading to shouts of alarm and one lost breakfast from the group watching. In a few moments, I had the ghoul messily bisected. I sat down on the ground a meter away from the ghoul's top half, then pressed the butt of my poleaxe into the creature's shoulder, holding it at a distance with one hand.

"This ghoul could stand up on its hands and run at me like a crazed rooster. But it won't do that either. It will continue to try to stand on legs that aren't there, or it will crawl toward me because that's what a human would do. Don't get me wrong, ghouls won't act completely human, especially the older ones, but it's a good rule of thumb."

I stepped away, walking out of the circle and accepting an old rag from Blondie that I used to clean the gore from my poleaxe.

"And there's only one way to kill a ghoul. Watch!" I ordered.

The acolytes gathered the ghoul halves with thick gloves and stepped up onto the cart bearing the balefire flame. They whispered prayers too softly to hear, then tipped the ghoul into the hungry fire. Purple light flared, and the corpse was consumed in a shower of violet sparks. Whatever necromantic energy that powered them was ignited by the purple flames, and the fire reduced both flesh and bone to ash in an instant.

"*That*, that is your goal," I shouted, pointing at the flame. "Every move you make, every attack, needs to be with the goal of either hobbling a ghoul or throwing it into the fire. In my line of work, the goal is usually to escape, but you all won't have that option," I shrugged. "You're up, Wallin. Make it count, watch the teeth."

Wallin, to my surprise, backed down, taking a step back into the crowd while looking a bit green.

"I believe I will pass. Thank you for the demonstration, Archdeacon. We . . . we'll keep your advice in mind."

Oh, the urge to rub it in his face was overwhelming but as fun as it would be, I didn't need to stir up any more animosity.

"I appreciate your attention, good luck tomorrow," I told them as politely as I could, then turned and walked away before they could respond.

XVIII

"Oh gods, that was terrifying," I sighed as we walked toward the last group.

"I know what you mean. You never get used to fighting a ghoul up close, do you?" Blondie commiserated.

"Ghoul? Oh, I meant dealing with all these soldiers, but yeah, that wasn't pleasant either. I think we've managed well so far, though. Maybe I missed my calling as a teacher," I boasted sarcastically to Calliope.

"You just cut a ghoul in half and fed his still struggling remains to a fire . . . ," Calliope argued, looking a bit ill.

"Hmm. Yes, good point. Maybe a biology teacher," I mused.

"Uhm . . . yes. Well, I hope my unit can be the one to impress you. We've worked hard, and I would vouch for every one of them.

We made our way over to the last section, and Calliope gave a piercing call from a whistle around her neck. Her soldiers immediately snapped to attention, forming a rectangle of fighters five wide and three deep, each armed with a long spear twice their height and a wooden shield rimmed with metal. I even noticed Curtis, the leather worker among the ranks, as well as other craftsmen I had seen in passing; knowing that I would be talking to working folk, my people, made this far less stressful than the previous interactions. As I addressed them, Blondie set up nearby, setting the remaining ghouls to dig a pair of holes in the dirt.

"Hello. I am sure you've already heard me shouting my name, so I'll skip introductions. I've been spending my morning embarrassing all your friends. You do not have to like me, but you do have to listen. Captain Deimos speaks very highly of you, so let's see what you've got," I called out.

"More ghoul stabbing?" Calliope asked.

"With a twist. That last demonstration slipped away from me a bit, so I'd like to give you a practical test. This is a simplified version of how some of the northern villages exterminate the small groups of ghouls that they split off from larger hordes." I explained, talking quietly with her before I restarted with my louder tone.

"OK, everyone, I want you to line up your formation right here!" I gestured to an area just in front of the two holes that had been dug by the ghouls.

"Imagine these two holes are balefire braziers set into the ground. Our ghouls are going to take a charge at you, and it is your job to get them into the holes whatever way you can. We will count the ones that fall in as burned up and order them to retreat. Good luck."

Calliope asked for a moment to get her troops ready, then reappeared shortly after, now armored in the Mycenean fashion to match her soldiers. The basic attire was royal guard standard, but there was some foreign flair thrown in as well, with each soldier sporting a metal helmet, sturdy greaves protecting their shins, and a skirt composed of strips of leather. Calliope's helmet bore a crest of dyed horsehair in the shape of a blue mohawk that distinguished her from her subordinates. The captain gave another piercing whistle, and the group lifted their shields and tilted their long spears forward, with each rank tilted slightly higher to create a bladed barricade.

"How do you think they'll do?" I asked Blondie as we retreated behind the cart. He had more practical experience using this method to dispatch wild ghouls.

"I think they'll stop them fine, the first few at least. Even my friends back home could manage that. Where it gets dicey is when you throw half a dozen ghouls in the mix, then they start squeezing through the gaps and biting people. We'll keep the muzzles on for this if you don't mind." A suggestion I heartily agreed to.

"Here comes the first one!" I warned, ordering the first ghoul into the fray.

It crossed the open space at a sprint, diving headlong into the phalanx of spears waiting for it. Three of the weapons swung to meet it, piercing into its rotting flesh. The weapons lacked cross guards, and the ghoul would've pushed right through a single spear. But the three spears spread out the force and increased the chance that some-one would find bone—holding the creature at bay. Now there was a stalemate, though, the ghoul couldn't get at them, but they couldn't do anything else but hold it at bay . . . Or so I thought.

"LEFT!" Calliope shouted, and the three spearmen pivoted their feet, hauling together to wrench their spears in the same direction, dislodging the ghoul and sending it tumbling into one of the holes.

"Not bad!" Blondie laughed, clapping his hands together.

I grinned back at him. It did look like we had found one piece of this army worth their salt. But how much worth they possessed was still to be discovered.

"Let's crank up the difficulty then. Maybe we have a diamond in the rough here," I replied, sending two more ghouls after them, with a third following a second later. I kept my mind leashed to these, giving them subtle directions to influence their attack.

The first two ghouls spread out and slammed into the formation a short distance apart, the spears shifting to intercept. This opened a gap in the center of the spear line that the last ghoul eagerly dove into. No spears were there to meet it, and it slammed headlong into one of the wooden shields, skeletal hands clawing against the rim to get at the man behind. The soldier almost went down to his knees from the weight bearing down on him, but his compatriots came to his aid, supporting him with their own shields. With a shout, he shoved the ghoul back, then deftly speared it as it tried to run back in. There was another moment of struggle, but Calliope's booming directions soon saw all the ghouls tumbling into holes soon after.

"Halt! That's enough!" I ordered, mentally pulling the ghouls back.

The soldiers dispersed from their tight formation, pulling off their helmets to reveal smiling faces still flushed red with exertion.

"Is that the first time you all have fought live ghouls?" I asked.

"Yes, Archdeacon." Calliope gave me a feral grin, looking more vibrant and alive than I'd seen her yet. "We've done drills with dull staffs and armored volunteers to stand in for ghouls, but this is the first time they've fought the real deal."

I pondered that, looking around at the circle of soldiers that had gathered to watch, the other groups were taking an interest in the phalanx's success. We had gone hard on these people to prove our point. Maybe it was time for a bit of positivity. I called Blondie over to where Calliope and I were conversing.

"Hey Blondie, maybe a bit of good guard, bad guard? I laid into them pretty hard; they could use a pick me up," I suggested.

He grinned and nodded, striding over to Calliope's soldiers.

"Now, that was some of the finest ghoul fighting I have ever seen! What are they feeding you all in the capital!?" he hollered to the mirth of all who could hear him.

Blondie looked the part of the dashing courier; with his strong but lean physique and long blond hair blowing in the wind, the soldiers immediately took to him. He moved through the group with confidence, shaking hands and patting shoulders. The effects were palpable, and even the soldiers from other groups began to look more hopeful. Seeing their own comrades finally succeed did wonders to disperse the depressing miasma that had settled over the field. While Blondie worked his magic, I made my way back to the pavilion, where Berg still stood, watching over the proceedings.

"Well, that could have gone better," he grumbled, turning to face me.

"Yeah, it could have . . . ." I paused for a moment, unsure of how to approach this. "I just want to say that you have some good soldiers here. They know their business well; I want to make that clear. I didn't see any poor equipment maintenance or any lax training. But it was obvious that they did not have the necessary experience when it came to dealing with ghouls. I don't have any doubts you can fend off Fin tribesmen, but I worry about how they'll fair against this horde you've built up." I explained, becoming increasingly aware that I had spent the morning embarrassing his troops.

"Do not worry. I believe that your intentions were good, even if your methods were a bit . . . overt. After your demonstration, I have chosen to alter the structure of our exercise. We will push back the horde from the safety of our walls, as you initially suggested," he relented.

"Thank you, sir. I understand it must have been a hard choice. I'll do everything I can to help you prepare," I told him. My small victory at changing his mind made me more than happy to assist however I could.

Berg sighed, then walked over to the table, pouring himself a generous glass of red wine. "Deacon, during your showing, I received some worrying information from the scouts. It seems that the incoming horde has unexpectedly increased in size. From how the reports read, the path of the ghouls crossed with that of two other hordes that went undetected until now."

"Well, that's not great, but we can probably manage a couple more ghouls now that we're using the walls," I laughed.

"Courier, there are six hundred soldiers under my command here, and the original plan called for three hundred to take part in the coming exercise. The undead force bearing down on us now numbers nearly eleven hundred," he explained. "Our original estimates were less than half that."

"Well . . . shit," I stated eloquently. "What are you going to do?"

"What can we do? In the last few days, local fur trappers have informed us that parties of Fin raiders have been reported *behind* us. If we abandon our fortified position and retreat home, we run the risk of being attacked on the road, with Fins at our front and ghouls at our back. I have dispatched our fastest riders south for aid. Even with the raiders, some of our men will make it back to the border, but any reinforcements they might rally will not arrive in time to see us out of this predicament. This outpost is our best hope for survival now. I'll be calling a meeting with my captains shortly to discuss this new development."

"Understood. May I suggest including the deacon and vicar in your planning?" I asked.

"Well, I'm not sure they have anything to contribute to military matters . . . ," Berg waffled.

"Sir, if I may, this situation seems to be rapidly souring. I do not understand your command structure, but I do understand mine. If we get overrun, and the survivors tell tales of how we all refused to cooperate, my boss is going to be in real hot water, and I imagine you'll have some explaining to do as well," I reasoned.

"Are you threatening me, courier?" he asked in an icy tone that made me abundantly aware of how close his guards were standing to me.

This is why I hated dealing with people. All these hidden conversational traps that I didn't realize I was stepping into until it was too late.

"Nonono," I backpedaled, "I just mean that I don't want to see us defeat each other before the ghouls even get the chance, and we will need as much balefire as can be produced."

Berg turned to look out over his soldiers, then took a deep drink from his wineglass.

"Fine. We will be convening at the keep in thirty minutes to discuss new developments. Please pass along my invitation to the bishop," he relented, dismissing me with a wave of a hand. I retreated from the pavilion, leaving Blondie to continue ingratiating himself with the soldiers.

The bishop received the information with surprising stoicism, outwardly reacting as if I'd told him that they would no longer be serving his favorite food at dinner. He called for the vicar, then questioned me further as he pulled a heavy coat over his robes.

"What would you say of our chances?" he asked.

"Maybe fifty-fifty? If we had more time or planned to fight from the wall from the beginning, it would be different. I don't have the military experience to make an accurate guess, though."

"Thank you, Archdeacon. I appreciate your insight and understand your inexperience in large-scale conflicts. But those in my employ regularly find themselves forced to exceed their limitations in pursuit of the cause. Just trust that I put no weight on your shoulders that I do not believe you are capable of carrying. Now, let us have a chat with our dear lieutenant colonel." The bishop smiled, departing the chapel with the vicar and me at his back. "Our own plans remain the same, just so you know, though it may be more difficult to enact now that we plan to fight from within the outpost. Our men will be prepared to clear a path for you regardless. Just be ready."

The meeting at the keep that followed was . . . tense. Berg sat on one long side of the table, with his four captains standing behind him at parade rest. The bishop sat opposite, with the vicar, Blondie, and I at his back. On the table between our two factions was a roughly sketched map of the outpost and its surroundings. Wooden tokens dotted the vellum, representing our own troops and the last reported positions of the ghouls. The rough-cut tokens of the undead far outnumbered our own.

Nobody here had planned for an attack of this magnitude, but the soldiers benefited from the experience of those that came before them and had a military manual written to deal with almost any situation, real or imagined. The tome looked a bit moth-eaten and worse for wear, but the relevant pages of the manual were intact, outlining a defensive structure to be used when a horde of overwhelming size was attacking. The keystone of the design was a long, high-walled pit leading in from the gates and terminating in a balefire brazier set into the ground. If all went as planned, ghouls could be funneled through the gate and into the flames while other soldiers held off the creatures trying to scale the walls. In a perfect situation, the design could funnel an infinite number of ghouls to their demise. We did not have a perfect situation, though; we had unprepared soldiers, short walls, and not nearly enough time.

But the ghouls were coming whether we did something about it or not. It was almost calming in a way, overwhelming danger like this quashed most of the dissent that would usually crop up. The church needed soldiers, the military needed balefire, and we could all kill each other later if we survived this.

There was one point of contention, though.

"The manual does have one optional feature," Berg stated, tapping his finger on the final page of the instructions. "As it stands, the horde will just slam blindly into our walls. A small portion will stumble through the gate, but it will be a trickle instead of a flood. If we do not funnel them in fast enough, the rest will pile up against the walls until they overwhelm our defenses."

"And what does your manual say about alleviating that issue?" the bishop asked.

"It suggests a scout lead the horde through the gates, using themselves as bait," Berg told us, reading the section again.

"Well, shit. I've done that a few times back home. Get me a fast horse, and I'll lead those ghouls on a merry dance all the way back," Blondie volunteered, nervous at the prospect but clearly confident in his abilities.

"I'm surprised your star courier hasn't stepped up to volunteer," Captain Foss scowled at me.

"Very subtle, Fossy," I shot back. "But I don't like horses. They're dangerous at both ends and unpredictable in the middle. Plus, I'd make sure to get some hazard pay. If you've got two hundred suns to spare, I'll take a crack at it."

"I think Courier Haakon will do the job admirably, though I'm sure we will all have our parts to play before this is over. I believe our best course of action is to lower one of our grand braziers into the ground for your trap. The other should cover the entirety of the outpost on its own, and I will get to work on creating balefire immediately to supplement, though we are limited by the number of braziers that we brought with us. Now, unless there is anything else to discuss, we all have work to do." The bishop rose to the table, nodding to the lieutenant colonel.

Berg didn't seem happy about the dismissal, but he couldn't deny facts; The oncoming storm was mere hours away, and if we did not properly brace for the impact, we'd soon find ourselves joining the legions of the dead.

The outpost soon resembled a kicked-over anthill, with workers running supplies and crawling over buildings. Whole structures were torn apart for resources; the half-finished workshops were especially vulnerable and were soon cannibalized for other projects. The epicenter of the chaos was at the gate, where dozens of soldiers and ghouls dug into the frozen earth at a near-frantic pace. Slowly, a trench began to form, starting at the gate and heading straight toward the heart of the outpost.

Even I found places to pitch in, though collaborating with the soldiers while so much animosity brewed among our superiors still felt odd. But there weren't enough soldiers with experience running a ghoul team, and it showed. After seeing the third man almost get eaten by his own ghouls, I decided to step in. The soldiers were happy enough to give me a dozen skellies from the paddock and set me to carting back lumber from a nearby copse of trees that had managed to avoid the axe up until now. These thin trunks were sectioned out and tied together into impromptu hedgehogs, the same defensive structures I'd seen at Zeb's ranch. Placed in front of the walls, they would hopefully blunt the ghoul's momentum and keep their slamming charge from damaging the defenses. As I walked beside my work team, I watched an impressive scaffold slowly sprout up alongside one of the grand braziers. According to Bishop Rimkus, the grand brazier would take far too many resources to relight if extinguished, so the military engineers had the unenviable job of lowering the metal cage to the ground while it was still aflame.

After delivering another load of freshly felled trees, I was assigned a different job, then another after that, and another, and soon developed a pounding migraine from the continuous mental strain, building like the worst kind of hangover. The balefire bond always took a toll, and I imagined it like what an orchestra conductor might feel. If you had a small, well-trained group like my sled team, the exertion was minor; everyone already knew their part and only required the slightest correction. But try doing the same with a band of musicians who had never played together before, had never even read the music? Well, that required constant, exhausting levels of attention. I held on as long as I could, though, even pitching in to help lower the brazier into its new resting place in the ground. When an acolyte came to relieve me, I almost dropped to my knees in relief. The sky was already starting to change color with the coming sunset, and all I wanted to do was find a nice dark place away from the balefire light so I could get some sleep, though I lingered for a few last moments to survey the progress we had made.

It wasn't pretty, but it didn't have to be. The long trench we had dug had been reinforced with wood planks along the sides, creating a corridor that would hopefully funnel the horde from the gate all the way to their demise in the balefire. I wanted to confer with Blondie, I wanted to get a drink with Calliope and relax for one gods-be-damned second. Instead, I checked over my sled and team, wolfed down a quick dinner, then showered off. We had prepared as much as we could in the short window given to us, and I tried to keep my worries at bay as I curled up in my little cot. If I were going to face death tomorrow, I'd at least face it well-rested.

XIX

If there was one constant in this crazy world, it was that waking before the sun was always a miserable experience. Your chest ached, and the cold shivers through your limbs made you long for your warm bed. The only thing worse than waking up before dawn was being *woken up* before dawn, a fact I recalled as a soft knock rapped against my door, stirring me from my light slumber. I cracked open the door a sliver, trying to keep the warmth of my room from leaking out into the night.

"Wakey, Wakey," Blondie whispered. "Time to get up and smell the . . . rotting ghouls."

"How could I resist? Give me a minute," I told him groggily.

"The soldiers are cooking an early breakfast. I'll meet you over there," Blondie told me, then retreated.

I pulled on my layers slowly, but the allure of warm food and hot coffee was enough to draw me out into the cold. The line at the mess hall was nearly silent at this predawn hour, with the half-asleep soldiers accepting their portions from a line of steaming pots. I accepted my own plate and found a spot on a bench nearby, next to Blondie and across from Dupont.

"What's the news?" I asked the vicar, shoveling food into my mouth.

"Scouts are starting to trickle back in now. The first ghouls will be coming through in an hour or so, with the full horde somewhere behind them. Then it will be up to our dear Haakon to come through," he told me.

"You nervous, buddy?" I asked, nudging him with my elbow.

"Me? Naahhh. This isn't my first rodeo, though I've never tried it at night before. I walked the path back yesterday with a squad of soldiers, though, and cleared my route of debris and such. Should be a smooth gallop back once I get their attention," Blondie bragged though the tremor of fear in his voice was obvious.

"Hey, just think of the tall tales this will spark: 'The Tale of Blondie: The Man Who Faced the Horde.' You'll never have to pay for a drink in a military bar again," I laughed, though the stress robbed it of any real mirth.

"Yeah, yeah. Well, I should get ready. They let me borrow a spirited little gelding from the stables. I want to take one last look at him before I head out," Blondie told us, standing up.

"Good luck, brother," I told him.

"May the light of the Balefire be with you, my child," the vicar intoned, nodding his head.

I had my own preparations to make and departed soon after, making my way back to my sled, where most of my team would sit harnessed and ready to depart at a moment's notice. The exceptions were Champ and Scramble, who would be accompanying me as my bodyguards throughout the battle, as both had valuable skills in that regard. To complement those skills, I dug into the wooden trunk again. For Champ, there was a pair of leather gauntlets, padded to protect the small bones in his hands. He had no skill with weapons, but the gauntlets would complement his direct brawler style. For Scramble, there were padded additions to his harness, turning his shoulders into handles and hipbones into footrests. The freakish strength of the older ghouls meant that skelly powered piggyback was a fast way to traverse the battlefield, even if it was an uncomfortable and risky ride.

My own equipment was sparse since carrying around a full set of armor wasn't practical for a courier on the move. Instead, I rolled up one sleeve and buckled a boiled leather vambrace around my offhand forearm to serve as a shield against ghoul bites. To protect my neck and shoulders, I had a thick leather gorget that fit under my coat. I always packed two sturdy coats for the trip and wore the lighter one now. It didn't ward off the cold entirely, but I knew that the events of this morning would have me warmed up soon enough, and sweating in these temperatures could be just as dangerous as the ghouls. I likely could have scavenged more armor from the soldiers, but I intended to avoid fighting as much as possible and didn't want unfamiliar armor slowing me down, regardless. I buckled on the coalblade as well and took a few extra moments to fiddle with the straps, making sure the sheath wouldn't hinder my movements or be visible once my coat was on. Drawing the weapon in an outpost full of church officials was the height of stupidity, but I still wasn't willing to leave the weapon behind when there was a battle about to commence.

Once fully kitted out, I spent a moment standing with King, trying to impart our escape plan into his mind, the route to the gate and the path we would take once clear of the outpost. Who knew how much would stick in his mind when the time came, but every little bit helped. With every preparation I could think of completed, I lifted my poleaxe and made my way to the wall, ghoulish bodyguards in tow.

I had accrued an abundance of skills in the wilds, but the battlefield was as alien to me as the surface of the moon. The silence was ... palpable, a hush that fell over the outpost like a heavy blanket. A long line of soldiers stood along the outer wall, ready to fend off any ghouls who tried to climb up. Small braziers were set at intervals in the ground in front of the wall, giving the guards a place to toss attacking ghouls into. More fighters stood in small groups near the wall at intervals, ready to reposition and shore up the defenses where necessary. The trench had been completed in the night, with the grand brazier lying ready to consume the rush of the horde. On the far side of the brazier were Calliope's special troops, given an unenviable but crucial task. Their long spears could reach across the flames to strike at the horde, while their living flesh would serve as a tempting meal to keep the ghouls moving forward once Blondie had drawn them in. I found Calliope there, armored and giving her troops last-minute instructions.

"How we looking?" I asked as she finished with her team.

"As good as it's going to get. A few ghouls have wandered out of the woods downhill, but the scouts haven't had any issues leading them into the outer fires. Reports coming in say that we will be seeing the real push in a half hour or so. Your courier is getting ready to depart, I was planning to observe from the top of the gate if you would like to join me."

I agreed though Calliope's demeanor towards me seemed to have cooled. I was a bit worried that I'd alienated her with my display yesterday, but in the end, I just chalked it up to the situation. This was Captain Deimos, not Calliope, and she had a job to do. The gatehouse had a set of stairs that led to the top of the outer wall, and I was thankful to be climbing that instead of the rickety ladders spaced around the other parts of the fortification. From the top, the view of the field was clear, with various nonmagical bonfires being lit to provide light across the snowy landscape. We watched as Blondie departed on his horse, heading out into the cold at a swift canter. He held a burning torch off to his side, and we watched as the orange dot disappeared into the woods.

Berg stood nearby, the lieutenant colonel resplendent with his steel armor glittering in the torchlight. A long-feathered plume stuck up from his helmet, which would make him easy to spot in the heat of battle. As we waited, a soft susurration began to push away the silence, like the whisper of the ocean lapping against a beach.

"What is that?" Calliope hissed at me.

"It's the horde. Some ghouls make noise when they get riled up . . . Like when they spot prey. Get enough of them together, and it sounds like this."

But then the noise pulsed louder . . . and louder, rolling in now like whitecaps pounding the shore. Scouts began emerging from the woods, galloping back towards the open gates. The soldiers had placed temporary wooden ramps near the grand brazier so the horses could be led out of the kill box, though these ramps would be removed once Blondie was clear.

Ghouls were starting to emerge now, though slow-moving and sparse in number. A flicker of torchlight appeared among the trees again, growing brighter in time with the growing roar. Finally, Blondie burst into view, leaning down low over the saddle of his galloping horse. Once free of the trees, he skidded to a halt, turning his horse back to shout abuse to the ghouls at his heels; the creatures had been stirred into a hunger craze and would hopefully stampede directly into our waiting trap. Blondie took off again, widening the gap as he led the horde back to the outpost.

Then his horse stumbled, so suddenly I thought it was a trick of the light from Blondie's torch sputtering in the wind. A moment later, the animal pitched forward with a scream of pain, throwing Blondie from the saddle in an explosion of snow. His torch was immediately snuffed, casting man and horse into darkness. All we could see was the prone shape of Blondie's gelding, its struggles fading, and the oncoming horde closing in on a suddenly stationary meal.

"Fuck . . . fuckfuckfuck." I swore, thudding down the stairs with Calliope at my heels.

"What are you doing?" she shouted as I jumped the last steps and landed heavily in the snow.

"Getting Blondie back," I growled, running over to a group of soldiers and yanking a balefire torch from a nearby scout still sitting on his horse. This design was long and thin, like a wine flute, designed to keep its single coal from falling out from the rigors of a galloping horse. I'd put that to the test.

"You can't go out there. You'll never make it in time!" she argued, trying to step in front of me.

I shouldered her out of the way, nervous energy giving me the strength to push aside the taller woman. Going out there was lunacy, even by my standards, but I would *not* let the ghouls take Blondie if I had the strength to stop it. The couriers of the Balefire Express were family in every way that mattered, and we looked after our own.

"You're a soldier, I'm a courier. You're gonna be doing your job soon enough." I told her, running over to Champ and Scramble even as I ordered them over to the open gate.

"So, save your energy and watch me work."

I jumped up onto Scramble, crouching on his back so that my feet found purchase against the footrests on his hip bones. Then I held the torch aloft and ordered my ghouls into a dead sprint. It had been a while since I had ridden with Scramble, and his freakish acceleration nearly sent me tumbling backward into the mud. I didn't have a pedigree for him, but I'd pay good money to know who he had been in his past life to be able to move the way he did. Ghoul riding was an experience that was hard to put into words; I was crouched on the back of a man barely a hand's width taller than me but with bones that contained the strength of a thoroughbred racehorse. He thundered forward, torso bent forward to keep my weight centered. Champ loped behind us, his light body allowing him to cover the distance in long, gliding strides. The roar of the horde grew stronger, as did the sickly-sweet scent of rot that accompanied them. It was going to be a close thing; they had the head start, but I had the speed.

I closed in on where I hoped to find Blondie, though I had lost sight of his position after descending from the wall. My ears picked up the slack where my eyes failed, alerting me to the scream of a horse in pain coming from the darkness slightly to my left. I adjusted Scramble's course towards the noise, and the sight we came upon would stick with me in the long nights to come. Blondie's horse was lying on its side, weakly kicking as three ghouls dug their teeth into its belly, pulling out loops of intestine in their frenzy. Blondie himself was trapped with his leg pinned between the horse and the ground. A fourth ghoul had taken an interest in the courier, and he was desperately fending it off with his extinguished torch.

"Champ. Deal with it," I ordered.

Champ lengthened his stride, sailing through the air in a long jump and landing next to Blondie's attacker. He punched forward, driving his armored fist through the belly of the rotting ghoul and grasping its spine. With a twist, he pulverized the vertebrae, leaving the ghoul to helplessly fold in on itself.

Slipping off Scramble's back, I ran over to Blondie, who was still swinging wildly at the shapes of the darkness.

"Blondie! Haakon! It's me. Calm down!" I shouted, planting my torch in the ground. Dammit, his leg looked badly twisted under the horse, though there was no way to tell how serious the injury was. The horse had succumbed to the onslaught, and its dead weight stood as a sizable obstacle.

"Move that horse, you two!" I shouted, simultaneously commanding my ghouls and throwing my will at the monsters shambling into the purple light. As my bodyguards moved to follow my orders, I lashed my mind out at the incoming creatures, turning their aggression against each other and buying us precious extra seconds. Black spots danced in front of my eyes for a moment as more ghouls poured in, adding more weight to the mental assault.

Then my ghouls set to work, rolling the horse's carcass up and off Blondie's leg. The man cried in pain as the weight was removed, and I turned back to look at him, the reaction automatic. In that instant, my concentration slipped, and the wild creatures renewed their assault, running around or jumping over the dead horse.

"RUN!" I barked, yanking my torch from the ground. Champ bounded by, scooping up Blondie's protesting form as he went. Scramble ran to me a moment later, slowing just enough for me to leap onto his back again. The horde had emerged in force now, and the ghouls at our back were packed so densely that if the leaders stumbled, they were immediately trampled by their compatriots behind them. Every time they closed the distance, I threw my will back to slow them, but it was like a sandcastle resisting the tide. There was always a new pursuer to replace the one I had pushed back, and they were closing the gap.

At least we were still performing Blondie's original task. The horde had strung out behind us, the center of the line bulging forward, outpacing the ghouls on the flanks. This fact was of little comfort to the pair of idiot couriers about to be eaten.

"They're getting closer!" Blondie shouted. Champ had thrown him over his shoulder so he was getting a clear view of the creatures gaining on us. He cast his own will at the pursuers, but the injury had sapped his strength, and they barely slowed.

In seconds we had reached the gatehouse, flying through it at a ludicrous speed. The men above us cast a net of hempen rope onto the leading edge of the horde, but it only bought us a second as the ghouls behind trampled their tangled compatriots.

"Get Blondie out of here!" I yelled as we raced down the trench, the grand brazier looming ahead. Champ looked at me, looked at Blondie, then grabbed him under the armpits.

"No, no, what are you—AAAHH!" Champ flung him bodily out of the trench, his scream of surprise fading as he crested the wall in a high arc.

"Not like that! Uuughhh! Get out!" I shouted, ordering Champ to get clear. He gave me a mournful look that, even with a skull of bare bone, managed to convey *I just did what you told me to*. Then he crouched down and launched into an explosive leap, clearing the trench in a single bound.

"Just you and me now, buddy; show me what you've got. Go! Go! Go!" I cheered, urging Scramble on.

I had never suspected that Scramble had another gear hidden away, but he found it in that moment, leaning forward and putting on a final burst of acceleration. The guards had removed all the ramps but one and were poised to haul it up as soon as we crossed. My mind pulsed with fatigue, and I felt a skeletal claw scrabbling for purchase on my coat. But then the crunch of boots on earth became the thud of wood, and we rocketed up the ramp to safety. Our combined momentum was so great that Scramble's feet left the ground as we reached the top of the ramp, flinging us both in a long parabolic arc through the air. My white-knuckle grip failed at last, and I tumbled free, seeing a dizzying swirl of sky, ground, then sky again before I closed my eyes and tucked into a ball. When the impact came, the breath was punched out of my chest, leaving me collapsed in a pile on the dirt, gasping for air. Hands closed in on me, and I lashed out, catching something heavy with my foot. They would not take me. Those creatures would not take—

"Winona, calm down, you're safe!" Vicar Dupont's voice cut through my mental haze like a foghorn, louder than I'd ever heard from the soft-spoken man. The grasping hands disappeared, and I eased myself up into a sitting position, cradling my aching head.

The vicar squatted down next to me, then held something under my nose, a tiny package wrapped in a twist of paper. My next breath blasted my senses with a kick of ammonia, causing a deep reflexive inhale that brought me back to reality.

"Gah! What's in that!?" I asked, coughing and stumbling unsteadily to my feet.

"A little church secret," The vicar grinned, pocketing the paper. "Are you OK? Have you been bit?" He asked.

"I think I'm good," I told him, patting myself all over in a quick inspection. Adrenaline could mask the pain of small wounds, and it only took one bite to be fatal. The wind had been knocked out of me, and I would need a few minutes to recover, but it seemed that everything was in order, at least for me.

"Blondie, my ghouls, they make it?" I asked.

The vicar shuffled out of the way, and I could see my duo safe and sound. Scramble was hanging from a nearby scaffold, content to watch the scene unfold. Meanwhile, Champ was holding Blondie high above his head, refusing to relinquish his charge to the medics crowding around him, much to the chagrin of everybody involved.

"Put him down, Champ!" I ordered, hobbling over to him while the vicar hovered near me protectively. He laid the man down and retreated so the medics could do their work, and I caught up to Blondie as they loaded him onto a stretcher.

"Hey . . . It's my savior!" Blondie managed a weak smile and stretched out a hand to squeeze my arm.

"Just don't make a habit of it," I teased him back. "You gonna be OK?"

"I don't think my leg's broken, but everything's . . . fuzzy. Get me a splint, and I'll be good as new. I'll hobble back into the fight as soon as I can!" he mumbled, already trailing towards unconsciousness.

I laughed, letting the medics start to pull him away, but his arm lashed out, and he pulled me back in with surprising strength.

"Winona. My horse didn't trip; he was *shot*. I saw it after we fell. Two bolts sticking out of his chest, maybe more. But we were facing the wall when we went down. We were *facing the wall*." A medic stepped in to pull Blondie's hand away, and they hustled him off to a tent already set up to receive the wounded.

"Everything in order?" The vicar asked as I turned away from watching Blondie go. I noticed now that Dupont himself was clad for battle, wearing the standard leather armor along with a hatchet threaded through his belt.

Ooooh, that was a tough question to answer. I had struggled with figuring out who I could trust since I arrived at the outpost. But lying to the vicar meant lying to the bishop, which seemed like a heavy risk to take with little chance of success.

"Blondie said his horse didn't trip; it was shot with crossbow bolts, at least two. He said it was shot in the chest as he ran back to the gate." I explained, wondering if he would come to the same conclusion I had. He did not disappoint.

"If the horse was shot in the chest as they returned . . . that means the shooters were on the wall, here in the outpost," he stated, leading me a short distance away from the nearby soldiers.

"So, Archdeacon, let's see if the bishop is right about you. Talk me through why you think this happened," he instructed.

"Uhm . . . Isn't there a battle taking place that we should get back to?" I asked, fidgeting with anxiety as the sound of fighting clamored behind us.

The vicar dismissed my concern with a wave. "You've already done your part. Now they must do theirs, so back to the topic at hand. Who shot courier Haakon's horse?"

"Two soldiers, must have been, or one with two crossbows, I guess." I told him.

"More likely two attackers firing at once. After the horse was shot once, judging the second shot would be far more difficult, even assuming you could switch weapons that fast. But now, the million-sun question. Why?" he asked.

"You want to do this now?" I asked again.

"Absolutely."

"OK. Well, they were trying to take out Blondie." I thought out slowly. "Maybe someone wanted him dead? I thought he got along with everyone, but I guess he could've made an enemy."

"Possibly, but why take a risky crossbow shot at a galloping horse when you could just knife him on his way back from dinner? Try again," the vicar chided.

"Can we at least get a bit closer to the action? I'm getting antsy standing here," I snapped, tired of this interview and wanting to get back in the action. I didn't have the size or skill to be a front-line fighter, but hearing a massive battle occurring just out of sight was sending my anxiety through the roof. I did make an effort to keep my tone restrained, though the vicar seemed far too familiar with the various methods of assassination.

The vicar nodded, and we began walking back to the front line, though his stare made it clear he still wanted an answer. Maybe it was his attention, maybe it was my eagerness to get back to the fight, but inspiration finally came to me.

"OK, if it's not about Blondie, then it must have been about what he was doing. So, he's leading the ghouls into the trap, gets shot, and turned into ghoul chow. So, the trap doesn't work, and maybe we don't burn up enough ghouls before they flood over the wall . . . Did the people who shot him want this fight to go wrong?" I asked him.

"I have no idea, Courier Winona. Maybe it was that, or maybe the assassin truly did have a personal vendetta. At this point, we do not have enough information to know. But what I am trying to say is that you need to be looking at all the angles. Not every problem in this world can be solved by having one of your ghouls hit it. But for now, stay sharp and help where you can. As soon as this battle turns in our favor, we're getting you back on the road."

"What if it doesn't turn in our favor?"

Vicar Dupont pondered this for a moment. "Well, then, I guess we all die, and you won't need to worry about it," he answered, then strode off towards the sounds of battle.

"Wonderful. C'mon boys, let's see what we can do," I called to my ghouls, jogging after him.

XX

———

M ost soldiers I'd had drinks with said the thing that surprised them most about battle was the smell. You know, blood, gore, shit, whatever. But I spent my days working with dead bodies, so my nose would take far more than that to turn against me.

For me, the thing I didn't expect was the noise. Weapons cracked into bone, skeletal hands screeched against armor, soldiers screamed, and wept, and died. And, above it all, was that horrible horde wail. Ghouls were packed in the trench like cattle to the slaughter, funneling inward towards the flames. Calliope's troops stood at the far side of the brazier, luring the ghouls to their demise and deftly spearing the intrepid few who tried to leap over the fire to reach their meal. There were also soldiers stationed on either side of the brazier, using hooks and long poles to pull the unburnt clothing from the flames before it could pile up. That must have been backbreaking work, but it was a vital job; if the grand brazier was smothered, the ghouls would have a straight shot into the heart of our camp. Even as I watched, one soldier almost fell in as he lifted his pole over to scoop the detritus out. A comrade caught him by the belt and hauled him to safety, but it highlighted how tenuous our plan was.

Even without any military experience, I couldn't help but be impressed by the level of discipline on display. The presence of the Grand Brazier meant that every person here was feeling a direct connection to the ghouls tumbling into the flames. I had the training and knowledge to tune out the worst of it, but the influx of sensation could be debilitating to an inexperienced mind.

But the tight phalanx held firm, presenting an impenetrable wall of spear and shield to the horde, stabbing and shoving against the oncoming tide with mechanical perfection. The front line was visibly tiring, though, those soldiers having withstood the worst of the punishment so far. As one, that front line turned to the side and pivoted away, allowing the second rank to step forward and take their place. The other ranks cycled forward as well until the front rank emerged at the back, where they could step away to rest before rejoining the formation. One of the resting soldiers had their helmet off, the blue crest instantly identifiable.

"Calliope! How you holding up?" I asked, kneeling down beside her.

"Hey!" She smiled grimly, then took another long drink from her canteen. "We're doing as well as we can. My soldiers are green, but they're tough. That was quite the stunt you pulled, by the way. Good work."

"Thank you . . . And sorry about brushing you off earlier. Time was of the essence and all that," I apologized.

"Nonono, don't sweat it. I should be apologizing. I never even thought a rescue like that was possible. I'll try to back you up more when you make a move like that in the future."

"It's water under the bridge. I appreciate you looking out," I told her. "And anyway, I very nearly ended up getting myself eaten, so your worries were well founded. I was out of it for a bit after we made it back. How's the outpost holding?"

"Not sure. I've been here with my squad since the start. Foss or Petersen would know more." Her smile faded. "We're holding on this front, one fatality and a pair of injuries that took soldiers out of the fight, but we're adapting. I need to cycle back into formation, though. If you're looking to pitch in, I think Petersen is up by the gate. Good luck, courier."

"You too, captain, stay safe," I told her, then departed off towards the gate, following the trench outward. Soldiers were posted every few meters to keep anyone from straying too close and tempting any ghouls to leap out of the trench and wreak havoc. At the base of the wall, an impromptu command post had sprouted up, various tables laid out showing maps and other charts I couldn't make sense of. A near-constant stream of messengers would run in, give a quick report, then bolt off again as officers updated the charts with the latest information. Here I found Petersen and Berg in deep conversation, with a large map of the outpost laid out in front of them. I also found my poleaxe leaning against the stairs nearby. I had dropped it in my rush to grab a balefire torch earlier and was grateful to have the familiar weapon back in my hands.

"Excuse me, lieutenant colonel, Archdeacon Winona reporting in. How can I be of assistance?" I asked, standing at attention the way I had seen the soldiers do.

"Winona!" Berg laughed, clapping me on the shoulder. "Oh, at ease, at ease, look at you, my little soldier. We're certainly breaking our men in now!"

Berg looked . . . Ecstatic. He reminded me of a boy who always sat on the bench, finally getting his chance to play.

"Uhm, yes, that's one word for it. What can I do to help?" I asked again.

"Hmm. It's going as well as we could hope, to be sure," he mused. "We did lose a juggernaut over the wall. Sent it down to clear out the ghouls stacking up. We can keep the horde thin near the entrance where they funnel in, but they are piling up quite high on the outskirts. Our juggernauts have been clearing them out, but one of the handlers suffered an accident of some sort, and the juggernaut was swarmed soon after."

"What kind of accident? If you don't mind my asking," I questioned. Such things were likely common in the heat of battle, but the attack on Blondie made me wary of anything that felt even remotely off.

"Ah, I believe he slipped off the wall, too many soldiers squeezing by. Broke his leg, poor man, though it's still a better fate than if he'd slipped the other way!" Berg chortled, blasé about the sea of death beyond his walls.

"He lost focus when he was injured," Petersen cut in. "Now we have one of our finest war ghouls lost in the press beyond the wall. Is there anything you can do to help?"

I thought about that for a moment, unwilling to commit aid to a problem I couldn't solve. The juggernauts were incredible and represented the sole example I was aware of where a person had been trained for the express purpose of passing their skills onto their ghoulish form. Before they were juggernauts, they were royal guards who trained relentlessly to hone their skills. The military still swore up and down that they upheld the golden rule of never adding another ghoul to the world, but clearly, the juggernauts were a planned experiment in ghoul crafting.

"This is a long shot, but did anyone know the ghoul when he was still living?"

"Living?" Petersen asked. "Why would that matter?"

"Quiet captain. That girl has done more to ensure our victory today than any of us. The juggernaut unit is a tight-knit group; if there is a spare handler, they might be of more help. I can have one sent over to that portion of the wall as soon as they are available."

That was a lucky break, to be sure. Picking the juggernaut out of the pile would be like finding one specific grain of sand on the beach, but my own experience with a horde had given me an idea. If I could learn a bit about who the ghoul had been and how they had behaved, maybe I could use that to home in and pinpoint them. It was the same method I'd used to locate my own ghouls before, but this would be a less familiar mind and a far larger horde.

"Thank you, sir. I'll do what I can." I bowed, then departed.

The walkway above was too crowded with soldiers to travel along, so I had to jog down the path below while listening to the sounds of battle echoing from above. Curiosity soon overcame me, and I stopped at an observation tower along the way. One of the single-story buildings had been outfitted with a small watchtower on top, giving a commanding view of the surroundings. The ladder leading up to the top was busy with messengers coming or going, so I had Champ boost me up to the nearest support and scaled it that way. I did end up giving the scout at the top quite a scare, though, as I crawled up right into the view of her telescope.

"How's it going, boss?" I asked, hooking a leg over the wall and pulling myself over onto the platform.

The scout gave a high-pitched squeak and nearly brained me with the telescope before coming to her senses.

"Ohhh, sorry about that, must have given you quite a scare. Don't worry, the bad guys are still on the right side of the wall." I explained.

From the raised vantage, I could look down and see the scope of the entire conflict; the good and the bad. As for the good, it seemed like our plan was working, with the grand balefire consuming a staggering number of ghouls as they stampeded down the trench. Even if they had wanted to stop, the weight of their brethren pressing in would have shoved them onward, and none of the bloodthirsty fuckers seemed inclined to slow down. On the bad side, the horde was absolutely, pants-shittingly massive. I'd never seen a group of ghouls that large outside a ranch, and it made our brilliant trap look like we were using a pinhole to drain a bathtub. The rushing ghouls and flickering light made an accurate estimate impossible, but I would wager that nearly fourteen hundred ghouls were hungering for our flesh. It was also clear to see the problem that Berg had highlighted. Our balefire was consuming the ghouls at the center of the horde at a prodigious rate, but those farther from the gate were reaching the walls unscathed. Here they piled on top of each other, unintentionally forming a ramp of flesh; if those ramps were allowed to grow higher, the ghouls would be able to climb up and over the walls, nullifying our best line of defense. At least morning was close, and the sky to the east had begun to lighten at last. Now that I had a lay of the land, I bid the scout farewell and climbed back down the way I came. My guardian Champ stood below, and he caught me deftly under the arms as I leapt the last two meters to the ground.

"It's getting bad out there, guys," I explained to dead ears. "Let's hustle."

We rushed along, arriving at our destination where the wall abutted against the towering cliff face. A harried-looking junior officer was issuing orders at the base of one of the ladders. I ordered my ghouls to a safe distance, unwilling to trust them with so many wounded nearby.

"Hey, I'm here about the lost juggernaut. What's the situation?" I asked, trying to sound professional.

"Good to have you. Yes, we lost the juggernaut over the—"

"AHHHH!" A soldier fell from the top of the wall, screaming until she thudded to the ground between us.

"MEDIC!" the officer shouted, leaning down to check on the woman.

"They're climbing over the wall!" the soldier gasped, alive but thoroughly winded.

"Dammit." the officer breathed as another soldier came crashing down. This one had leapt instead of falling and managed to break his fall with a roll.

"To the wall!" the officer shouted. "Push them back!"

Then he was shouting, and his men were shouting, and I was shouting, and next thing I knew, I was halfway up the ladder, hollering a battle cry with the rest of them. The ladders were set at an angle so that you could almost walk up them, which I was grateful for as I climbed upward with my unwieldy poleaxe balanced in one hand. Another screaming form fell past as I crested the fortification, stepping onto a packed walkway no more than a meter and a half wide. The surface was already slippery with blood and coagulated ghoul bits, likely attributing to the multiple falls that had already occurred. A few meters away, four guards struggled at an impromptu shield wall, pushing back against a ghoul clambering over the edge. Every balefire brazier that could be spared had been placed at the base of the wall, consuming any ghoul that stumbled into them. But there wasn't nearly enough to fully protect us, and ghouls were piling up in the spaces between. Even worse, I could already see gaps in the balefire perimeter, places where the braziers had been toppled or smothered. The top of the wall was at least three meters off the ground, not including the extra depth the trench added; it must have taken dozens of ghouls stacked below to form the ramp this ghoul was standing on.

"Keep your heads down!" I shouted, running up behind them and holding my weapon high above me.

The poleaxe thrust forward, stabbing into the creature's shoulder as I tried to send it tumbling back down the pile. The ghoul had a firm grip on the outer rim of the wall, though, and more ghouls were climbing up behind, further anchoring it. My feet began to slip on the filth, forcing me back centimeter by centimeter.

"I'm losing it, help!" I called out to anyone listening. I slid back further, then felt a jarring impact as an armored form slammed into my back, halting my slide.

"Push, you bastards! I'll not have some courier waif out-soldiering us!" I recognized the gruff voice of Sergeant Greaves.

Another pair of arms wrapped around my waist, anchoring me further. Hands rose from both sides to grab onto my weapon, and together we heaved the ghoul back, starting a domino effect that toppled the entire pile off the side of the wall. Many of the ghouls fell into a nearby brazier set into the trench, and a ragged cheer rose from the ranks, though the reprieve was short-lived. We barely had time to catch our breath before another wave of ghouls crashed into the wall, threatening to spill over. Then we were rushing, slipping, fighting, the minutes blurring together in a swirl of light and sound. Certain moments stood out in vivid detail, though, like the way the world lights up when lightning strikes at night.

A young fawn, still wearing the dress she'd died in, biting into the leg of a soldier as he ineffectually slashed at it with his sword.

Stab, Slip, Fight

Stabbing my poleaxe into the ribs of a ghoul, its hands vainly tugging against the spike. It tumbled back as a body beneath it shifted, and my trusty weapon was wrenched from my hands, another casualty of the fight.

Punch, Claw, Slide

Falling to the slick floor as a skelly tackled me, jamming my armored forearm into its mouth to keep the snapping jaws at bay. Feeling the viselike strength of the bite bruising me even as the leather creaked and kept teeth from piercing flesh.

Scream, Panic, Kick

Sergeant Greaves clamoring up on top of the ghoul, eyes wild as he jammed a broad knife into the space at the back of the creature's mouth. With a hard, jerking motion, he broke the ghoul's jaw away like he was shucking an oyster.

Stand, Rally, Push

More spearmen arriving, stabbing downward with their new crosspiece-adorned weapons. Ghouls falling, tumbling into the balefire braziers below. The cheers rising, our voices pushing back the roar of the horde.

XXI

———

The tide had abated ... for the moment. Ghouls still piled up against the wall, but the soldiers had become far more adept at repelling them before they could spill over the top. A pair of juggernauts had arrived as well, their hammers pulverizing any ghoul that made it over the wall. With the first crashing wave finally thrown back, a sizable portion of the fighters was given their first break, collapsing where they stood as the sky continued to brighten with morning light. Acolytes of the Balefire Church moved amongst the tired ranks of soldiers, distributing water and carrying off the wounded. Blondie found me sitting against the wall of a nearby shed, my coat open to the cool air. The juggernaut handler I had hoped to meet had never shown up, and I had given up on retrieving the armored ghoul from beyond the wall.

"Nice ensemble you have there." I gave a weak chuckle upon seeing him, his head covered in a thick swath of bandage and a crutch under one arm.

"Uuugghh, don't even get me started. I get a battle wound to show off and it's because my horse fell on me ... ," he lamented.

"Ha! ... Haha ... hahaHAHA!" The laughter burbled from me with a tinge of madness, the battle strain making itself known through the oddest avenues.

"You sure you should be moving around on that thing?" I asked, pointing to his splinted leg.

"Probably not, but the medic's tent is already filling up with worse wounds than mine. It'll hold my weight, just hurts like a bastard. I can still fight or at least use balefire to give you a hand."

Then the moaning was rising beyond the walls again, along with shouts from above. Another clump of ghouls had emerged from the tree line, bolstering their numbers and stirring the remaining creatures into a fresh fervor.

"On your feet, maggots!" Sergeant Greaves shouted as the noise rose. "These dead bastards are looking to recruit for their own army! Too bad you poor bastards already promised your hides to the Empire!"

Creakcreakcreak

Sergeant Greaves paced back and forth, stomping through the mud in front of the culvert.

"I don't care if you've never fought ghouls before; I don't care if you're scared, or hurt, or shitting your britches!"

CreakCreakCreak

"We're gonna burn every last one of those monsters! And we're going to toast the Emperor while standing on top of the ashes!"

CREAKCREAKCREAK . . . CRACK

Sergeant Greaves stamped his foot, throwing up a spray of muddy water. "Damn it, I'm trying to speech here! Who's making that rack—"

The sergeant slammed to the ground, falling as if his legs had been cut out from under him. The man barely had time to scream before he was yanked violently backward, disappearing into the darkness of the culvert. There was a moment of stunned silence, then he emerged again, climbing unsteadily to his feet.

But . . . the clothes were wrong, the skin was grey . . .

"Oh gods," I realized in horror. "We didn't block the culvert . . . They've broken through."

The first ghoul stood tall, regarding the buffet of prey before it. It gave an ear-splitting screech, then launched forward as more of its brethren spilled from the hole.

"Breach!" a soldier shouted. "There's a breach in the wall!"

Half the soldiers turned and ran even as the other half charged into the fray. I couldn't blame anyone for turning tail in the face of such an attack, but it was truly the worst possible thing to do. We needed to stem the flow of ghouls here and block the hole before too many pushed through. If we retreated now, we'd be overwhelmed in minutes. With that in mind, I waded into the battle, swinging an axe I'd grabbed to replace my lost weapon. Blondie and I didn't have the armor or training to go toe to toe with the horde, but we did what we could to help, casting our wills out to slow the ghouls' advance. The soldiers with us didn't have the training to subjugate ghouls the way a courier could, and it took all their concentration just to resist the waves of ferocity pouring through the bond. The defenders had managed to surround the emerging mob, but we were losing ground with every moment. Like a balloon, the expanding horde was stretching our line thinner and thinner. Without reinforcements, our thin defense was soon going to rupture.

"Do they know we need help!?" I shouted to Blondie.

"No idea!" he shouted back, throwing out his hands to mentally pull a nearby ghoul off its victim. He had been pushing himself hard, and I imagined he was suffering the same vicious migraine that was digging into my own skull.

A horn sounded behind us, signaling a charge of reinforcements to bolster our flagging line. Along with the men, a pair of juggernauts plowed forward, smashing into the line where ghouls had begun to pour through and cutting into the horde like a hot knife through butter. Each juggernaut wielded a massive two-handed hammer that they whirled around them in effortless arcs, pulping the flesh of any ghoul unfortunate enough to venture close. With these two leading the counterattack, we finally had something to anchor our efforts around. Acolytes had brought a pair of balefire censers as well, allowing us to permanently dispatch the ghouls we had maimed. We'd stopped losing ground, though we still couldn't quite push them back to the breach.

Abruptly, a scream rang out from everywhere and nowhere, echoing off the cliff walls. In the depth of our struggle, I don't think I would have taken any notice, except the sound was repeated a few seconds later. I pulled away from the fight, gaining some space from the melee. The sound wasn't coming from the battle line, though the cliff acoustics made it hard to pinpoint. I looked towards the cliff top, outlined by a sky-tinged green as the last vestige of aurora borealis filtered through the morning clouds. A human form appeared in silhouette up above, then stepped forward, tumbling into the open air. I caught sight of the falling figure once again, bouncing off a rocky outcropping before tumbling out of sight. Then another . . . and another.

"What now!?" I groaned, watching the strange sight continue. "Hey, Blondie, help me out here!"

I pulled Champ in to watch our backs, then had Blondie turn those bright blue eyes on the new development. Maybe my brain had been rattled too much during the fighting, but it only took Blondie a moment to put together what was happening.

"Shit . . . It's another horde. I don't know how they got on the hill above us, but now they're tumbling down," he whispered in shock. "There could be a dozen up there or a hundred . . . ."

"They must be pretty smashed up after that fall, but if even one in ten can still move, we're going to be trapped between the hammer and the anvil. I'm gonna check it out and raise the alarm!" I barked, dropping the heavy axe and climbing onto Scramble's back once more.

"What should I do?" Blondie asked, leaning more heavily on his crutch.

"I don't know!" I shouted, my voice cracking with fear.

I saw Blondie look away sharply, and it made me feel guilty for the outburst. We were all at our limit right now. I didn't know Blondie's experience or even his age, but it was clear now that he had been looking to me for direction. I couldn't be the person he needed, though; I was as out of my depth as he was; all I could do was try to get us through the next few minutes.

"OK . . . Find Dupont and the bishop. Let them know what's going on. They've got the clout to rally people, maybe get to the keep."

"I can do that. Are you still gonna try to get out of here?" he asked.

"If we're truly losing, then yeah. It's not like I could get my sled up to the keep anyway. The only way through this for me is getting out," I reasoned.

"Good luck. Your sled should be all set, but I'll double-check everything if I have a moment," he promised.

"Thanks, Blondie. If I don't see you again, good luck."

Then I was off, leaning forward as Scramble bolted through the camp, living up to his name as he deftly scrambled over boxes and barrels. He could never compete with a horse in a straight sprint, but in the clutter of a dense forest or crowded camp, nothing could match him. We swiftly traversed the outpost, the sun's strengthening glow bringing more and more detail to the chaos around us. Other soldiers farther from the fighting had seen or heard the same disturbance I had and begun to trickle in the same direction, and I broke out from behind the last tent to come upon a scene of true horror.

Ghouls tumbled from thirty meters up, smashing into a pulp against the hard earth. There was already a sizable blob of ruined flesh at the bottom of the drop that the ghouls were adding to with every fall. None had survived the landing intact, but there were already over two dozen partially destroyed ghouls dragging themselves around on shattered stumps. Another ghoul plummeted down, landed on a cushion of its pulped brethren, then climbed to its feet. One arm was snapped off at the elbow, but the creature was otherwise unharmed and eagerly shambled towards us before I ordered Champ to intercept. More ghouls were tumbling down now, and more were surviving the drop.

A sonorous note echoed out nearby as a soldier raised a horn to his lips, sounding the alarm and alerting the rest of the outpost to the danger.

But, as another group of ghouls dropped down, the truth became clear . . . this outpost was lost. Even if there were at most another few dozen assailants up there, it would still divide our troops when we were barely holding the wall as is, and if we became trapped between these two forces, we'd be crushed. With that in mind, I pulled Champ back and sent Scramble running again, curving back towards the gate where Berg had set up his command tent. Every soldier I passed heard my shouted warning, though I was gone before I could see how they reacted. There were ghouls in the camp now as well; I could sense them through the light of the grand brazier that still stood. Just a few so far, but the fact that there were any roving the camp unchallenged boded ill.

Breaking out into the center of the camp, I discovered that they were experiencing their own difficulties. Ghouls were beginning to climb out of the sides of the trench even as the purple flame consumed others by the score, and the soldiers nearby were desperately trying to shove the escapees back into the press. Calliope's soldiers were still holding strong, but I could see injuries and signs of exhaustion even at a distance, and the formation looked smaller than before. Scramble galloped past it all, skidding to a stop in front of Berg's table and spraying a nearby soldier with cold mud.

"Uhm, sorry about that . . . ," I apologized, climbing off Scramble's back and stretching my sore muscles. Riding Scramble required a sort of awkward crouch to stay mounted, and my legs were aching from holding the position.

Berg was easy to find, an island of calm as various junior officers flowed around him in a panic. Petersen, on the other hand, was swamped; he was standing on another table and shouting new orders to each messenger as soon as they ran into view.

"Sir!" I shouted, running over to Berg. "There are ghouls coming down off the cliffside behind us. I don't think we can hold!"

"Oh, hello, Winona! I didn't see you there. Wonderful exercise we've set up, and such a toll against the ghouls. We're cooking them by the hundred!" he laughed ruefully.

"SIR! We. Are. Going. To. Die!" I shouted, grabbing him by the lapels and shaking the larger man. Two officers grabbed me from behind and pulled me away, directing me over to Captain Petersen as Berg returned his attention to the table.

"Leave him be, courier," Petersen ordered. "He departed his senses when the undead started falling from the cliff walls, he's refusing to admit we could be losing, and I have temporarily relieved him of his command."

"Well, we are losing. I've seen both the outer wall and the ghouls coming from the cliff." I looked back, verifying that creatures were still tumbling down in the grey morning light. "I don't think we can deal with ghouls coming in from both sides."

Petersen sighed, rubbing his temple with a palm. "I know. We're already starting the retreat to the keep. We're also sending additional scouts out the back gate to bring word back to the border, hopefully, they can dodge the Fins. Get the bishop to the keep now. Leave anything you can't carry," he ordered, dismissing me with a wave.

I nodded, then backed away from the chaotic command center and ran off in the direction of the keep. Once I was out of Petersen's line of sight, I leapt onto Scramble and doubled back, racing towards the storage bay where my sled was kept. There were so many people I wanted to check in with. Did the bishop still have his men in position to let me out? Were Dupont and Calliope making their way to safety? Would Blondie be able to retreat fast enough with his injuries? These were questions that would have to remain unanswered. It was past time to get the hell out of here while I still had the chance.

Even moving at speed, it was easy to see the battle turning. Ghouls roamed the camp unopposed or closed in on knots of fighting soldiers. A fire had broken out in the panic, greedily consuming wood and canvas, adding an orange glow to the balefire purple.

"Woah there!" I shouted, yanking Scramble into a skidding stop as a trio of ghouls stumbled into our path. Two ghouls were of the horde, but the third was a soldier, one who had clearly been bit and then killed, leading to a near-instant reanimation. A sheet of blood coated one side of his chest, bubbling from a ragged neck wound.

Scramble wheeled back to flee in the direction we came, but Champ was already fending off another ghoul that had been stalking us from behind. Damn it. There were too many ghouls loose in the balefire light; the mental noise battered my focus to the point that controlling any ghouls besides my own would be hard. Even just keeping track of the exact number of creatures closing in on us was growing more difficult by the moment, though it wasn't hard to discern that there were far too many to fight.

"Up and over Scramble, Let's go!" I shouted, sending him clambering up the side of a long, low-storage building. Champ joined us a moment later, easily leaping the distance. Then we were running again, footsteps thudding over wood and canvas. I could see the sled bays not too far off, and the path looked clear, once we—

A brief feeling of weightlessness, a vast silence, then a jarring impact, throwing me off Scramble's back. I rolled with the fall, tumbling head over heels once before coming to a stop.

For a moment, I thought I'd gone deaf, though an involuntary groan from the impact dispelled that concern. I looked up to see a single shaft of purple light streaming down, emanating from the hole in the roof I'd fallen through. That explained the silence at least; I was in darkness, out of the balefire light, so the riotous cacophony of the horde no longer pressed in on my mind. I had lost my torch in the fall as well. No bones were broken, but the wind had been knocked out of me once again, and it took a few moments of gasping like a fish out of water before I was able to move . . .

Eyes adjusting, I could dimly see other holes above as well, still covered in canvas. Damn, this must have been one of the buildings they had started cannibalizing to reinforce our defenses. It was a miracle the roof hadn't collapsed as soon as we had put our weight on it.

Something clattered to the ground nearby.

Wait, *we* had put our weight on it . . . Scramble had fallen too.

I dove to the side as Scramble careened through the space I'd been occupying a moment before, pulverizing a wooden box as momentum carried him past. The darkness had severed the balefire leash I used to control the ghoul, and he was once again a beast of mindless hunger.

"ShitShitShit!" I tried to stand, slammed my head on something, then began to blindly crawl forward. The sound of another collision rang out, and I was showered with debris as what sounded like a full set of cutlery clattered around me. I employed an old courier trick, directing my vision straight ahead while focusing on my peripherals. Shapes materialized in the dark, and I vaulted over a crate, landing in a cleared corridor that stretched the length of the room. Nobody knew why the borders of your vision worked better in the dark, but the technique had helped me through more than a few scraps. What it couldn't help with was the cold truth that Scramble was now between me and the balefire light. He was faster too; if I tried to run past him, he'd tear me apart in a blink, so my best chance was to find a different exit.

There was silence behind me again, which was far scarier than the crashing sounds. At least when Scramble was knocking things over, I knew where he was. I padded softly down the corridor, my panicked breathing and the distant rumble of battle the only sounds. The outline of a door was visible now, light leaking in through the gap in the bottom. Once I was outside, Scramble was sure to follow, and the balefire light would reestablish my control.

The unnerving silence sent a chill down my spine, and I risked a glance back.

Scramble was standing motionless in the corridor, no more than ten meters behind. The purple light behind him cast the creature in silhouette, the curves of his ribs given the appearance of black fangs. Silently, he crouched down, disappearing from sight. A moment of stillness, then the click-clack of bone on wood growing louder as he scuttled towards me on all fours.

Throwing myself backward, I desperately clawed at the supplies stacked around me, tearing them down, anything to slow his charge; the door had to be close. I just needed to stall him for a moment. Scramble plowed into the first few obstacles, tossed them aside, then leapt over the rest, crossing the last two meters between us unimpeded.

"Nooo!" I screamed in terror, hurling myself to the side and pulling another pile down on top of me as an impromptu shield. Scramble slammed into it, through it, and into me, bearing me to the ground. Skeletal claws reached out, grabbing handfuls of my coat and tearing through it like tissue paper. Training took over, and I reflexively threw my arm forward, aiming to jam my armored forearm into his mouth. Scramble was old and likely strong enough to bite clean through the vambrace, but if he sunk his teeth into my neck, it was all over. Instead of teeth, I punched metal, and the shock forced my eyes open, revealing the reason I was still alive. The last object that had fallen between us was some sort of metal grate, a rectangular lattice of iron bars, maybe a meter square. Scramble had thrust his arms through, but his head wouldn't fit, and in his ravenous state, he kept trying to push through the bars instead of simply tossing the lattice aside.

I splayed out my arms and legs to the sides of the barrier, pushing the bars away from me as far as I could. The lightweight skelly was lifted bodily off the ground for a moment, then planted his feet and attacked again, pushing against the barrier and sending us sliding across the floor. I threw one arm above my head just as we collided with the door, knocking it wide open. Cold swept in, and it should have been followed by blessed salvation: balefire light streaming in, infusing me with its power.

We had come out on the far side of the building, though, opposite the outpost center. This meant that the grand brazier was behind us, and the doorway was still cast in deep shadow. I had landed hard on my side, half in and half out of the doorway, and began to crawl forward towards the slanting border where shadow met light. But Scramble was too quick, his hands catching me by the arm and yanking me back. The grate was too wide to fit through the door, trapping Scramble on the other side for the moment, but his hands could still disembowel me with ease.

Then my life was saved, not by training or experience, not strength or agility, but by a few weak stitches. One of the toggles holding my coat closed ripped free under the strain. This put more strain on the next button, which tore off a moment after. I twisted and leaned forward, using the extra space the move created to slide my arm free of the sleeve. Scramble yanked the now empty sleeve through the grate, tearing into it with rotting teeth. All at once, the rest of the fasteners ripped free, spraying little bone toggles in every direction; I fell forward, and my coat disappeared in an instant, Scramble ripping it through the grate.

With an undignified scurrying leap, I threw myself into the balefire light, letting the madness of the horde pour back in.

Gods, there were ghouls everywhere, and any attempt at defense had failed. I could feel the flow of them like a shoal of fish, the dead pouring over the walls unimpeded. Most surged together in the same direction, harrying the survivors as they tried to retreat to the keep. But that still left dozens milling about nearby, and I could feel their attention beginning to turn, picking up on the lone human who had been separated from the pack, isolated and vulnerable.

Not completely alone, though. Champ still squatted sedately on the corner of the roof above, watching the events with a blissful detachment. I called him to my side a second before Scramble tossed the grate away and lunged into the light. Champ caught him by the scruff like a recalcitrant cat, and I sent a lance of thought through the ghoul, seizing control once again. Having a creature by my side that had tried to murder me mere moments ago was unnerving, to put it lightly, but we had bigger problems.

A flash of movement—a dark shape bolting between two tents nearby. Then a clang as a bucket fell from a shelf, knocked over by an unseen force. There were maybe two dozen ghouls circling us now, drawing closer, tightening the noose, too many to fight; Champ and Scramble were likely far older and stronger, but they could not be everywhere at once. Eventually, a ghoul would slip by and bring me down. We couldn't make a run for it either; they would swarm us and pull me from Scramble's back as soon as we tried to break through their line.

What we needed was balefire, some way to destroy a chunk of this hunting pack and give us an opening to run for it.

We needed balefire . . . or a coalblade.

"Damn me for a fool!" I cursed, yanking the sheath off my back. I had been so worried about concealing the coalblade that I'd ceased to think of it as the weapon it was.

A litany of rumors surrounded the coalblades, most of them almost certainly false. They were attributed with a variety of magical powers that ranged from the unlikely to the certifiable insane. Coalblades could make you fly, coalblades could raise the dead, coalblades could cure gonorrhea. There was one rumor that persisted, though, and it was the reason I had taken the risk of taking it off Oleg's hands. Coalblades were said to contain the power of the balefire, the blazing coals somehow forged into a deadly black glass. Just a single cut could burn a ghoul to ash as effectively as plunging them into the sacred flame. *Allegedly*.

The sound of my outburst rippled through the pack, and one ghoul broke from cover, bounding through the mud toward me. The bladed club slid free of the leather, polished wood glimmering in the firelight as I turned to face my attacker, nauseous fear pooling in my gut. The coalblade felt more work of art than weapon, I just hoped it was tougher than it looked.

Champ stepped forward, raising an arm to intercept the ghoul. I could taste bile on my tongue.

Then a realization struck me. It was so simple but so fundamental that it went against the core of everything I had been taught as a courier.

I ordered Champ to stand aside and stepped forward to face the monster alone. This was insane; Every courier was taught that you didn't fight ghouls; you *survived* them. Maybe you could tip one into a brazier if you were lucky, but attacking the undead head-on was suicide.

The ghoul leapt, and I whirled to the side, the coalblade flashing down in a short arc. The weapon hit the ghoul in the spine and cut through with barely a whisper of resistance, continuing downward to bury itself in the snow. The two halves of the ghoul tumbled away. There was a spark, and a tiny purple flame bloomed into existence at the point of contact. Then the fire blossomed as if the ghoul had been soaked in oil, racing along the bones, consuming it all. In the span of a heartbeat, all that was left was ash.

Oh, *Fuck* yes.

See, so much of the fear in a courier's life came from uncertainty: inclement weather, bandits, the things you could never fully predict or plan for.

But with the balefire light embracing me, I could sense every ghoul in the area, their position, their intention even. Instead of trying to drive the horde back with willpower alone, I merely opened myself up to the noise, absorbing it and divining the patterns beneath: Champ moving to defend, another assailant focusing on my throat and preparing to leap, even Scramble behind me and the rest of the pack closing in.

I had cultivated that sense for years, but it was always a defensive measure; bind ghouls to your will, force others away, or slow them down.

Don't fight; run, hide, survive. Don't. Get. Bit.

But now I had a weapon that could bite back and a perfect understanding of my opponents. It was like the ghouls were trying to bluff me, but as long as I had balefire, I could see all their cards.

Now I'm the one that can fight, and these monsters will have to survive me.

The next ghoul leapt at me from behind a nearby crate, out of my line of vision. But I could *feel* it. I spun around and sliced clean through its skull.

Then another, this one bursting out of a tent nearby, still clad in soldier garb. Out of the firelight, I hadn't sensed it and barely got the coalblade up in time to intercept. The ghoul's momentum carried it to its own demise, dissolving even as it slammed into me. A quick blast of heat, a flare of purple, and it was gone, leaving me coughing in its ashes.

"OK, keep it together, don't get cocky. You're not invincible. You can feel them coming, but you're still human; you can only move so fast. You'll get tired; they won't," I talked myself down, beginning to shiver. I had lost my coat to Scramble, and my shirt underneath was sweat-soaked. Morning had now emerged in full, but the sun shone weakly through the clouds, doing nothing to dispel the cold seeping into my bones; if I didn't keep moving, exposure to the cold could become a real problem. I grabbed a balefire torch that had been planted in the ground nearby, brandishing it in my off-hand. I had already experienced how dangerous the deep shadows devoid of balefire light could be, and I refused to be caught in one again.

I hefted the coalblade, adjusting my grip. Those first strikes had been like cutting through paper, I didn't need to waste the energy on a full-strength swing to dispatch these ghouls. A mental order pulled Scramble and Champ behind me, forming a wedge with me at the point. They would keep me from getting swarmed, but I wanted enough distance so that there was no chance of hitting them by accident. I could see the sled bays a short distance away, a dozen ghouls between me and my goal.

One of the ghouls screamed, and I screamed back, charging madly into the crowd, outrunning the fear that tried to bind me. I remembered the darkness, the sound of Scramble skittering through the room, the power of his grip on me. I took that fear, compressed it into white-hot anger, and rammed it forward.

The first ghoul was cut down. Another lost a hand, flames spreading up its stump. The next charged straight on, and I ran to meet it, holding out the blade and bracing the tip against the torch. The creature was split in half on contact, and I ran straight through the ghoul, the halves separating on impact. The top of the creature scrabbled at me as it arced by, but it fell to ash before it even scratched the fabric.

"Help!" A voice nearby, high and panicked. There was a clump of ghouls nearby, just out of sight. They hadn't noticed me. Rounding the corner, I saw two soldiers and an acolyte standing atop an overturned cart, desperately fending off the trio of ghouls that were trying to climb up to them. I held the coalblade at shoulder height and simply ran by them, letting the stone edges catch and cut through each as I went.

"Get to the keep! Now!" I shouted, turning away and moving on before I heard their response.

A handful of creatures still blocked my path, but it was as if they were converging on the grand brazier that had already consumed so many. Scramble and Champ funneled them in, and I cut them down.

We reached the deserted bays soon after, my team stirring as we drew near. I ordered Scramble back into position, buckling him back in line while leaving Champ free to roam in case more wild ghouls attacked. Once Scramble was strapped in, I ran back to the cargo bay, finding the box of medicine strapped down again with a fold of paper tucked under one of the straps.

Your battery is good to go. Tossed in what fresh supplies I could find. Get going. I'll do what I can here. Good Luck!

—Haakon (Blondie)

"Good man!" I grinned, shaking the box to make sure the straps were secured.

Fortunately, it seemed like everything was in place. My knees threatened to buckle for a moment, the toll of the battle catching up. I considered myself a decent runner, but prolonged fighting was an entirely different experience and not one I was accustomed to. My arms and shoulders burned, the coalblade now feeling leaden in my grip. A collection of scratches, bruises, and abrasions covered my body; each was inconsequential on its own but borderline debilitating when layered on top of the fatigue. The shivers were getting bad now as well, wracking my whole body, the soaked fabric leaching heat away. My other coat was in the living area, and I pulled the door open, laying the coalblade on the floor as I grabbed the door frame to haul myself up.

"That's far enough! Hands up if you please!" a familiar voice called from ahead.

"You have got to be kidding me," I muttered, thudding my head against the sled in frustration. Slowly, I complied, standing up and raising my arms above my head. A quick glance confirmed my suspicion. If the gods were real, they had a sick sense of humor.

"Hello, Captain Foss. Having a pleasant morning?" I asked, unable to even try to keep the contempt out of my tone.

The captain sneered, leveling a strange pistol at my chest; it was quite compact and squarish in shape, not a design I had seen before. Foss gestured for me to step forward, away from the sled.

"Captain Foss? Oh, so formal now, aren't we? It's amazing how a loaded gun inspires courtesy," he snapped the fingers of his free hand, and an armored juggernaut lumbered into view.

"We've got bigger fish to fry, captain. Ghouls coming over the walls, let's just—"

"Shut your mouth!" Foss snapped, his grip making the weapon shake. "Cut the bullshit. Despite our antipathy, let us not doubt each other's intelligence. You intend to continue your journey to Skyroost. Given that we never supplied you with a battery, the bishop must be assisting you. No way you'd be able to obtain one on your own."

"OK, OK. No worries. I'll come with you. We can go to the keep. Everyone stays happy," I reasoned. There was a muffled crash nearby, closer than the other sounds of battle. Most of the ghouls would be drawn to the forces fleeing for the keep, there wasn't enough prey on this side of the camp to interest them, but the few stragglers nearby were beginning to take notice of us.

"We could, those are my orders after all. But, let's be honest, you'd try to slip away as soon as we took our eyes off you. So, I guess that only leaves us with one option . . . ," he sighed, seemed to hesitate for a second, then refocused, decided. "I know I must seem quite the villain to you. Yes, you are a jumped-up peasant brat, but I take no pleasure in this. Duty is what separates us from the ghouls, the willingness to act beyond our own self-interest. We both have our orders. Today, those orders just happen to put us on opposing sides."

The sun was rising at my back, causing Foss to squint against the brightness. It might throw off his aim slightly, but who knew if it'd be enough to cause him to miss at this range.

"C'mon Foss. You can't just shoot me. People will ask questions," I stalled.

"There won't be enough left of you to identify once the ghouls are done. I'm sorry, courier, but the time for conversation is at an end. I need to make my own retreat to the keep, and that path is growing more dangerous by the minute. It's a shame, that skelly of yours is quite the specimen. I would have enjoyed pitting it against my juggernaut. I'm known as quite the ghoul duelist back home; I've never lost a fair fight," Foss boasted, hand tensing as he began to pull the trigger.

"That's good for me. I've never fought a fair fight," I snarled, springing my trap and throwing myself to the ground. Since the moment Foss had pointed his gun at me, I'd been projecting my will outward, coaxing the wild ghouls roaming nearby to venture closer. Foss would be able to sense the ghouls through the balefire, same as I could. But he lacked a courier's experience, and I was banking on him dismissing their stalking movements as random shambling. Imparting any sort of complex plan on so many unfamiliar creatures was impossible, but painting Captain Foss as a fat juicy meal was as easy as reinforcing their natural hunger.

Three things happened at once:

- I dove to the ground, aiming to land behind a nearby pile of boxes.
- Four ghouls burst into view from various points around us, careening towards Foss.
- Foss shot me.

There was a sharp crack of sound, then I felt a strong tug against my shirt, pulling my arm back sharply as I tumbled to the ground. With the adrenaline pumping, I barely even noticed the wound at first; just a stinging line of heat added to my other myriad aches. Two more shots rang out, and I pressed myself against the cover, but it soon became clear that Foss was no longer aiming at me.

The juggernaut was doing an admirable job, as evidenced by the pair of ghouls already torn to pieces at its feet. Another trio tried to rush Foss, but his protector intercepted with surprising grace for such a heavily armored form. One ghoul received a boot to the chest, the next a war hammer to the face. The last almost slipped by, but the juggernaut caught it by the scruff at the last minute, lifting it up single-handedly and slamming the creature back into the dirt. Foss fired the pistol at another ghoul, snapping its head back; the attack did little more than stagger the ghoul, but it gave the juggernaut time to whirl around and smash the ghoul to splinters.

But there were dozens of creatures now converging on Foss, and he only had a single ghoul to protect him. Foss fired the pistol, commanded the juggernaut, and pushed the ghouls back with his raw will, but it was a losing battle. A duo of wild ghouls found an opening and slipped by, leaping on Foss as he fired one last desperate shot. One ghoul went low, scything his legs out from under him and knocking his pistol flying while the second pounced on his struggling form. Foss let out a horrified scream. There was a dull crunch of bone, then the scream cut off abruptly, Foss's body disappearing in the press as more ghouls joined the feast. The juggernaut continued its assault even as more slipped by, trying to protect a master who had now joined the ranks of the dead himself.

That pain in my arm was radiating outward, and I looked down in shock as the hand I had pressed to the wound came away red. I groaned as a wave of nausea hit, but I managed to stand, then immediately trip over the length of my balefire torch. I must have knocked it over when I dove for cover, and now the flaming coal lay dead and inert in the snow. I threw the torch in the cargo bay, then hauled the cab door open and pulled myself inside.

"Get going!" I shouted, spurring my team forward. "Head to the rear gate!"

My head was pounding now, focus severely diminished, but most of the ghouls were distracted by Foss's body or the juggernaut's rampage, a fact I was grateful for. Craven and Heist did stumble as one of the blood-painted ghouls lunged closer, but Champ intercepted, yanking the creature away. As we made our way through the camp, Champ continued to fend off any curious ghouls while I saw to my wound. The layers of shirt were already soaked with blood, and I slit them open with a slice of my knife to clear the space around the wound.

I had a small first aid kit stored up front, of course, though I'd never expected to be treating a gunshot wound with it. I fished out the small leather package, spilling the contents on my map table. There was a paper packet that I ripped open with my teeth, dumping the entirety of its powdered contents directly into the wound.

"OOOHH! That smarts!" I shouted, smacking my other hand against the dashboard as the injury flared with pain again. The powder would help stem the bleeding for the moment, though, and I followed it up by hurriedly binding the area with a fresh bandage. It was ugly but should hold until we made it out of danger. We continued on relatively unscathed, the feral ghouls drawn away to larger concentrations of prey. The sun began to burn off the morning cloud layer, shining out in a cheerful blue sky that was a sharp contrast to the growing chaos below. Several smaller fires had broken out, isolated events for the moment, but all it would take was a shift in the wind to stir up a true conflagration.

I was surprised to see that the back gate was still manned, with a half dozen guardsmen anxiously brandishing their weapons from raised positions. King almost took a crossbow bolt to the chest before the soldiers realized he was part of a sled team, though the shooter's nerves had sent the projectile high over King's head.

"Hey! Stop shooting at my team! They're the only ghouls here not trying to eat you!" I shouted, continuing to disparage them until they lowered their weapons.

"The surviving soldiers are all rallying at the keep. If I were you, I'd head that way. The camp is lost." I advised, cracking my door wider so they could better hear me; I was too tired to dismount.

These men wouldn't be inclined to obey a courier, but the fact that they were terrified to a pants-shitting degree certainly helped. I doubted that most of them had been assigned here, judging by the blood and ash that coated a few of them. More likely, they had fled from the fighting and banded together when they saw the gate guards still holding position., Two of the men still had pristine uniforms that hadn't seen combat, and they gave me a meaningful glance as they approached. The pair brought order to the mob and quickly had them setting their backs to heave the heavy wooden gate open. As one continued to oversee the work, the other pulled himself up to my open door.

"Bishop Rimkus wishes you luck on your mission," the scarred veteran grinned. "We'll get these survivors to the keep and inform him of your departure. Good luck, courier."

"Much obliged. Be careful, the soldiers seemed like they were retreating in good order, but with all the chaos, it might be a full-on rout by now. Ghouls were falling from the cliffs too," I warned.

"The balefire lights our way. Whether we survive or not, it will be the will of the flame," he intoned with a worrying level of religious fervor. And that's an observation coming from a member of the clergy.

"Uhm . . . Yeah . . . Good luck," I nodded to him, then spurred my team on, driving them through the gate the moment it was open wide enough. The soldiers closed it behind me as soon as I was through, and I leaned out gingerly to get one last look before we rounded the bend. The flames were no longer visible, but the smoke certainly was, curling up in long grey fingers towards the morning sky. I shouldn't have expected anything to go to plan on this insane trip, but the sheer scope of this catastrophe exceeded even my wildest expectations. I muttered one last prayer for the good people I was leaving behind, then let the wilderness envelop me once again.

PART TWO

XXII

The severity of my wound was becoming more apparent with each passing minute, red splotches of blood beginning to seep through the white of the bandage. A bit of wilderness medicine was in order, but it wasn't a procedure that could be performed as my sled bounced through rough country. Every moment we rode on took us farther away from the horde, but every bump in the road jarred the injury more. Given a choice, I would take pain over the chance of running into feral ghouls, so I gritted my teeth and pushed farther north over the next few hours.

By late afternoon, I had endured all that I could. The bandage had staunched the bleeding for now, but even the slightest twitch sent a bolt of pain arcing through my arm. My other wounds had also made themselves known, and my body felt like little more than a collection of various injuries, with an extra helping of exhaustion to really enhance the experience.

After a bit of searching, I found a copse of spruce trees alongside a clear mountain stream and pulled my team under their boughs. The trail north called to me, but between the early wake-up, the exertion of battle, and my injuries, I had pushed as far as I could today. Making camp with just one working hand was taxing, but I could direct my team to take care of many of the more labor-intensive tasks. Once we had a fire going with a pot coming to boil, I called over Heist to help me see to the wound. She had no training with first aid, but I needed another pair of hands, and Heist's fingers had been boiled and cleaned until nothing but gleaming white bone remained. Some of my younger ghouls might be more useful here, but I wasn't stupid enough to let those rotting hands near an open cut. King and Heist were also the two on the team with the least voracious appetite for living flesh, though I still took the time to muzzle Heist and tighten the straps on King's mask. Any ghoul would be tempted by the sight of an open wound, but I was confident that even my flagging willpower would be adequate to smother any hunger my two assistants might be feeling. King poured boiling water over Heist's bony digits, sterilizing them to the greatest extent we could out here. As they prepared, I cut away the ripped and bloody remains of my sleeve, then unwound the stained bandage, stopping right at the end where it still stuck to the clotting wound. King came over with the pot of water, steaming hot but no longer boiling.

"OK, let's get this cleaned out," I ordered, then placed a small roll of leather in my mouth to bite down on. I reached out, gingerly extending my injured arm and grabbing hold of a railing on the sled. King began to pour, streaming the hot water over the cut as Heist gingerly lifted the bandage away.

"UUuugghh!" I groaned as the bandage pulled free, taking the half-formed scab with it. Blood trickled anew, tinged to pink as it mixed with the water. Steeling myself, I looked over, getting my first clear look at the damage Foss had dealt me. The flesh had been ripped away in a shallow divot, down to a yellow layer of fat that I could see glistening as the water poured over it, which meant that damage hadn't gone deep enough to pierce muscle. I wasn't out of the woods yet, though. The weapon injuries I had accrued before now were mainly acquired in short knife fights, wounds that could be stitched together. But the projectile had torn away an entire line of flesh, carving a long diagonal furrow up across my bicep; there was no skin left to draw together; it was just . . . gone. I looked away in disgust for a moment and found Amelia once again peering down at me from a nearby tree branch. Those eyes still seemed far too clever, and the extra attention was even more unnerving now that I was wounded.

The pain was flaring up now, fresh blood welling as the last of the water streamed away. I had never expected to treat a gunshot wound one day, but I did the best with what I had, cleaning the area and smearing it with a healing paste before wrapping it firmly, leaving enough pressure to stop the bleeding while avoiding the risk of cutting off circulation. I made a sling from the ruins of my bloody coat to support my arm and as a reminder not to overuse the limb. The fact that it was my left arm was a silver lining; the situation would have been even more dire if I'd lost the use of my dominant hand.

"Well, that was unpleasant . . . ," I griped, then looked over at the ruined remains of my coat. Most of it was unsalvageable, but I made a mental note to save what I could in case my remaining coat needed to be patched in the future.

With plenty to do, the rest of the day passed swiftly. I washed thoroughly; the cold was biting, but I needed to make sure all my injuries were clean. Catching an infection this far out in the wild could be lethal, especially with my body already so beat up. The supplies Blondie had packed helped augment a bland dinner, and soon enough, I had a full belly, clothes hung out to dry, and a comfortable spot to rest, reclining on a fallen log as the fire crackled and the stars slowly came out.

From the bandit ambush to the outpost attack, it felt like I had been stumbling from one mess to the next, cutting it closer every time. There were too many outside forces with their fingerprints on this job, too many variables. What was truly plaguing Skyroost? And along those lines, why had the bandits that kidnapped Blondie been heading in that direction? Rimkus had mentioned a new force throwing their skull-branded gold around and pulling the strings, but where did that factor in? I'm sure there were plenty of ghouls between here and my destination waiting to kill me, but at least they didn't pretend to be my friend first. For now, I was simply glad to be back in my natural habitat, just me and my team against the world.

Part of me feared that the horrors I had witnessed that morning would keep me up, but the combination of early wake-up and hard exertion was an effective sedative. My sleep was deep, though my dreams were strange. A young woman tugged my arm through a faceless crowd, pulling with a strength that far exceeded her size. The dream transitioned in that peculiar but effortless way dreams do, and I was falling from a tree the size of a mountain, giant pine needles tumbling down around me in slow motion. I awoke just before I hit the ground.

I tensed up as I woke, throwing my hands up and bracing for an impact that would never come.

"OOOWWW!" I shouted, cradling the injured arm I'd yanked up without thinking. "Uugghh, that's going take some getting used to."

I redressed the wound and took the time to catalog my other injuries as well. To summarize: Everything fucking hurt. My joints felt like they were coated in rust, and every movement seemed to aggravate some scab or bruise. But the honest truth was that I had been lucky; other than my arm, my other wounds were superficial, though it certainly didn't feel that way when they all hit me at once. I left the warmth of my sled and made a note to save and boil my used bandages when we stopped tonight. I hadn't packed enough supplies to have a new bandage every day, it just wasn't practical, so I'd have to sterilize and reuse the old ones as best I could.

Stepping out of my sled, I felt beaten and worn down but ready to face the challenges of the day. Most challenges, that is. I could honestly say that I was absolutely not ready for the scene I stumbled into. It was common for wild ghouls to wander through the camp during the night, but they were easy enough to disperse come morning. That is unless they encountered Amelia. Somehow, she had managed to snag one around the neck using the rope leash she'd been tied to and suspend the pitiful thing a meter off the ground. As the creature struggled to free itself, Amelia hung upside down from a nearby branch, methodically cutting into its flesh with a short knife.

"It's too damn early for this shit," I protested, heading towards the fire pit. Whatever mischief she was performing could wait until I'd had coffee. Not far from her, my ghouls sat in two perfect rows of four, watching the demonstration like school children in class.

"King! Aren't you supposed to be keeping her in line?" I asked, throwing my hands up in frustration and wincing again at the pain the gesture caused.

King shrugged as if to say, "She's very persuasive."

I ignored the show, cooking up a quick breakfast along with a bracing cup of coffee using some new grounds I'd pinched from the outpost's stores. Those royal guards were fancy folk, and I was more than happy to enjoy their fine taste in morning refreshments. Once I was fed and caffeinated, I turned to face . . . whatever the hell Amelia was doing. Her knife was short, but ghoulish vigor meant she would never tire, and it looked like she'd been at her task for some time now. It wasn't just random butchery either; her methodical approach made it clear that she had some sort of goal. The creature's chest had been laid open, and a fist-sized rock lay bloodstained at her feet, which explained how she had managed to bash through the creature's ribcage. As disturbing as the behavior was, it also stoked my curiosity. It was rare for ghouls to interact so actively with each other unless prompted, but Amelia clearly had a purpose in mind. So, I let her continue and turned to deal with the other ghoul, who was complicit in this odd behavior.

"Hmmm . . . I wonder how Amelia got that knife?" I asked, pacing in front of my crew. "I know I didn't give it to her . . . I know she didn't have it on her when we found her . . . So where did she get it from?" I wondered aloud, stopping in front of one ghoul in particular.

If a skeleton could look sheepish, Heist did a respectable job of conveying it. She even tried to scooch back and hide behind Bonk, inadvertently revealing the knife sheath on which she had been sitting.

"You know the rules, Heist. I let you keep your trinkets if you behave . . . ," I chided. "Champ, grab her legs!"

She tried to scrabble away, false jaw clacking comically. There was a moment of struggle; then Champ had Heist suspended by the ankles, the ghoul wriggling in a vain attempt to escape.

"OK, hand it over!" I barked, reaching into her chest cavity with my good arm. Heist vainly tried to batter me away, but my mental grip kept her from putting up more than a token resistance. She wasn't a bare skeleton, but what little flesh that still clung to her had long since dried and withered to the consistency of jerky, so it wasn't hard to look straight through her ribcage and pluck out the leather bag where she hoarded whatever she could get her bony hands on. I wasn't sure how much the negative reinforcement of taking her stash altered her behavior, but it was a good idea to check what she'd gathered up every now and then, regardless.

The items I dumped out across the fallen log formed a road map of our trip so far. There was a small bracelet, a leather cord laced through round amethyst beads that picked at my memory. For a moment, I thought it was a piece we had stripped from the dead bandits, but I could have sworn I'd seen it on a living man's wrist. I slipped the jewelry over my own hand, which triggered my memory.

"This is Ronny's!" I laughed, remembering seeing it on him while we drank at the bar. "But how'd you get it?"

It was a question that would remain unanswered, though if I had to guess, I would say she'd slipped the item off him when he'd run afoul of Tybalt back in Ozero. After that, there was a slip of paper money from the Song Islander we had met, the varied trinkets from the bandits, and . . . a pistol.

"Gods above Heist! You're a menace!" I shouted, running a hand through my hair in shock. It . . . it had to be Foss's; that odd design was instantly recognizable. The weapon must have been knocked away when Foss was dragged down. I couldn't imagine any other time Heist would've had the opportunity to get her hands on one. This left me with a bit of a conundrum . . .

This was pre-cataclysm technology; it had to be. The craftsmanship was so far beyond anything I had seen, and there wasn't a flintlock mechanism or any visible mechanism for that matter.

"How do you work?" I mused aloud, pointing the gun away from me while I examined it. I stayed clear of the trigger but found a small button in the handle that I pressed after a moment's hesitation. I nearly had a heart attack when a long rectangle dropped from the bottom of the pistol, falling into the snow at my feet.

"Oh, please don't tell me I already broke it." I grabbed the rectangle, wiped it off on my coat, then pushed it back into the recess it had fallen from. The piece locked into place with a satisfying click, and I breathed a sigh of relief.

There was no doubt this was a useful and lethal weapon in the hands of an expert, the few times I'd witnessed the effectiveness of similar weapons had left an impression. But I wasn't an expert, and trying to use an ancient firearm I didn't understand felt like an unreasonable risk, even by my standards. It wasn't something I was comfortable keeping on my person, so I figured I'd keep it stowed up front as I traveled just in case I needed one last line of defense. By the time I had the pile sorted, Amelia had finished her task, pulling the wild ghoul's arm off with a grisly crack and taking a large section of shoulder off with it. She immediately sat on the ground, ignoring the hanging creature as she began to carve off the arm's flesh.

"OK, that's enough of that, weirdo," I interrupted, ordering her to drop the knife as well as the arm. The knife was old and rusted. Heist might have found it at one of our campsites, likely discarded by a traveler. The arm was still animated by magic even after the separation and was inch-worming around the campsite in mindless circles. Amelia chuffed irritably, dead eyes never leaving the flailing limb.

"What are you trying to do? Looking to replace the one you lost?" I joked, throwing the knife away and regarding the severed limb flopping aimlessly on the ground. After a moment of deliberation, I kicked the limb into the brush, though curiosity almost convinced me to keep it. Amelia was clearly acting on some mysterious echo of her past life, and letting her play it out would teach me more about her. But we had enough to deal with on this trip.

"I promise, once we're done, you can have all the arms you want," I placated Amelia, sending calming tones through the bond.

That just left the hanging remains of Amelia's catch to deal with. I retrieved the coalblade and stalked over to the ghoul, hefting the weapon in my good hand. So much had been going on in the battle, the noise, the chaos; I wanted to take this opportunity to get a better look at what this blade was doing to a ghoul when it made contact.

With one last breath to steady myself, I struck, swinging the weapon down in an arc toward the ghoul's remaining shoulder. The blade bit into flesh, then just kept going. Instead of cutting through it, the blade seemed to unbind the creature, effortlessly parting flesh with no more resistance than cleaving through a snowman. The creature was cut from shoulder to hip, purplish light sparking from the point of contact. These sparks bloomed into purple flame in the wake of the weapon's passing, eagerly consuming the ghoul's flesh. The strike passed through so effortlessly, in fact, that my blow continued downward, and I almost ended up driving the blade into my own thigh before I managed to halt the momentum of the strike.

"I need to remember that if I keep swinging this like an axe, I'm going to end up lopping my own foot off."

I checked the weapon for damage, but the sole evidence of the strike was a long twist of rotten fabric caught in one of its teeth. So, the blade was deadly to ghouls, but the effect didn't extend to mundane materials, same as balefire. That was something to keep in mind; if the ghoul was wearing thick clothing or armor, I would need a heavier blow to ensure the black glass pierced through to flesh.

Still, this purchase was paying off more than I ever could have imagined.

I looked around, but there were no other feral ghouls wandering the area that I could test the blade out on. Maybe I could round up a few when we camped tonight and start practicing with the weapon in earnest, as much as my wounds would allow.

"You are beautiful," I told the coalblade, grinning like a child presented with an unexpected new toy, though the elation faded a moment later.

The situation had been looking grim when I left the outpost, and there was no way for me to know what the end result had been. I was sure that at least a handful of survivors would have retreated to the keep before the camp was overrun, but I had no idea if my comrades were among them. Blondie and Calliope both had the competence to make it out alive, but in the chaos of an endless horde, no amount of skill could promise survival.

"Let's get going. We're burning daylight," I sighed.

We packed up camp and resumed our trek northward, venturing into even more remote country. People who trekked along these wastes were the kind who just disappeared one day, swallowed up by sudden snowy whiteouts, lost and never seen again.

Thankfully, Bishop Rimkus may have provided me a solution in the form of a sheaf of papers detailing secret courier routes I hadn't seen before. My own documents showed a single safe path up to Skyroost, a well-defined inland road that weaved around peaks and through valleys as it followed the mountain range north-northeast. I had taken that route many a time with no problems outside adverse weather, but as I looked at it with new eyes, all I could see were a dozen spots where a weary courier could be ambushed. Amazing how a changing situation could make an old, reliable trail seem so . . . sinister. I hoped that the bishop's gift would open up some new options and unfurled the sheets across my chart table as we pulled northward. Overlaying the thin papers on top of my map revealed the hidden courier routes that had been compiled over the years. After examining the added information, it seemed like I had two available paths beyond the conventional route.

First option: I could run farther east, break free of the mountains, then sprint through the lowlands before cutting back in. The advantages were that the lowlands would give me plenty of room to maneuver if attacked, and I would be spared from pushing through the toughest terrain. The downside was that it was a long, circuitous route that was new to me and would take considerable time to navigate. The battery running the heater would keep that medicine warm for five days, one of which was already behind us. My planning told me that we could make it, barely, but only by putting in long days and getting a lucky break of clear weather. If we became bogged down taking the long way around, the medicine would freeze, and the whole journey would be for nothing.

This left me with the second route, a path that led in the opposite direction. Instead of going east, we would head west, towards the ocean. From there, the route took a straight shot to Skyroost, running the journey in fewer kilometers than even the traditional road would take. To make up for the shortcut, I would be riding through a route pulled straight from a courier's nightmare; there was a glacial cave, a frozen lake, and even a portion of forest that just had a crude drawing of an angry bear next to it.

"What kind of frozen-brained lunatic blazed this trail?" I wondered aloud, writing out the calculations to determine how long this route would take. Given the difficulty of the trail, I added in a generous budget of time for negotiating the more treacherous areas. Even with that buffer time added, it looked like I could make the journey in three days' time.

"Damn, that's tempting." This was one of those moments where choice was a curse. At the end of the day, there was no way to know which was the right call. Each had pros and cons, but nothing outside a prophetic view of the future could tell me what the right path was. My biggest fear was that some part of the glacier had collapsed over the years, blocking the route. If that were the case, I would need to backtrack and make a no-sleep sprint up the main route to have a chance at making it in time. The best I could do was rely on my fall-back method of decision-making and ask what my father would have done. The long road could leave me arriving too late, the middle path could have me attacked by bandits, and the shortcut would be . . . ice and angry bears?

"Well . . . Dad always said that when faced with some bad choices, go with the one you haven't tried yet. Let us go fight some bears."

I double-checked my calculations, jotting down every major way-point we would need to hit to stay on course. Tonight, I would sit down with King and go over it again in detail. King would be leading us into uncharted territory, and I would need to send him highly specific instructions to keep the team from straying. I whispered a quick prayer to the balefire, then set my team to work. Minutes later, we were turning to put the rising sun at our backs and kicking fresh powder up in our wake.

XXIII

Now that our path was chosen, I took a moment to take stock of our supplies for the coming challenges. The glacial cave was worrying and not an obstacle I'd faced in my capacity as a courier. There were similar caves further south, but most were well-marked tourist attractions for Song Islanders or southern colonists returning to visit the homeland. I had visited a handful of those with my father as a child and racked my brain for any details I remembered that might be useful here. Low ceilings, pools of ice-cold water, a floor of unstable rocks dredged up by the ice. It had been a fun diversion at the time, but navigating it with a full sled would be far less pleasant. On top of that, I was missing my lost poleaxe, the sole weapon I carried that had a chance of fending off those bears the map hinted at. I could use Tybalt or Champ to fight them, but the bears up north could easily tear a ghoul in half if threatened. Either ghoul should be able to kill an animal that size, but it was a poor trade if one of my best fighters was crippled or destroyed in the process. Maybe I could cut a branch into a makeshift spear if I found a suitable length of wood, then lash my long knife to the top as a spearpoint. That would be a last resort, though; a bear had layers of hide, fat, and muscle, making it difficult to strike a fatal blow before the animal could get its teeth in you.

In contrast to the challenges ahead, our current road was smooth sailing. The ghouls' steady lope ate up the kilometers, and we arrived at the general location of the glacier just before noon, hopefully giving us plenty of time to navigate the labyrinth before nightfall. I had just started to worry that we might have somehow missed the turnoff when the sled rounded another bend, revealing the glacier in the distance, a massive slab that dominated the landscape. This particular section of the glacier was far longer than it was wide, and cutting through its heart would be a perfect shortcut . . . if we weren't drowned . . . or crushed by falling ice . . . or eaten by the ghouls that had wandered in.

The sheer ice wall loomed even higher as we drew close, the ground nearby littered with massive shards that had broken away to shatter across the rocky ground. Grey clouds were building on the horizon, and my barometer had been on a steady drop throughout the day. Hopefully, this journey through the cave would also give us some shelter while the incoming weather passed overhead. With the aid of the route's notes, I tracked down the entrance, a low half-circle opening in the wall with a small stream, now frozen, snaking out from it. The stones inside ranged in size from fist to boulder, ready to tear apart the metal runners of my sled.

"Well, looks like we'll be carrying the old girl," I ordered, stepping down from the cab. "I figured as much. Let's get to it."

I knew my team could lift the sled; it was one huge advantage of running one of the lightest long haulers in the north. That didn't mean it was a straightforward process, though, especially in this situation. Having my ghouls hoist the sled on their shoulders and ford a river was one thing, but trying to shuffle through the low caves and rough terrain ahead would be far more difficult. With that in mind, we prepared as best we could. There were three brackets along each slide of the *Ridgerunner*, just below the main body. Each of these brackets had a slot reinforced with metal that was shaped to fit a set of hardwood poles tucked at the bottom of my cargo pile. I dug them out and slid them into their slots, giving my ghouls a sturdy place to lift from. The task also meant reordering my team a bit to take the strain: Champ and Tybalt would still be at the back, where the sled was heaviest, while my middle-aged ghouls (Grah, Craven, Scramble, and Heist) would be up front, two a side to compensate. Bonk and Amelia were still young and had less strength to add, so they would be in the middle. Hopefully, they could help stabilize the whole ensemble if it started to slip. Once that was done, I grabbed my personal equipment since I would be walking to avoid putting any more strain on the team; I had my ice axe, an oil lantern, the sheathed coalblade, and a sheet of paper further detailing the route through the cave. There was a note by the underling who had copied the map, stating that a portion of the page containing written notation had been lost to water damage but that the part detailing the cave's layout was free of any distortion. King would be with me; we would range in front of the sled to spot dangerous terrain before the sled encountered it.

"OK, I'm betting this is gonna be a story for the grandkids. Let's get moving," I ordered, slowly leading us into the darkness.

Or at least, that's what I expected. Surprisingly, light extended far deeper into the cavern than I would have believed. The blue ice was pitted but translucent, reflecting a surprising amount of light to form a tunnel of glowing sapphire glass that stretched inward. I hated defacing such stunning natural beauty, but I hated getting lost more and scratched a broad arrow into the ice wall with the tip of my axe. It wasn't a perfect trail of breadcrumbs, but the abundance of ice made marking my trail far easier than in a traditional rocky cave. I was also surprised to see signs of a campsite just inside the cave mouth; it was long abandoned, with little more than a ring of stones and a few scraps of detritus to mark the spot. But this path was marked as a courier route, so it made sense that I wasn't the first person crazy enough to try this shortcut.

We pushed onward. The light from the tunnel mouth faded, but cracks from the surface above dug down just deep enough to let in more blue light at random intervals. The going was slow, but my team remained surefooted as mountain goats and the *Ridgerunner* crept forward without even a wobble.

After half an hour, we reached our first intersection. The paths appeared identical, though a cold breeze from the right side hinted at a crack marked on my map that snaked all the way down from the surface. I turned back to check the way we had come and was hit with a wave of confusion that bordered on vertigo. The path behind me was identical to the one I was facing, to the left, or was it the right?

"You're losing it, girl, get yourself together! It's too early to be cracking now," I chided, closing my eyes for a moment, then opening them and reorienting myself. I had my sled pointing forward, the arrows on the wall, my own map, and even the cool breeze could be a guide, but only if I kept my wits about me. We turned left and delved deeper into the blue.

The glacier must have been thicker here as the light faded from a bright sapphire to thin veins of cobalt to nothing at all. All we had now were lanterns and the balefire, keeping the darkness at bay in a circle around us. The featureless tunnel and primordial darkness warped my perception of time, the air felt old, thin, and stale. I took another step and slipped as my foot skated across something. I found myself flailing with one arm in the sling and the other holding my lantern, then dropped to my knees before I tumbled all the way down the shallow decline. The move wasn't graceful, but at least I had kept my lantern from shattering against the stones.

"*Ugghh, I bibt mah tun,*" I spat, tasting a hint of blood in my mouth.

Spitting did little to alleviate the taste, and I looked down to see what I'd slipped on. I had expected a slick wet rock or patch of ice but instead found a perfect rectangle of slate, something that clearly wasn't formed naturally. As we continued, I spotted more of the slate tiles, many snapped in half or reduced to shards. Now that I was looking for irregularities, my eyes picked out more unnatural shapes in the gloom; there were large blocks of stone out there, their edges long since worn down by time and ice.

"King, I think these were houses," I told him, thinking aloud. "Or some other kind of building. Either way, I've never heard of a settlement out this way. If it's been crushed this far inside the glacier . . . I can't imagine how old this stuff is."

We continued, turning at another split and barely slipping the sled through the gap. It was marked as the thinnest portion on the map, and we had to lift and tilt the sled forty-five degrees to fit the opening. It was a tight fit, and I had to send Scramble up to chip away at an outcrop of ice that hindered our passage. With some effort, we heaved the old girl through and resumed our course. Up ahead would be the largest open space in the cave, a natural amphitheater of ice and stone we would have to cross before beginning our ascent back toward the world of the living. It wasn't a massive space, or the weight of the glacier above would have collapsed inward, but it was still wide enough that our light couldn't reach all the way across the void. When we emerged out of the thin tunnel, it felt like stepping up to the edge of a cliff. The darkness drank in the light; this was a cold, lonely place. We began to creep around the edge of the space but soon came across a thick wall of ice that didn't appear on my map. Glaciers were always moving, shifting, and collapsing, so it wasn't a surprise that a portion of the ceiling had fallen inward since the map was first drawn.

I would have liked to keep following the outer wall, but this obstacle meant we'd have to venture inward to the center of the amphitheater to skirt around it and hope that the rest of the route remained unobstructed. The terrain slanted down as if we were descending into a bowl, with pools of perfectly still water dotting the landscape.

"Don't step in those," I ordered. There was no way to tell if those dark pools were six centimeters or thirty meters deep, and I was not going to risk getting swallowed by one.

A gloved hand gently grabbed my shoulder, pulling me to a stop. I was thankful that I sensed King coming up behind me, or else the contact might have given me a heart attack. He pointed his finger forward, indicating to some point in the blackness that I could not yet see. His mind pulsed a rhythm of concern; there was something out there.

"Let's go check out what's spooked you," I told him, and we crept forward together.

It took a few more meters before the creatures were revealed, crouching around one of the pools. One ghoul stood slowly, watching me, while two others were hunched over at the far end of the pool, darting their hands into the ice-cold water. I could only imagine what kind of strange cave-dwelling fish they were snatching at. It seemed as good a time as any to get another test of my coalblade in, though I had to awkwardly roll my shoulder forward to pull the weapon out of its sheath with my good hand. Once I had the ghoul's attention, I stepped back, trying to draw him into the light of the balefire. The creatures looked like young fawns, still wearing layers of crude furs that had staved off the cold while they lived. Their strength would be little more than that of a human, but I was injured and wanted to be able to subdue them with the balefire's influence before striking with my coalblade. I ordered King back to the sled so he could help guide the team forward over the uneven terrain.

"C'mon, you ugly bastard," I whispered, taunting the gaunt-faced monster. "Just a few steps further . . . Gotcha!"

I reached out with my mind, subduing the ghoul as he stepped into the purple light, except . . . I didn't. When I tried to connect to the creatures, there was no rhythm to latch onto. The ghoul stepped forward, baring its rotten teeth as if in a feral grin. The light reflected oddly off the ice around us. Maybe that was interfering with the balefire's power?

I tried again, redoubling my efforts as I took a step back from the ghoul. But no matter how I strained, the slippery bastard would not appear in my mind's eye. He inhaled deeply, preparing to unleash a rasping undead scream.

"Take them!" he hollered, his voice deep and heavily accented.

"You're not a ghoul . . . shit," I swore, momentarily dumbfounded. It was all I had time to say before the man charged, reaching out to grab me as I stumbled backward. I swung hard as he closed the distance, aiming to bury the coalblade in his shoulder. The blow thud-ded into his collarbone, staggering the man but not stopping him as he grabbed at me, clamping one dirty hand on my injured bicep. I let out a hoarse scream of pain as his fingers tightened on the wound and twisted away in desperation, dragging the coalblade across his neck as he bore me to the ground. His stench was a horrific mix of body odor and old fish, an oppressive miasma that made me gag as I scrambled to push him off, ramming my elbow into his temple over and over until he slumped on top of me, half unconscious. My mind reached out to call my ghouls for aid even as I levered the man off me with my good arm. The lantern had fallen nearby, and I crawled for it, fingers closing around the handle as hands clamped around my ankles. I turned blindly, swinging the lantern and bashing it into the head of another cave dweller, spattering her with burning oil that transformed my assailant into a screaming column of flame that lit up the area with orange light.

There was movement around us as new attackers rose from the ground, the darkness and rocky terrain rendering them invisible until I walked right into their ambush. Torches streamed in from the tunnel we had entered as more dwellers entered, the group fanning out to encircle us. The first man was still splayed out on the floor, hands at his throat as he gurgled the last of his lifeblood away. My coalblade had done little in terms of blunt damage, but my panicked twist had dragged the obsidian blades across him, opening ragged wounds across his neck.

My team shambled up behind me, sled in hand, and we began to retreat from the mob, shuffling across the open space. The dwellers maintained a set distance, hovering just at the edge of the purple light. I kept Tybalt close, letting his ravenous hunger flare up to a barely repressed inferno.

We had passed the halfway point now, but when we reached the far wall, there were more gaunt faces waiting for us. We were surrounded. My order went out to lower the sled to the ground, and I retrieved my bow, stringing it and nocking an arrow. Drawing the weapon would be excruciating with my injury, and I would run out of arrows before they ran out of people, but maybe I could scare them off if I put an arrow through the first one that charged. There were so many people, and they had materialized far too fast; this had been a trap from the start, and I'd blundered right into it. I couldn't begin to fathom how a group this size could survive in these caves, but they were living people, and people could be bribed or intimidated.

"My name is Win—" I began, but the words died in my throat.

A rhythmic chant had begun to rise around us, starting soft as a whisper but rising to a shout.

Bjor.bjor.bjor.Bjor.Bjor.BJOR.BJOR!BJOR!BJOR!

I distantly recognized the word, an ancient one for an animal, a bear maybe? Despite, or maybe because of the horrific absurdity of our plight, I barked out a short laugh. All I could think of was that stupid drawing of an angry bear from my map. Strange, the things that come to mind when you're about to be killed by mole people.

The chanting reached a crescendo as a single individual separated from the crowd and swaggered toward me. A loincloth covered his waist, and he wore the pelt of a bear across his head and shoulders, the beast's dead eyes staring out forlornly from their perch. The man was otherwise nude, though the bare skin glistened as if oiled. Instead of bulging muscles, he was all bone and sinew, though no less intimidating for that. Bjor drew a pair of short, simple axes and raised them above his head, eliciting a cheer from the crowd.

"Great, looks like we're the entertainment for tonight . . . Or the main course," I growled, sending mental orders to my team. Pulling through my bond, I brought each of them to full attentiveness, focusing them on a singular goal. Once this bastard was down, we would make a break for it. I was tempted to fire an arrow at him, but then I hesitated. This scene had a feeling of ritual to it, like they had chosen a champion and were now calling me out. My gut told me that if I tried to shoot him down, it would be seen as some sort of violation of honor, and they would swarm us. No, this situation required a more personal exertion of violence.

"Tybalt, the locals aren't afraid of us yet. Change that!" I barked, setting him loose. My will did more than just release him to the hunt; I pushed him harder, stoking his bloodlust until the discordant drumbeat of his mind sent my head pounding.

Bjor began to spin his axes in quick, circular motions, weaving a pattern of whirling death around himself. I couldn't remember the last time Tybalt had been confronted in such a direct manner, and my ghoul seemed mesmerized by the display, swaying hesitantly just outside the warrior's reach. Tybalt tried to smack at the blades like a cat with a toy, but Bjor leapt forward, a whirlwind of flesh and iron that closed with Tybalt before the ghoul could react. A chip of white flickered off the skeleton; Bjor's axe had taken a finger clean off Tybalt's hand. Then Bjor feinted high with one axe and struck low with the other, shearing the tip off one of Tybalt's ribs.

For the first time I'd ever witnessed, Tybalt retreated, giving ground under the frenzied assault. Bile rose in my throat, panic building as I saw the ghoul falter. If my best killer couldn't fell their champion, then there was little hope that we could fight our way out of this mess.

The one thing that kept the fear at bay was the rhythm of Tybalt's mind: Calm, eager, hungry.

Tybalt leapt back farther, scooping a square of slate from the floor and slinging it at Bjor in one fluid movement. The man sidestepped the projectile with ease, but the people behind him weren't so lucky, and one took the spinning chunk of rock to the face, skull shattering in a fountain of blood. Tybalt gleefully let more tiles fly, and I worried for a moment that the ghoul had finally lost it—if insanity were possible for an animated corpse. He threw tiles at the ceiling, at the floor by Bjor's feet, and at any bystander that caught his eye. One projectile even shot our way, and I turned to see Grah flailing, the shard of stone now jutting from his forehead, the world's most forlorn unicorn. Bjor was kept at a distance by these antics, but the champion was far enough away to continuously dodge the assault, and Tybalt would eventually run out of shit to throw at people. At least the dwellers' excitement had quelled, with a sizable portion of them crouched low to the ground after another bystander had taken a roofing tile to the sternum.

Tiring of the ranged assault, Bjor waited for a lull, then sprinted forward as Tybalt looked around for ammunition, turning his back to the man. Bjor let out a victorious cry, raising his axes high for the deathblow. Then he . . . stumbled. It was the smallest of blunders, just a slight quiver as his foot came down on one of the razor-shards of broken slate that Tybalt had littered the arena with. But . . . It was enough.

Tybalt made a blind dodge, letting the blade pass by as he pirouetted in a tight circle, catching the haft of an axe with one hand and ripping the weapon free. Bjor tried to cancel his momentum and turn to face the ghoul, but Tybalt's axe was already in motion, swinging down into the warrior's shoulder. A meaty thud resounded from the impact, and Bjor's entire arm dropped low, the joint violently dislocated.

The dwellers began to scream in outrage, some stepping forward to save their champion, but they were far too late.

Tybalt wrapped both hands around the broken limb of the kneeling man, then placed one foot on Bjor's head and *pulled*. With a hideous squelch, the arm ripped free. Tybalt held his trophy aloft in silent exaltation, then turned to finish his foe. Bjor grinned widely, teeth cracked and stained, then spat a gob of bloody phlegm across the ghoul's feet. Tybalt seemed to pause for a moment as if he were acknowledging the warrior. Then he bludgeoned Bjor across the face with his own arm, sending him tumbling to the blood-soaked stones. Then Tybalt hit him again . . . and again.

Bjor must have been dead from the blood loss by that point, but the attack made an impression, and even the most vengeful dwellers were momentarily paralyzed by the brutality.

"Fuckin' leg it!" I hollered, bolting forward with my ghouls thudding along behind me, angling towards what I hoped was the right tunnel out of this underworld pit.

Between the death of their champion and our crazed charge, the dwellers ahead broke and ran even as the ones behind us roared and charged. I turned to usher my team into the tunnel, then nocked an arrow as I pulled Tybalt back to us. The idiot was just standing there, apparently prepared to kill every living thing in the chamber, spinning his new weapon in a grisly parody of Bjor's attacks, spattering himself with flecks of blood from the severed limb. Coaxing the ghoul to abandon the slaughter and return to us required a herculean effort that I might not have managed if not fueled by terror of imminent death. Reluctantly, he rejoined the group but made no effort to help carry the sled.

"Leave that damned thing and help!" I ordered, noticing that Tybalt was *still* carrying around that severed arm. He gave me a pulse of emotion that could only be described as childish petulance, then hurled the arm at our nearest pursuer and lent his strength to the sled as we made our escape. I stopped for a half second to loose an arrow into the mob, grunting in pain as my injured arm protested, then turned to chase after my team as they rounded a corner. The tunnel ahead narrowed to a diagonal oval, worn smooth by some ancient subterranean river. Angling the *Ridgerunner* to squeeze through the gap took time, and the crowd was closing the distance at a worrying pace. The arrows helped to stall our pursuers, as every dweller wanted to chase us, but none wanted to be the first to round the corner. I kept them pinned at the bend, allowing my team to work until I reached out for another arrow and found the quiver empty. One dweller poked his head around the corner, then another, until their anger overpowered their fear, and the whole mob came thundering towards us.

With a scrape of metal runner on stone, we were through, and I let a sigh of relief slip as the dwellers howled in frustration. We were going to make it. It'd be damn close, but if the map was right, they wouldn't be able to close the gap before we reached the surface. Then the *Ridgerunner* lurched to a stop so abruptly that I nearly collided with the back of the sled.

"King, we need to move!" I barked at him, running forward to see what the holdup was.

A slab of ice had given way some time in the distant past, sliding downward into our path and cutting the width of the tunnel by a third.

It was too narrow, I knew it was too narrow, but we had to try. My team began to tilt our sled again, pushing flush to the curve of the far wall as we tried to slip around the obstacle. For a moment, there was hope, then the balefire brazier clipped the icefall, bringing us to a halt with a shower of pulverized ice. I dove into the back and upended my toolbox, scattering its contents everywhere. The hammer was easy to find, though, and a moment later, I'd tossed it to Scramble. He was fast and strong; with proper motivation, he could chip off the ice around the brazier in half a minute.

But we didn't have that long. It would be maybe ten seconds before the dwellers flooded into the gap we'd just cleared. That narrowing of the tunnel would have been a perfect choke point if I had anything left to throw at them, any weapon left to use. My team was making me proud, though; Scramble hanging from the ceiling, scattering chunks of ice with every hammer blow. My skellies pushed while the fawns lifted, their minds still sharp enough to understand the angle we needed to fit through. Even Craven was lending a hand; the roaring crowd had pushed him into a frenzy, and he was smashing at the ice with a rock, moving even faster than Scramble. Almost everyone had their part to play.

And then I knew what I had to do. No time for hesitation, not a second to spare for even the shortest of goodbyes.

There was always a way out. You just had to be willing to pay the cost.

I projected my will through the balefire and drew Grah's attention to our pursuers, stoking his hunger into an insatiable craving that could not be ignored. I allowed myself a single glance as he ran past me, taking in his balding head, his filthy gambeson, committing to memory as much of him as I could in that singular moment. And, lest I ever forget, his voice.

"GRRAAAHHHH!!!!" The ghoul cheered, careening recklessly down the tunnel, falling, tumbling, and bouncing back to his feet, building momentum all the while.

Crack! A chunk of ice fell from the wall, sliding off the roof of the sled to shatter on the ground.

"PUSH!" I shouted, planting my feet and extending my hands in either direction as if shoving against two enormous weights. My team pushed harder; Grah ran faster.

The first of the dwellers had cleared the chokepoint but began to backpedal frantically at the sight of Grah barreling toward them. They tried to retreat even as their compatriots pushed forward, still unaware of the danger.

Grah slipped his shield on, though the panicked volley of axes and spears sailed overhead, the throwers misjudging his speed. He cried out again, the echoing war cry informing everyone in the tunnels that the hunters had become the hunted.

"GRAHglmaGLAGbaKAA!"

The ground slanted downward in the last two meters of his charge, but Grah leapt from the top, and the few fighters who had managed to brace spears to meet him panicked as the ghoul sailed overhead, bellyflopping into the mass of people trying to push through the gap.

Skkrrttt! The *Ridgerunner* screeched as if in pain, the frontmost tines of her brazier bending against the unyielding ice. Scramble continued to hammer away, now perilously close to the flames. One slip and the fire would consume him, but I needed him at work and had to put my faith in his preternatural dexterity.

CRACK! A huge chunk of ice gave way, nearly flattening Craven. But it was enough. With one last screech of protesting metal, the *Ridgerunner* slid through, frenzied ghoul strength propelling it into the snow-covered passage beyond.

"GRAAH!"

I turned towards Grah, looking down at him one final time.

So great was the press of bodies that he seemed to stand waist-deep in them, ripping and clawing with wild abandon. A young man tried to break from the crowd and continue the pursuit, but Grah grabbed him by a handful of dreadlocks and yanked him back into the scrum, clamping rotted teeth down on his exposed neck. Another tried to wrench her compatriot away and caught the rim of a shield across the face for her troubles. There were cries of pain, screams of fear and anger, and above it all:

"GGRRAAHHH!"

Then an axe fell across his exposed back, splitting layers of fabric and knocking him forward. Another plunged a knife into his side, over and over and over again, until it punched through, piercing a lung and silencing his battle cry. And still, he fought, even as they dragged him down, clawing and kicking and biting, biting, biting.

The balefire light was fading as I chased after my team, the connection between Grah and me growing tenuous. I didn't see the blow that severed his arm but could feel it through the bond, a disturbance as his essence separated into two separate physical boundaries. Then a leg, and after that, his neck. It was like listening to a musician frantically trying to finish his solo, even as the crowd hacked his piano to pieces. We rounded a corner, and the passage behind us was cast into darkness.

Grah, the enthusiastic, irrepressible, cacophonous fool, had been silenced.

The path beyond cut through the bottom of a deep crevasse. Flakes of snow swirled down to blanket the floor, along with a gust of fresh air that tasted sweeter than any breath I'd ever taken. We pressed on as the dwellers sprinted after us, trying to shorten the lead that Grah had won us. In that final stretch, with a circle of light growing brighter ahead, even I grabbed onto the *Ridgerunner*, willing to take the pain coursing through my injured body if my strength could make even the smallest difference.

Then we were free, bursting out onto the surface and straight into the teeth of a whiteout snowstorm. We lowered the sled and shifted from carrying to pushing. Ghouls tripped, fell, then stumbled back into place as I spurred them on. As the snow reduced everything to a white blur, I took one last look behind us, the cave, a single circle of darkness marring the white blanket. It was packed full of gaunt figures, their eyes locked on us until they faded from view.

XXIV

Pushing a sled along was a far harder task than pulling one. When my team led, the sled would glide along in their wake and naturally correct course to follow the ghouls. Pushing meant that it was a constant fight to keep the sled on course as it shifted and wandered across the snow. At long last, I called a halt, ordering the ghouls to ease the sled to a stop while I rushed around to lay out the gangline and other bits of harness that I'd packed up before entering the glacier. The whirling snow made it feel as if the world were closing in on us, with visibility dropping down to maybe a few dozen meters. This was exacerbated by the coming nightfall, the walls of white around us shading towards a steel gray as the light faded. I'd traded my bow and empty quiver for the coalblade; it may have lacked any magical power against living people, but those sharp teeth could still deal grievous wounds if it came to that. Dark shapes seemed to flit past in the corner of my sight, keeping me on edge. Maybe they were just animals or, even more likely, tricks of the failing light. But maybe they were the dwellers below, coming after me to finish the hunt. But they would not take me now, not after they'd already taken Grah. The tunnels might be theirs, but the frigid wastes above were *mine*.

"King! No way we're finding the trail again in this mess!" I shouted over the howling wind once everyone was harnessed up. "We're not sticking around here, though. North! North as fast as you can!"

My fear and anger flowed into the ghouls, galvanizing them to move. I ran beside them for a few minutes, trying to spot any pursuit, but the conditions had brought visibility down to almost nothing. Eventually, I had to admit that the exercise was pointless and pulled myself up into the cab. I had nothing to guide me but a compass and a vague idea of our position on the map, though even that became moot once night fully set in a short time later. Right now, it was all about putting the kilometers between us and that cave, and my team set to the task with gusto. Inside the sled, the world seemed even smaller, the flakes of snow-stained purple by the balefire swirling and curving around my windscreen. We stopped for a moment sometime past midnight, but I refused to make camp yet. Our tracks were clearly visible, trailing out into the white behind us, a stampede of ghoul feet and the double lines of the sled's metal runners. I couldn't do much about that, but I could do something about the blazing beacon of purple light atop the sled, which would give away our position for a fair distance, even in the howling storm.

From my gear pile, I pulled out a stack of square metal sheets, each as long as my forearm. These sheets would assemble to form a set of blinders around my balefire brazier, cutting off the light everywhere but directly ahead. The metal was light and thin, and it didn't take much effort to haul the stack up to the top of my sled, right under the mount for my brazier. Trying to set the pieces in place with my one good arm was tough, and my thick gloves made the task even more difficult, but handling metal with bare skin at these temperatures was a recipe for severe frostbite. Between that and the howling wind, the installation was a laborious process. I pushed through the discomfort, though, clipping the sheets into grooves in the mount, slowly encircling the blazing purple flame in metal. The plate on top had a small hole that stretched upward like a chimney to let as little light escape as possible. It wasn't perfect, but the sacred flame could never be fully covered, another quirk of the magic that infused it. The front portion was left unobstructed, allowing a wedge of purple to shine forward like a spotlight across my team. This configuration would make us drastically harder to spot at a distance, but that increased stealth came with its own drawbacks. The blinders meant that I could no longer sense or exert control over any ghouls that attacked us from our blind spots. It generally wasn't worth the trade-off, but I had planned to get them set up as we closed in on Skyroost to avoid detection, and the chance that we were now being pursued solidified that decision.

Once the blinders were in place, we started moving once again, though I did slow the team down to a steady jog as night fell. With visibility so low, it would be too easy to tumble into a crevasse or onto a patch of thin ice if we were moving at full speed. The falling flakes were lit by the flame and streaked past my windscreen like purple comets in the dark. During this downtime, I took a moment to care for my wound, reapplying more healing salve and re-wrapping it securely: the rigors of the day had cracked the newly formed scab and sent blood dripping down my arm. It would take the skills of a professional healer to get me on the path to recovery, but for now, there was little I could do except try to keep infection from taking root. Hopefully, there were still healers alive in Skyroost who could help.

Best I could guess, we had missed the frozen lake entirely, our due north sprint taking us through the woods that bordered it instead. Lucky for us, the mountains on our path ahead should funnel us inward, so being a few kilometers east or west of our planned course wouldn't be too problematic. So, we pushed on, me giving general directions but letting King plot our course from moment to moment. His echoes ran deep with knowledge of forest paths and wilderness survival, and I trusted him to find a route onward. I forced down a cold dinner, along with a cup of water dosed with a bitter powder. The powder couldn't hold a candle to coffee but would give me a boost of energy that should keep me alert for a while. That wakefulness came with a nasty case of anxious jitters, though, and I spent the next few hours drumming my fingers across the dashboard, jumping at flickers in the night.

My mind kept returning to that first dweller and the tugging sensation in my hand as the coalblade's teeth dragged across his throat. Seeing the blood pulse from those ragged wounds, in time, with his fading heartbeat.

I'd been forced to take a life before, but this one ... it just felt so horrific. I had killed those bandits, after all, the ghouls were my weapons, and I bore the same responsibility as if I had slain those people with a sword. But having my attacker so close, feeling him drag me to the ground, my panic, his weight, the sound he made as he died. That was going to stick with me for a bit.

With the blinders on, the view to the sides of the sled was nothing but darkness, and the inability to see a threat approaching further intensified my paranoia. Despite my body being wound tighter than a counterfeit clock, the night passed quietly. In the wee hours of the morning, I called a stop, admitting to myself that all the energy powder in the world couldn't keep you alert forever. We'd made solid progress, and I felt confident that, even if the dwellers had been following our tracks, there was no way they could match the distance we'd covered running through the night.

As the forest gave way to mountains, we found a shallow depression in the earth that would hopefully hide us from prying eyes. I threw together the campsite with less order than I'd normally tolerate, then took a deep breath, letting some of the tension ease out of my muscles. As if sensing my weakness, the events of the day came back to me in a rush, jumping me like a predator I'd momentarily turned my back on. The *Ridgerunner* was hurt, and I didn't yet know how serious her injuries were. I was aching too, the escape continuing to wear down my already battered body.

And my team had lost a member. I tried to look at that fact coldly, clinically, considering what we would lose in speed and how I could react differently if we were attacked again . . . .

Grah . . .

I'd made that classic mistake, the one every courier swore they would never make. My ghouls were just animated bones, no more alive than a wagon wheel or a ship's sail. They weren't . . . people, and their "personalities" were nothing but echoes, harmonies playing on long after the instruments lay silent.

All the rationalization in the world didn't alleviate the guilt, though, and it still felt like I'd sent a friend off to die.

There were a dozen tasks to attend to, but I just couldn't. My brain was fogged with fatigue, and my hands shook too much for anything more complex than drawing the tarp down to shelter my team.

In the corner of my mind, a timpani drumbeat, almost imperceptible, but rising now, faster, louder.

"No!" I shouted, spinning around as Tybalt's hands reached for my neck.

He hesitated for a moment as my willpower flowed over him, and I took the opening. One of my hands twined into his ribcage and pulled, causing him to stoop low enough for me to wrap my other hand around his throat and slam him into the side of the sled.

"Come on! DO IT!" I yelled, slamming him into the sled again. His fist came up to retaliate, but I froze it with a thought. The ghoul looked away in submission, feeling the situation turn against it.

"Look at me." Tybalt didn't. I hit him, slapping him across the pale dome of his skull with an open hand.

"LOOK. AT. ME!" I snarled, hitting him again, then yanking on his chin to pull his gaze up.

"Thought today would be the day, huh?" I shouted, barely recognizing my own voice. I projected my will into his mind, smothering him, forced the ghoul to open its jaw unnaturally wide, then stuck two fingers into the shocked creature's mouth. His attention became fixed on my bare hand, mere centimeters from that fatal bite.

"I'm right here, Tybalt. One bite and I'm a goner. Just bite down, bite down, and you win. COME ON!"

And oh, did he want to. The battle had soaked his rhythm in bloodshed. He was mad with it, a berserker just craving the next kill. And I was tired and hurt . . . and . . . sad, so profoundly sad.

But I was still the stronger.

"Remember this, get it through that empty skull. Remember that, on your best day, you're just my attack dog. And on my worst day? Well, you're still my bitch."

I heaved the ghoul to the ground, then climbed up into the sled. That was idiotic and suicidally risky. One scratch of those teeth, and I'd be in for a backwoods amputation. Stupid, stupid, stupid.

The tears didn't start until I tried to unbutton my coat with clumsy fingers: Failing at that last simple task shattered the dam that held the emotional deluge at bay.

Sleep should have set upon me in an instant, but it was proving elusive. I was jittery, overtired, in unfamiliar territory, and any sense of confidence I had held was left in that cave. Finally, I gave in and sought comfort. My hand quested out from under the covers, moving by memory to retrieve a small, soft shape from a nearby cupboard. My dad had given me Rune, a small stuffed fox, when I was born, and she had never been far from me since. There were good memories there. Sitting by the fire, watching my mom sew up some rip that Rune had sustained on one of our adventures. She always treated it seriously, as if it were a live patient in her care. That solemnity mattered greatly to a small child when their favorite companion was injured. I'd have to take some time off and visit Mom after this was all over; it had been too long. I had outgrown Rune years ago, and she spent most of her days packed carefully away in her cupboard. But, when those hard nights found me, her familiar weight still gave me comfort in the dark.

The gods must have decided to cut me a break since I managed to avoid oversleeping, waking up around noon the following day. Before departing, I had to wade through a mountain of chores; some I could sheepishly admit should have been done when we stopped the night before, exhaustion be damned. There were minor repairs of the sled and harnesses to be seen to, as well as reorganizing the gangline to account for our missing teammate. King would still be the lead, but then Bonk would follow behind him alone. He was likely older than Amelia, but I wanted his experience up front. Then it'd be pairs; Amelia and Craven, Heist and Scramble, then Champ and Tybalt. Craven did *not* look happy to be paired with Amelia and began to shy away. Before he could even flinch, she smacked him upside the head with surprising strength. After that, Craven was still scared of her, but he was even more scared of raising her ire, so he stayed in line.

At least I could treat myself to a big lunch; with us so close to Sky-roost, I was confident that I had ample food supplies for the remainder of the journey. Even with everything that needed doing, I was soon ready to depart, eagerness lending a spring to my tired step. If all went well, we should catch sight of our destination on the horizon before we stopped tonight. The weather had passed, and the sun shone brightly in a cloudless sky, the light almost blinding against the snow. I fetched a small tin from the back and smeared my hands and the lower half of my face with a liberal coating of the paste stored inside. My goggles protected my eyes, but the combination of sunlight, cold, and wind would wear down any exposed skin if I weren't proactive about protection. The snowfall had filled in last night's tracks to a degree, though the path we cut today would stand out clearly in the fresh powder.

"No use worrying over what we can't change, though," I muttered to myself, spurring my team on. They churned through the new snow, throwing it off in either direction like the bow wave of a ship. It was an awesome sight, bare-bones pulling with the strength of draft horses, but it did little to stoke my confidence after the blows I had taken during this trip.

We had to wander a bit to get our bearings but soon came across a tall hill with a decent view of our surroundings. It seemed that we had deviated a few kilometers in our blind escape last night, but nothing that would delay us too heavily today. If my reckoning was right, we were just on the edge of that bear-marked forest, the mountains funneling us into a thin valley before widening out to reveal the cluster of mountains that Skyroost perched upon. Any brown bears this far north should be sleeping in their dens, but any shred of optimism I'd had for this trip had long since been abandoned. With the way my luck was going, the bears will have woken early and constructed a toll booth, charging me thirty moons and two salmon as payment to pass.

The image brought a reluctant smile to my lips, and I spent the next hour or so sketching out the absurd scene. I was just starting the process of giving the bear a matching hat and vest when I felt a mental pulse from King up front. He'd begun to slow the team, clearly noticing something on the path ahead. I leaned out the door and stood to get a better view, seeing fresh markings in the snow, crossing our path as we joined up with an intersecting trail. My team slowed to a stop as I hopped off, jogging up beside King to examine the tracks.

"Looks like another sled," I muttered to my team leader, squatting down to get a closer look. "I'd guess a skimmer from how close together the tracks are, though their team is all over the place...."

Instead of an orderly row of footprints, the snow was churned across the entire width of the path, with various indentations showing where ghouls had stumbled and fallen. Either this courier had no control over their team, or they'd been pursued by a group of wild ghouls that had trampled the fresh powder during their pursuit. Either way, we would have to be careful moving forward. We were heading in the same direction as our mysterious track-makers, so I put my art supplies away and kept a careful eye on the path ahead. I highly doubted that we would catch up to whoever had made the tracks, but there were enough unanswered questions surrounding Skyroost to keep me on edge. I was also very aware that the bandits who had abducted Blondie must have had some destination in mind as they transported him northward. The tracks continued as we pushed on, drawing ever closer to that thin valley passage that opened up to Skyroost. The bandit ambush weighed on my mind; if you were going to pick a point to attack travelers, you couldn't ask for a better location than this funneling valley, though I hoped that this route was too far from the main road to be watched.

Maybe the person we were following had the same worry since

they swerved off the trail a few moments later, pushing uphill to hug the cliff wall. After a moment of deliberation, I decided to follow them, though my larger sled would have a slightly harder time navigating the wooded terrain. Even though I didn't know who I was following, I hoped that taking their route meant that I wouldn't run into them by accident and that they would stumble into any hidden danger ahead before we did. The incline and deep snow made for slow going, but soon enough, we were approaching a high bluff that would give a commanding view of the terrain. But that also meant that it would give anyone nearby who might be watching a clear view of us. With that in mind, I went forward alone, donning my snowshoes to avoid sinking into the soft powder. After about thirty seconds, I remembered something and swore, then shuffled back to my cab to retrieve my spyglass. I'd almost forgotten about it because, like most scientific instruments, it was as expensive as it was fragile. The tool rarely emerged from its case, but this seemed like a time when bringing it along might be worth the risk. Snowshoeing was demanding work when I was uninjured, and my legs were already starting to burn as I waded up the last few meters. The cliff fell away to reveal a spectacular panorama of the forest below, as well as my first glimpse of Skyroost.

The city was burning.

I could see the towers in the distance, peeking up from the far side of a U-shaped set of mountains, though these buildings were dwarfed by the massive columns of white smoke that rose beyond them. From the direction of our approach, I could only see the back of the city where it abutted a sheer cliff drop; the bulk of the settlement was built into the side of the sloping valley beyond. Whatever chaos might be occurring within the walls, it would have to wait until we could find a better vantage. One positive I could take from it was that the columns of smoke were a light grey color, almost white; white smoke meant water, so hopefully, the fires were well under control. I'd seen black smoke in my travels before, and it had always meant that buildings were burning unchecked.

Removing the spyglass from my eye brought a new discovery, drawing my attention back to the surrounding forest. There was a light moving through the trees below my vantage point, casting a greenish glow that filtered up through the evergreens.

"Uuuugghhh . . . Just walk away. Leave it be, Winona. It's just an odd green will-o'-wisp moving through an empty forest. It couldn't possibly be important."

I made it halfway back to my sled before I gave in, cursed quietly, then began tromping down the hill toward the flame.

Going was slow, snowshoes not being known for either speed or stealth. The crunching of snow felt deafening in the dead silence of the wintry wood, and I frequently paused, squatting down low and listening for any sound out of place. As I drew closer, it became clear that this light was no folk tale wisp, like the ghost lights that haunted some marshes of the Empire. I could hear movement ahead, snow-crunching footsteps that were suddenly drowned out by the bellowing roar of an irate bear.

The intensity of that primal call sent a spark of fear through my stomach, though I pushed the feeling aside and used the last echoes of the noise to cover the sound of my approach. The light grew brighter as the trees thinned, and I found myself at the edge of a wide forest glade, hiding underneath the lowest boughs of a snow-laden pine. Through the branches, I witnessed a hunt taking place. Four ghouls harried a massive bear, surrounding it on all sides and prodding at it with spears. A man, tall and pale, stood opposite me at the far end of the glade, watching the fighting, even though the angle unsettlingly made it look like he was staring right at my hiding spot. In one hand, he held a long staff planted in the snow, topped with a circular iron brazier. A fire glowed from within . . . A green fire. It was so strange, so out of place, that it took my mind a moment to comprehend.

There was a sudden second when I thought I was going to be sick. Then I managed to push the feeling back down. Despite my status in the church, I never thought of myself as particularly pious. But this . . . this was *heresy*, heresy of the highest order. The balefire's light was the one thing that had allowed us to survive the near extinction of our species, to hold off the endless hordes of risen dead while humanity clawed its way back from the brink. This green flame felt like a perversion, sputtering and spitting out sparks at seemingly random intervals. The man who held the torch seemed indifferent to the volatile flame, though. He was dressed strangely for the cold as well, wearing a simple animal skin vest with the fur still on it, and didn't even flinch as emerald sparks landed on the bare skin of his exposed arm.

An attacking ghoul stepped a bit too close, and the bear lashed out, sinking claws into the meat of its thigh and yanking it into range of the bear's crushing jaws. I could hear the audible crunch as the bear bit down on the ghoul's ribcage, knocking another attacker to the ground as it shook its head from side to side. This prey couldn't be killed so easily, and the ghoul in its mouth continued to scratch and scrabble at the bear's eyes even as its own bones splintered and broke.

A few moments more and the bear had taken all the punishment it could endure, dropping the broken ghoul to the ground and bolting away into the trees, passing so close to my hiding place that I felt the vibration of its heavy footfalls through the ground. The ghouls gave chase, hissing and grunting as they trudged after it through the heavy snow. The pale man followed, striding after them with the torch held high. Flickers of green light filtered through the branches of my hiding spot, and I froze. The light flashed across my face, and I felt . . . nothing.

No connection to the ghouls, no sense of their minds, nothing. I realized then that I hadn't felt any sort of power since I first saw the flame. It might as well have been a mundane torch for all I could glean from it. As the man chased after the ghouls, I turned to watch him and almost cried out as his movement revealed the gaping head wound that had caved in the back of the man's skull. It was a fatal wound, period. A chunk of flesh and bone was simply gone, carved away to reveal rotting gray matter underneath. This was no man. This was a ghoul, leading his undead brethren as confidently as any courier. He disappeared a moment later, chasing after the bear with long, loping strides. Once they were out of sight, I allowed myself to breathe again, leaning back against the tree trunk as I let my racing heart slow.

"What the actual fuck," I whispered to myself, putting my head in my hands.

The sight of that green flame had been terrifying enough, but the implications that settled on me after the group departed were just as dire. Those ghouls had operated in sync, showing far more cooperation than wild ghouls would have. A wild group didn't have the restraint to hunt like that anyway. You would need a living person with balefire to impart that level of skill. But there was no person, and no balefire, just another ghoul leading them. I had no idea what effect that green fire had on the creatures, but the evidence seemed to point to only one conclusion; it made these ghouls smart, smart enough to coordinate their attacks and act in concert without a human guiding them. Smart enough to ... what? To think, to communicate, to feel even?

The hike back to my sled was slow going and gave me far too much time to think. Did the fire truly make these ghouls smart? Or were they always smart, and the fire just ... woke them up? My line of conjecture became increasingly ludicrous as I trudged back, panic beginning to overtake me. Maybe the flame strengthened their echoes so that it merely seemed like they were smarter. Maybe it instilled them with some foreign intelligence. Maybe it called their souls back to inhabit their—

I cut that line of thought off as soon as it surfaced. Letting my thoughts go down that road was dangerous. Ghouls were nothing but animated meat, and the souls they once held had long since departed beyond the veil, a journey that nothing could return from. Still, the discovery had shifted something in me, and I looked at my crew with new eyes when I made it back to the sled. What would happen to my ghouls if that green light fell upon them? And how did this tie back into the skull coins and whatever was going on at Skyroost? Every discovery just seemed to raise more questions. It was quite the mystery, but it was also way above my pay grade. I intended to deliver this medicine, do the bare minimum of snooping to satisfy the bishop's curiosity, then get out of town before this adventure could go any more sideways than it already had.

My team started forward again, but I remained on foot for the moment, trudging along ahead just inside the balefire's range. It was supremely tempting to rush ahead at a sprint, putting as much distance as we could between us and the green flame ghouls, but I was more worried about missing any signs of their passing. After an hour of tromping along, there was still no sign of them, and I had to admit that they were either behind us or had taken a different path out of the forest. All that was left between us and the Skyroost mountains was a set of rolling hills, undulating in lines like ocean waves growing in height. These foothills were thinly forested, and we would be visible every time we crested a hill, so speed would likely benefit us more than stealth. With that in mind, I re-boarded my sled and gave King the order to get us moving at our best speed through the deep snow. The sky was beginning to darken, and I wanted to be flush against the mountain before we stopped for the night. This far north, the snow could pile up to truly monstrous depths, but it was here in the harshest conditions where ghouls proved themselves superior to any other form of transportation. Where horses or dogs would freeze, sink, or tire, the ghouls would push on through, crawling onward even when they sank down to their hips in the powdery snow.

There was little for me to do but keep an eye out and spur my team on, though I made sure we took every hilltop at an angle, riding parallel to the ridge before ducking into the next valley. It would leave us visible for longer but also keep our hooded balefire flame from flashing up at the mountain every time we crested the next hill. If the bandits had scouts on the mountainside, I planned to make spotting our approach as difficult as possible for them. I stopped for the night in a small depression at the base of the cliff. This low, we could still find the cover of trees, clustering around the shore of a frozen pond. From here to the mountain itself, it was just open ground and scree, the piles of fallen rock that collected at the base of mountain cliffs.

Here we made camp and offloaded most of my supplies. Tomorrow would be a sprint to the finish; our precious medicine was still warm; I'd either deliver it tomorrow or fall victim to whatever mystery tied this all together. Either way, any extra weight would just slow me down, especially now that we were one ghoul down.

With that in mind, I set my crew to work.

First, I pulled off part of the brazier blinder, creating a circle of balefire light to work in; I would set it back in place tomorrow, though, in case those ghouls or others like them were patrolling the area. Next, Tybalt and Champ dug a pit in the snow, which we lined with a tarp and began filling with clothing, extra rations, and other nonessentials. If it wasn't going to be of use tomorrow, it went in the hole. I snowshoed another fifty or so yards, then had Champ dig another, smaller hole. Into this went a watertight package containing nonessential maps, navigational equipment, a few personal effects, and Foss's pistol. I took care to disguise the path on my way back, as much as one could in deep snow; even if the bandits found my other gear, I didn't want to risk aiding them further by letting them uncover that hidden information.

With all that done, the *Ridgerunner* looked a bit forlorn, sitting there like a skeletonized husk of its former self. But she would be light, and she would be damn fast. I checked my sled, my team, and then my own wound before settling down for dinner. Afterward, I reclined against the cab of my sled, then pulled out the coalblade for inspection as an afterthought. I'd given that cave dweller quite a hefty whack and discovered that the weapon hadn't escaped unscathed. One of the lower blades had become loose in its housing, and I fiddled with it like a child with a loose tooth until the square of obsidian glass popped out into my hand.

"Ahh ... oops," I muttered, looking around guiltily. Amelia was watching me from a nearby tree, and I flipped her a rude hand gesture before returning to my work.

With a bit of glue, I could probably secure the blade back in place, but another idea occurred to me as I examined the weapon. I'd lost this chunk off the very bottom of the club, right near the handle; given that the rest of the weapon was intact, this missing blade would do little to reduce its effectiveness. But it did present an opportunity. We hadn't covered our supply stash yet, and I dove back in with gusto, extracting bits of wood, glue, and leather cord from a chest. I was no craftsman, so the end result favored function over form, but it didn't need to be pretty to do its job. Splitting a length of hardwood at one end, I created a fork that the little blade fit snuggly into. A liberal application of glue and wrapped cord left me with a sort of crude mini cleaver the length of a shaving razor. This coalknife wouldn't do much to a man, but if the coalblade was any indicator, even a shallow cut would be deadly to a ghoul. That was assuming I hadn't ruined its magical properties the moment I'd yanked it from its housing, of course. Either way, it'd be a weapon of last resort, wrapped in cloth and secured against the small of my back with a thin leather belt.

With nothing productive left to do, the trepidation settled in. Even if tomorrow went off without a hitch, I'd still find myself in some damn risky situations and would likely need to think and move at a rapid pace. That meant getting a good night's sleep, and even Rune could not quell the nervous energy churning in my gut. Reluctantly, I retrieved my father's briarwood pipe and packed it with pyreweed. Coaxing the pipe to light took a moment, as I was out of practice, but soon I had a little spark twinkling in the bowl and aromatic smoke wafting up. That first puff always made me hack and cough, but the soothing effect of the herb soon took over, filling me with a benign, calming warmth. I kept the pipe with me, pulling long draws from it as I did my last nightly checks around camp. When it was time for bed, I was warm, comfortable, clutching my little fox, and high as a kite. Sleep took me the moment my head hit the pillow.

XXV

———

The longer you spend in the wild, the more it wears you down. It's a slow assault that tires you out, dulls your senses, makes slip-ups more common and more costly. Even the few hard days since the outpost were enough of a strain for the effects to be felt. So, when I woke up after a night of deep, restful sleep, the difference was immediately apparent. I felt mentally sharper now, more present than I had been before, and less apt to let my mind wander. Given the implications of the green flame, I was glad to have the renewed lucidity calming my thoughts. My body felt renewed as well, though my arm still ached, and my bruises had yet to fade. Checking the wound, I saw that it had begun to heal, though the skin around it was starting to turn hot and red with infection. It would be mended enough to get me through today, though, and I felt confident that I could use my arm at full strength if I didn't mind cracking the scab open again.

My stomach felt a bit queasy from the pyreweed, but I remedied that with a hearty breakfast pulled from my remaining supplies. Once my meal was done, I arranged the rest of the gear in the pit, then piled snow on top. There was no way to completely disguise our campsite, but with some luck, our hidden cache would look like just another pile of snow to anyone tailing us. I felt a bit paranoid with the extent I had gone to but reminded myself that whether it was guardsmen, bandits, or those green flame ghouls, there were plenty of groups that could have stumbled across our tracks in the snow and even now could be closing in on our position. But if they wanted to catch us, we were about to make the chase far more difficult. The range of mountains curved in a broad "U" shape, and the road to Skyroost curved around the mountains and entered a valley on the opposite side, where a long field sloped up to the gates of the city. That would be the first place any prying eyes would watch, so we instead pressed inward from the opposite side, moving towards the mountain itself. Walls of rock rose around us as we left the safety of the trees and trekked upwards toward the base of the massive vertical cliff that dominated this side of the mountain. Piles of scree were everywhere, but after a bit of searching, I found us a clear spot where the path simply ended in a sheer wall of grey stone.

I stepped out, took one last deep breath to calm myself, then triple-checked everything, paying special attention to where the gangline connected to the sled. After I finished, I had to resist to urge to go back and quadruple-check. But there was something . . . off about the *Ridgerunner*. Nothing major, or else I would have noticed it before now, but I knew every centimeter of her and couldn't shake the sub-conscious nagging that some aspect was out of place. It took another slow revolution of my sled before I spotted the fault, a fist-sized stain right at the bottom edge of the crate. That itself wasn't surprising; we had taken a few bumps, and a small amount of water was bound to seep into the wood through those scratches, but this was different. Instead of a darker brown that I would associate with water damage, this stain was ink-black and sickly looking. First, I checked around the edges of the crate, but nothing was spilled there to explain the stain. With growing trepidation, I flipped the lid of the crate open.

A sickening vapor issued forth from inside, burning my nose and sending me into a coughing fit. Tilting my head away, I stole a few gulps of fresh air until the fumes had diffused enough to be bearable and pulled my goggles down to give my eyes some protection. The interior of the crate looked untouched, but clearly, something was amiss. Another wave of the miasma spilled out as I opened the inner case, so potent that I was forced to toss the top aside and retreat to a safe distance while it aired out. Then I climbed back up and peered inside, eager to unravel this mystery.

The battery had broken . . .

It was difficult to tell even looking straight at it, but the damage was obvious when I gently lifted one side of it with a gloved hand. The ceramic vessel had cracked at some point, a mere hairline fracture down one side. But it had been enough to let the acid inside begin to seep out, staining the bottom of the compartment black. I was certain that if I extracted the inner case, I would find a mass of soaked fabric and affected wood mirroring the damage I had seen outside. For a moment, I just stared at it, wondering what to do. My mechanical knowledge was topical at best, and I had as much chance of repairing the battery as I did of conducting surgery . . . .

"The medicine!" I hissed in a panic, looking over at the metal box sitting in its cradle like the smallest child of a nesting doll. I ripped off a glove and pressed my bare hand to the metal, all fear of electrocution long forgotten.

It felt cold, too cold? Or maybe my warm hand just made the metal feel chilly by comparison?

I slammed the top back on the case before any more heat could escape, then closed the crate and tightened the straps securing it to my sled. I couldn't do anything about that now. Either the medicine would survive, or it wouldn't. All I could do was pick up the pace and get this stuff where it needed to go.

"OK, boys . . . let's climb!" I urged my crew on, steering them directly into the sheer wall. King approached it first and lifted his head to methodically scan the rock, his practiced gaze taking in the entirety of the vertical surface. After a moment of consideration, he lifted a hand and slid it into a vertical crack in the cliff, pulling himself up onto the wall. As he began his slow ascent, the line drew taught, and the rest of the team began to follow. Bonk was next and an old hand at this by now, but I had my worries about Amelia. She was new to climbing with a team, even if she had already shown the dexterity of a mountain goat, though I was banking on her fawn cleverness to help her adapt. She proved my fears unfounded, though, scaling the wall with her climbing hook as if she had been doing it all her life. These first few members of my crew were vital, as it was the youngest ghouls who still retained the spark of intelligence necessary to chart a viable path up the mountain. While my leaders provided the brains, the rest of my team supplied to brawn, lending their undead strength to haul the weight of my sled skyward. The front of the *Ridgerunner* began to lift as Champ and Tybalt started their climb. It was barely perceptible at first, but the angle increased steadily until the sled was tilted back at a forty-five-degree angle. I leaned flat against the back wall, bracing myself for the shift.

"Gods, I hate this part," I muttered, clenching my eyes shut.

The team continued their ascent, taking more and more of the sled's weight. With a final effort, my skellies pulled themselves upward, and my sled was lifted entirely off the ground. There was a metallic clang as the runners swung into the stone, followed by a clunk of shifting gears from my balefire brazier. At some expense, I had installed a custom gimbal, creating a contraption that allowed the brazier to rotate freely as the sled tilted. So, while I was fighting vertigo from hanging in midair, my balefire had rotated to stay upright, not losing a single coal in the process. I peered out the door as we continued to move upward, verifying that the back of my sled was now hanging barely three meters off the ground.

"Drop check!" I called, projecting my orders while bracing myself as firmly as possible.

Tybalt and Champ climbed up farther, getting right behind their comrades ahead. Then they let go, falling back to the end of their tether and dropping my sled in a short freefall that pulled an embarrassingly loud squeak of terror from me. Then the gangline ran out, snapping taut and swinging the sled back into the wall.

I hated, absolutely hated, doing that. But when climbing an un-known route, one or two of my ghouls were bound to slip and fall at some point. If a sudden jerk were going to snap the only cable holding us together, I'd rather find that out at two meters than at two hundred. With that done, the ghouls went back to work, climbing up the rock face and hauling the *Ridgerunner* up the vertical surface. The sheer portion we found ourselves on extended a few dozen meters before shallowing out to an easier but still very terrifying seventy degrees or so. I had taken a good long look at the route through my spyglass yesterday, and we would be climbing at this angle for the next two hours, give or take, crabbing our way around the mountainside to a tiny outcrop, about three-quarters of the way up. Then I could stop, check my team over for damage, and see what the path looked like from there. It would be dangerous and painfully slow, but if any bandit managed to set up an ambush on the near vertical cliffside, they'd earned their payday.

We made steady progress from there, my anxiety ratcheting up in direct correlation to our increasing altitude. This wasn't my first time going vertical with my team but being experienced and being comfortable were two vastly different things. The gangline creaked, the sled swayed, and the ghouls slipped and scrabbled over the rocks. While it was an effective method of avoiding the main roads, it also felt insane, even with dozens of climbs under my belt. Scary as it was, this unique skill also kept me in business, though I was careful to keep my methods a secret. Even without the specifics, clients like Ronny knew I could slip into settlements without ever touching a trail, appearing like a ghost at the city gates just after dawn. Eventually, someone would put together that my ghouls were scaling the cliffs, but until then, I was happy to let the mystery continue to grow. The air of mystique let me add a hefty bonus to my prices after all.

King began to climb at an angle, following a deep seam in the rock, and my sled rattled along behind. I'd have to be careful; any lateral movement could cause the *Ridgerunner* to roll along the cliff side, smashing my brazier and cargo into the unyielding rock.

After about an hour, the incline shifted again, the steep mountainside giving way to sheer rock. From here, we'd be vertical all the way to the outcrop above. Being stuck in my sled somehow made the experience even harder to bear, as the inability to look behind me increased the feeling of height. Heist reached up for another hold, but the stone came loose in her hand, nearly dropping her down on top of Champ. She managed to hold on with her other hand, but the stone clattered down, rebounding off the wall again before smashing into my windshield.

"Godsdammit!" I cursed, shielding my face as the pane cracked violently with the impact. "Watch what the hell you're doing Heist!"

The impact had spiderwebbed cracks across the corner of the glass, though a quick inspection of the area confirmed that the damage hadn't been severe enough to break the glass all the way through. The wind had picked up as we gained altitude as well, buffeting the boxy sides of the sled enough that it began to sway in the sections of cliff where the metal runners no longer touched the wall.

"Oh boy, more things to fix," I muttered to myself, angrily rubbing at the glass as if I could wipe the damage away.

With little else to do, I tried to enjoy the scenery, our unique position giving me a stunning view of the mountains. Birds routinely roosted high on cliff sides, and I spotted a beautiful hawk gliding on the currents nearby. I had a special appreciation for those birds of prey when I was climbing. It had taken me so much time and effort to get the *Ridgerunner* vertical, to drive a sled up a sheer cliff in defiance of gravity. But that hawk did it effortlessly, instinctually, soaring and diving while I fought for every meter. It was humbling, in a way.

Less magnificent than the hawk was the smaller bird raising a racket above, darting around my ghouls. Maybe we had trod on its nest, or it just saw the mass of dead flesh as a free buffet, but eventually, the little nuisance fluttered a bit too close. Bonk casually snatched the unfortunate thing out of the air, regarded it curiously for a moment, then stuffed the entire animal down its rotting gullet. A few sullen feathers drifted down to rest on the windshield, and we were notice-ably free of avian harassment after that. I looked away as small bits of bird meat rained down and caught something out of the corner of my eye. There, near our old campsite, was that a flash of green? I called a halt for a moment, letting the sled settle into stillness so I could get a better look. Nothing. The white snow could cause all sorts of prismatic effects that might trick the eye. But if those green fire ghouls had come across our trail, it wouldn't have been hard to follow . . . I ordered the team to resume the climb; even if those ghouls had found my trail, there was little they could do to stop me now.

It was relatively smooth sailing from there, and we reached the outcropping I'd spotted earlier with no further issues except for the present one, how to maneuver the sled onto the ledge. The solu-tion seemed simple, as my ghouls would have had ample strength to scramble up and over the ledge, towing my sled up behind them. That assumption had nearly cost me my life the first time I had attempted such a traversal, back when I wasn't even sure if a climbing ghoul team was viable. What I'd failed to account for was that, as soon as the first ghoul climbed over that edge, they were blocked from the balefire's light by the ledge itself. They would get up there, then mill around aimlessly while more of the weight was put on the ghouls lower down in the chain. That attempt had almost ended in a fatal fall, and it was one of many lessons I'd learned while pioneering this climbing technique. The solution was an awkward but effective maneuver that involved climbing above the outcrop, then gently lowering the sled and crew down from there. We would have to take it slow to avoid damaging the *Ridgerunner,* but if I kept my ghouls in the balefire light, it should be a routine maneuver.

. . .

Wait.

. . .

I had kept the blinders over my balefire, limiting the light to a narrow cone directly ahead of the sled, like a bullseye lantern.

But as soon as I lowered the rear of my sled onto the ground, that pool of lantern light would tilt down, shifting off of my ghouls and severing my connection to them.

And they'd let go, and we would fall off the wall.

We would still land solidly on the outcrop, but that wasn't my main worry. Maybe the medicine would be damaged, maybe the ghouls would fall *onto* the top of the sled and get consumed by the balefire, or maybe the sled would roll onto its side, spilling the coals out entirely. Any one of those outcomes would be catastrophic.

...

"Dammit!" I shouted, slapping the dashboard so hard that my fingers tingled with pain. "We don't have time for this!"

Stupid, stupid. I should have thought of this on the ground, but I had never climbed with the blinders over my brazier before, and the limitations were just now occurring to me. My imagination conjured an image of medicine vials covered by a layer of frost, then shattering one by one from the brutal cold.

Well, as far as I saw, there were two options. The first was to just continue towards the top, without any idea of what challenges lay further up the wall. We could maybe make it, but there was no way to be certain. The second option was to climb out and shift the blinders by hand, moving a few plates to allow the light to shine out . . . while I hung suspended hundreds of meters above the ground.

Like in moments before, I asked myself a simple question: What would Dad do?

Then I swore loudly and started strapping into my climbing harness. It was a standard rig, a combination of suspenders, belts, and leg loops that I could secure over my cold-weather layers. There was a loop against my hip on either side, to which I secured a pair of short straps that ended in metal hooks. The idea was that if I kept one hook secured to an anchor at all times, I could not possibly fall.

In theory.

That safety net started looking a bit thin as I cracked my door open, getting my first glimpse of the drop below. That first moment came with a rush of vertigo, the yawning distance seeming to twist and expand in my vision. There was an immediate urge to throw myself back into the relative safety of my sled, but I resisted, bracing my arms and holding myself over the drop until my heart slowed its nervous pounding.

I clipped both hooks into a top rail and began the descent down the *Ridgerunner*, taking extra care to ensure some part of me maintained contact with the balefire light. It was funny, I'd hopped into the back of my sled a thousand times, but tilt the whole thing ninety degrees, and I was reduced to slipping and stumbling like a newborn deer. Each little slip sent a bolt of fear through me, causing an involuntary tension that left me clinging desperately to each new handhold. With one hand, I managed to reach up and wiggle one of the metal plates free, letting purple light spill out onto one side of the sled. The wind took it a moment later, though, yanking the thin plate from my hand and sending it spiraling off into the yawning drop. My eyes naturally followed its descent, and I was afflicted with another dose of terrifying vertigo.

"OK, I am done with this," I growled. If I didn't do something soon, the fear would eat me up, and I'd never get off this damn mountain. I had to trust in my gear and trust in my sled, neither of which I could do while clinging to the side like a baby bird too afraid to fly. Slowly, I gathered my feet under me, leaning away and letting the two straps take my weight, then I let one hand fall away from the safety of the rail. I didn't immediately plunge to my death and let the other hand fall away a moment later. Lastly, I reclined back, opening my arms wide and closing my eyes. The wind buffeted my little sled, but my feet were solid, and my ghouls were strong.

The air up here was . . . intoxicatingly pure. It was also thinner this high up and lacked any scent beyond a slight hint of pine and stone. This was . . . this was my realm, one that I laid claim to in a far more visceral way than any duke could. While they drew lines on a map, I fought ghouls. While they planted flags, I climbed heights that they feared to tread. If I were going to die, it wouldn't be here, doing what I did best.

Plus, I was over three hundred meters up, and any fall over a few dozen would have been fatal anyway, so why worry about it?

Newly centered, I began to descend with more confidence, clipping in and out of various rails and gear loops as I scurried around to get a better angle on the panels behind the brazier.

"Damn, Winona, you really jammed these things in there," I grumbled to myself, dangling from the back of my cab while I wiggled the next panel loose. This time, I was ready for the wind and kept the metal plate tucked close to my body as soon as it was pulled free. Instead of trying to climb back up with it in, I decided to tuck it into the straps of my cargo bay; I could get it packed away properly when I was not swaying from the side of a mountain.

Once finished with the last plate, getting back to my cab was a far quicker journey, the promise of perceived safety serving as a powerful motivator as I scurried along.

"Well . . . I'm never doing that again," I grumbled to myself, laying out along the back wall, which now served as the floor. With the blinders removed, I ordered my team onward, directing them up at an angle to get in position above the outcrop. As we climbed up parallel, I took my first look at the space, a jagged recess in the gray rock likely created when a large chunk had broken free years ago. All that was left was a pair of stone slabs, jutting out above and below the recesses like rotten teeth.

If they were teeth, then my team played the part of a tenacious piece of apple skin, squeezing in to wedge ourselves between. Crabbing my entire team sideways was a complicated affair, as it meant my ghouls lower in the chain had to find their own handholds instead of just copying those above. But, with aching slowness and careful coaching, we executed the maneuver, lowering the *Ridgerunner* down onto the outcrop. A few fallen chunks of rock littered the thin platform, but I set Champ to task, and he eagerly pushed the stones off the edge, his simple mind pulsing with contentment.

With that task completed, there was enough room to push the *Ridgerunner* flush against the wall, giving me enough room to step back onto solid ground, stretching my back with a long, satisfied groan. A realization hit me as I looked back at my sled, and I flushed with embarrassment. In my rush to take action, I had performed my brave excursion over open air instead of just shuffling the sled over the outcrop first, which would have reduced the fatal fall to a survivable few meters. Though, if I had fallen there, the sled would have likely fallen on top of me a moment later, so I decided not to dwell on it.

That was easy enough to do, as the view from our perch left me speechless. The panorama that stretched before me was a perfect moment of contrast, the vibrant blue of the afternoon sky meshing with the white snow and gray crags. I'd seen the Duke's oil paintings once during a ceremony at his manor, they were incredible works of art, massive things that must have taken hundreds of hours to paint. Even the grandest of them paled in comparison to the vista before me. I'd love to spend a night beneath the stars, perched on this cliff at what felt like the edge of the world. Sadly, time was not my friend, and what little we had was rapidly ticking away. With that in mind, I did a bit of scouting, scaling the wall towards the upper slab six meters above. There was a rope that connected me back to my sled, but a fall right now could still end in severe injury, as I would either slam into the outcrop or tumble past until my tether swung me back into the unforgiving cliffside. But I would never have been able to coach my team through such terrain if I weren't an experienced climber in my own right, and the rough stone provided little difficulty until I reached the upper slab. Here I found a true challenge: the slab created a sort of ceiling that forced me to bend backward until I was nearly upside down, clinging to the underside like a spider until I could find a solid enough handhold to pull myself up and around. By now, my hands were aching from the cold and strain, but I kept up the slow, methodical pace until I eventually crested the slab, leading to a small, flat platform where I could rest while surveying our path forward.

I couldn't lie, it didn't look good. We still had maybe a hundred meters left to climb, much of it like the rough stone we'd scaled so far, pitted with holes and cracks that made our climbing attempt viable. That all changed in the last thirty or so meters, where stone gave away to a sheet of thick ice wrapped around the top of the cliff like a crown. It was difficult to imagine how I'd missed the feature earlier, but angles and lighting could have easily caused the sheer wall of ice to blend in with the pale stone. The reasons behind my folly were honestly irrelevant since we were already up here and would have to conquer this obstacle one way or another.

But first, I had to get back down. I withdrew a small cam from my belt and jammed it into a nearby crack, sliding and twisting the device until it lodged firmly in place. The flared head would catch in the stone, jamming tighter into the gap as more weight was put on it. I threaded my safety rope through a loop on the end of the cam, then used it as an anchor to repel back to my waiting team.

"Well, that's a problem . . . ," I muttered to myself, sinking to the ground and shaking out my tired hands as I pondered the obstacle. Getting my ghouls to scale mountainsides had been so difficult that I would have abandoned the training years ago had it not provided me with such a unique niche of well-paying courier contracts. But even with the skills I'd imparted, an ice wall like that was beyond most of their abilities. If one of my ghouls slipped and fell on rock, the others could tighten their grips and hold fast until the fallen one could recover. If a whole portion of the ice wall gave way as we climbed . . . Well, there was no recovering from that.

"OK, keep it simple. Let's break the problem down," I spoke aloud, pacing back and forth across the small sliver of open space, pointedly ignoring Scramble, mirroring my pacing like a court jester. "We need to get the medicine to the city, but I don't trust taking the weight of the sled up that ice . . . So can we just take the medicine?"

I went over to reexamine the crate in question and realized it still wouldn't work. Maybe I could rig the harness so the team could just pull the crate up, with me clinging to the box as we went...? No, leaving the sled behind would make us far lighter, but I still didn't trust that the bouncing of the heavy crate against the ice wouldn't lead to some sort of catastrophic collapse. Plus, I needed the balefire brazier to control my team anyway.

Maybe we could do the opposite, climb up without the package, then haul it up behind us?

Nope, I didn't have nearly enough rope, and we would need some sort of crane boom at the top to keep the crate clear of the wall.

The best viable option I could think of was climbing up alone, then somehow getting into Skyroost and recruiting their aid in retrieving the medicine. That felt promising until the sheer scale of the climb set in, plus the fact that I would be switching from rock to ice after I was already tired. I was only human, and you would need a ghoul's endurance to make that climb.

You would need a ghoul's endurance...

There it was, a little spark of an idea, blossoming into the fire of a plan as the possibility took hold. It was absolutely, insanely stupid, but hey, at least no bandit or green flame ghoul would ever see this one coming.

XXVI

"Scramble, old buddy, there's a non-zero chance that I might have made a bad call on this one," I groaned, clinging tightly to his back as he scaled the rock face. We were at the center of the rope line, with King climbing a few feet above us and Bonk an equal distance below. Each of the two carried a small pack of gear strapped to their backs, while Scramble had the unenviable task of carrying me up the mountain, though, to be honest, he barely seemed to notice my weight. I would have loved to close my eyes and hold on for dear life, but I had my own valuable cargo to carry.

See, the decision to continue without my sled had been hard enough to imagine, even without considering the most obvious hurdle. My ghouls needed balefire, and the metal brazier atop my sled was far too cumbersome for even my strongest ghouls to bear. The solution was buried in my sled, an item I had acquired in the days past and nearly left at the bottom of the mountain when we started our climb. It was a balefire torch, the same one I'd grabbed during the battle at the outpost. Without its coals, it was nothing but useless metal, and without the blessings of the Balefire Church, I was unable to transfer my own brazier's coals to it. To meddle with those rules was heresy.

At least, that was what the church taught.

I mean . . . That green fire was *true* heresy, radiating an unnatural aura with every guttering crackle, and I had always viewed the church as more of a work union than a religious organization, at least when it came to my part in it. Yes, I had to wear certain clothes and chant certain scriptures from time to time, but that was just the price of membership for a group that offered good wages and amazing adventures. Maybe there was some floating deity in the sky who bestowed us with magic flame and led us from the dark, or maybe it was just magic, and trying to figure out how and why it worked was pointless. But rules were rules, and only a priest or higher could transfer the sacred coals from one receptacle to another. To break that tradition was to invite all sorts of holy smiting from the powers above.

So here I was, with a brazier amply filled with coals and an empty torch that I might be able to carry as we scaled the mountain . . .

My self-control ran out in about five minutes . . .

"Uhm . . . Here I gather to gift . . . myself a portion of our blessed balefire so that . . . I . . . may brave the wicked wastes beyond . . . this giant fucking wall. Godspeed, and please don't smite me," I intoned nervously, then plunged the torch into the brazier and fished out two of the coals. I could feel the heat against my hand as I levered the coals out, but it was not as intense as I expected. I didn't handle balefire as often as the priests did, and it was easy to forget that balefire had little in common with natural flame. You couldn't use it to boil water, light a torch, or burn anything but ghouls. There was even an ongoing ecclesiastical debate on whether balefire was actually "hot."

Yes, if I had tried to grab fiery coal with my bare hand, it would have roasted the skin off in a heartbeat. But nobody could determine if that was due to the heat or just the effect of trying to hold raw magic in your palm.

I didn't know why balefire behaved that way but was happy to leave that question to the scholars. What I *did* know was that it infuriated and foiled many inventors who were determined to use the coals to power some sort of perpetual steam engine. The practice of using balefire for industrial purposes was banned by church doctrine, of course, but progress marches on.

Which led me back to the present, clinging to Scramble's back with the torch pole haphazardly strapped to my own body. Strange did not even begin to cover it. As ridiculous as it was, we were making fantastic time. Free of the sled's weight, King was able to climb at full speed, nimbly picking a path up the cliffside with the confidence of a mountain goat. For my own part, I held on for dear life and sent mental words of encouragement, doing little else until we reached the boundary of the ice wall. Each ghoul had a set of crampons and ice axes strapped to their back, perfect for the ice climbing ahead but worthless for the rock we currently clung to. The ghouls would need to switch to using that gear to continue the climb but lacked the intelligence to do so on their own. So, I would have to earn my keep.

First, I projected my orders to the trio, instructing them to bunch up vertically below the ice wall until they were in a column so close that I could reach up and touch King's foot. Traveling light was obviously necessary, but I had still brought along a handful of pitons and a small hammer. Wincing at the cold, I bit the finger of my glove and pulled my hand free, tracing my fingertips across the nearby cracks in the rock face. My father had taught me to climb, passing along his knowledge in a series of quips and sayings that managed to stay lodged in my mind, even all these years later. The one that came to me now was, "You climb with your hands, not your eyes. Trust them."

The rock of this wall was pitted and cracked, the various striations and shadows making it difficult to see where one crevice ended and another began. A light touch saw through all that, though, and I located a thin crack in the wall I could jam a piton into. A few swings of the hammer lodged the piton into the stone and gave me a firm anchor to wrap my rope around in case we fell. Now secured to the wall, I was able to work my way up this ghoul ladder until I was standing on Scramble's shoulders and could reach the gear strapped to King's back. I carefully freed the ice axes and passed one into his hand, bracing myself as he swung upward, sinking the tool deep into the overhanging ice above. A chunk the size of my head fractured off, plummeting past us. I let slip a shout of fear, hugging close to the wall as shards of ice speckled my head and shoulders. I had known that the bottom of the ice would be the most precarious, the border of ice and stone likely the weakest part, and this incident reinforced how dangerous trying to bring my whole sled up would have been. King struck again, at a point slightly higher and to the right of the first attempt, and his axe bit into the ice without issue. Once secure, I climbed down and fastened the crampons over King's boots, a strange moment of nostalgia reminding me of the times I would have to tie my little cousins' bootlaces while they squirmed with impatience. Once secured, King stepped up, kicking the barbed crampons into the ice, and pulling himself higher, taking up the slack of the rope as he went. Outfitting the other two was easier, as that piton gave me a firm anchor to hang from. There were a few tense moments, but soon I was back on Scramble, holding on with a white-knuckle grip as the ghouls picked their way up the ice wall. We were doing it slowly but surely. I was acutely aware of my injuries now, my body ached, and the rigors of climbing had cracked the scab on my arm, sending fresh blood dripping down

At one point in the climb, a thin fissure spiderwebbed through the ice from the spot where an axe had landed, cracking and spreading haphazardly with a deep sound like distant thunder. We all froze, waiting to see if the whole slab would give way. With aching slowness, the sound abated, and we continued, sidestepping over to reach a more secure patch of ice.

"The sled would never have made it," I whispered to myself. It was a fact that had already been made clear, but remembering it helped me justify this colossally risky plan I had come up with.

At last, we came to the final stretch of our journey, ice once again giving way to rock and snow as the vertical incline slowly diminished. Soon enough, I was able to dismount and climb alongside my team, the four of us crawling up toward the city walls that were now emerging into view. One final push and we made it, spilling out onto the short rocky expanse in the shadow of the wall. My ghouls may have had limitless endurance, but I was more than happy to collapse flat onto my back as soon as I'd planted the torch into the ground. A few blissful moments were spent gulping in greedy breaths, the thinner air starting to take its toll, but soon enough, I levered myself upright, groaning in fatigue as I surveyed the area. The wall stood nearby, maybe four meters high, and built from large blocks of stone in varying shades of gray. I remembered the walls of the city being clean and robust during my past visits, but clearly, maintenance was not a priority this far from the main gate. The blocks were pitted and crumbling, with gaps so large that even an unskilled invader would be able to scale the wall without rope or ladder. I guess nobody who ran the city thought anyone would be foolish enough to try scaling the cliff face to approach the city from the back.

I couldn't wait to see the look on their faces when I told them.

XXVII

Scaling the city's wall proved as simple a task as I'd imagined, and we scrambled over the crenelated top and onto the walkway above with little difficulty. I fully expected to be met by a cadre of soldiers and had already been working on an explanation for our sudden appearance. That proved unnecessary, though, as the path along the wall was completely devoid of life. That was the first thing I noticed that unnerved me, but the second realization was just as disconcerting.

It was too damn quiet.

This close, we should have been able to hear the hustle and bustle as the people of Skyroost went about their day. Even a cholera outbreak wouldn't be enough to turn this place into a ghost town.

Would it?

Cautiously, I peered over the edge of the opposite wall, looking down into the cityscape below.

Not a damn soul in sight. The wind swept through empty streets, piling up snowflakes to form tiny drifts in every corner like cobwebs. Many of the nearby buildings were built high enough to be level with the wall, but every window I could see was shuttered or dark. A faint smell of old rot lingered even at this height, though I couldn't spot any corpses or refuse that may have caused it. The inner side of the wall was in relatively better condition than the one we had climbed, and I didn't relish the idea of climbing all this way just to break an ankle falling off a city wall. There had to be a way for guards to get up here, though, a stair or ladder, so I picked a direction at random and started walking. I guess I could have called out for someone's attention, but breaking that oppressive silence just felt . . . wrong. There was a stubby tower not far away, and our walkway merged into it, with a stout door leading into the interior. I led my shambling crew over, then briefly regarded the door before giving it a tentative knock.

"Uhm . . . Hello? I've had an exceedingly long, exceedingly cold day. Can you let me in?" I asked. There was no reply, and the door seemed unwilling to budge.

There were no windows visible, and I still wasn't willing to risk that drop, so I ordered Scramble to force it open. He could not compare with Champ or Tybalt for pure strength but was still a powerful ghoul. It took just one swing of the ice axe and a firm thud from his shoulder to slam the door open. After we passed inside, I noticed that the door hadn't actually been locked, only jammed by the warped wood. Scramble seemed so pleased with himself, though, that I didn't have the heart to tell him. The interior was abandoned, with one broken stool lying forlornly in a corner. The room was a simple square, with no stair leading lower, so we continued along the wall, departing through a door on the opposite side. As my eyes adjusted to the light, I caught a flicker of movement below, as if something had ducked into the shadow of an alley. I ran along the wall a bit farther until I could see down the length of the alley but found that the path was littered with rubbish and anything that may have been hiding there was long gone. We continued towards the next tower, above which could be seen a tiny ribbon of smoke twisting out of a short chimney.

"Finally! Warm bed, hot food, and an end to this gods-cursed trip." I ran up to the door and knocked once before shouldering the door open. Inside were three soldiers, bundled up for the cold and sitting in a semicircle around the glowing coals in the fireplace.

"You're a sight for sore eyes, got any—"

The three soldiers recoiled as if a bear had barged into their room, one diving for a crossbow leaning against the wall as the others drew swords. I stood nonplussed at their reaction, only snapping out of it when the crossbow was leveled at my face. I stumbled back, almost dropping the torch as I pulled my ghouls in front of me. There was a heavy *THUNK* as the crossbow fired, and Bonk's head snapped back, the bolt lodging in his helmet. Every instinct told me to rush my ghouls in and take out the threat, but I held myself back. King might be capable of taking prisoners, but the other two would rip the men to shreds as soon as I let them off the leash.

"Listen up!" I barked, climbing back to my feet and regarding the men through the gaps in Scramble's ribs. "My name is Archdeacon Winona of Ozero. I am here on a mission to deliver *medicine* to your city! If you do not drop your weapons right now, I will let my ghouls paint the walls with your insides, then go find some soldiers with better manners!"

There was silence from the room, then a flurry of panicked whispers. I couldn't pick up much, but the words "Church" and "Purple Flame" could be made out. A moment later, the clatter of weapons falling to the ground could be heard.

"We're unarmed . . . Please, Deacon, you just startled us. Nothing should have been able to enter the city from this side . . . There's a lot that's happened here . . . ," the deep voice of an older man called out.

Cautiously, I crept forward, ordering Scramble to lean to the side enough for me to peer in. Each of the men was standing now; their weapons dropped at their feet.

"Kick them over," I ordered.

"Really?" The older man regarded me with a mixture of concern and embarrassment at the order. He had the look of a career military, not a noble officer, but one of the hard bastards that survived to old age by being smart, practical, and ruthless. He had short-cropped grey hair and dark stubble-like sandpaper across his cheeks. A horizontal scar cut a line over a nose that looked to have been broken and reset multiple times.

"Yup, you lost weapon privileges when you took a shot at me. Kick 'em over, boys," I replied, waiting to enter the room until their weapons were sent over.

Once that was dealt with, I cautiously moved inside, taking a seat set apart from the stools the men had been sitting in. The three soldiers slowly sank down into their own seats, the older man leaning forward so that the folds of his cloak fell forward to hide his arms and chest. I'd be willing to bet a heavy handful of suns that he had a knife out, aimed right at me under that cloak. I couldn't blame him; it was exactly what I would do in his position. But the excitement earlier had riled up my ghouls, and I kept my mental leash on them razor thin. If any of the soldiers so much as twitched in an aggressive way, Scramble would splatter their entrails across the floor . . . and the walls . . . and the ceiling . . . He was one of the most even-tempered ghouls I'd worked with but could still summon brutality on par with Tybalt when pushed. He might have been a boxer in his past life, given the flurry of punches he could dish out, and ghoulish strength meant that any blow he landed could shatter bone and mulch a target's vital organs into the consistency of pulled pork.

With that comforting thought in mind, I forced myself to relax a bit, lest my own twitchiness set off the soldiers' violent response.

"OK, let's start from the top." I began, "I'm Winona, a courier out of Ozero. Who are you all?"

"I'm Sergeant Stein, this is Ivar, and that's Fat John," the older man gestured to each in turn.

"OK, so I apologize for barging in like that. I've had a damn tough time getting here and was a bit excited with the finish line in sight, but that's no reason to be taking a shot at me. I thought you all had a cholera outbreak. What's made you so twitchy?"

"Hah!" One of the younger men, a heavyset ginger with a patchy beard, let out a sharp bark of mirthless laughter, but Stein quieted him with a wave of his hand.

"Cholera . . . Gods, I remember when it was just the damn cholera.

I'm going to be straight with you, Deacon, though I bet that you'll call me a liar when you hear it. Skyroost . . . We're under siege. I don't know how you slipped in, but it can't have been the usual way, or you would have seen it. There's an army at our gates, we're trapped," he explained.

"Damn it. Those stuffy capital bastards were right! I never thought the Fin Tribes had it in them to try something like this," I thought aloud.

"Fins!?" Stein looked nonplussed. "I wish they were Fins! We could just bribe the bastards to slink back to their forests. No, it is the dead that lay siege to our city, Deacon Winona. The fucking ghouls have started thinking for themselves, and they are not happy."

"That's ridiculous. It must just be a larger-than-average horde," I reasoned. However, the recent encounter with the green flame ghouls, the ones that seemed intelligent despite having no living human there to guide them, had depleted my conviction even as I said the words.

"Let's say you're right. I gotta ask . . . These ghouls, do they carry a green flame with them?"

"So, you've seen them too? How did you get away!?" Ivar asked.

"I was lucky enough to see them before they saw me. Just a small hunting party south of here. What do you know about them?"

Stein shifted, leaning back against the wall and shrugging his cloak back over his shoulders. His hands were revealed to be empty of weapons, which I took as a good sign.

"Not much more than you, I assume. We had a few people go missing up north, but nothing too unexpected given the toll that ghouls and wildlife usually collect up that way. Then the cholera hit, and we stopped caring about anything happening beyond these walls for a while. Something was wrong with the wells, some filth we couldn't eliminate. Every time we closed one well, another would come up fouled. I can't speak for Skyroost's leadership, but I know that we on the wall didn't know we were under attack until refugees started pouring in from the northern villages. Bastards caught us with our pants down, that's to be sure."

"The ones I saw . . . There weren't any people with them." Just the sight of a handful of intelligent ghouls shook my Balefire Church teachings to their foundation. But a whole army?

"They do still have people with them, but . . . It's complicated, and I'm not the man to explain it to you," Stein told me, rising from his seat. "Now, please, how did you even get here without getting caught by their forces or noticed by ours? If you managed to enter the city unseen, so could those monsters, and our defenses are already stretched thin."

"I . . . uh . . . I wouldn't worry about them following my path here. I came up from the other side, never even saw the front gate." I explained vaguely.

"The other side is a few hundred meters of bare rock and ice!" Ivar stated incredulously.

"Mmm, yup, that does sound like the route. My cart is on a ledge about a hundred meters down, couldn't get it past the ice. I climbed the rest of the way to find some help to retrieve the cargo. It's medicine, and it's getting colder every minute we waste," I explained.

"Save your breath, courier. You'll be telling your tale again soon enough. We need to inform the Duke immediately. John, Ivar, spread the word to the others that I want the patrols doubled; if she could get in, so could they. I'll clear it with Captain Rusco later. Courier, with me," he ordered, descending a ladder that extended through a hole in the floor.

Both men looked like they wanted to argue, but a stare from the sergeant sent them scurrying for the exit. I began to follow the man down the ladder, then paused, regarding my ghouls still crowding around the doorway. It seemed that using one of these portable torches had its drawbacks, as I now had to figure out how to get down the damn ladder while keeping the ghouls in the purple light. It took a bit of planning and far too much squeezing close to dead bodies, but we eventually made it down the ladder and out into the street below.

"That was . . . quite the ordeal. And you say you taught these ghouls to climb the cliff?" Stein asked skeptically as we spilled out onto the street. The wind seemed to howl even louder than it had on the wall as if the buildings of the city compressed it into a gale.

"Everyone's a skeptic. Where are your grand braziers? I've seen them in the city center and the Yard, but I can't see one from here," I asked as he led me purposefully down a side street.

"Don't have them the same way you do. Buildings are too tall, and the city layout is too unique to cover the entire place in balefire light. The only grand braziers we have are those you've already seen. We confine most of the working ghouls to the lower tiers, and a horde would be forced to attack from the front, so we don't worry about it as much as you lowlanders do."

I threw a pointed look at the three ghouls that had scaled the walls but said nothing. The warren of twisting alleys began to reveal other people further in, most either gawking openly or scurrying away at the sight of my ghouls. I'd been to Skyroost before but never explored any neighborhoods so far off the beaten path. The slipshod buildings seemed to almost lean over the space above us, diminishing the light that streamed in. Two such houses had even partially collapsed into each other, forming an arch overhead that had been reinforced with a haphazard lattice of wooden beams. Some areas seemed to be little more than rubble, with shacks protruding out at random intervals, like mushrooms on a rotting log.

"How did the ghouls manage to hit you this high up?" I asked. "No way a catapult could lob a rock this high."

"You're right about that. The ghouls don't have any siege weapon with that range, though they've been happy to pound the lower tiers relentlessly. No, the Warrens have always looked like this, and the Duke has never had the funds or inclination to clean the area up."

After a few more minutes of walking, the alley spit us out into a huge thoroughfare, a giant horseshoe of a road that ran a long loop around the most wealthy and influential part of the city.

As we turned to follow the lane, I glanced back to memorize the exit we had emerged from but found that I couldn't distinguish our alley from the half dozen others that spilled out from the walls.

Stein caught my look of confusion and let out another short bark of tired laughter. "The Warrens will do that to you. They try to keep the upper tiers prim and proper, but those slums snake up here all the way from the lowest tier. There were always more building collapses on that side of town. Nobody wanted to fix it up, so those with nowhere else to go made home in the rubble. I was born there, and it's still taken me a lifetime to learn all the twists and turns."

I told him a bit more about Ozero, and we spent the rest of the journey amicably swapping stories about our hometowns until we reached the city square. It was not the largest of such constructions I'd seen, space in the mountaintop settlement being at a premium, but the builders had sought to make up for that with incredible artistic expression. The expanse was built primarily with tiles of slate gray mountain rock, but the monochrome expanse was broken up by a path of smooth river stones set into the ground. These stones had been sorted by color and formed a beautiful mosaic of blues, teals, whites, and grays that twisted through the square with the fluid grace of a mountain stream. As the swirling hues flowed past each major building, a single ribbon of color would split off, creating a curving path to each structure. The remaining river stones spiraled inward at the center of the square, swirling around a grand brazier of equal size to those in Ozero. Last time I was here, the children of the rich and powerful could play a game of who could run the "Frostpath" the fastest, all while the square was festooned with carts and tents advertising street food, palm readings, and other cheap diversions. There was no such frivolity taking place today. The square was barren except for pallets of supplies and a few squads of armed guardsmen on the move, their shoulders hunched against the biting wind.

"I hope you've got more soldiers stashed away," I told him, counting a few dozen at most.

"Most are asleep, the ghouls like to attack at night, plus they are forced to attack us from the front, so we only keep a skeleton guard on the higher tiers. We may lack professional guardsmen, especially with illness so rampant, but we do not lack fighters. When you know what the ghouls will do to your family if they get in . . . Well, let's just say we don't have issues with conscientious objectors."

The Duke's mansion loomed ahead, the centerpiece of the square a stark contrast to its twin in Ozero. Ozero's mansion was a tall structure of wood, built to resemble a giant hunting lodge while retaining all the opulence due to the Duke's station. It always reminded me of an elk, with the soaring spars reminiscent of the animal's antlers. If Ozero's was an elk, Skyroost's mansion was a toad. Heavy and squat, the building seemed like even it had tried to flatten itself into the earth to avoid the deep chill.

But I was here, in Skyroost, despite the best efforts of ghouls, bandits, soldiers, and crazy cave people. Yes, it was under siege, and yes, my cargo was still perched on the edge of a cliff, but I had made it, despite the odds. That final realization hit me, and I slowly trudged to a stop, leaning against a nearby lamppost. It felt like I'd been running on adrenaline ever since crossing the Wilderness Arch, and seeing the finish line in sight momentarily let all that fatigue crash onto my shoulders. All I wanted to do was take a bath and sleep in a warm bed, but I could feel Stein glaring at me with impatience as I took a long, steadying breath. Groaning, I hauled myself back into a walk, determined to fight through this last portion of my journey just as fiercely as I'd done so far, though the moment of fatigue once again brought the ache of my various injuries back to the forefront of my mind.

"Anything I need to know going in? What's the Duke's name again?" I asked, catching up to my guide again.

"You don't know the Duke's name?" Stein asked incredulously, coming to a stop.

"Listen, man. I've had . . . such a long damn day. Also, do you have a medic nearby? I kinda got . . . shot a few days back, and it hurts like a bastard. I'm worried about infection."

"Uhm . . . yes . . . ," Stein took a moment of shocked silence to process that before continuing. "I've taken a crossbow bolt before; it's an ugly wound. Pulling the bolt out can do more damage than the initial injury."

"It was a pistol, actually," I corrected him, still trying to shake off the wave of exhaustion that had hit me. "Lucky for me, it was just a bad graze. I'm not sure how I would have managed with a more serious wound."

"Who shot you? You almost never see firearms this far north, pistols especially. Professional military are the only ones who have the weapons in bulk," he replied. His statement came a bit too fast, though, as if he'd been expecting my answer and already had a rebuttal waiting.

Damn it all, Stein was sharper than I'd given him credit for, and he had caught me flat-footed. He was right, gunshot wounds were a rarity, and most guns were in military hands, so the nature of my injury would raise suspicion in someone who put the clues together. I couldn't exactly tell him that I had been shot at by a royal guard captain, though, even if I left out the part where I goaded a horde of ghouls to tear the man apart . . . .

"Bandits. I was ambushed on my journey here. A few had bows, but clearly, one had stolen a pistol and knew how to use it. No idea where he got it from, though . . . ," I trailed off, the explanation feeling weak even to my own ears.

Stein leveled a suspicious glance at me, then turned and strode towards the mansion's entrance. I didn't think that he had bought the lie, but hopefully, he would let his suspicion go since there was no evidence to refute my story.

"As I was saying, we served Duke Hagen, though he was lost during the first attempt at negotiation with the invaders." Stein began to explain. "Now we serve the new Duke Hagen, his eldest son, though much of the defense of our city has been helmed by the old Duke's chief adviser." Stein began but cut off the explanation as we reached the mansion. He turned to regard one of the two soldiers guarding the doorway, and both hastily snapped to attention. One of the guards looked well past retirement age, while the other was so young that his helm was too big for his head and kept sliding forward over his eyes.

"Soldier! Is the Duke in?" Stein shouted with the impressive volume that all sergeants seemed to possess.

"Eh?" The old man regarded Stein myopically.

It might have been a trick of the light, but I could have sworn I saw a vein pulse in Stein's forehead.

"The. Duke. Where is he?"

The old man squinted at the sergeant. "Didn't ya hear? Duke's dead, strung him up like a damn scarecrow, they did."

I thought violence was going to break out, Stein turning shades of purple while the old man nodded his head, happy to have been of service, but the youngster broke into the conversation with a high voice not yet deepened by age.

"Duke Hagan is at the gates, sir! He's with adviser Toussaint surveying the defenses," the boy piped up.

Stein nodded, ordered the boy to run ahead with word of my arrival, then turned, stalking off in the opposite direction. I turned my face to the sky and groaned loudly in annoyance, then hustled after him, remembering how tiring it was to navigate the city on foot.

The original plans for the city that would become Skyroost were ambitious, to say the least. It would be constructed at the head of a glacial valley, protected on either side by high cliffs. The steep triangular slope of the valley head would be cut into long, curving terraces of diminishing size, giving the city the look of pie slices stacked on top of each other, each slightly smaller than the last. Every tier would be distinct in its purpose; the lowest layer would contain the city's huge smelters, while the highest held the city square and Duke's residence, along with other governmental buildings. It would be a center of trade and a defensive bastion against any assault from the Fin tribes to the northeast.

That was the plan, at least. The local mines ran dry before the city's ambitious architects could fully realize their vision, leaving Skyroost unfinished, with construction projects simply abandoned and left to the elements. One could find beautiful mosaics on one street and a stinking refuse pile the next lane over. The city seemed trapped in a haphazard sort of half-life, like an ancient marble statue held together by rusty iron plating. Now it scraped by as a small trade hub, smelting and shipping any ore that could be brought in from the mining towns scattered throughout the nearby expanse. It was still the largest northern colony under Empire control, though it stood so far beyond the realm's northern borders that it functioned with almost complete autonomy. The Empire seemed happy to keep it that way as long as the tax payments found their way to the capital on time.

We reached the edge of the highest tier, where the road cut through an ornamental wall and snaked down into the tiers beyond. Stein hesitated, stopped, then turned away, leading me to an overlook that would give the privileged few an awe-inspiring view of the city, the valley, and the mountains beyond. A few clerks had erected telescopes and were scribbling down hurried observations, shoulders hunched against the wind blowing in from downhill. The air tasted of smoke.

"This is the best view in the house," he sighed, waving me forward. "See for yourself. The sight will certainly do a better job than my words ever could."

Skyroost's location made it a defensive bastion, but the thing I always remembered most about the city's lofty position was the landscape. The last time I'd been here was mid-spring when the valley below was a paradise of untamed beauty. Wildflowers had bloomed across the landscape in a dozen vibrant hues, sprouting up in wide swathes like daubs of paint on a palette, broken up by streams of clear mountain water and a single winding road.

Today, it was a scene of carnage. The white snow had been churned into a muddy brown sludge by the passage of thousands of feet, turning the ground immediately beyond the walls into a knee-deep swamp of sucking mud. The muck seemed to be moving in places as if giant earthworms were surfacing to escape rain.

I threw a puzzled look at Stein. "That mud, it doesn't look right."

"Brace yourself," he warned, then gestured to a telescope.

It should have been a simple task to focus the lens on that area, but I kept fiddling with the focus, unwilling to comprehend what I was seeing until there was no other explanation.

That muddy pit was strewn with bodies, the unmoving corpses of guardsmen and . . . the still-twitching forms of ghouls. Hundreds of them.

The creatures must have been too damaged in the fighting to retreat but still retained their magical automation. Many were missing entire limbs and simply dragging themselves in mindless circles. Craters from catapult shots collected pools of dirty water and ballista bolts, each a meter long, still stuck upright in the ground like reeds.

A long muddy line extended from the pit downslope, less a road and more a dirty path tramped into the snow by thousands of passing feet. It snaked across the snowfield before disappearing into one of a handful of large tree groves that hugged the southern ridge wall. As the story went, those groves had originally been planted as orchards, but time and neglect had let them spread into chaotic sprawl, much like Skyroost itself.

At least, that was how I remembered it the last time I'd been here. Now it was a hive of activity as invaders tore down the trees to build their encampment. There were fewer tents than I would have expected, and those few I saw seemed haphazard constructions at best, though I could only see the northernmost tip of the camp as the bulk of it trailed back into the grove. Even at this distance and obscured by scrubby trees, it was still easy to spot hundreds of dark forms, shifting and crowding in on each other like an upturned anthill.

And above it all stood a blasphemous grand brazier, casting its sickly radiance down into the settlement like the gaze of a baleful eye. It was set on a small rise near where the curve of the cliff began to climb and was further elevated on a scaffold of fresh wood, the bark still clinging to the logs. Contrary to the smooth glow of balefire, this new flame seemed agitated, angry even, belching out sparks and tongues of flame at random intervals.

"They have a grand brazier, same as us, but lit with that fire that gives them life again. You can't see it, but that whole scaffold is on wheels, and they push it up with them when making an assault. We've tried hitting it with a lucky ballista shot, but bolts weren't made to pierce something that sturdy, and our best volleys during the last skirmish just made it look like a pincushion, with no lasting damage to show for it. Let's keep moving," Stein sighed, turning away from the sight.

At least we didn't have to descend the tiers of Skyroost on foot, as the incline elevators had avoided major damage so far and remained operational through the siege. Each was an open platform, maybe five meters square, and they were mounted side by side atop a large viaduct that ran diagonally down the slope of the city, from the top tier to the bottom. A giant capstan manned by ghouls was set at the top, and we jogged by them, hopping onto a platform just as it began its descent. There was a large wagon filled with canvas sacks strapped down to the center, with maybe a dozen people, soldiers and civilians alike, sitting around the edges. My three ghouls were still trailing behind me, bound by the balefire coal in my torch, so the other passengers gave us a large birth.

The howling wind at this height further discouraged conversation, and I took advantage of the viaduct's height to get a better look at the city itself.

I was no architect, not a military strategist, nor an engineer. My domain was bone and wood, not iron and stone, but even I could see the one inevitable truth:

Skyroost was dying.

The city walls held for now, shielding the lowest tier from siege weapons, but the tiers above were in ruin. A few buildings were burnt husks, but the true toll was in the dozens of collapsed structures. With tiered levels and shoddy workmanship, one collapsing building could easily fall on top of the tier below, causing more buildings to collapse and furthering the destruction. Multiple points in the city had been reduced to manmade scree fields, the landside spreading out into wide cones of rubble. Gods, it made it look like the city was in its death throes, crying tears of crushed brick and plaster.

"DOWN!" Somebody roared. Startled out of my reverie, I fell to my knees and pulled my will inward, gathering the ghouls about me in an impromptu shield.

Nearby, there was a sharp *Crack!* A soft rumble of falling stones, then nothing.

"Clear!" The same voice called out, and I rose back up, searching for the source of the disturbance. The whole city was too pockmarked for me to tell old damage from new, but the locals knew what to look for and drew my attention to the impact site. With their help, I spotted the tower that had been struck by the catapult shot. As we descended past it, I saw that a large hole had been blown straight through the building, the missile of stone crashing through both wooden walls before tumbling into the street below.

Stein sat down beside me, his expression grim. It seemed he had something to say but was working himself up to it, and I wasn't going to press him. We passed the halfway point down the city slope, and the elevator didn't even stop; it just slowed long enough for a few passengers to jump on or off as we drew level with the loading dock. The elevator's twin platform passed us by, the interconnected cables pulling it upward even as we were lowered down.

"You know..." Stein began at last. "I felt happy seeing that boulder land. Seeing it crash through that building. Even if it missed hitting anyone directly, the people inside that room would be riddled with splinters the size of daggers. What a way to die. And I felt happy about it...."

Another pause, shorter this time.

"I felt happy because that rock didn't cause the building to collapse. It didn't slam into a supporting wall, causing the houses above to avalanche downward onto those below. It didn't hit the elevators, cutting the last artery this city has," he sighed, running a hand through his graying hair.

There was a chorus of deep *thrums*, like bow strings but deeper. Half a dozen ballistae fired, hurling massive bolts into the snowy fields beyond. I didn't see where they landed.

"When the ghouls first started bombarding us, we wreaked bloody havoc on their siege engines. Our ballistae aren't nearly as destructive, but you can take a ghoul's head off at a few hundred meters, and we reduced their weapons to kindling."

Stein spat over the side, then looked out over the wastes beyond the wall.

"Now they've gotten smart; there are trenches out there, carved into the hill where the valley starts to drop off. Getting scouts out is damn near suicidal, but the ones who return say that the ghouls have their siege weapons sunk into pits they've dug, out of line of sight. They're hurling rocks at us blind, just hoping to hit something important. But it's nearly impossible to lob a ballista shot back at them, and there's enough loose rock nearby to feed their weapons for months."

"Scramble, stop that!" I berated the ghoul, who had been surreptitiously sidling closer to the edge of the platform. That thing loved heights, but I wasn't about to accidentally drop a ghoul on some innocent passerby below.

"Do you have family in the city?" I asked Stein, thinking of Ronny and eager to change the subject.

"Mhmm. Got a wife and a little girl. My father is still around, too," he said, and I saw real warmth in his expression for the first time.

"They're sheltering in the Warrens," Stein continued, pointing to the southern edge of the city, where a mass of collapsed architecture seemed to have been fused into one giant edifice that threaded up through the tiers like a tumor. "Ironically, that might now be the safest place in the city. The tallest building over there collapsed years ago, and the ghouls don't seem to think it's important enough to hit too hard ... Silver linings of a rough upbringing, I suppose."

Our mood had become somber, and I felt I was somewhat to blame for asking about Stein's family.

"So, this chief adviser, does he have a goatee?" I asked, trying to lighten the mood.

"What? Why would you ask that?"

"Well, haven't you seen those street shows the actors do around festival time? There's always like an evil vizier with a goatee ready to betray everyone," I explained.

Stein thought about this for a moment. "You are an incredibly odd person. You know that?"

The elevator thudded to a stop, settling into a recess in the floor so that the platform lay flush with the ground around it. We hustled away the moment it landed, jogging clear as the platform was swarmed with activity. Horses were being maneuvered to pull the wagon away, and people of all shapes and sizes were jostling to get on. The elevator station lay at the end of a wide plaza that formed a half circle around the imposing city gates. Those massive wooden doors were three times the height of a man and stained black with age, though there were now a few portions reinforced with boards of fresh lumber. A half dozen message boards lined the edges of the plaza, each covered in scrawled notes searching for loved ones. So many families had been separated during the siege, and the building collapses only added to the terrible confusion.

Dad,
Albert, Eric, and I made it out. Mom didn't make it. We're sheltering
at Grandma's.

—Karin

Looking for Jory. Young boy, eight years old, black hair, scar on forehead. Last seen wearing a green cloak. Bring to Emperor's Arms Tavern on third tier.

Mom,
Collapse knocked out a balefire torch, ghoul at the forge bit Laila.
She's gone now. I'm joining the guard, don't come looking for me.
—Logan

There were . . . hundreds of them, stacked so thick that new notes had been pinned over old. A few people paced these boards, some searching with panicked alacrity, others drifting like wraiths.

With silent agreement, both Stein and I picked up the pace. In short order, we made it to the outer ramparts, taller, thicker, and better kept than those I had scaled earlier. Stone steps climbed up the inner wall, wide enough to allow us to ascend side by side. We crested the top of the steps, and I was treated to an up-close look at the carnage I had spied from the top of the city.

XXVIII

The smell of death was horrific, even by the standards I was used to, and more than a few soldiers walking the battlement had lengths of cloth covering their nose and mouth. That muddy pit was even more disturbing up close, as the distance had blunted some of the most stomach-churning details. Ghouls flopped and crawled, leaving trails of blood and filth behind them like corrupted slugs, painting the landscape with their viscera. Most wore little more than roughspun tunics, but interspersed throughout the scene were bursts of color, soldiers of Skyroost that had been dragged down and converted to the legions of the dead.

Stein led me along the wall towards a large tent that had been erected over one of the gatehouse towers. As we walked, I kept my head turned, trying to catch a glimpse of the enemy camp. Wooden boards had been affixed to the wall to form crude crenelations, so my vision was cut into a series of quick flashes as we passed alongside them.

"Oh, uhm, sorry . . . ," I muttered, nearly colliding with a soldier patrolling the wall.

"Courier! Keep up," Stein snapped.

I hadn't realized that I'd slowed, and I caught up as he entered the gatehouse tower. A narrow staircase ascended along the inner wall of the tower, blocked at the base by a single guard. Stein leaned in close and exchanged a few whispered words with the woman, who then turned and disappeared up the steps.

"She's just announcing us to the council," he explained. "You'll have to leave your ghouls here for obvious reasons." He gestured for another soldier, this one a young boy, to take the torch from my hand, but my grip remained firm.

"These ghouls are my livelihood," I told the boy, glad for once that I didn't have to crane my neck up to meet someone's eyes. "If anything happens to them, you'll be replacing them on my sled team," I growled. The boy nodded, eyes wide with fear.

A minute went by . . . then five . . . then ten. I pulled a strip of jerky from a pouch and began absentmindedly chewing on it. After another few minutes, I pulled out another strip and offered it to Stein.

He peered suspiciously at the offering. "What kind of meat is that?"

"*Ah dun oh,*" I mumbled around the food in my mouth, shrugging.

The guard returned and gestured for us to follow, leading us up the right-hand spiral steps to the roof of the stout tower. We emerged from a hatch in the floor onto a platform lined with stone-crenelated walls. A pavilion tent of gold and burgundy fabric had been raised to block the howling wind, and the material fluttered and snapped against the gusts. One cloth wall had been rolled up to give a clear view of the battlefield. A pair of small braziers burned with seasoned wood, dispelling the cold enough for me to do away with my hood and thick gloves. Under the tent, a half dozen people in noble attire stood arguing around a rectangular table.

"We cannot continue to hold a defensive position. Their siege weapons are getting more accurate, and we keep having to relocate the sick and wounded. Their conditions worsen every time we are forced to move them," a thin man in blue raiment argued.

A different man, this one towering over the rest with bald head and hairy arms bare even in the cold, chimed in, "Their weapons are protected now as well; we cannot even hope to return fire with any real effectiveness. On top of that, we are still repairing the gatehouse after the last attack. Some of the ghouls we reeled in had firebombs, barely kept the blaze from spreading."

"We need the fishhook defenses working again. They're our best bet to keep the ghouls from breaching the gate. Take whatever manpower you need to get it done." This order came from a younger man at the head of the table, with a burgundy mantel that matched the decor. A mop of black hair tumbled down to the top of his shoulders, and a wispy black mustache clung to his upper lip.

"Duke Hagan, what of the latest casualty reports?" This from a severe-looking older woman wearing a fur-lined cloak over finely made skirts. "We've moved people from the most vulnerable buildings, but those collapses took so many. Our number of missing is more than double that of confirmed casualties. We're stretched too thin."

"Then . . . Pull the rescue workers off the oldest sites," he said at last, shoulders sinking as if bearing a great weight. "We can't keep wasting our manpower searching through week-old ruins."

The woman looked like she wanted to argue, but a heavyset older man stepped forward to stand next to the young Duke. He wore a heavily brocaded red coat, and his long white beard fell almost to his waist.

The two nobles stared at each other in silence for a moment, and Stein jumped on the pause in conversation to cough politely and draw the eyes of the older man.

"A moment, my lords and ladies!" The heavyset man announced, his booming voice cutting through the chatter. "I believe we may have some good news at last. This is the courier that has made it through the enemy lines. Allow me to make introductions. I am Chief Adviser Toussaint, loyal servant to the young Duke Hagen."

Mr. Wispy Mustache bridled at the "young" part but quickly brushed it off and sketched a graceful bow. "Your presence has warmed our hearts during these cold . . . uhm, you're bleeding . . . ."

I looked down and saw that a slow drip of blood was indeed falling from the end of my sleeve, the fat drops forming a small puddle on the stone floor.

"Oh crap, sorry. I mean . . . my apologies, Your Grace, I was shot during a battle at a military outpost north of the Wilderness Arch," I explained.

"We'll have a medic called immediately," he snapped his fingers and gestured to a nearby assistant. "An outpost, you say? So, reinforcements are on the way!" He smiled, turning to pat his chief adviser on the back. Smiles and laughter flowed through all present as if the weight they had carried since the start of the siege had begun to lift.

"Uhm . . . Sorry, Your Grace, but the outpost was overrun by ghouls. I'm not sure how many survived the assault, but they'd be in no condition to give aid if they even knew about what was happening here."

Any cheer that had begun to build immediately deflated, leaving the mood even more dejected than before.

"We've sent out runners since the beginning of the siege. We had hopes that they would have been able to return with aid by now," Toussaint explained.

"It's possible, sir, but the journey here was beyond treacherous, even for a courier. I can't conjure up fighting men, but I am with the Balefire Express, and I have a contract to deliver supplies. There were rumors of a cholera outbreak, and an arrangement was made to deliver a crate of medicine. I know it's not what you hoped . . . ."

Toussaint cut in, "No courier, it isn't, but you have still brought us some relief. We are not a city that was ever prepared for a siege, and these monsters attacked us at our weakest during the height of the outbreak. We found ghoul remnants floating at the bottom of many wells, so there is the concern that even this outbreak was part of their attack, though we do not know how that could be possible. Regardless, the attacks have hindered our ability to care for the sick and wounded, so I'm sure your supplies will be greatly appreciated. I'll detail some men to see that the medicine gets where it needs to go."

There was something in his eyes for a moment, recognition, maybe? Ronny clearly knew people up here. Maybe they had worked together in the past.

Toussaint flicked his hand in a clear dismissal, but I took a step forward instead, sliding into a gap that the nobles had cleared around the table when they had moved back to face me.

"I'm sorry, sir, but it's a bit more complicated than that. I scaled the cliffs to reach Skyroost but couldn't take my sled the whole way. It's waiting on a ledge about a hundred meters below the cliff top, with the medicine still on it. It might take more than ropes and a few strong backs to haul it up. My sled is stuck where it is, and I'll need help retrieving it, but the medicine is my primary concern right now," I explained.

"Wait . . . Did you say you scaled the cliffs . . . with your sled?" An older man in a green frock coat asked.

"Uhm . . . yeah. Long story. The important part is that I need some help getting it the rest of the way."

"This council has greater concerns!" The young Duke Hagen snapped, slapping a palm on the table, silencing all discussion.

Hagen looked up, took in our expressions, then sighed. "My apologies, courier, we are all very weary, you even more so, I'm sure. Engineer Maki, can you task some of your people to deal with the retrieval of the medicine?"

"Yes, Your Grace, I'll see to it personally." The bare-armed man answered, turning to leave and gesturing for us to follow. I took one last look at the map before departing, some sense tugging at the back of my mind.

The Duke's voice faded away as we descended the stairs. "That giant brazier of theirs casts its light all the way to our city. If we can destroy it, we may be able to scatter them."

"Well, that was . . . a lot," I sighed wearily, retrieving my torch from the young soldier.

"Heh!" Maki chuckled, coming down after Stein. "I am inclined to agree. This warfare by committee . . . It makes me fear for the city."

Stein seemed to bristle at the comment but remained silent. Given that Maki had been at the meeting and Stein had been on guard duty, it seemed likely that there was a large gap in seniority between them.

"How would you do it?" I asked, wanting to learn more about this strange new person.

"In wartime, one leader, one voice. Others can advise but not over-rule. It gives the tribe a unity of purpose. The young Duke still has much to learn, and a siege is no time for teaching," he explained.

Stein could keep silent no longer. "If you Fins had the right of it, it'd be you with the walls instead of freezing your savage asses off in the wastes," he rumbled.

"Fin . . . ?" Maki tapped his chin with a sausage-thick finger. "No, I am good Empire man like you. Cold must have got to your head. Heh, heh. Now, to business."

Maki asked me questions; the exact location where I'd summited the cliff, the weight and dimensions of the package, and how far down the outcropping was.

"This can be done, though we will need to construct a crane boom to keep the medicine from hitting the cliff as we hoist it. My concern is for your team; if I send a soldier down on the rope, we may just be using him as bait for ghoul fishing, eh?" Maki poked Stein in the rib with a playful elbow, but the older man remained taciturn.

"Ugh . . . Yeah, figured I'd be the one going back down. I started this trip; I'll be damned if I'm not the one to finish it," I sighed.

"Heh, heh! I like you, little one. If all our soldiers had your fire, we would have thrown the ghouls back by now. It will take some time to prepare, though. Maybe you get some rest while you can; it will be a long night. I must head to the wall to plan anyway; would you like me to watch your ghouls while you rest?" Maki asked, smiling amicably.

After a moment's hesitation, I agreed, handing over the torch. I needed rest before getting back on the mountain again, which meant I'd need to entrust the ghouls to someone eventually. The Fins treated their ghouls far better than the Osgil Empire did, as they were an integral part of the life they eked out in the northern wastes. I trusted him to safeguard them, for a while at least.

"That's . . . an interesting man," I wondered aloud, casting one last look at King and the others as he departed.

"I still can't fathom how a culture that lives in hide tents ended up producing the best engineer in the city . . . I'm glad we have him, though; man's brilliant, even if he is a pain in the ass." Stein shook his head as if clearing away the thoughts. "You must be exhausted. Let's get you taken care of."

One result of a city under siege is that it left a host of abandoned buildings in its wake. The rich had fled their mansions, retreating to hidden bunkers or reporting to the Duke. The poor fled their homes to find safety in numbers, flocking together to pool strength and resources . . . or to go ransack the now-empty mansions. One such mansion, set on a higher tier just out of trebuchet range, had been converted into a field hospital. The large double doors were open wide, admitting a constant stream of wounded soldiers, many limping, a few motionless on stretchers. Stein handed me off to a flustered orderly with a promise to retrieve me in a few hours when Maki was ready. The orderly, a rotund woman with hair pulled back into a tight bun, led me into the madness, moving easily between cots and people with the grace of a ballerina. I followed behind, wincing and muttering apologies as I occasionally bumped into the wounded, eliciting grunts of pain.

"I can find my own way to a bed," I called ahead to the orderly, feeling guilty that I was distracting her from people in need.

"Nonsense, dear. You'd be doing me a favor. The Duchess sent her ladies in waiting to help care for the wounded. The daft girls can stitch crochet, but not a wound, apparently. One fainted on top of the first soldier I sent her to care for. Pawning them off on you gets them out of my hair," she explained, leading me to a corner where a pair of tall, willowy girls stood, a blonde and a brunette pressing themselves into a corner to escape the bustle of moving people around them.

"I'm more than happy to help, though I did get shot a few days back. I'd appreciate it if you could have someone take a look who actually knew their stuff," I added. This would be the third time I had mentioned the injury in Skyroost, and I was starting to lose faith in northern hospitality.

The orderly spun on her heel, regarding me with new interest. I could feel her eyes roaming me, taking in the way I cradled one arm close, trying to keep it from being jostled in the press.

"You hide it well, or maybe I'm just tired. How long has it been?" she asked.

I thought back, the days seeming to smear together in my exhausted mind. "About three days. I patched it as well as I could the first day, but it's not like I've been able to rest and relax since then. It's a long graze across my bicep. Not deep, but a wound that wide is hard to stitch up. It felt infected last time I checked it."

She nodded tersely. "I'll tell your helpers to run a bath and send someone competent to check that wound as soon as I can spare them." The orderly snapped loudly, and the two girls darted to her side, their posture making it clear that they were terrified of the woman. She issued them a quick set of instructions, and they led me from the crowded ballroom.

XXIX

The two girls led me up a broad flight of stairs, and the bustling noise began to fade away as we reached the second floor. Here, people moved quietly, speaking in hushed voices as they passed rows of cots where the sick and wounded slept. Many patients were missing limbs, the hurried amputation a sure sign of ghoul bites. Past this open space was a hallway lined with closed doors, which the brunette, Gertrud, told me had been converted into staff housing. So constant was the influx of wounded that many healers spent their entire day, from sunup to sundown, without ever leaving the building. From there, they led me to a thick door, which the blonde, Erika, opened with a firm tug. Inside was a small room of paneled wood with benches and shelves lining the sides and another door at the far end. Plush towels and robes of white cloth were stacked high on the shelves.

"You can leave your clothes here," Gertrud told me, gesturing to the shelves. The washerwomen have been so busy, but I'm sure they can make time for your attire."

"Good luck to them. I think the dirt is holding it together by now. Where's the bath?" I asked, stepping into the small space and gingerly slipping my heavy coat off. Both women shed their clothes, exchanging them for light shifts.

"In the next room, mistress," Erika answered, reaching up to unlace my overshirt.

"No!" I shouted instinctually, pulling away, then immediately regretting it, realizing my mistake when I saw the hurt look on her face.

"Sorry," I apologized. "Been through a lot, still jumpy. Go on ahead. I'll join you in a moment."

Erika looked like she wanted to argue, but Gertrud put a hand on her shoulder and pulled her away, cracking the far door open enough for them both to slip inside. Steam flowed out from the gap, curling into dissolving spirals as the door was pulled shut again.

Damn, I felt bad for that, but I was still on high alert. Usually, I could relax once I made it inside city walls, but with a package still undelivered and a city under siege, I was still wound tight as a cheap watch. Plus, there was just the base idea of stripping naked around other people that I wasn't too enthused about. Maybe Song Islanders were happy to strut around nude in their public baths, but we were a bit more demure up north. Personally, I blamed it on all the layers we used to protect ourselves from the cold. After a while, all that clothing could feel like a second skin, one we were loath to remove among strangers.

But none of that could distract me from a simple truth: I *stank*. It was easy to ignore out in the wilderness surrounded by ghouls, but in the clean changing room, the stench rolled off me like a thick miasma, filling the small space with the smell of sweat, dead flesh, and woodsmoke.

"Gods, that's rancid. Do I always smell like this?" I wondered aloud, slowly stripping off the various layers, careful not to aggravate my various injuries further. My body exhibited a patina of mottled bruises, with my ribs and shoulders displaying the worst of it. In a compromise between modesty and practicality, I wrapped a towel around my waist, then slung my belt across my uninjured arm. Along with the tiny coalknife I'd made, there was a more utilitarian long knife, its broad blade equal parts camp tool and defensive weapon. Maybe taking weapons to the bath with me was an overreaction, but the comforting weight helped to set my mind at ease. I also wasn't planning to let the coalknife out of my sight for any reason. If either girl asked about the wrapped package on my belt, I would have to play it off as something innocuous.

Tentatively, I cracked the door open, letting warm steam pool out over my bare toes.

"Hurry, mistress, you'll let the heat out!" Erika called out. I took a deep breath and stepped into the room, pulling the heavy door shut behind me. The moist heat settled over me like a blanket, surprising me with how thick the air felt. The frigid air outside was dry as a bone, and my chapped skin reveled in the influx of moisture. This room was larger than the one I'd left but retained the same floor-to-ceiling wood paneling.

Gertrud raised an eyebrow at the weapons slung over my shoulder but made no comment, leading me over to a clawfoot bathtub set in one corner of the room. I approached it cautiously, feeling like a mud-encrusted dog that just realized it was bath time.

There was also a small stone pool of steaming water set into the floor on the opposite side of the room. It looked chest deep, with a broad lip halfway down so that people could sit. Erika was collecting water from it with a large bucket and methodically filling up the tub, humming a jaunty little tune to herself as she went.

"I've never seen a room like this," I told the women, watching the steam curl off the surface of the pool in thin ribbons. "Where's all this heat coming from?"

Erika beamed with pride, launching into an excited explanation before Gertrud could quiet her. "Oh, it's amazing, isn't it!? Our Duchess had the first one built. Then it became all the rage among nobles in Skyroost. Some crazy Mouse inventor set them up!"

"Mycenean," I corrected softly, thinking back, but Erika didn't seem to hear.

"The room is right above the kitchens. I saw the construction, there's a maze of metal piping that moves the heat of the ovens up to here." Gertrud explained further, offering a hand to help me as I stepped unsteadily onto the tub's slick porcelain bottom.

"Easy there," Gertrude muttered, catching me under my uninjured arm as I began to slip. "Apologies, mistress, the Duchess prefers bathing in the pool directly, but we considered that to be unwise given your . . . state."

I looked down, seeing the grime and dried blood that coated me. "That's . . . that's fair," I admitted.

A hiss of pain escaped my lips as the hot water flowed around my leg, but after a moment of bearing it, the pain faded into a lovely feeling of deep warmth. I sank into the tub, wincing as the water flowed around various cuts and scrapes and easing down to sit on the porcelain bottom. The tub was shaped vaguely like a heeled shoe, with a raised rim on one side that was the perfect height to recline against, though the position did leave me in an awkward spot, my injured arm over my head to keep the wound dry. A bolt of lightning pain shot down the limb with even the slightest moment, the abuse of the day catching up with me. The bandage was dotted with pinpricks of blood that had soaked through, and the skin around the wound had turned an angry red, the affected area looking larger than the last time I had checked. Gertrude appeared at my side a moment later, setting down a small table that I could set my arm on, keeping it clear of the water.

"Thank you," I murmured sleepily, allowing some of the tension to leak out of my tired muscles. Gertrude drained the tub part way, the water taking with it the layer of road dust that had coated me for many days, then replaced the loss with more buckets from the pool. I noticed her hands for the first time, deeply tanned and callused.

"Those hands look too well worn for a lady in waiting," I observed, then blanched. That had been blunt, even by my standards. Small talk had never been a skill I'd excelled at, and the weight of exhaustion was not helping.

"Oh, I didn't . . . I'm sorry—" I began to apologize.

Gertrude's short bark of laughter surprised me, the first sign of genuine mirth I'd seen from her.

"I'd feel like I should take offense to that, courier, but I know you work hard to put food on the table, same as I do. My parents were hunters who found employ with the old Duke, bringing in hard-to-find game for his table. Erika's parents were dressmakers for the Duchess. They were kind enough to take us in as ladies in waiting when we came of age. It was quite a jump in social standing for our families, and if I marry well, I'll be able to provide for my parents in their dotage. But, even with the nice dresses, we never forgot where we came from." Gertrude looked over at Erika, still humming, and I saw unalloyed warmth for the girl in her expression.

Erika pulled up another stool behind me and attempted to wrangle my hair with a stout ivory comb, but I shooed her away after she snagged it on the first of what would have been numerous tangles. She changed tactics smoothly, rubbing a rough soapy stone over my shoulders, the ministrations loosening knots of muscle that had not relaxed since Ozero. Her efforts were hard to resist, and I soon melted under her touch, allowing the pampering to continue until a sharp knock at the door awoke me from my reverie. An older woman, all bone and sinew, stepped in, a basket under one arm.

"My name is Healer Alwyn; I was sent to tend to your injury courier. There are plenty of other patients to see, so let's have at it." She gestured to the short stool, and I stood from the water, sighing as I left the soothing embrace behind. Gertrud pulled on a looped chain by the wall, ratcheting open a vent in the ceiling that dispersed the rising steam, while Ericka helped me dry off with a fluffy white towel before draping a robe of absorbent cloth across my shoulders.

The healer went to work as soon as I sat down, cutting away my dirty bandage with a short, curved knife. I winced as she pulled the bandage away, hissing with pain as it stuck to the wound.

"Oh gods," Erika whispered, turning away from the sight.

"That bad?" I gave a rueful laugh, focusing my attention on the opposite wall so I wouldn't see the extent of the wound.

"I can see you performed some basic first aid, but the infection has already taken root. This needs to be drained and stitched, which means I'll also have to remove the scab that's begun to form over it. Why didn't you stitch it earlier?"

"I thought it was too wide. I've only stitched clean cuts before. Didn't know how to do it right when there was so much skin gone . . . ," I explained.

She sighed, then offered me a wooden dowel wrapped in leather to bite down on.

"I hate gunshot wounds; nasty, messy affairs. Thank the gods, we don't get many. We are low on almost everything right now. The one anesthesia I could offer will leave you in a torpor for the rest of the day."

"I have a few hours to rest, but then I need to be back out there. Just get it done," I grimaced, bracing for the pain.

Alwyn grunted skeptically, then pressed the flat of her knife to the scabbing wound. I hissed in pain and snatched my arm away; even that gentle pressure was too much to bear.

"I'll go find the anesthetic," Alwyn said, rising to her feet with a grunt. "You won't be out of bed till tomorrow, but there's nothing for it."

"STOP!" I shouted with a ferocity that surprised even me. Gods, I seemed to be doing a lot of shouting today. "I'm going out to retrieve medicine for the city. We originally thought you just had a cholera outbreak, but I'm sure you can still find some use for it."

Healer Alwyn seemed to waver for a moment, indecisive.

"Please. I don't trust anyone else to get to it, and the medicine might be frozen solid by tomorrow. Hold me down if you have to. I don't care." My vision blurred, and I realized after a moment that I was on the verge of tears. "I can't fail so close to the finish line. Don't let it all be for nothing . . . Please."

"It's going to hurt; however much pain you're expecting, I promise that it will be worse," she cautioned.

"That's why you gave me something to bite down on. Let's get this done."

It took a bit of rearranging, but Healer Alwyn was soon ready to begin. I sat on the floor now, back against the wall. My injured arm was laid across the table, a tourniquet bound tight above the wound, while my other arm stretched out to grasp a metal bar on the wall. Gertrude and Poor Ericka had been drafted into the procedure as well. Once they had returned in their original attire, Healer Alwyn ordered them into position; Ericka sat astride my legs, ready to hold my shoulders down, while Gertrude grasped my wrist and leaned away so that I couldn't wrench the limb free at the first taste of pain.

"Hold as still as you can, please."

I nodded, then placed the leather-wrapped dowel between my teeth and seized the bar once again, my grip already white-knuckled in anticipation.

The metal of the knife felt blessedly cool against the fever-hot skin around the wound. The tip of the blade probed across the perimeter of the scab until Alwyn found whatever sign she was looking for.

"Here we go," she warned.

I tensed up, ready to endure, but the pain hit like the thundering of an avalanche, obliterating my self-control in an instant. It wasn't just in my arm; it was in my chest, behind my eyes, sinking its teeth into every part of me. I bucked against the pain, trying to escape it, to flee from it, anything to make it stop.

"Hold her!" the healer barked.

Dimly, I heard Gertrude swear, and my arm was pulled taut again, chaining me to this torture. My body tensed and twisted, and I nearly threw Ericka off, the waif giving a squeak of surprise as she held on.

I couldn't breathe. My lungs wouldn't work. The stick fell from my mouth as I gasped for breath, but all I could manage were the smallest of inhalations that left me panting in a rhythmic *hik hik hik* sort of gasp.

Everything began to feel far away for a moment as if I were looking up at Ericka's face from the bottom of a deep well. Her mouth moved, but I couldn't hear the words...

With a rush, I was thrown back into my body again. The pain was still there but diminished and...purer in a way. It had the sharpness of metal and frigid air instead of the sickly pulsing of warm rot that had been growing over the last few days. A clean pain.

I sobbed once, trying to hold the tears back. Then Ericka was around me, blanketing me in an embrace, whispering encouragement to me as her hand massaged the back of my neck.

And I broke, I broke down hard, sobbing into the rough cotton of her dress. I cried for the pain, and for the people that had been lost along the way. Sergeant Greaves, and the other soldiers that had died when the outpost defenses fell. Blondie and Calliope, who I had abandoned when I fled the camp, and were now either besieged by the horde or already dead. Ronny's family and the other citizens of Skyroost, fighting and dying and still waiting on the medicine I had yet to deliver. It felt pathetic, but I even cried for Grah, ripped apart to buy us the time to escape the tunnel dwellers. Mostly though, I just cried for myself. I felt so . . . small. Not the hero or the ace courier, just another kid lost in a warzone, stranded hundreds of kilometers from hearth and home.

I must have passed out for longer than the scant seconds it had felt like, and Healer Alwyn had nearly finished her work by the time I composed myself. After the wound had been sealed, she applied a cool poultice and wrapped it loosely in cloth, with instructions to find a healer to inspect it before I departed later. I managed a weak nod of thanks as she left. Gertrud and a pale-faced Erika led me away without protest. I found that my feet hurt too, my heels had drummed against the stone floor in my struggle, and Gertrude crouched under my good arm to help support my shaky legs. The pair cleaned me up, helped me change into a clean shift, and guided me to a quiet room full of sleeping women, all bearing some sort of injury. The cot was small but clean, and I drifted off to sleep in moments.

XXX

Learning to be a light sleeper was one of the first survival strategies new couriers cultivated. Though to be honest, it might be a skill I needed to practice more, as I'd slept through a horde wandering into my camp earlier in this misadventure. Slight changes in your surroundings; the smell of smoke in the air, the quieting of nighttime animals, the sound of branches snapping, anything could be the first warning sign of impending disaster. So, when a woman gently shook my shoulder to wake me, I woke in an instant, tensing for action before realizing where I was. That being said, waking quickly and getting out of bed quickly were two different things.

"Mistress, it's time," Erika whispered.

"Ugh," I pulled the blanket closer and rolled away from the noise.

"Please, mistress, the soldiers are waiting." she pleaded, voice soft.

"Meh," I muttered and sank deeper into the warm embrace of the mattress.

Slowly, the blankets began to recede, pulled away by unseen hands.

"Noooooooo," I tightened my grip on the fleeing blankets.

With a sudden jerk, the covers were yanked away, exposing me to the cool air of the room.

"Mistress, the soldiers are waiting for you! Please get up!" Erika whispered plaintively.

At long last, I gave in, sliding my legs under me and pushing up into a sitting position on the bed. A yawn escaped my lips before I could speak, evolving into a full-body stretch that I let run its course.

"What time is it?" I asked, scooting to the edge of the bed and searching for my boots.

Gertrude brought them over, along with my clothing, now neatly folded. They were still far from clean, but at least the various rips and abrasions had been patched up. "About two hours after nightfall, mistress."

"What!? How long does it take to get some pulleys and rope together?" I had hoped to reach the crate with the sun still up. Doing it at night ratcheted up the risk another notch, and it meant that the medicine would be cooling down even faster. The tarp I'd rigged would help keep the wind from stealing what little heat remained, but there was no way to tell how much time was still on the clock.

Erika pulled a folding screen in front of the cot, giving me a little privacy as I pulled off the shift and donned the various layers of my courier garb. It was funny, I could tramp through the wilderness for a week and not notice the grime but get me squeaky clean, and I could instantly note the dirty cloth slipping over my skin. I grimaced against the feeling but continued, leaving off the outermost layers so that the healer could take another look at my arm. This one was a man, wrinkled and bent with age.

He regarded my half-dressed state, taking in the old blood stains still marking the arm of my coat.

"Should I even try to tell you to rest while you heal?" he asked wearily.

"Uhm, you can if it makes you feel better," I shrugged, which garnered a sigh of disapproval from him as he began to rewrap my injured arm.

"Well, I wouldn't usually do this, but we've been instructed by Chief Advisor Toussaint to provide all aid available to you." He pulled out a slim wooden vial stoppered with cork and wrapped with a leather cord. "This is a tincture of henbane, an extremely potent substance.

Only use it as a last resort. I have been told you have some strenuous work ahead, retrieving medicine for us. We need that package desperately; this siege has nearly depleted our medical stores. It . . . I don't want to give this to you, honestly. It feels like a betrayal of the ideals a healer should stand for."

"Henbane?" I muttered to myself, trying to dredge up my old lessons. "I vaguely remember that, but it's been a while . . . Wait, isn't it a poison?"

"Yes, yes, it is," the healer sighed, then handed me the vial. I slipped the cord around my neck, burying the tiny vessel under layers of clothing. "Too much medicine can kill, and a small amount of poison can heal. The line between the two is not as defined as many might think," he explained.

"So, what will this 'medicine' do? Is it a painkiller?" I asked, feeling as if the vial had become as heavy as a chunk of lead against my chest.

"Honestly, it might kill you or leave you in a helpless stupor. I must reiterate that this is a *last* resort. In the best case, you can still expect hallucinations, restlessness, manic episodes, and a pounding heartbeat."

I started to pull the vial back out of my clothes. "Maybe you should just keep this."

The healer held up a hand to stop me, then continued.

"We learned it from the Fins, whose berserkers consume the drug before battle. Terrifying creatures, mad with rage and able to move and react with inhuman speed. They are purported to be twice as strong as a normal man and nearly impervious to blades, but I believe this is an exaggeration derived from the pain-dulling effects; it is amazing what humans are capable of when neither pain, fear, nor fatigue can make them falter."

"Berserker in a bottle . . . " I mused. "Well, I won't turn that down."

"No, it isn't a magical potion courier. It's a dangerous drug. Maybe it will help you push through the pain, maybe it will pop your heart like a bursting bubble, it is not something to ingest lightly. I watched a captured Fin come down off the drug after a battle once; he was weak as a kitten for days. He almost died, both from the effects of the drug and from the wounds he had sustained and ignored during the fighting," he warned.

"I get that, really, I do. But almost dead is still far better than completely dead. Some might call me brash, but I'm not stupid, and I won't use it unless things are looking dire. Thank you, truly."

I shook his hand with my good arm before he departed, then shrugged on the rest of my gear, patting myself down to make sure everything was secure and fitting comfortably. Erika and Gertrude were still watching me, and I figured they deserved thanks for helping me out as well. I turned to face them, but Erika beat me to it, throwing her arms around me in a tight hug, the taller girl crushing me against her chest.

"Thank you for your service, Winona! We owe you so much for bringing the medicine all this way!" she squalled, nearly lifting me off my feet with surprising strength.

"*You're crushing me . . .*," I grunted, wincing at the pain.

Erika dropped me self-consciously, brushing at my clothes as if she were the one covered in dirt.

"Sorry! I'm just—You go out there in the wilderness, saving lives; it's amazing! I just wish there was more I could do to help," she explained.

My immediate reaction was to shy away from the compliment, but denying Erika's enthusiasm felt like kicking a puppy.

"Thank you, Erika, it's not all adventures and riches, but I'm glad there are people who appreciate the effort the Balefire Express puts in."

She gave me one last quick hug, then backed away so I could leave. Gertrude was far less emotional, which I appreciated, giving a quick nod of respect that I returned before departing. A nondescript soldier met me outside the room and led me away, carving a path through the chaos as we descended to the first floor. The ghouls had made another probing attack against the walls, striking in the fading light with scaling ladders. They had been rebuffed, but our casualties were now flowing into the hospital, adding more bodies to the crowded space. The chilly air of the city was a relief after the packed heat inside, and I took a moment to acclimate to the temperature. The truly cold months were just beginning, but Skyroost's altitude and northern location made it feel like dead winter.

My arm still ached, though the sickly heat was gone from the wound. The few hours of sleep had done some good, but it was nowhere near enough time for a full recovery. I felt feeble in a way that was deeply unnerving, as if my body was held together by little more than spit and string. But the end was in sight, and I refused to waver when the finish line was so close.

The soldier who guided me was respectful and direct, informing me that the engineers had almost finished the construction of a crane capable of lowering me down to my sled and bringing the package back up. While the structure was opposite the main wall, it would still be visible to anyone looking at Skyroost from the way I had come. Even if the ghouls couldn't do anything to stop us, I hated that I might be giving away where the *Ridgerunner* was hiding to any keen observers.

We retraced the path I had taken earlier that day, though I still found myself instantly lost as soon as we entered the Warrens. The soldier seemed to know his way, though, and the twisting maze of tunnels soon spat us out near the guard tower where I had first met Stein. Two other guardsmen stood at the entrance to the tower now, their spears crossed over the opening until the soldier approached them with me in tow. I had the distinct feeling of a child with a rotating cast of babysitters as one of the guards bowed to me, then asked me to follow him up the steps. It did not take long to reach the spot where I had climbed the wall, though it looked far different now. A pair of large wooden wheels had been mounted on either side of the walkway, with a thick cable strung in between, dropping down either side of the wall. A pair of engineers fiddled with the contraption, then one put a brass pipe to her mouth and let out a short whistle. The wheels began to creak and rotate, and I peered over the city side edge to see the rope being pulled through a series of pulley blocks by a team of skellies. From the far side of the wall, a wooden platform began to move, rising level with the pathway so that guardsmen could pile various supplies onto it.

"Pretty clever!" Maki's voice boomed behind me, causing me to jump in alarm. It was difficult to sneak up on a courier, but the giant Fin had seemingly materialized from thin air.

"Gods, you nearly startled me off the wall!" I barked, though there was little malice in my voice. Maki just had an earnestness to him that made it hard to believe he ever meant you ill.

"My apologies, little courier. Your ghouls are waiting below, and we are about ready to start. Shall we?" He gestured for me to climb onto the platform, but I saw a rope net thrown over the wall nearby and chose to descend that way instead. My arm still felt stiff from the healers' ministrations, and the descent let me check what my damaged limb could take. I could still hold my own weight without too much difficulty, though any abrupt movement still sent a line of pain across the wound. Maki arrived at ground level on the descending platform at about the same time I finished my climb.

"Heh, you are so eager to climb! Good, good!" He patted me on the uninjured shoulder, then led me towards the cliff edge, which had been transformed into a small worksite. Balefire torches had been driven into the snow at regular intervals, blanketing the area in purple light. I also spied Stein nearby, directing a team of guardsmen to watch the perimeter. The few sparse trees had been cleared, replaced with metal spikes sunk deep into the frozen earth. These were bound to ropes and served as anchors for the large wooden construction that leans precariously over the cliff edge.

"She is very pretty!" Maki beamed, slapping a wooden beam with obvious pride. "Not bad for a few hours of work!"

He was right; lineage aside, the man knew his work. A small wooden platform had been built, with a tall A-frame standing at the far end. The frame was hinged so it could hang out over the cliff edge, with ropes securing the upper portions to the ground. A vertical wheel lined with spokes was mounted farther back, with another four skellies standing ready to winch it up or down. I spotted my ghouls nearby next to one of the torches, a thin rope tying them to one of the spikes to keep them from wandering. They seemed no worse for wear after the separation, and Scramble was perched upon a waist-high mound of snow he seemed to have piled up.

"I hate to be critical, but did we need all this set up for just one crate? I would have preferred just rigging a few ropes and getting this package up here while we still had daylight to spare."

"I would have liked that as well, little courier. It would have been done sooner, but we have few skilled builders left, and there are many broken things in this city to fix. As for size? We needed a long boom, or else you and cargo just get dragged over the rocks, bump, bump, bump. Not good for fragile cargo. And long boom needs sturdy support," he shrugged, seemingly unbothered by the questioning. "Plus, if you can climb up here, so can bad ghouls. We plan to lower a man down to survey the cliff, maybe find a way to stop them from coming up. Maybe you help us with that too."

"We'll see. I'm still injured, and I think the healers might be cross with me if I just go out and bust my arm up again. So, how are we doing this?" I asked, stepping onto the platform and tightening the straps of my climbing harness.

"After you climb this wall, going back down should be easy." Maki gestured to a pair of workers rigging a bosun's chair to the end of the tether. "Have you used one of these before?"

"It's been a while, but my father showed me how to use one," I answered.

"Good. Good! We will lower down a bag of straps with you. You slide down, tie up the box, and we pull you both back up."

"Sounds like a plan. Damn, I hate having to leave the *Ridgerunner* down there. Plus, I still need to figure out how to get her up. I could downclimb with the sled, but it would be far more difficult than the ascent had been. Maybe I can sidestep to a better route. Actually, I'll take you up on that offer to help tomorrow. Seeing the cliff in daylight might help with my problem as well."

"I am glad you are up to helping!" Maki laughed, gesturing to his workers to start their final preparations. "Though, for this, I can put your mind at ease. We will not be able to get to it soon, but I am confident we can retrieve your sled with the crane as well. I have seen them before; they are not so heavy. Though we may need to break down the heavier parts for separate trips."

Relief flooded my body, letting loose a tension I hadn't even been conscious of carrying. The *Ridgerunner* was my livelihood, my calling, my home. Leaving it perched on a mountainside had felt like abandoning a dear friend. Bringing her up here in jigsaw pieces wasn't ideal, but it was worlds better than abandoning her on some barren outcrop.

"Thank you, Maki," I told him, patting him on the shoulder though I nearly had to go to my tiptoes to accomplish the gesture. "Not a lot of people would understand how much that sled means to me."

"But I would, courier, my people are . . . largely nomadic. We rely on our sleds and our *kuolematon* to survive. You do not have this word; I think the closest translation would be 'immortal ancestor.' It is a more respectful title than 'ghoul' to my ears, at least. I see that you understand this respect, so there is no need to thank me," he replied, dropping that booming tone of his for the first time.

"But I'll thank you anyway," I told him. "Let's get to work."

XXXI

I had no reason to distrust the engineers' work, but that didn't stop me from double-checking every centimeter of the bosun's chair before I let it take my weight. A worker had approached to help tie me in, but I shooed him away with a gesture and a click of my tongue. I'd spent enough time on mountains to only trust knots tied by my own hands.

Regardless of the preparation, there was no way to completely quell the fear that arose when I leaned out over the edge, night's darkness making the thousand-meter drop look endless.

"I do feel like the bait on a fishing line, to be honest," I wondered aloud, dangling in the bosun's chair over the sheer drop below.

"Heh! Let us see what we can catch then!" Maki laughed, signaling to an engineer to begin. A large ratchet holding the vertical wheel in place was lifted free, and the ghouls went to work, slowly letting the wheel spin and paying out the line.

I began the descent, which was far smoother than I had expected given past experiences, though those had been slapdash affairs done by a team of men paying out rope. The boom kept me clear of the wall, and for the most part I could just relax and enjoy the ride. An oil lantern hung from a hook attached to the chair, enveloping me in a small bubble of warm light. Off to my right, I could see a green glow reflecting off the low clouds, the sickly viridescence of the enemy's brazier visible at even this distance. Out over that way, the cliff slanted lower, revealing a waste of bare snow and gnarled trees among crags of rock, with gaps barely wide enough to fit a skimmer sled through.

Barely wide enough to fit a sled . . .

"Oh, gods!" I shouted, jerking upright and accidentally sending myself spinning in circles.

"You OK!?" Maki shouted, peering down at me from above.

"Yeah!" I hollered back, getting my motion back under control. "Keep going!"

Damn it, I'd been too focused on the mission and too injured and fatigued for my mind to work out anything not related to my own concerns. But now I finally made the connection that had failed to click into place earlier. Bishop Rimkus' courier routes had been a blessing to me, letting me plot an alternate course to Skyroost, but there had also been a host of other routes that had no bearing on my path. One of those paths started at the bottom of the valley, snaking through trees and cliffs up to the doorstep of one of Skyroost's small side gates, all of which had been boarded up and abandoned years ago. There were many situations where someone might want to stop you from making your delivery, and this path would have been a fantastic way for someone to reach Skyroost while avoiding any prying eyes watching from the walls. My memory of the route was hazy, but I knew the terrain well enough, and that route had to pass damn close to the enemy camp if it wound around that part of the ridgeline.

If we could find the path, Skyroost could surprise the invaders, maybe even take that profane brazier down.

But, if the enemy found the path, they could pierce into the heart of the city without the defenders ever seeing it coming.

Either way, I would need to double-check if my recollection had been right. Luckily for me, my maps were in the *Ridgerunner*, and she was coming into view now, enough light leaking from behind her shelter to dye the snow purple.

The wall tapered away, leaving me dangling in open space as I descended the last few meters, calling up for the men above to stop when I drew level with the outcrop where I'd stashed my sled. I had done the best I could to protect the *Ridgerunner* in my absence; my team and I had pushed her snug against the wall and secured her with ropes, then rigged a tarp across, providing a bit of cover for my ghouls while hiding the light of the purple flame from prying eyes. That cover had come loose in one corner, the fabric now flapping in the wind, but I was just happy to see my old sled in one piece. That warm feeling faded a moment later as I realized there was still one more obstacle between me and my goal. The cliff we had scaled earlier sloped outward as it neared the top. That incline meant that I now hung awkwardly in space, five meters away from the ledge.

I tried swinging my legs to build momentum, but with no starting push and such a long rope above, it was damn near impossible to get any useful motion going. The wind wasn't helping either, and even the lightest gust killed any movement I tried to build.

"What is the problem?" Maki shouted down.

"I'm too far from the wall!" I barked back. "I'll try to figure something out!"

Damn, if I'd thought ahead, I could have brought a hook to throw and reel myself in. I could always let them reel me up, then come back down once I was more prepared, but I hadn't forgotten that we were running out of time. Couriers had some of the best cold weather gear in the Empire, and even I could feel the tips of my fingers start to go numb. I didn't know what Ronny's fear had been; maybe the glass would shatter, or maybe the cold did something to the composition of the medicine. The specifics were irrelevant. My goal was five gods-be-damned meters away, and I was going to reach it.

One thing I had going for me was that loose tarp flapping in the wind, giving me intermittent glimpses of the purple flame. I centered my focus on the fire, reaching out mentally for my team. The connection was there but tenuous, the flickering link spiking my head with something akin to vertigo.

"Champ! Get your big ass out here!" I hollered, his presence easily found even through the less-than-ideal conditions.

He poked his head up a moment later, looking around to find me. Amelia also scurried up into view, though I could have sworn I'd left her tied securely to the sled. After some trial and error, I coaxed them to pull the tarp down, Champ snapping the ropes with ease and bundling the fabric under the sled. That left the light of my balefire unhindered, allowing me to form a stronger link with my ghouls.

"Get the hook!" I called out, imprinting an image of the metal claw into Champ's mind. "Throw it to me."

If I managed to catch it, Champ would have no problem reeling me in. The big skeleton hopped into the back, digging around in the small pile of supplies we hadn't discarded at the base of the cliffs, but soon lost focus and started wandering around the sled. Ugh, Champ was strong as an ox, but time had worn his mind down until only his core behaviors remained. He could lift, climb, and fight, but getting him to do anything else was like trying to grasp smoke.

Casting my mind out, I began to pull Heist and Amelia forward. Either of them would still be smart enough to stay on task, and I still needed them to tie a rope to the hook first.

A pulse of simple contentment pulsed back along the link, drawing my attention back. Champ had found the hook and was holding it aloft in triumph. Then he followed through with the last order he'd been given: I had told him to throw the hook to me after all, and he was nothing if not eager to please. He hurled the metal hook with all his undead strength, sending it hurtling at me like a shot from a ballista.

"Shit!" I screamed, grabbing the rope above and pulling myself up with fear-fueled strength. The hook missed by a span of centimeters, continuing its long arc toward the ground below.

"If we survive this, I'm turning you into fertilizer!" I barked at him as I swung in the wind, sending the big ghoul sulking off.

"Uhm, should we pull you up?" Maki asked loudly.

"No!" I replied grumpily, trying to figure out what to do next.

So lost was I in my planning that I didn't notice Amelia at first digging around in the sled. Her mind caught my attention, though, pulsing with rhythms of determination and something else, something I rarely felt in the minds of the undead: Initiative. There was no better way to put it. Amelia was planning. I could feel the thrum of her mind growing louder as if she were putting the pieces of a puzzle together. Even after acclimating to her personality over the trip, the behavior was still a bit unsettling. To have retained this much focus as a ghoul, Amelia couldn't have been dead more than a few months, maybe even weeks. What was her story?

But that was a mystery for another time. I didn't have a better idea, so I flowed encouragement into her, curious to see what she was up to. Amelia emerged from the sled with a rope knotted into a loop, and I felt my hopes drop. I'd already thought of that but knew that the rope was far too light to be thrown the distance without something heavy to give it weight. There must be something in the sled heavy enough for the task, a spare tool maybe?

Amelia apparently had a different plan, though, as she slipped the loop over her shoulder and began to climb. The ghoul confidently made her way up the wall, following the same path we'd taken earlier until she reached the slab above, just at the edge of the balefire light. She sank her climbing hook into a crack in the stone, then squatted upside down, compressing herself back against the rock face. She looked outward with a rhythm of deep focus, stance reminiscent of a crouched predator preparing to spring . . .

"Oh no . . . nonoNO!" I reached out with my mind to stop her, but already knew I'd be too late.

Amelia flung herself into the void. The world seemed to slip into slow motion as she flew, arms stretched out like wings as she twisted in midair, a hawk diving down onto her prey. The world sped back up as she slammed into the rope four meters above, sending me swinging wildly as she began to fall, scrabbling for a grip with her one intact hand as she plummeted towards me. Moments before collision, she succeeded, wrapping an arm and leg around the rope and rapidly slowing in the final two meters before impact. Amelia ended up coming to a stop straddling my bosun's chair; her expressionless corpse face mere centimeters from my own. Zeb's ghoul docs had done a respectable job, and rot hadn't yet laid its touch on her. One could have believed she was wearing a porcelain mask bearing the visage of a young woman if not for her milky eyes and sunken cheeks.

The light around us dimmed, and I looked down to see my lantern in free fall, a speck of light tumbling, shrinking until it winked out in the blackness below us. I was sharply reminded of exactly how far off the ground I was and turned to the ghoul in my lap to distract from the fear.

"You just earned your nickname, Hawk." I panted, very much aware of the closeness and that the purple flame reflected in her glassy eyes was the sole force keeping her from ripping my throat out.

There was a clamor of excitement from above as the engineers looked on, some shouting in alarm while Maki hooted with joy. I kept one eye on Amelia, whose name had already become Hawk in my mind, then reached out to Champ, calling him to reel in the rope attached to her. I needed to coordinate a bit with Maki, paying out extra slack as we went, but soon I was back on solid ground, reunited with my beloved *Ridgerunner* and her crew. Like any good courier, I saw to them before anything else, making sure that no damage had befallen the sled or ghouls in my absence. I was relieved to see that the tarp had shielded both from the worst of the weather; there was some minor damage where a loose bit of tack had knocked against the chassis, but overall, I was quite happy with how they had fared.

"Give me a minute to check things out!" I called up before ducking into my cab, enjoying the subdued silence after the constant howling of the wind outside. Even a thousand meters up and perched on a cliffside, this place was home. The calm of familiar territory washed over me, adding a surety to my movements as I dug around my maps, locating the translucent pages that contained the secret courier routes.

"Oh, you beautiful little bastard." I breathed, tapping a finger against the page. The path was there, starting at the grove near the ghoul camp and snaking along the ridge all the way to the side gate. You didn't need to be a brilliant tactician to see that this information might hold the key to ripping the undead heart out of the besieging army. Though it pained me to deface such a valuable map, I drew my long knife and cut out the section containing the secret route, along with the map overlay needed to make sense of it. The people of Skyroost and I were on the same side, but that didn't mean I was planning to hand over any more courier secrets than strictly necessary. With that task complete, I grabbed the ledger I'd need to officially complete the contract, then glanced around, wondering if there was anything else I should take care of while I was here.

It was difficult to leave the coalblade behind, but it wasn't something I could explain away that easily. I decided to have a talk with Maki, then smuggle it up when I surveyed the cliffs tomorrow. That power it bestowed had been . . . intoxicating. I had some skill at fighting ghouls, but that blade had transformed me into an avatar of destruction on the battlefield. I imagined leading a counterattack against the ghoul camp, cutting monsters down in great swaths like wheat before the scythe.

But this fight was bigger than me, and I had to let logic dictate the path instead of my ego. It was unlikely that I could convince anyone that I had stumbled across the weapon out in the wilds, and even if I could, what then? With balefire on my side, I could tear through ghouls; I'd proven that to myself. But I wouldn't be fighting a mindless horde in the purple light whose intentions I could read and predict. I would be fighting intelligent creatures, ones that could apparently think and strategize. No, if that coalblade was going to turn the tide, it had a far better chance of doing so in the hands of a trained warrior.

So, once I had the coalblade in the city, I would give it to Stein. I didn't know who else I could trust, and Stein seemed the pragmatic sort. My bet is that he would happily lie to his superiors about how he came to find the coalblade if that was the price of acquiring such a game-changing weapon. I didn't know any other soldiers I could trust, and I felt confident that he would see it used in the most effective way possible.

After a moment's deliberation, I retrieved my battle gear, buckling on the vambrace and gorget. Given the situation, I would rather plan for violence and find peace than hope for peace and get blindsided by violence.

Once suitably equipped, I bid the familiar space farewell and went back to the task at hand. The crate had been tied down so securely that even the vertical tilt of the climbing sled would not knock it loose, so getting it free proved difficult through the thick fabric of my gloves. So close to the finish, I was tempted to just reduce the straps to shreds with my knife, but such wanton waste would have my old teachers turning in their graves. So, I took a breath and set to work, getting the package free, then retying the straps into a cradle to haul the crate skyward. It took a bit of coordination, Tybalt and Champ lifting the crate up while I scuttled underneath with lengths of rope, but soon enough, the task was done. Before I departed again, I made sure to check over my team, resecure the tarp, and just generally make sure that they would be safe on their own for the near future.

The departure went smoother than my arrival, at least. The engineers slowly took up the slack while Champ took the strain on a second rope from his position. As the line winched up, the crate and I began to slide towards the edge, swinging like a pendulum outward until Champ's strong grip arrested the movement, paying out the line until I settled directly below the crane above. I cast Champ's rope away and gave him the command to return to his position with the others. The final order I gave him was to pull the last flap of the tarp up, cutting off the balefire's light and severing our mental connection.

XXXII

There are certain moments in life that just radiate raw, unadulterated audacity. That sort of belligerent shout into the void that you are alive despite the world's best efforts, and it will take far more than that to bring you down.

As the crane reeled in the last few meters of line and drew me level with the platform, I felt that moment flow through me. I also made a mental note to commission a giant oil painting to commemorate it once I retired. Courier Winona, armored and grinning, standing astride a crate of medicine above an endless drop. Firelight lit her face while darkness swelled behind her in black and gray swirls. I would sit by the fire, bounce my grandkids on my knee, and point to the painting, dazzling them with tales of Courier Winona and her adventures.

The engineering squad cheered as they pulled the crate onto solid ground with long, hooked poles, then clapped me on the back as I untied my harness and stepped down. Waiting soldiers moved in, shepherding skellies to lift the crate and bring it back to the city. I breathed a long sigh of relief, my job done, and gratefully accepted a balefire torch, reconnecting with King, Scramble, and Bonk and calling them to my side.

"That was amazing!!!" A familiar voice called out half a second before Erika collided with me, almost knocking me over as she pulled me into a tight hug.

"You were down there! And then you rode that big crate up! And then—" She finally noticed my ghouls and scurried behind my back with a squeak of surprise. "Are those . . . yours?"

I chuckled, then put a reassuring hand on her arm. "Don't worry. They're quite tame if we stay in the firelight, though I still wouldn't get too close. Erika, meet King, Bonk, and Scramble."

"Uhh . . . Hi . . . ," Erika murmured, waving a hand in greeting while carefully keeping me in between her and the ghouls.

Sensing her discomfort, I led her a short distance away. "Erika, it's nice to see you, and I don't mean to be rude, but what are you doing here? It's too dangerous for you outside the walls."

Her demeanor recovered instantly, regaining much of her former energy. "Well, I was thinking about you and all you're doing to help Skyroost, and you're not even from here! So, if you could do all this for us, there had to be something I could do!" She looked over my shoulder, eyes catching on something.

"Hey! Make sure everybody's had one before you get seconds!" she shouted with surprising force.

I turned to see a group of men pouring drinks from a pair of large ceramic jugs. Each jug was wrapped in cloth and had wisps of steaming issuing from its open mouth.

"I brought you some mulled cider and bread too! Went down to the kitchens not long after you left and hauled them all the way here!"

She was beaming now, and I couldn't help but smile. It was a small gesture in the scheme of things, but a hot drink was always welcome on a cold day, and I knew that her kindness would bolster the good cheer that my delivery had fostered for the soldiers of Skyroost. I thanked her for the efforts, and she nearly skipped away to help distribute steaming mugs of cider and slices of still-warm bread.

"Stein, could I have a moment?" I asked, sticking the torch upright in the ground and waving to the sergeant.

"I think you've earned far more than a moment, courier. That medicine should help us get the sick back on their feet, and I'm sure the healers will find a use for it with the wounded as well. The situation is still dire, but you've given us a much-needed breath of hope." Stein grinned, his dour mood lifted by the delivery and the mug of cider cupped in his rough hand. "What can I do for you?"

"Well, I'm gonna do you a big favor, then you're gonna do me a small one." I grinned, savoring his confused expression before letting him in on what I had discovered.

"This . . . is a map of a courier route, a trade secret among my order that we *never* share with outsiders. These routes let us dodge bandit ambushes, beat oncoming storms to our destination, they keep us alive," I told him, holding up the folded pages. "And unless my geography is off, this route details a secret path from one of Skyroost's side gates, alllllll the way down to the rise where that damned green brazier sits."

I handed the pages over, watching his face go from skeptical to puzzled to incredulous as he looked over the treasure I had just given him.

"Can I?" he asked, turning back towards the walls.

"Give it to a runner. I still need you for a moment. Use that information well, but please, destroy the original once you've made a copy. And if anyone ever asks how you found that path, you didn't get it from me." I winked at him, caught up in his excitement. Stein let out a shrill whistle to summon a young assistant, the teenager's guardsman uniform too small for his lanky frame. Stein put the fear of the gods in the poor boy, then sent him scurrying back into the city, along with the map and orders to get it to the Duke with all haste.

"What do you need me for?" he asked, turning his attention back to me.

"Yes, as recompense for this gift, I require your firstborn child." I intoned, deadpan.

Stein blanched, sputtering for a moment in confusion.

"Hah! I'm just fucking with you. I need a signature for the crate. I swear, the Balefire Express has so many forms and contracts you'd think it was a part of the treasury instead of the church. Usually, I would have been given the name of a specific person at the destination to sign off, but I forgot to ask Ronny in all the rush of leaving."

I sighed for a moment, the scenes of destruction I'd seen earlier resurfacing. "I was supposed to get it to Skyroost, so having the ranking member of their city guard sign off on it should do well enough to close the contract."

I talked him through the process, opening the compact ledger and unfolding the contract Ronny had signed in Ozero all those long days ago. The leather case contained a bone-handled fountain pen supplied by the Balefire Express, its ink a secret blend used for the signing of contracts. Stein signed on the line, using a hapless subordinate as a makeshift writing desk.

"One last thing," I told him as I accepted the pen back. Another pouch on the case produced a thin needle with a three-pronged head like a trident.

"Ugh, I've heard about this part," Stein complained, presenting his hand to me. I jabbed him in the pad of his thumb, drawing three small beads of blood across the callused surface. I spread the blood evenly across his thumb with the tool, then turned his hand over and pressed it into an empty space on the journal, leaving a bloody thumbprint on the page.

"A bit archaic, don't you think?" He stuck his thumb in his mouth, sucking on the wound.

"You're a big tough soldier. You'll recover, and hey, if you're looking for progressive thinking, don't look to the church," I laughed, waving the journal to dry the thumbprint before folding it back into my coat.

Whumpwhumpwhump

"What's that noise?" I wondered aloud. Stein had noticed it too, a low rhythmic humming that was increasing in volume, drawing our eyes to a cluster of trees that clung to the cliffside a short distance away.

"Get down!" he shouted, drawing his sword and stepping in front of me.

The foliage erupted with ghouls, green light shining as the creatures unveiled their partially covered lanterns. Ahead of their charge flew a wave of projectiles, plunging arrows and whirling bolas spinning with that distinctive *whumpwhump* sound. One bola shot overhead, tangling around a soldier's balefire torch and ripping it from his grasp. The coals hissed and died as they fell into the snow, allowing the darkness to pool in closer around us. More projectiles were launched toward Stein and me, still standing on the platform. I gave a shrill whistle and sent Scramble rushing forward. I was not about to let him get close to that green light, but I could create a makeshift shield using his body to intercept the projectiles.

Stein wrapped a thick arm around me, diving behind the base of the crane as Scramble fell into a jumble of bones, tangled in a lattice of bolas chords. The soldiers nearby attempted to form a ragged line of battle, but the hail of arrows had them wavering before the ghouls could even close the distance. At the last moment before the sides met, the green-eyed ghouls skidded to a stop, avoiding the purple torch glow as if it were a ring of fire. Instead, they channeled their momentum into an attack, hurling short spears into the soldiers. Two more torch bearers went down, one with a spear driven clean through his chest. Their torches fell with them, and the true intent of the attack became clear. As the purple light faded, our own skellies went feral, going wild as they tore into the soldiers who, moments before, had been controlling them.

"We need to go!" I shouted, now pulling Stein along and gathering my remaining ghouls around me.

Whumpwhumpwhump

I never saw the bolas that hit, never even had time to brace for it. All I felt was a sudden tug, and then the torch was ripped out of my hand. The coals scattered out over the drop, becoming little purple meteors before winking out in the distance below.

Stein and I looked up at each other as the light faded, then over at King and Bonk, the purple light fading from their eyes.

My heart stopped, fear seizing it in my chest. "Oh shi—"

Then they were on us. King leapt at Stein, knocking the big man back a step and bringing his mouth down for a bite. Stein was saved from a gruesome end by King's mask, which kept the necrotic teeth from making contact. The soldier roared as he fell, trying to force the ghoul's face away with a meaty palm.

Then my world spun, Bonk tackling me to the ground as I turned to face him, gasping, the breath knocked out of me by the impact. Bonk went for the neck as well, biting into my gorget so deeply that the leather creaked in protest. Snow and cold mud splashed across my face as panic began to bubble up in my chest, hands punching ineffectually at Bonk's thick helmet, the blows failing to dislodge the creature. Every instinct screamed at me to keep trying to push him off, but training saved me, muscle memory taking over even as my composure broke and I cried out in fear. My hand dropped away, allowing Bonk to bite deeper into the leather while I drew my long knife from my belt.

Terror coursed through me, then was pushed away by a bracing rush of anger. With a scream, I hammered the handle of the knife into Bonk's jaw again and again until the bone snapped. All his magical strength meant nothing if the bones were no longer connected, and his bite went slack against my armor. Capitalizing on the advantage, I pulled my feet up and set them against his hipbones, kicking out with all my strength to hurl the ghoul away. He tumbled, gained his feet, and hurtled back at me in the span of a heartbeat, giving me no time to draw my coalknife.

If I ran, he would chase me. If I fought, he would rip me apart.

I sank down into a low stance, arms forward, hands open as if warding him off. With no sane option, I'd have to risk it all on an insane one.

It would never have worked with an unknown feral ghoul: too unpredictable, too many unknowns. But I had spent every day on the job looking out my windscreen, watching how my team ran, how they moved, internalizing their motions until they were as familiar as my own.

When Bonk began to crouch low for his leap, I saw the move coming a kilometer away. He flew forward, and as he grasped for my shoulders, I pivoted, reaching out to draw him closer. Then I slid my hip under him, turning sharply with a shout and flinging him over my shoulder. Ghouls were strong, but they were light, and Bonk flew much farther than his size would have implied. He bounced off the snow once, scrabbled for purchase, then disappeared as he skidded off the cliff edge, plummeting out of sight.

I hauled myself to my feet, watching a creature that had saved my life more than once get swallowed by the blackness. He had been a wild animal and a merciless killer, but he'd been mine, and a part of me would mourn him, same as Grah.

My arm wound stung, but the healer had done their work well, and the stitching held. I turned away to help Stein, but my vision was filled by sudden movement as the haft of a spear swung towards my head.

XXXIII

Consciousness returned as it always did after a knockout: slowly, then all at once.

First was a sense of movement, a rocking motion like I was swinging back and forth on a hammock swaying just a bit too fast. Then the sounds, the crunch of snow, muffled whimpers of fear. Lastly, the pain, a dull ache deep in my head matched by sharper jabs in my arm, wrists, and ankles.

With a gasp, I woke, flailing in panic. The world was upside down, swinging wildly in a blur of color. I twisted, fought, tried to right the world. Then something jabbed me hard in the side, the sharp impact jolting me into full awareness.

I was . . . hanging upside down. My wrists and ankles were bound to a long pole with a ghoul at either end, carrying me between them like a fresh deer carcass. Groggily, I glanced around, squinting through the green light flooding my inverted perspective. Other ghouls stalked nearby, many leading prisoners along the edge of the city walls. It was tough going, and discomfort shot through my wrists and ankles as one of the ghouls carrying me slipped on a loose rock. The wall on this side had been built to leave little more than a dirt path between it and the cliff, just enough for engineers to be able to inspect the fortifications from the outside.

There were people on the wall too, Skyroost soldiers mirroring

our movement. I wondered why they didn't attack, didn't rush out
to capitalize on the terrain and pin the ghouls against the fatal drop of
the cliff edge. Then I realized that all the prisoners had a captor at their
back, and each ghoul that walked behind them had a weapon close at
hand. I could even make out Stein, the big man limping in pain as a
short ghoul stretched up to press a blade against his face.

So not just prisoners, then, hostages. The raiding party that captured us would stroll right back to their camp, and there was nothing
the soldiers above could do about it. And that was exactly what they
did. They followed the line of the wall back to the killing fields I'd
witnessed earlier in the day; being carried on the jostling pole was
thoroughly nauseating, but this was one part of the journey that I
was glad to be carried through. The cold mud here had not refrozen,
and many of the captives tripped and fell into the frigid muck. With
their arms bound behind them, the prisoners couldn't even break their
falls as they collapsed into the filth, wriggling like maggots until the
ghouls eventually hauled them back to their feet. The ghouls themselves were far more surefooted, trampling through mud and over
bodies with little difficulty. Tiny will-o'-wisps flashed in the dark,
creating a miniature starscape whose mystery I only solved as we left
the killing field behind, and the lights began to wink out. They were
ghouls, bodies too shattered to move, eyes reflecting the green light
as their heads turned to follow our passage.

Even if we could escape, I could scarcely imagine a more terrifying task than wading through that mud in the pitch-black night,
surrounded by the squelching movements of hungry, broken monsters.

The party trudged onward, beginning the trek downhill as we left
the carnage behind. I counted twenty or thirty ghouls, though keeping
track of the headcount in my current predicament was difficult. Some
of the ghouls wore the regalia of the Skyroost skellies, now walking
alongside their attackers without any restraints. The observation made
me wonder where King and Scramble had disappeared to, but my position severely limited what I could see around me. Had they survived

the onslaught? Or had they tumbled over the cliff in the fighting, plunging down to shatter on the rocks below? We soon entered the trees, and the last vestiges of outside light faded. Our group existed in a pool of sickly green light, pure blackness pooling around us as if eager to spill inward. Discerning any direction should have been next to impossible, but our captors continued on an arrow-straight course until the trees ahead began to thin.

"I'd like to walk," I protested, twisting to look at the ghoul slouching along next to me. He looked relatively fresh, but his nose had been ripped away, leaving a gaping hole behind. "My legs work fine. Just let me off this thing, and I'll stroll right along."

The creature glanced at me but made no move to comply.

"Hey, you arrogant sack of rancid meat, I'm talking to you!"

He poked me with the butt of his spear, not hard, but enough to get the message across.

Shut up.

I kept my mouth shut after that.

The trees began to clear a few moments later. The green light glowed brighter, the giant brazier becoming visible as the trees thinned out, giving way to a field of stumps that ended in a long wall of piled stone and dirt. There was no gate, merely a hole cut in the earthen barrier with sharp-eyed sentries perched on either side. The ramshackle tents I'd spied from the wall were scattered around, though they appeared deserted now that night had fallen. Our captors stopped before the sentries for a moment and seemed to gesture back and forth at each other wordlessly until the sentries turned aside and allowed us entry. Beyond, I expected to find a continuation of the dilapidated tent city, ghouls squatting amid structures of rope and canvas. Instead, we entered a marvel of earthmoving, the product of having an undead workforce that neither tired nor slept.

The entirety of the hill had been hollowed out, the slope cut into a series of descending terraces that curved out into the distance, merging into a trench that stretched across to seal off the mouth of the valley.

Torches of green fire twinkled like a scattering of fireflies, paling in comparison to the verdant bonfire that blazed in the grand brazier overhead. The ghouls relaxed their grip on the prisoners after we entered camp; after all, where were we going to run to? Stein managed to maneuver himself beside me as we were led down a series of dirt ramps, descending deeper into the encampment.

"Are you OK?" he muttered, keeping his eyes forward.

"Oh, I'm all sunshine and wildflowers," I groaned.

"Do you think they can understand us?" Stein asked, glancing around at our captors.

"Hey, you, where are you taking us!?" I called to No-nose walking beside me, but received no reaction. "Were you that ugly before you died, or has death improved your looks?"

"Are you trash-talking the ghoul?" Stein whispered.

"If he gets mad, then he understands me," I explained.

"Or he'll just hit you because you're loud!" Stein hissed.

"Hey, jackass!" I growled, pressing a thumb tip between my fingers and wiggling it against the bindings. "Got your nose."

I braced myself for the rebuttal, but the spear butt still stung as he jabbed me in the ribs, harder this time.

"Owww, yup, felt that one . . . Yes, Stein, I'd say they can understand us," I grunted.

The trees that had been felled were found here, carved into supports to keep the dirt walls from spilling into the excavation. It seemed so much work for an army that had little to fear from the elements, and I said as much to Stein.

"I thought so too. Seemed crazy to me; any guardsman could take the high ground and fire a rain of arrows down here. Then I realized, so what?" he explained, gesturing at the walls. You could turn a ghoul into a pincushion of arrows, and it would do little to hamper them. We would need siege artillery if we wanted to hurt the undead at a distance, and there is no way to hit them from the walls with their camp set into the ground like this. It also hides their true numbers;

I'm not sure what the estimates were, but from our walls, you'd have guessed that this army was half the size. They've hidden their numbers, shielded themselves from artillery, and cut off the mouth of the valley completely, all by digging a hole. I don't know what's going on here, but these things are smart . . . ."

I pondered that as we descended onto a terrace midway down the slope, a large crescent cut wider than the levels above or below it. Nestled against one wall was a sprawling tent structure comprised of a wide conical main tent with a pair of rectangular rooms jutting off to either side like wings. The canvas of the entire structure was black chased with motifs of interlocking golden chains. It looked like the most macabre circus tent I had ever seen. Our party stopped a few meters away from the entrance, and the ghouls carrying my pole dropped it abruptly, dumping me onto the ground. I lay there stunned for a moment, then began to roll onto my knees as the pole was pulled from between my bonds. The frozen ground was uneven against my back, pressing into me uncomfortably as I wriggled over onto my knees. Stones ranging from the size of a head to the size of a carriage lay strewn across the terrace, still half embedded in the ground and apparently deemed too much effort to remove. With a careful hop, I managed to balance on my bound feet but would have fallen over if not for Stein lending a steadying arm. Our captors pulled and prodded at us until we formed a curving line around the tent's entrance. On one side were the humans: Stein, I, and maybe a dozen guardsmen and engineers, with Maki standing towards the back, catching my eye with a nod. With a shock, I recognized Erika as well, slumped on the ground and shaking with fear. I'd completely forgotten about her in all the intervening chaos. On the other side were the captive ghouls: four of the skellies used to power the crane, as well as King and Scramble. My heart sang to see them safe, though there was something . . . off about them. All the captured ghouls peered around at the camp surrounding us with far more perceptiveness and energy than would be expected from their normal placid behavior, and their eyes now reflected the green light of the profane brazier.

ShkaShkaShkaShka

A dry rattling of bones echoed from within the tent, building to a crescendo like water pulling back from the shore as a wave built. Then the wave broke, and a tide of bone spilled out of the tent. Dozens of small skeletons, most not even half my height, tumbled out into the open. Each had a metal round shield strapped to their backs as large as they were, giving each the appearance of a baby turtle crawling frantically for the ocean.

"Gods," Stein whispered, color draining from his face. "They're children."

The sight of them was disturbing in a way that went beyond fear. I had seen child ghouls before, of course; children could succumb to a bite just as easily as an adult. But seeing such a mass of them, crawling all over each other, bones polished to a brilliant ivory shine . . . it twisted my stomach with the wrongness of it.

I could not imagine a sight more perverse and twisted . . . Until the abomination emerged from the darkened interior of the tent and shambled into the verdant glow.

XXXIV

The creature that appeared from the darkness was a thing of nightmares, a massive skeletal golem pieced together from a dozen disparate creatures. The spine and ribcage were enormous, like those of a draft horse. The monster's legs were stubby and squat, while its arms were long enough to reach down to the dirt; Instead of walking, it paced forward on all four limbs, supporting its bulk by hunching forward and pressing the giant knuckles of its hands into the ground.

Gold finery adorned many of the polished white bones, encrusting the surface with jeweled rings, chains, and nets. The decoration was concentrated in the center of the skeleton's ribcage, where the bone itself had been scrimshawed into elaborate shapes and inlaid with precious metals. Heavy metal shackles bound the ribs with chain, creating a lattice inside the abomination's chest. From this lattice hung a large metal censer, blazing with that sickly green flame. The fire lit the creature from within, creating a lambent glow that spilled out from its chest, casting nightmarish shadows across the faces of those gathered before it. A very human skull perched between the massive shoulders, wreathed in smoke and flickering light.

Everyone reacted differently. Stein's hand twitched for a sword he no longer carried while I crouched low, trying to seem small and not worthy of notice. An engineer nearby vomited loudly while a soldier behind her simply . . . broke. His scream filled the night air as he recoiled, shoving the ghoul guarding him and sending them both falling onto the ground. There was a quick scuffle, but the soldier stood up first, whirling on the abomination. He had the ghoul's crossbow in his hand.

"Die, fiend!" he screamed, pulling the trigger as ghouls closed in on him from every direction.

The bolt that spat from the weapon had no real hope of killing the monster, but the projectile never even reached its target. The child skeletons, which had been crawling in placid circles at the abomination's feet, reacted to the danger like a kicked hornet's nest. They swiftly piled up onto each other, forming a precarious barricade in front of the abomination. A metal ping signaled that the bolt had ricocheted off one of the shields, then the whole wall collapsed forward, cutting off the soldier's scream as they crushed him under the weight.

There was a heartbeat of frenetic movement, then the children retreated, pooling once again around the abomination's feet. The soldier was dead, his remains torn to unrecognizable chunks in seconds.

The abomination did something with its knuckles, knocking them together to produce a rhythmic pattern of clicks. A slight figure detached itself from the shadow of the tent opening, stepping forward into the green firelight emanating from the creature's chest cavity. This figure was a woman, a living woman, though her hairless head made her appear ghoulish in her own right. A heavy silver collar was clasped around her throat, with a metal chain trailing off it, winding across the ground until it disappeared somewhere within the body of the abomination. If she was alarmed by the scene around her, she did not show it, instead positioning herself off to the side and turning to face the giant skeleton.

The monster sat back on its haunches, then began to gesture, twisting its massive digits into a rapid series of intertwining shapes. The woman began to speak, projecting her clear voice out into the crowd as she watched the hand movements, apparently translating them on the fly.

"You stand before the Grand Scapula Ramses, The Shoulder that Supports the Arm of the Continuum. He Who Carries the Flame Within Him. The Lambent One. The Heart of the Shield Swarm." The woman bellowed the myriad titles with surprising volume. "All shall kneel before him in deference to his majesty!"

I obeyed the order, sinking to my knees and pulling Stein with me. I loved nothing more than spitting in the face of authority when given the opportunity, but even I could tell when discretion was the better play; we gained nothing by antagonizing this creature.

"Humans of this feral waste! You stand accused of the following crimes: Slavery, heresy, genocide, and the use of foul magicks! Each of you will stand before the Grand Scapula to answer for your crimes and beg his mercy. Those who can prove their dedication to serving the Continuum may find redemption. Those who refuse will be punished accordingly," she intoned, never even turning to look at us.

The abomination shuffled, turning to look at the captured ghouls, his translator pivoting to follow.

"As for the Undying forced to live in servitude, you are free. Throw off the shackles you have been bound by! You were slaves before; now take your rightful place as rulers! You may depart if you wish. We will not stop you." At this, the abomination stuck out a long arm, gesturing expansively to the darkness beyond the firelight.

"You may take the path of darkness but know that your minds will be stolen as soon as you leave our torches, turning you back into the dull beasts that these humans saw fit to shackle. Or you can stay and start anew as a child of the Continuum."

The captured ghouls, both the imperial skellies and my own team, looked at each other. One clacked its jaw together over and over as if it were trying to speak. The green fire had . . . awoken something in them, filling them with a level of intelligence that even the most exaggerated legends had never spoke of. King stepped forward, moving up to the edge of where the shield children curled around their master. Then he placed a fist against his chest and bowed deeply.

The other ghouls looked at each other for a moment, then followed King's example, bowing to their new master.

"Good, Good. Welcome to the Continuum, my children." He rotated his bulk again to face the humans. "Take these vermin from my sight. See that their . . . biological failings are cared for. Bring the first to my pavilion for questioning at sunrise."

He turned away, knucklewalking back into the darkness of his tent, the child-swarm flowing inside behind him. I felt a light kick in my ribs and looked up to see a ghoul prodding me into motion. My limbs had recovered enough to let me stand without assistance, and our captors herded us together, leading the humans further into the encampment. I craned my neck to get one last look at King and Scramble before we were pushed away, but my boys were being led in a different direction, and neither looked back.

XXXV

As the guards led us deeper into camp, I began to calm. Adrenaline had carried me through the last few hours, but you can only remain at red alert levels of terror for so long before the fear begins to burn itself out. Yes, we were in a bad way. Yes, torture and death were imminent, but breaking down and crying wasn't going to do me any good. That's not to say I was fearless, quite the opposite. I was as scared as I'd ever been. But I had been scared when the bandits attacked, when Foss shot me, when the champion of the cave people had fought Tybalt. And now all those bastards were stone dead, and I was still breathing. There was always a way out, a way to survive, if you were willing to pay the cost. And I would pay just about anything to watch that abomination's plans crumble around him.

"You OK?" Stein asked, catching up to me. "You're smiling . . . ."

"More like 'baring my teeth', I think," I told him, sighing ruefully.

Thick poles had been pounded into the earth at irregular intervals along the path, with large metal cages dangling from each. Maybe I was simply overtired, but my first thought was puzzling over the logistics of dragging the cages all the way from wherever they had come from. That thought was swept away when I realized that a quarter of the cages were . . . occupied. Each contained a person, crammed in so tight that they needed to sit with their knees tucked beneath their chins. A few of the individuals tried to call out, reaching thin arms

355

between the bars to get our attention. Our guards put a stop to that quick enough though, sending the cages swinging with a whack of their spears.

We were shepherded into a wooden shack, a sturdy construction of fresh timber bound with metal, with the guards frisking each of us before we were pushed inside. It was fortunate that the ghouls were amateurs at the task; they took away the long knife on my belt and my courier ledger but missed the coalknife and vial of henbane secreted on my person. There was a moment of trepidation as I crossed the threshold, fearing that we would find ourselves crammed into some dank cell, but my worries were unfounded. This building had clearly been purpose-built to hold living prisoners in relative comfort. A small fire pit crackled in the center of the room, the smoke trailing up through a hole in the roof. A length of fabric hung across an alcove leading to a privy that was honestly nothing more than a bench with a hole cut in it. Wooden benches lined the walls, though, with a dozen of us in here, some would have to sit on the frozen earth. The building was cozier than a few courier shacks I had slept in, though there were plenty of reminders that this was a prison cell, first and foremost. The heavy click of a metal lock was audible behind us as the door was shut, and the hole in the roof above the fire was also covered with metal bars. Even the privy had been secured, the hole below it lined with heavy stones to prevent us from trying to tunnel out.

"I appreciate your ... thoroughness," Stein remarked as I gave up on rattling a wooden board I had hoped to wiggle loose.

"It was worth a shot," I muttered, slumping down onto the bench next to him as he fed another log to the crackling flames. Erika sat on my other side, gently leaning against me until her head rested on my shoulder. The position was a bit awkward, as Erika was taller than me by a fair margin, but I couldn't bring myself to shift her. We were all beaten up, but the trauma of our capture must have been magnitudes more severe for a girl who didn't have the mental calluses that came from fighting and living around the undead.

Between the fire and the packed bodies, the small space warmed up soon enough, allowing us to shed our coats and use them as cushions over the hard ground. I checked my arm and was unsurprised to see the white bandage spotted with red. The pain was minor, and the limb could still move well enough, so I figured it was the least of my problems.

"What happens to us now?" a soldier asked, staring mournfully into the fire.

"They're gonna eat us, idiot." an engineer scowled, leaning back against the wall. I felt Erika tense against me at the words, and I rubbed her back in slow circles until she calmed again.

"Easy now, let's not get too worked up. If they're smart, they'll wait till right before their next attack to eat us. Though who knows if they still have a taste for it . . . ," I murmured, realizing after a moment later that this reasoning was of no comfort.

"What are you on about?" the engineer snapped, pulling me from my reverie. I had just been thinking aloud, a habit born of spending too much time alone on the road.

"She is a courier, and I would talk to her more respectfully, engineer Frida," Maki spoke up for the first time, scolding his subordinate. "She fought them, threw a ghoul off the cliff while we tried to flee. I would believe she has more experience with ghouls than the rest of us put together. So maybe we listen."

He gestured for me to continue, and I took a moment to gather my thoughts. Yeah, I had a wealth of knowledge on the subject, more than most. But outside of a newbie courier like Billy, I rarely found an audience for it. The attention pulsed a minor jolt of stage fright through me before I pushed through the feeling and began to speak.

"Ghouls . . . they don't need to eat. They crave living prey, but it's not necessary for survival. They can continue walking for years without ever getting a meal. As far as couriers have been able to figure, ghouls . . . how do I say this . . . ? They drain your life away when they eat you. The meat they swallow doesn't get digested; it's not like their dead stomachs work. Whatever magic gives them life also steals life from their victims. It's why no medicine can cure a bite, and it's why their prey needs to be living. When they feed, it gives them a boost; they become faster, stronger, more alert. But that boost is temporary and lasts a day at most. If they are smart enough to do all this—" I gestured to the shack we were in and the camp beyond "—I assume they'd want to use that energy for something."

"Like attacking Skyroost again." Stein understood.

"Yeah. We know these ghouls are smart, like human-smart. Maybe that means that eating another human might not be as appetizing anymore," I shrugged.

"That big one could even talk, in a way," Frida added. "Like you were saying, they're smart. Do you think . . . Do you think they're the people they were when they died? Have the souls of the dead come back to their bodies to live again?"

Dammit, I was a courier, but I was also a deacon, though religious questions of this magnitude were far beyond my purview to contemplate. But these people wanted answers, they wanted guidance, and I was the sole representative of the Balefire Church present to give that to them.

"The holy scriptures tell us that when we die, our souls join with the balefire, living on eternally, safeguarding those still living from harm," I told them, trying to sound convincing. "I've seen fawns—fresh-turned ghouls—act strangely, showing far more personality than one would expect. It's very possible that this blasphemous flame enhances the echoes of life latent in all ghouls, gifting them with a twisted mirror of humanity."

The others accepted that answer, relieved by an explanation that fit their worldview. Erika seemed to steady herself as well, picking her head up and taking a greater interest in our discussion. Maki looked distracted by his own thoughts, though, and was staring out into space. The Fin man would have been raised with different beliefs and was probably wrestling with his own questions of faith as well. As for me,

I had told them what the church taught, but had chosen to leave out my own thoughts on the subject. What if... what if this green fire really did bring souls back? That would mean ....

I shook my head to clear away the thoughts. Idle speculation was not productive now, though there was precious little else to do. I still had my coalknife, but even if I could slay the next guard who opened the door, we would still be stranded in the center of the enemy army. Nothing to do for the moment but wait and conserve our strength. The space was cramped, but most of us managed to snatch a few hours of sleep where we could, even if that meant slumping against the person next to you. I wasn't sure if Stein found any sleep, but he did make a surprisingly good pillow.

I was startled awake by a noise, wood scraping on wood. Early morning sunlight was staining the sky through the hole in the roof, and the fire had burned down to coals. The noise had come from a slot beneath the door, which had been pulled back to allow a tray of food to be pushed through, along with a pair of water skins. The others were stirring, and soon we were all regarding the tray, piled high with bread and hard cheese.

"Do you think it's safe to eat?" Erika asked, eyeing the food hungrily.

"If they wanted to kill us, they wouldn't need to rely on poison." Maki reasoned, taking a large bite from a heel of bread.

Never one to pass on food and unable to find fault in his logic, I joined him, with the others following suit. If death were coming for us, I'd rather face it on a full stomach.

We had barely managed to finish our breakfast before they came for us. The door creaked open, revealing the hairless woman from last night, flanked on either side by armed ghouls.

"The Grand Scapula has summoned you to answer for your crimes. Who will be the first to be judged?" she asked.

No one moved for a moment, then Stein stood, straightened his armor, then strode forward, his gait stiff. He paused before stepping outside, turning back to regard us.

"If I don't come back, look out for each other," he ordered, then he ducked under the low doorway and into the morning light.

An hour went by . . . and Stein never returned. When the woman came back for another victim, nobody volunteered. The woman didn't wait long and pointed to a soldier at random, who was seized and dragged away by the ghouls that accompanied her. He never came back, either. And so it went, the woman returning at intervals; sometimes an hour would pass, and sometimes it felt like she had only been gone a few minutes. Frida was dragged away, then lunch came soon after, more bread along with some kind of salted meat, maybe pork.

Four prisoners remained when the bald woman pointed her finger at me, and the ghouls closed in. Fear coursed through my chest, but I had seen how futile resisting was. I hopped up, raising my hands in surrender and stepping towards the door.

"Good luck," I called to those left behind, now whittled down to just Maki, Erika, and a soldier whose name I didn't know. The shack that had once seemed cramped now felt cavernous with the void of those missing.

"You as well, little courier!" Maki put on a good show of cheer, though even he was not immune to how grim our situation had become. "I will see you on the other side of this, eh?"

I squinted in the harsh sunlight of a new day and pulled my coat tighter around me. The strange, half-buried construction of the camp served as an effective windbreak, but the air was still holding onto the previous night's chill.

"You must get cold dressed like that," I observed conversationally, glancing at the woman's bald head. "You should ask your master to get you a hat."

No response.

"What happened to the other prisoners, the ones you took before me?" I asked.

Again, silence.

"Do you have a name, at least?"

"My designation for the duration of this campaign is Translator PH-453, but I ask that you not address me directly. I serve only to be a conduit for the will of my masters."

"That's a bit of a mouthful. I'm just going to call you Phillis." I needled, trying to antagonize her enough that she would let something slip. "Oh wait, even better, I'll call you Phase, cuz the four-five-three part would look like letters . . . if you squint. It's a shame you didn't get better letters; we could do like a four-five-five—" One of my guards raised a hand to strike me, and I quieted down. The slim chance of getting something out of this woman wasn't worth another injury.

Phase gave me a cold stare but didn't take the bait. Having failed to gather any information that way, I tried to take in every detail of the camp as we walked, the sunlight giving me a far better opportunity to map the camp's layout than I'd had last night. It was a bustling place too; the sounds of construction and labor had echoed through the camp without stop since we had first come upon the place; no need for work breaks when your laborers never tired or slept.

My captors led me back to the abomination's tent, the black and gold even more striking in the sunlight. Our guards stepped aside, joining the two standing at attention by the entrance to the tent.

"The Grand Scapula Ramses will ask you questions, and you would do well to answer truthfully. He is famed for his ability to sense untruth, and you would find his methods of punishing lies . . . unpleasant," she warned, though it felt that her statement was more a form of intimidation than it was a sign of honest concern.

But, ready or not, it was time to face the monster. Phase held a tent flap aside, and I straightened my back, marching into the gloom beyond with all the false confidence I could muster.

XXXVI

The interior was dark, the only light available streaming in from the open tent flap behind me, stretching my shadow ahead. Phase stepped in and let the flap fall back into place, extinguishing the light completely.

Every instinct told me to run, to bolt for it and make my escape. I resisted the urge with difficulty, forcing myself to wait as my eyes adjusted to the darkness. We were in a small canvas antechamber, with the barest hint of green flickering from the gap beneath the curtain drawn across the far side of the room. After a moment, Phase stepped forward, placing a hand on my shoulder and ushering me into the main room beyond. As I pushed the curtain aside, I found myself in a larger space awash in the verdant light emanating from the chest of the Abomination. The creature that called itself Ramses crouched behind a broad wooden table, sitting upon a strange, saddle-shaped chair that must have been built to accommodate its twisted anatomy. I heard movement from a corner and noticed a section of the room piled high with rugs and cushions. The skeletal children nested there, heaped on top of each other like rats, their green-spark eyes tracking my every movement.

For all the horror, the most off-putting part of the scene was it appeared that I had caught the monster in the middle of . . . paperwork? He had a quill in his hand and was writing away at a roll of parchment illuminated by his own internal glow. The bastard didn't even stop working when I entered, scribbling away for long minutes while I stood at attention. In the oddest way, it felt like I was back in class, getting called into the headmaster's office for a scolding. After letting me sweat for what felt like hours, Ramses lay the quill down, leaning back to stretch his over-long arms before beginning to gesture at Phase in that strange sign language.

"The Grand Scapula Ramses bids you welcome. He had heard of your kind, those who ply the ice in sleds pulled by the Undying. You call yourself 'Couriers,' correct?" she asked, relaying his message.

"Yes, I am Archdeacon Winona, based out of Ozero," I answered in a flat tone, careful not to give any more information than necessary.

"Have you seen much of this land?" she asked next.

"More than most, less than some." I was trying to be cagey, but it was hard to beat a skeleton's poker face.

There was an awkward silence after that, the three of us regarding each other carefully before Ramses began to sign again.

"My poor, stupid child, you think you are so clever. I am . . . ageless. I have studied texts from before the fall and spent more time in forgotten libraries than you have spent living. If you were twice as smart as you thought you were, you still wouldn't be half as smart as you needed to be to match wits with me."

Oof, that was quite the burn. This creature certainly had a way with words. I'd give him that, at least.

"Your crimes are myriad, courier. The other prisoners I have questioned, their crimes are of a passive nature. They merely existed in an empire built on the slavery of the Undying. But you . . . you are the slaver. You have yoked the Undying, forced them to work like animals pulling your sled. What do you have to say in your defense?"

Gods, that was a loaded question. There was no way I was going to come out of this looking good, so I might as well just shoot for honesty and gather what information Ramses might let slip.

"Sir, we have never seen the green flame in our lands before, never known its influence. You yourself spoke of what happens when a ghou—an Undying one, is separated from that flame. My people have never known them as anything but beasts, creatures whose sole objective was to consume. We thought that the soul fled when the body died. We didn't . . . " I faded off, unsure how to continue.

Ramses clicked his knuckles together rhythmically *clickclickclickclick* and Phase let out an emotionless laugh "Hahahaha."

The bastard was *laughing* at me.

"You are still unsure, it would seem. You do not know what we are." More clicks, more laughter. "Are we a new intellect? Or are we the same souls that once left our bodies? Tell me, courier, do you want to know if I can remember who I was before I died? What would that revelation mean for the religion your empire holds on to so tightly, I wonder?"

As much as I was desperate to know the truth, it wasn't hard to spot the creature's attempt to manipulate me. Coming to terms with the idea that the ghouls might still be . . . people to an extent, I don't know what that would do to me. But it wasn't something I wanted to try dealing with while Ramses grilled me for information. So, I deflected.

"On the topic of who you were before death," I began carefully. "I can't imagine that your living body had such . . . magnificent proportions."

Ramses stood and came around the table, knuckle-walking toward me until he was less than a meter away. Even with his hands planted on the ground, he still towered above me.

"I have served the Continuum faithfully for many decades, child. And the Continuum, in turn, has rewarded me for my service, molding and altering my form so that I may better serve. It is the greatest honor that can be bestowed on an Undying, to have our bodies elevated beyond the frail echoes of our past."

Ramses made a gesture, and there was a rustling, then a clank of metal on stone as two of the skeletal children dragged out a thick bar of pitted iron. Ramses proceeded to pick it up at both ends, then bent it in half with a screech of tortured metal. He tossed it aside with the same contemptuous ease, though the bar was so heavy that I felt the vibration when it struck the ground.

Champ was one of the strongest skellies I had ever seen, and he wouldn't have been able to put the slightest bend in a bar that thick.

"I hope this puts your situation into perspective," Phase continued as her master signed. "We are smarter than you, we are stronger than you, and we are inexorable."

"So, what do you want from me?" I asked, seeing no other option but to feign cooperation.

Ramses gestured to Phase, who moved to a corner and pulled on a length of rope. Some hidden mechanism ratcheted above, and a section of canvas ceiling above pulled back, letting the sunlight in. Ramses moved behind me, placing a giant hand against my back and leading me to the table he had been working at.

"You are not the first courier I have had the pleasure of meeting. Clever, resourceful little creatures you are. I like to think of you as little foxes. Like foxes, you know there are far more dangerous predators than you in the wild, and your survival depends on being smarter than those predators. I require knowledge, young one. The knowledge only a courier would have. If you can provide that, we will see about pardoning you of the crimes you have been charged with."

Spread across the table was a map of the Empire, drawn in stunning detail. Not just every city, but every town, even most of the smaller hamlets that the regional maps routinely missed. There were mountains, forests, and rivers, all labeled in elegant script. Phase withdrew a folder, and placed two thin sheets of paper down, rotating them into place to highlight routes connecting the various cities. One sheet detailed a section of the Empire's eastern shoreline; another covered the mountain lands further south. I wasn't familiar with either of those areas, but I knew enough to guess that those overlays must be secret courier routes. I also spied my own ledger on his desk and cringed inwardly at the information a creature like Ramses might be able to extract from it.

"You are not the first courier to stand before me. The others were . . . stubborn at first, but they found their voices in time. Sadly, they destroyed their documents before capture and could only recall routes closer to their home bases. But you said you are of Ozero, yes? That is . . . quite a bit closer than the cities the others called home. I wonder what you can recall."

His grip tightened, fingers encircling my neck with room to spare.

"If I tell you what I know, what happens then? You just let me walk out of here?" I asked skeptically.

Clickclickclickclick

"Maybe I would lie to another, but I believe you to be far too clever for such blatant deceptions. No, you will not be released: You have proven yourself able to bypass our encirclement of Skyroost, and I will not risk you alerting the rest of your empire to our presence. Instead, I will reward your aid with a gift far greater. You will be allowed to join the ranks of the Continuum."

There was an awkward pause, and I looked over to regard Phase. "I don't think I could pull off the shaved head look, no offense," I told him.

"Oh no, you are far too valuable to join the living chattel. We will release you from the bonds of mortality, and you will rise again as one of the Undying," he explained.

"Oh . . . Well, that is quite the honor," I stalled, wracking my brain for a way out of this.

The grip tightened further, and I could feel my gorget creak with the strain. If Ramses decided to exert his full strength, the thin armor wouldn't stop him from popping my head like a ripe berry.

"You make a compelling argument, Grand Scapula. I can't say that I am eager to accept such a . . . change, but I'm not stupid, and I know what refusing means. I will give you the routes I can remember, though I do not have the documents on me," I relented. With no other option, I would have to give him something to earn his trust, to buy myself more time. Hopefully, the opportunity to escape would present itself if I could just survive long enough.

Ramses released his grip on me, and Phase spread a new sheet of paper across the northern portion of the map, from Skyroost to Ozero. I took the quill and began to draw, connecting points of the map. If the bastard wanted courier routes, I would use his own ignorance against him. I kept the routes around Skyroost close to what I remembered but omitted the cliffside path I'd told Stein about. None of the other paths would help the ghouls attack Skyroost, but if Ramses sent men to confirm them, he would find the trails where I'd drawn them. After that, though, I let my imagination run wild. One route would lead across a lake that was notorious for thin ice; another path snaked under that glacier I had passed below, though I made sure to add a few wrong turns that would leave them hopelessly lost in those deep caverns. Ozero had some thickly forested areas that would be difficult to cut—

A sense of movement behind me, then blinding pain, lighting up the right side of my body from hip to shoulder. I was flying, spiraling through the air for a moment before I slammed back into the cold earth.

"You insolent *bitch*," Phase hissed, emotion evident in her words for the first time. I wasn't sure if the words were her own or if she just agreed heartily with the translation of her master.

I groaned, slowly levering myself onto my hands and knees. The abomination had slapped me, blindsiding me with a swing of his massive hand. Pain stabbed through my side whenever I took a breath, and at least one rib was likely cracked. If his hand hadn't been so broad, or my clothing hadn't been so thick, the damage could have been crippling. That hand encircled me again, lifting me into the air. The grip sent more bolts of pain through my chest as I struggled vainly, Ramses dragging me back to the table with little apparent effort. Phase placed a new sheet over the map, this one already covered with routes.

"That was a test, one that you have failed, little courier. One of your captured Undying was quite eager to give us the information we desired, and I trust his honesty far more than your own."

Ramses discarded me with a flick of his wrist, tossing me back to the exit. This time I was ready and managed to roll with the impact, though it failed to completely negate the pain of the landing.

"You would have been an asset to the Continuum, so we set up this test to see if you would be willing to collaborate with us. Such wasted potential . . . Bring her to a holding cell for execution." Phase waved a hand and spat the dismissal.

A moment later, the strong arms of the ghoulish guards yanked me to my feet, eliciting another yelp of pain. Pushing the discomfort aside, I walked under my own power, stumbling towards the exit of the tent before the guards could exacerbate my new injury further. Ramses and Phase were already deep in conversation, my presence immediately forgotten.

XXXVII

The cage they threw me in was a far cry from the accommodations I had shared with the other prisoners prior. On one side of camp, the ghouls had carved deeply into the hillside, leaving a sheer cliff of frozen earth. At the base of this wall, shallow caves had been dug, their mouths lined with metal bars to form individual cells. It was into one of these dark maws that I was thrown, the cage door slamming shut behind me. Most would consider me shorter than average, but even I had to bend forward to avoid striking my head on the stone ceiling, which slanted down to meet the floor at the far end. Cold, muddy water pooled on the floor in one corner, forcing me to press into the opposite side where the uneven ground offered a dry island to sit on.

"Well . . . shit," I swore dejectedly, bumping my head against the wall again and again in frustration. Now that the meeting with Ramses was behind me, I found my options swiftly shrinking. My best chance to break out had likely been when all the prisoners were still together. One of the soldiers could have subdued Phase, and Stein might have been able to destroy our guards with my coalknife. But even then, we would still have found ourselves stranded in the middle of the enemy camp, with only a single tiny weapon capable of harming our captors.

I briefly debated shifting that knife to the inside of my sleeve for easier access, but these guards had already hauled me around by the arms more than once. If one of them noticed the extra bundle under my sleeve, it would give away the last card I had to play. Instead, I settled the belt a bit higher across my stomach; the last thing I wanted was for some guard to spot the thing dangling below the edge of my coat.

So, it would all come down to the execution then. If Ramses had simply wanted me out of the way, he would have snapped my neck like a twig without delay. Opting instead for an execution meant he wanted a spectacle. If it were in any way like the executions I'd seen before, he'd want to march all the prisoners out and make a big speech espousing the virtues of his "Continuum" before killing us by noose or blade. I would love to sink my coalknife into Ramses, to watch the purple flames eagerly consume his form, but I had seen how fast his little shield bearers reacted to a threat; they had deflected a crossbow bolt and killed that soldier in a heartbeat of furious motion. There was no way I was getting into stabbing range, and even if I could, his massive strength would flatten me in an instant.

If I couldn't get to him, my last hope seemed to lie with Phase. Maybe I could cut down a guard and take the woman hostage, then do . . . something? The plan felt flimsy even to me. Ramses hadn't treated her as anything more than a pet, and I had no idea if threatening her life was enough to force his hand into letting us go free.

But I didn't have a lot of other options. Maybe Stein or Maki would come up with something better. Maybe their own deceptions would play out, and they could get close enough to make a move.

Too many fucking maybes.

There was nothing more I could do now, though I briefly contemplated attempting to dig my way under the bars before accepting the absurdity of the idea. So instead, I prepared for the oncoming shitshow as best I could. First, I checked over my wounds; the graze on my arm, the new colony of bruises forming from the impact of Ramses' hand, and the ribs underneath. Taking a deep breath was uncomfortable, but it seemed like I had avoided any broken bones. Overall, the injuries hurt like a bastard, but none would slow me down if I were willing to push through the pain. I took what rest I could, curled up in the corner, knees against my chest and arms wrapped around them to conserve body heat. True sleep escaped me, but I floated just below the surface of consciousness, conserving energy for the trials to come.

After an indeterminant amount of time, a rattle of bars stirred me back to wakefulness. I lifted my head blearily to see one of the guards, a ghoul I'd dubbed Broken Skull, placing a tray of food into the cell, accompanied by another translator, this one male, his head shaven bald like Phase's.

"The execution will take place soon. Eat, The Grand Scapula wants you to put on a good show. Gather your strength, make peace with your heretic gods," he intoned before stepping away.

I shuffled over to the tray, guessing from the angle of the sun streaming in that it was just before sunset. I only hoped that the oncoming darkness might aid whatever escape plan presented itself. The food was surprisingly hearty, including a hot stew of beef, potatoes, and carrots. They hadn't given me a spoon, so I slurped right from the bowl, luxuriating in the warmth that filled me. A heel of bread looked like it could withstand some travel, so I tucked it away for later; if I did manage to break free from the camp, who knows when I'd be able to find another meal? Something about the thought of a full stomach nagged at me, but the feeling slipped away a moment later.

After that, I did a few easy stretches, working out the kinks and warming up my muscles best I could.

Not long after, Broken Skull came to collect me, glaring at me for a moment, then signing angrily. The translator walked up beside him, looked into the cell, then gave a soft chuckle and extended a hand to the guard. The ghoul grumbled petulantly but dug a thick, gold coin out of a pouch and dropped it in the translator's hand.

"My silent friend here just lost a bet," the translator explained. "He believed that none of the prisoners would touch the food, fearing poison, but you all devoured your meals like the wild beasts you are. At least you will die with a full stomach."

A full stomach . . . poison . . . a full stomach . . . the henbane! I still had the henbane, the small vial forgotten in the excitement.

The ghoul opened a small hatch in the doorway, then signed to his translator.

"Put your hands through the hatch," he instructed.

Alarm bells rang in my head, but I quieted them after a moment of panic. I needed to think.

The henbane was a gamble. Maybe the painkiller would give me the edge in my escape, or maybe it would leave me a half-conscious sheep stumbling blindly toward the slaughter.

The ghoul pulled a long hardwood baton from its belt, then rattled it across the bars, a threat that required no translation.

A tincture like that might take time to digest. I can't just guzzle it a moment before my escape.

I began to walk towards my captor, taking each step slowly, deliberately.

It's gotta be now or never. There's always a way out if you're willing to pay the price. But is this the right price to pay? The right risk to take?

. . .

. . .

Fuck it.

I began to cough, an ugly hacking sound that did not take much effort to fake. Turning around, I trotted over to the remains of my meal and bent down to retrieve a half-empty mug of water. A little sleight of hand slipped the vial from my shirt and the contents into the mug.

Medicine never tasted good, but the flavor of the henbane was so heinous that I almost spat it out on instinct. The liquid was horrifically bitter, almost acrid, but the smell was worse, like rotting fish and rank body odor.

On the plus side, the disgusted look on my face sold the lie that I had just coughed up something nasty, and the ghoul seemed none the wiser as I placed my hands through the hatch.

Broken Skull pulled my vambrace off, then brought out a pair of manacles connected by a short chain. He affixed them with quick, practiced motions, only releasing me from the cell once he had double-checked that my restraints were locked shut. It was a stroke of luck that I had decided not to move my knife, as it would have been discovered otherwise. The manacles did leave me unable to draw the weapon from its place on my back, though, so it wasn't all good news. But hey, at least I'd face my execution while absolutely blitzed on berserker poison, which was . . . good?

Other cells were being opened as well, and I recognized Stein, Frida, Erika, and a few others. We were shoved together, and I did a quick head count. There were eight of us now, leaving six unaccounted for, Maki among the missing. We were herded off before I could ponder their absence further, leading us to a section of camp we had not yet seen, situated at the lowest section of the hill. As we descended, I realized that the enemy camp reminded me of a giant tadpole, with the body of the camp thinning into a long tail that cut across the valley. I had to bring my eyes back to the ground as we continued, though; the long sloping path was thick with patches of ice, and trying to keep my balance was even more difficult with my hands bound.

"I hope you have a plan," Stein muttered, using a stumble on the ice to inconspicuously move up next to me.

"I was gonna say the same to you." I managed the summon a grim smile, but having my hands bound made the situation feel even more hopeless. "You wouldn't happen to have a hidden talent up your sleeve, would you? Maybe you moonlight as a lockpicker?"

"Heh. I wasn't always a sergeant, led quite the life before I found my way to Skyroost, but no, nothing that would get these manacles off," he sighed.

"Well, the best play I can think of is to make a grab for one of the translators, maybe hold them hostage."

Stein gave me a skeptical look, and I shrugged. I knew how thin the plan was.

"Damn it. I don't have anything better. Let's spread the word." He moved away, slipping further down the line as I dropped back to talk to the captives behind us.

Erika was stumbling along, head down, and I wrapped an arm around her in support, using the moment of closeness to whisper in her ear.

"Get ready to run. Just stay glued to Stein or me when it kicks off. We'll keep you safe," I murmured under my breath.

"I'm . . . I can't do this, Winona. We're going to die here," she whispered back, voice quavering and hands gripping my arm with white-knuckled intensity.

"Listen, I know it's scary, but I've survived worse. This doesn't even make my top five." I lied, pulling her closer. "Ghouls have been trying to kill me for years, and they haven't succeeded yet. Just watch me and stay close when we make a break for it."

A guard seemed to notice our hushed conversation, so I gave Erika one last reassuring squeeze, then moved back in line.

With one final twist of the path, the camp opened further, revealing an amphitheater of earth and wood set into the hillside. On the high slope of the hill were rows of terraced seating that led all the way down to a circular arena, with small green fire torches spaced at set intervals to blanket the entire space in light. On the opposite side of the arena was a raised dais, crowned with a throne resplendent in black metal and gold filigree. Ramses was already perched on the seat of honor, his light spilling out across the terraced seats, and his shield bearers crouched at his feet like loyal hounds. He was flanked on either side by two figures, one standing, the other given a chair of the same black and gold style.

The figures gained detail as we moved closer until I could identify them. The standing figure I recognized as Phase, that bald head was easy to spot in the green light. The other looked vaguely familiar, though his face was obscured as if he were wearing a mask . . . .

"Oh, you rat-fuck bastard," I growled.

King, the leader of my team, sat in the place of honor at the right hand of Grand Scapula Ramses.

XXXVIII

Well, that answered two questions that had been nagging at
me. First, I now knew who had given Ramses the courier
routes. Second, I could also now confirm that these ghouls were not
inhabited by the souls of the people who had died. I knew who King
had been when he was still alive, and that man would have spat in the
face of anyone willing to collaborate with these monsters. Though,
that did mean that whatever King was, he still must have been able to
recall memories from before he was "awakened," which had all sorts
of terrifying implications. Regardless, there was clearly some form of
intelligence behind his eyes, even if it were just a twisted mirror of
the man King had once been.

Contrary to his usual attentive stance, the "awakened" King reclined
in his seat, one leg causally thrown over the chair arm as if he were
a drunken reveler enjoying the festivities. I hadn't realized that I had
stopped walking until a guard poked me in the back with his spear
butt, growling until I started moving again.

"That ghoul next to the leader, isn't that one of yours?" Stein moved
back beside me.

"Yup, I don't know how smart that green fire made him, but clearly,
he's clever enough to remember the routes I showed him and to switch
to the winning side," I trailed off, struggling to separate this creature
from the leader of my team or the human that once lived. I had fallen for

the same trap many other couriers had, getting too damned attached to a ghoul. At the end of the day, King had been nothing more than a beast of burden with a particularly useful skillset, and pretending he was anything more was an act of sentimentality I could ill afford now. The prisoners were led down to an open platform at the bottom of the terraced seats where a roughhewn log had been mounted at waist height. We were directed to line up in front of it and place our manacled hands on the rough wood. Then a skelly came by with an armful of metal hooks shaped like crude horseshoes and simply pushed them into the wood, pinning the chains of our manacles against the log. It was a crude form of restraint, but I could not deny its effectiveness. I gave a quick tug against the hook when I thought no one was looking, and it didn't so much as wiggle.

"Don't pull," Stein whispered beside me, having had the same idea. "Twist it back and forth. Maybe we can loosen them." I nodded, then passed the instruction down the line.

The ambient noise slowly grew as the seating behind us filled in, though the cacophony was far removed from any human crowd. Instead of the susurration of murmuring voices, there were rasping exhalations from lifeless lungs. Instead of the soft vibration of footfalls, there was the clack of bone against hard earth.

Eventually, Ramses stood, and the noise behind us petered out in seconds. Usually, I would expect a leader to raise his voice or bang a gavel to be granted silence, but it was clear that the absolute power Ramses wielded required no such aid.

"We are here to welcome our new brothers and sisters to the Continuum and to punish those who would seek to threaten our sacred order," Phase called out, her voice carrying across the space as she translated Ramses' hand signs.

The crowd roared, those without lungs stomping their feet to show approval.

"But we are not the ones who bind with chains! We are the ones who break them!" Phase roared, real passion entering her voice. Given that she wore a collar and I was manacled to a log, I found the statement slightly hypocritical.

"So, we will not curse these wretched souls to bondage! Instead, their fate will be determined in the Circle, where they will be given the very same chance that they stole from you! Let them fight! Let them fight and earn their freedom!" she crowed.

The mass of ghouls behind us couldn't effectively jeer, but they showed their displeasure in other ways, including throwing clods of dirt that rained down around the prisoners. It was a clever ploy Ramses had here, this "Circle." Give prisoners the illusion of hope; give those watching the illusion of fairness. But Ramses had no such need to lie in private, and he had told me himself that this would be an execution. A guard came up, pacing down the line to the far side of the log and unlocking Erika's manacles. The girl rubbed her sore wrists but had little time to recover before the ghoul grabbed a fistful of her hair and dragged the screaming girl toward the pit.

"Hey! She's not a soldier! She's not part of this! Let her go!" I shouted, pulling uselessly at my restraints until the skin on my wrists was raw. Stein took up the cry, but the ghouls carried on without hesitation.

Erika was dumped on the ground by the rim of the pit, where a rope ladder dropped about three meters to the floor below. She very clearly did *not* want to climb down, but the spears at her back presented little choice in the matter. Erika gave us all one last look, and my heart broke for the fear in her eyes. The girl was putting on a brave face, but it wasn't hard to see the tears brimming.

"Hold on," I mouthed to her, then went back to work, desperately trying to pull free of my restraints.

"Here stands a servant of the Osgil Empire! One who serves the whims of those who would enslave us even as she herself is shackled by disparities in wealth and class! But does she understand that we have all been wronged by the injustice in this land? Does she choose to join the Continuum? No! This woman continues to hold loyalty to this corrupt domain! Well, let her fight in the Circle and see for herself if her precious Empire will come to save her! Her opponent is a recent addition to the Continuum, an Undying once forced to work under the yoke of the humans, and now eager to prove his loyalty!"

From a long tent near the raised dais, a ghoul emerged, this one a bleached white skelly still marked by its imperial harness. I had not been watching them closely at the time, but from the livery, I would guess it was one of the ghouls we'd used to operate the crane. The creature could have easily leapt the distance to the ground but instead descended a ladder opposite Erika.

"Our new brother is a weapon unto himself, but our poor prisoner has no such advantage." Phase declared with mock sympathy. "Let us show that we are not without understanding for the weakness of her pathetic form."

A guard tossed something into the pit, a thin silver shape that clattered to the ground midway between the two combatants. The amphitheater echoed with the knuckle clicks that the ghouls used in place of laughter.

"Sick bastards, they gave her a fucking bread knife," Frida growled, stretching against her bonds to peer into the pit.

"Begin!" Phase shouted, and Erika startled at the noise, pressing herself against the wall as if to make herself a smaller target.

It should have ended right there; Erika was paralyzed with fear, not even trying to make a grab for the pitiful weapon her captors had supplied. I'd never seen a ghoul fail to make a meal of such helpless prey until now. Instead of an all-out attack, the ghoul approached her with something akin to caution.

"ERIKA!" I shouted hoarsely. "Fucking MOVE!"

Erika snapped out of her trance and dove for the knife, scrambling in the dirt, then bringing it up in a clumsy, two-handed grip, the tip pointed toward her opponent. Amazingly, that brought the ghoul up short.

"What's going on here? That thing should be all over her." I wondered aloud, yanking uselessly at my restraints.

Stein was silent for a moment, ruminating on the question as the combatants warily circled each other.

"I think . . . well, they act like people, right? They think they *are* people," Stein pondered. "They were . . . What? Dead, sleeping? Then that green light hits them, and they're back? Awake in a damn corpse. The only thing that kept your ghoul King from finishing me off was the light hitting us. He was going at me as any ghoul would, but the light made him stop, hesitate. Gave me the opening to throw him off."

"I don't follow." The skelly was closing the distance with noticeable caution, backing Erika against the wall.

"What I'm saying is that this skelly might have all those memories of being alive. Even if I were nothing but bone, I'd still be real careful getting too close to a big knife if I remembered being human."

Stein was right, a point proven moments later when Erika, cornered and fear-crazed, went on the attack. Screaming in terror, she darted forward, swinging the knife back and forth in clumsy arcs. In response, the skelly did more than just retreat; it fully panicked, falling back and scrambling on the ground to get away. Emboldened by this reaction, Erika waded forward, swinging wildly until she landed a solid blow, the blade thudding into the vertebrae of its neck as it tried to stand.

Both froze, a momentary tableau caught mid-combat. The ghoul raised a hand to where the blow had been struck, then looked at it in surprise as if expecting blood. It repeated the gesture, then fluttered its fingers as if noticing the bones for the first time.

Slowly, the creature began to walk forward. And the next time Erika swung, it flinched but stood its ground. The knife slammed into the creature's hip this time, chipping away a sliver of bone but doing no real damage.

The skelly looked down at its own scratched pelvis, then back up at Erika.

It charged.

The girl managed to land another frantic strike before the creature slammed into her, sending them both tumbling to the ground. Before she could swing again, the skelly clambered on top of her and wrapped its hands around her neck.

Then it ripped Erika's head off.

The skelly yanked up, skin and muscle tearing as her head was pulled away from her body. It was not quick, like an executioner's sword, not clean, like a hanging. Blood was everywhere; on the ground, on the ghoul, on what was left of the woman.

More than one prisoner vomited, leaning over the log and losing the remains of the hearty meal they had been given. The skelly, it seemed, was equally horrified. It dropped the head, still connected to the body by a few strips of viscera, then stumbled away, slapping at itself in a hopeless attempt to wipe red blood from white bone. Phase ordered the panicked skelly to return to the tent, but it was deaf to the order, pressing itself against the wall and feverishly grabbing handfuls of earth to scrape the blood off., Two guards were forced to descend into the pit to contain him, but he lashed out madly, cracking the sternum of one before more guards piled in. The last we saw was it being carried into the tent, still struggling even with four ghouls, each holding it by a limb.

"The whole world's gone fucking mad." I heard one of the soldiers mutter next to me, his beard stained with vomit.

"Congratulations to the victor!" Phase called out. "The awakening can be a difficult adjustment for some. The strength and influx of sensation can be . . . overwhelming. We wish our new comrade a speedy recovery."

It took me a moment to realize that Phase, and by extension Ramses, were giving words of comfort to the same ghoul that had just torn a girl's head off as easily as a child twisted the head off a doll. Heat flushed through me, sweat pricking my skin under the layers of cloth as blood pounded in my ears. With one foot on the log, I heaved against the restraint again, not even trying to hide my actions. The hook didn't shift in the slightest.

Then the guards came for the next person in line, Frida, the engineer. Phase gave another brief introduction, denouncing Frida as "a builder of the Empire's cruel war machines" and pairing her against another of the captured ghouls.

When the engineer was tossed in, a metal hammer was thrown in beside her. Stein confirmed that it was a common engineer's tool, so it seemed to confirm that our captors were returning the items they had confiscated upon our capture. Frida had a chance, at least. Without balefire, she would need to dismantle the ghoul, crushing joints until it could no longer physically move; a long shot, to be sure, but her hammer might have the heft to make it happen. Knowing her survival lay in swift victory, she attacked, driving the ghoul back until the hammer slammed into the junction of collarbone and arm with a resounding *Crack!* The joint wasn't entirely broken, but the arm hung low at an awkward angle. The ghoul stepped back as Frida swung again, the hammer missing its target by centimeters.

And then it was over,

Without the expected impact to halt its momentum, the hammer continued its arc, pulling Frida off balance and momentarily drawing her focus.

This skelly's response was lightning fast, throwing a wild haymaker that slammed into Frida's side just below her armpit. The blow lifted her off her feet and hurled her to the ground over a meter away. She lay there for a moment, then pressed one arm into the ground to lever herself up. Frida began to rise to her knees, then . . . stopped. She wavered, staring blankly at the earth, then collapsed back to the ground, unmoving.

The slaughter continued. The next victim was a young soldier, a heavyset boy no older than sixteen. He never even tried to go for his weapon, instead turning tail and making a running leap for the lip of the pit. Shockingly, he actually made it, finding a foothold on the uneven wall that he used to push himself upward. His fingers just barely caught the wooden lip of the pit, and he pulled himself up, feet scrambling in fear as he heard the ghoul in the pit closing the distance.

He never saw the guard standing over him or the spear that lanced down to plunge through his neck. Gravity took hold, and his body flopped lifelessly to the ground below. At least it was quick.

We kept working at our bonds whenever we thought our guards were watching the fight, but the hooks holding us were driven in too deep. Maybe, *maybe*, the last few soldiers in line might be able to pull free before their time came, but the rest of us would be dead long before that. And even the ones that freed themselves would have little hope of salvation.

The next soldier maintained his composure, scooping up a short spear and hurling it at Ramses. The weapon arced towards the great abomination, on a perfect course for the green flame brazier in his chest. I didn't know what effect damaging that cage might do, but we would never find out. The shield bearers rose in a wave to deflect the weapon, then cascaded into the pit, burying the man in a seething mass of tooth and claw before his opponent could even react.

"I guess that's it then," Stein murmured, now the next in line, looking at the empty manacles stretching out in front of him.

"No, no, I can get this loose!" I hissed, yanking at the hook, the skin around my wrists worn bloody. There was movement now, a minuscule shift, my constant twisting beginning to weaken the wood's grip on the hook.

A guard casually strolled over, placed one foot on my manacles, and stomped down, driving the hook down even deeper than before.

"NOOO!" I screamed, seeing red, flailing against the bonds.

"Winona . . . Winona, look at me," Stein murmured softly, nudging me with a shoulder. I picked my head up with effort, wiping the snot and tears off my face with a grimy sleeve.

"It's OK, kid. We've done our part. It was all looking grim before you showed up, Skyroost was on the edge, and it wasn't going to get better. But then you came, and now they have medicine and—" He looked around. "—that other thing you found. At least there's some hope, even if it's only a fool's hope."

"You're pretty good at speeches." I gave a weak laugh, feeling the hot teardrops roll down my cheeks and turn cold before they reached my chin. I wanted to say more, to comfort him, to bolster him, anything, but the tears were coming faster now, turning into sobs of hopelessness.

"Good luck to you, Winona. Now ... let's see if this old bear has one last fight in him."

XXXIX

Stein caught the longsword that was thrown to him, hefted it with easy familiarity, and drew the weapon free from the dark blue scabbard mottled with the stains of hard use. It was a beautiful weapon, though of an uncommon design. Most rank-and-file soldiers were given simple short swords with broad, chopping blades. Nobles might use a longer blade, but they generally preferred rapiers, which were seen as more stylish and unobtrusive. This sword was longer than the short sword and thicker than the rapier, the double-edged blade tapering to a triangular point.

"For our next contest, we have a commander of the enemy army. A man who has not only fought the Undying but directed others of his kind to do so. His orders have brought untold suffering to those on both sides of this war." Phase announced, eliciting an even fiercer negative reaction from the crowd than that garnered by the previous prisoners. Stein made an admirable show of ignoring them, though I couldn't imagine that even a hardened fighter could entirely tune out the undead cacophony. Ramses raised one massive hand, and the crowd quieted.

"But his opponent will not be one of the Undying he sought to enslave, like our new brothers that have proven themselves in the previous bouts. He shall instead face a traitor from our own ranks! One who was rewarded by his superiors and given the Change to better serve the Continuum. But this child has squandered his gifts, seeking self-enrichment at the expense of the cause. I give you Commodus, The Shamed!" Phase proclaimed.

The ghoul emerged from the tent at a jog, pushing one of the guards away before leaping into the pit. It landed on one knee and slammed one oversized fist into the ground to punctuate the impact. The body was nearly skeletal, though skin still clung to its ribs and head, time and the elements reducing the flesh to the texture of dry jerky. A horseshoe of long stringy hair trailed down to his shoulders, circling a bald spot that showed patches of skull through the skin. Like Ramses, this ghoul had been . . . altered, though not to as extreme an extent. The "Change" Phase mentioned must have been their name for whatever heretical magic they used to alter the form of a ghoul, and it was evident in this creature's arms. The right arm was miniaturized as if the limb of a child had been grafted on, and the ghoul kept it tucked protectively against his chest. In contrast, the other limb was massive. In many aspects, it was like Ramses' own, an assembly of oversized bones which formed an arm that stretched down past the ghoul's knee. Each fingertip ended in a talon, black and curved like that of a bird. If the jeers had been loud for Stein, they were riotous in reaction to this newcomer. Rocks and clods of dirt rained down into the pit, and even Ramses needed to slam a nearby gong with a skeletal fist before the noise was returned to a more reasonable din.

Stein still maintained his composure through all this, and even I was surprised that his stoicism had held in the face of this monster. His mouth moved as if he were talking to the weapon, but whatever he was saying was lost in the clamor. Then he sank down into a fighting stance, leaning forward onto his bent left leg, sword held close, the tip facing out at a forty-five-degree slant. Commodus might be the dead one here, but the ghoul paced and twitched like a rabid animal while Stein remained statue still.

"Begin!" Phase barked.

Commodus showed none of the hesitancy the other ghouls had.

He dug those talons into the ground, then used them as an anchor to launch himself forward, bounding across the distance between them in the span of a heartbeat. Mid-leap, he thrust the arm forward, sending his razor-tipped fist flying toward Stein's face.

"HAH!" Stein barked, stomping his lead foot forward.

The movement was so quick, so precise, that I nearly missed it. The tip of the sword lashed out, swatting the hand aside. There was no way to halt the ghoul's momentum, but the move had shifted the attack enough for Stein to move clear, swaying like a reed in the breeze. Effortlessly, he turned the defensive move into a powerful counter, twisting the blade into a horizontal swing that passed through the ghoul's empty belly cavity and *thunked* into its spine. Commodus flailed, the blow seeming to impact with far greater force than I had expected. Stein slid the blade free and spun with a dancer's grace, pivoting to face the creature again as it tumbled end over end.

"That's the trick, isn't it?" Stein called out as the ghoul hopped back to its feet. "You're strong as an ox but light as a feather. I doubt those dry bones are a third as heavy as I am."

Commodus rushed again, and Stein stepped forward to meet him, jabbing the tip of the blade toward the ghoul's head. While the thrust couldn't have done any real damage, Commodus reared back instinctually, unable to avoid flinching away from the flashing silver blade. Stein stabbed forward, capitalizing on the opening and driving the tip into the ghoul's eye socket in a powerful thrust. Commodus flew back, his feet leaving the ground with the force of the blow.

"You've got all the strength in the world; you'd rip me apart in a grapple. But without anything to grab onto, you're outmatched," Stein growled, his breathing barely increased from the exertion.

I had to wonder why Stein was narrating his fight, why he was telling his opponent exactly how he planned to counter the ghoul's monstrous strength. Then he glanced up, catching my eye for a moment before returning his concentration to the fight. The bastard, he was doing it for *us*. Giving the remaining prisoners knowledge and a chance at winning their fights even as it put him in danger.

Commodus sprinted forward again; Stein switched stances to meet him. A meter before impact, the ghoul drove his oversize claw into the ground and pole-vaulted over it, slamming a kick into Stein's chest. Commodus used the arm like an anchor, pushing off it to leverage his full strength into the blow and send Stein tumbling backward. The ghoul closed in for the kill, and Stein barely managed to scramble up and dive away from the follow-up strike. Commodus wasn't giving him any room to breathe now, slamming him about with shoulder charges and kicks, using that damned arm to plant himself for every strike, knocking the man around like a ragdoll. Stein faltered, the tip of his blade dropping as pain and fatigue overtook him. Commodus jittered in anticipation, dancing from foot to foot. When Stein tripped over a divot in the earthen floor, the ghoul launched a lethal haymaker without a moment's hesitation.

Stein spun into the ghoul's reach—his movements quick and precise—feigned fatigue disappearing the moment Commodus took the bait. They were so close now that the ghoul's momentum sent him stumbling into Stein's back, giving the absurd impression that he was embracing the soldier like a lover might. Rather than fall beneath the ghoul's weight, Stein put all that energy to work. He grabbed the oversized arm and pivoted, throwing his body forward and taking the ghoul with him. He completed the throw as Commodus flew over his shoulders, slamming the ghoul violently into the ground. The creature might not have felt pain, but the sudden lurching spin must have been disorienting, and Commodus took a moment to steady himself before trying to rise.

Stein did not give him that moment.

In a move I had never seen before, Stein's grasped his longsword by the blade, lifted it above his head, and swung it down like a sledge-hammer, the cross guard of the sword hammering into the ghoul's lower spine.

Crack!

Then again, Commodus now flailing.

Crack!

And once more, swinging wildly as the ghoul began to stand.

Crunch!

The vertebrae of the ghoul's spine shattered. His top half fell one way. His bottom half fell the other.

The crowd went so silent; you could have heard a pin drop.

I don't know why Stein paused at that moment. Maybe it was hard to believe that a creature could be a threat after being cut in half. Maybe the beating he had endured was finally taking its toll. Regardless, Commodus seized the opportunity. His hand lashed out with the speed of a snake, tightening around Stein's leg and pulling him close enough to bite down on the man's calf with rotted teeth.

Stein screamed in pain, stumbling back, dragging the half-skeleton with him as he tried to escape the hold. Commodus released the bite but used that iron grip to pull himself close again, sinking his teeth even higher into Stein's leg. The man's cries intensified even as he pushed through the pain and tried to free himself. First, he tried to pry the hand away with his blade, but the massive fist's grip was so tight that Stein cut into his own flesh with the tip of the sword. Commodus was tearing away at him now, ripping away chunks of meat until his teeth were stained red with blood.

Stein pulled away again, then stopped, his whole body tensing as he planted his injured foot, fighting the panic. Stein raised his sword above his head, one hand on the grip, the other on the blade just past the cross guard.

"Die!" Stein hollered, stabbing down into the ghoul's scapula, the point skittering off the flat plane of bone. Commodus ignored him, ripping out a gobbet of leg muscle.

"Die!" Stein's yell broke into a pained sob, the sword point finding purchase and sticking into the shoulder until he worked the blade back and forth to dislodge it.

His wounded leg collapsed, and he fell back into the wall, pressing hard onto his good leg to stay upright.

"FUC-KING-DIE!" Stein cried, stabbing down, his whole body collapsing as the sword fell one last time.

Neither form moved for a second, merely lying motionless in a jumbled pile. Nobody spoke, nobody moved, nobody even breathed, though I guess most of the spectators no longer needed to anyway.

Then . . . movement. Slowly, achingly, Stein began to crawl, pulling himself away on his hands and elbows. Behind him, Commodus lay broken. His shoulder lay in pieces, the massive arm now detached and floundering like a beached fish. The shrunken arm still flailed on his other side but accomplished little other than to carve futile furrows in the dirt. Grimacing, Stein pulled his belt loose and fashioned it into a rough tourniquet just above the wound.

The man stood, pressing the point of his sword into the ground for stability. His wounded leg was nearly useless, but he managed to hobble over to Commodus, avoiding the detached lower half that had almost managed to stand before toppling over again. The ghoul's teeth gnashed frantically, head craning to follow a target it could no longer reach. Balancing on his one good leg, Stein raised his sword, arm shaking until the point aimed directly at the sitting form of Ramses. The shield children reacted to the perceived threat, piling into a wall in front of their liege as if Stein could have leapt the distance to strike at him.

Stein managed a grim smile, his own teeth stained red from some internal injury. Then he brought the sword down, hacking into the back of Commodus' neck. After the second strike, the bone shattered, and Commodus' skull rolled away from his twitching body.

Stein growled something weakly, the satisfied scorn evident even if the words were inaudible, then fell back against the wall, sinking slowly to sit on the ground.

XL

———

Attendants filed into the pit with haste. A pair of humans loaded Stein onto a stretcher, though they needed a guard ghoul's assistance to lift him out of the pit. Another ghoul clamored down moments later, hauling a large wicker basket into which Commodus' still twitching remains were placed. The ghoul's severed limbs would continue to move indefinitely after the separation, though scholars had never been able to figure out if a ghoul were still aware or in control of these separated limbs. Commodus did not seem to be in the mood to answer that question, though, gnashing his teeth so hard that he almost rolled out of his basket.

I knew what was coming next, but my mind seemed unwilling to grasp the idea, sliding off the realization of my impending death as if it were made of ice. Anyone, anything was better to think about than the rapidly approaching conclusion to my story.

As Stein was carried away, I wondered what his fate would be. Would they bring him to a healer? Did they even have healers in this army? Or would they be more concerned with trying to get all the King's horses and all the King's men to put Commodus back together again? And Stein had been bitten . . . The necrotic magic would grow like an infection, stretching black fingers up his leg, toward his heart. He needed an immediate amputation, physically separating the infected limb before the magic spread to the rest of the body. If Stein didn't get that leg chopped up soon, he wouldn't live long enough to worry about his other injuries.

A shadow swept over me, bringing me back to the present as a guard ghoul approached. Numbly, I held up my manacles for release. Instead, the ghoul grasped the short length of chain and pulled, yanking the hook out of the wood while keeping my hands bound. Instead of being allowed to walk, I was dragged, the ghoul's draft horse strength pulling me bodily over the log, then dumping me at the ledge where the rope ladder was tethered. I raised my hands in one last attempt to get the manacles removed, but another guard approached with a wooden baton, clearly ready to provide some encouragement for me to get moving. I scurried down the ladder before he could draw closer; climbing with my hands bound was a challenge, but the guards seemed more than happy to fling me into the pit if I didn't comply.

While the workers had removed the previous bodies, they had neglected to do anything about the blood and various bits of viscera scattered about the circular arena. Something squished under my foot as I stepped forward, and it took a conscious effort not to look down and see what I had trod on. Under the guise of stretching, I tried to reach for the coalknife nestled against the small of my back. It was hopeless, though; the short chain made reaching behind me impossible; if I hadn't repositioned the weapon while I was in my cell, I might have been able to reach it now. Instead, I was defenseless, with salvation stuck mere centimeters away.

All of it felt . . . a bit surreal, to be honest. This whole time I had expected an opening, a chance, some strange cosmic possibility that would allow us to make a dash for freedom. At least, that's how the stories always went. Maybe I was a bit too old for stories, a bit too jaded to believe in those twists of fate that always saved the heroes, but I had honestly thought I would pull through this one by the skin of my teeth, just like all the times before.

At least I didn't hurt anymore. The accumulated aches of the journey had been a constant nuisance, slowing me down, making me just a hair clumsier than I should have been. Now, the memories of that burden felt distant, indistinct. The pain, the exhaustion, the cold; all of them tried to sink their claws into me, all of them failed. The potent cocktail of henbane and adrenaline coursed through my veins, soaking me in a heat that battered away any sense of frailty.

It brought a manic smile to my face for a moment, and I surrendered the last of my fear to the fire in my blood. A half-mad bark of laughter spilled from me, and it felt good. There was nothing left to do but the doing, and I would not face the end cowering for Ramses' amusement.

"And now, we have a special treat!" Phase announced, more animated now than during the previous fights. "Here we have a true monster, a living, breathing symbol of the corruption that has taken root in these forsaken lands. While all the captives brought before you today have supported this corrupted regime, this 'courier' is a true slaver, wielding the yoke and the lash to subjugate your brethren!"

The crowd jeered, and I hollered back at them, a raw animal howl. The ranks of the dead had become blurred in the flickering firelight, their outlines indistinct as if each wore the burial shroud they should have been entombed with. By contrast, the arena was in sharp detail, the grand brazier like a verdant sun casting its rays down on me.

After a moment to allow the crowd's jeers, Phase cleared her throat to continue, but Ramses cut her off, signaling her and passing a message through a quick series of motions. Phase moved away, and I lost sight of her, the depth of the pit keeping me from being able to see anything farther back in the camp. She returned almost immediately, though, leading two prisoners. At least, I thought they were prisoners. I couldn't see any chains or manacles. Instead, they were led forward by a thin length of colorful cord that was looped loosely around each of their necks. Both wore simple robes identical to Phase's and shuffled after her with the slow gait of sleepwalkers.

Ramses soon made their purpose clear, scooping up one prisoner in a single giant hand and lifting her to his mouth. The woman didn't even have time to scream before he bit down, severing her arm in a fountain of blood.

"UHHH . . . Uuuhh . . . ," the woman gasped, floundering in his grip.

They must have drugged these two before they brought them up. That woman should have been screaming bloody murder, not mewling as if her fatal injury was a stubbed toe. Ramses rotated his meal to take a bite from her leg, then another from her side. The chunks of flesh fell uselessly from his mouth, but I could see the sparks behind his eyes flare with renewed energy. Like all ghouls, these creatures didn't need to feed, but it was clear that these sentient monsters took a sort of pleasure from the rush of energy they drained from their victims. Regardless of intellect, Ramses did share a trait with his mindless, feral cousins; he had no self-control when it came to feeding. The woman's twitches were already subsiding after a few bites, blood loss claiming her. With a casual wave, Ramses flung the corpse away as carelessly as if he were tossing aside a chicken bone.

Then he waved to Phase, who led the other slave over to King.

"Oh Gods," I whispered, turning away as King began to lift his mask up.

Whatever King proceeded to do, it certainly was not quick. The weak, confused moans of his victim seemed to continue for an eternity, though, in reality, it could not have been more than a minute. By the time I turned back, King was seated again, his mask back in place. The mask could not hide the blaze of green fire in his eyes, though, or the dark blood staining the chest of his coat.

"As I was saying!" Phase continued. "We cannot allow this . . . slaver, this forger of chains to go unpunished! Let her face her opponent manacled so that she may understand her crime of binding the Undying to servitude!"

The crowd cheered at this; their vigor instantly restored to a fever pitch once again.

"We find ourselves truly blessed tonight, my friends! Because here, now, we bear witness to this courier, her punishment doled out by the very same being she chose to enslave."

There was a flash of movement, and a ragged shape dropped into the pit, turning the landing into a tumble that brought it back to its feet in one smooth roll. I regarded the familiar ghoul, taking in the new gleam of green fire behind its eyes.

"Hello, Scramble," I muttered.

XLI

————

A guard tossed my long knife into the pit, and I watched it tumble end over end until it stabbed into the dirt an equal distance between us, but closer to the wall than the center of the pit.

"The beings you tried to enslave are still recovering from their awakening," Phase told me, gesturing to Scramble, then to King. "It will take some time for them to fully recover their faculties from the long slumber you imposed on them. But each has begun to remember some small element of their former selves. By our laws, each was given an opportunity to address the one that wronged them before we mete out your punishment."

She removed a rolled length of parchment, then turned her attention to Scramble.

"From this one, who has yet to earn his name or prove his loyalty: Hey kid, it looks like I get a second chance at living, and that's more than most get. But sadly, you're in my way. I think I remember you, but everything is still foggy. I don't think you were a bad person, but it seems like we're on different sides of this, and I ain't dying again. So, it's nothing personal. I'll try to make it quick." Phase finished, the casual cadence of the words seeming awkward on her lips. Or maybe she was just uncomfortable with the idea of Scramble not immediately condemning me for my wicked ways.

Then she turned to King. "And from this one, who, by virtue of the vital information he has contributed, has been granted the right to take a Name of Antiquity so that he may live on forever like the conquerors of old! He has taken the name Wallace and been granted the position of Third Carpal under Grand Scapula Ramses."

"To the fire with him and all the rest of you!" I spat, but was ignored. It felt like the floor of the pit had tilted, like Scramble was standing downhill and I was wavering on a cliff edge. It would only take the slightest effort to move forward, to tilt and fly down towards him.

"Third Carpal Wallace states: Your path has been altered; every route twisted to lead you to this judgment. You believed there was a way out, a way to survive. Now you must pay the cost. I wish you the bravery and stoicism to face the pain ahead."

It seemed like the malevolent spirit that now inhabited King's body fancied itself a poet.

"Goodbye, courier," Phase announced a moment later, then waved her hand. "Begin!"

Scramble moved to close the distance, but I was buzzing with energy, moving even as the first syllable left the translator's mouth. Realizing he would lose the race, the ghoul changed his angle slightly, moving to tackle me as I stopped to retrieve the weapon. I didn't stop, though, couldn't stop, the heat inside me demanding motion. As Scramble leapt, I dropped, sliding across the blood-soaked ground feet first. The wild slide nearly careened me into the knife, but I managed to pop up with it in hand at the same second Scramble rolled back to his feet.

"COME ON!" I yelled, running to close the distance. Rage flooded me, and maybe it was the drugs or the dead prisoners, or just my mind finally snapping under the pressure. All I knew was that I would bring this creature down if I had to rip him apart with my fucking teeth.

The ghoul retreated from the attack as if he were still human, but I could tell from the tilt of his head that he was glancing down at his skeletal hands as if trying to remind himself that he no longer had flesh that a knife could harm. Even if I managed to land a blow, he would just get to that realization sooner, so instead, I stabbed outward, aiming to *just* miss him. He gave ground, and I followed, striking with short jabs that never quite connected. His panic was fading, though, and Scramble's movements became more fluid, relaxed, both hands up like a boxer as he bobbed back and forth.

For a moment, I thought I could keep him at bay long enough to think of . . . something, anything, some way, some hope. But then he countered, ducking below one of my stabs and delivering a devastating right hook to the body. The strike was too quick to avoid, but I dropped an elbow to block while twisting my body to absorb the force of the blow. If a human had punched me, the defensive reaction might have let me shrug off the hit and reply with a counter of my own. When the punch came from a ghoul like Scramble, my reaction barely kept the blow from crippling me. I was thrown across the arena, rolling, falling, then stumbling again until I fetched up against the far wall.

There should have been pain pulsing through my arm, sharp and searing, but all I felt was a dull ache. That . . . that wasn't right, though. My breath came in short sharp inhales as if my chest were in a vice. The arm I'd used to block the blow felt sluggish as if it were half listening to the orders I was giving it. The heat in my chest was faltering, a deathly cold edging in, darkening the corners of my vision.

I could have pushed through, but . . . what was the point? I fought an opponent I could not physically harm, and the greatest irony was that I had a coalknife that could end the fight in one cut if my hands weren't bound.

I was going to die here. Even worse, I had handed them King on a silver platter. Now they had every damn courier route they could ever want. They knew every path to take.

Your path has been altered.

King's words came back to me, quiet through the numb haze in my head. But it wasn't Phase's voice I heard. No. Instead, I heard the message in the voice of a man, the man King had once been.

Every route twisted.

Scramble was moving in for the kill now, hands still up in a ready stance, even though I was lying in a senseless heap on the ground.

A way out, a way to survive, now you must pay the cost.

And there it was, something important, something I had missed. Or maybe it was madness, my drug-addled brain making wild connections in the last moments before death, desperately flailing for a way out. But I remembered something then, a quick snap of memory that I had never thought to reflect on. When Ramses had shown me the map King had drawn, when he had triumphantly thrust my face towards it to witness his victory, the route between Skyroost and his camp had been missing.

I had instructed King in every route. He knew every path to or from Skyroost, including that one. But Ramses' map was missing that one critical detail. His map was wrong.

And that meant there was hope, if only a fool's hope. And that cut through the despair, dispelling it just enough to rekindle the fire and beat back the darkness.

So, to take stock:

Hands: Bound

Weapon: Out of reach

Allies: Injured, dead, or far, far away

Plan: Nonexistent

Fucks given: Zero

Bravery and stoicism to face the pain.

I latched onto the thin hope as if it were a lifeline, pulling myself back to my feet as Scramble closed in. The coalknife was the solution, and the manacles were the problem. I didn't have the strength or skill to free myself from my shackles... but I wasn't the only one in this pit, was I?

An idea bloomed, but it was going to hurt. I wasn't sure how much more punishment I could take, but my battered body didn't need to last forever; it just needed to last long enough.

Letting Scramble get within arm's reach was terrifying, and I pretended to shy away, coiling myself into the corner like a compressed spring until he cocked back a fist to strike. Then I sprung forward, driving the long knife into the space where his groin would have been.

Scramble did not have any groin to speak of, and the knife failed to even chip the bone, but I couldn't imagine a man, alive or dead, that wouldn't instinctively react to an attack between the legs. Scramble seemed to agree, leaping clear then backpedaling furiously as I followed, his own imperviousness forgotten in the heat of my renewed assault. When his back hit the opposite wall, I leapt up, wrapped the short chain behind his neck, and yanked, kicking my feet against his pelvis as I hauled back with all my strength.

The skeleton was strong as a bull but light as a feather, just like Stein had demonstrated in his fight. Scramble tumbled over with me, rolling on the ground until I came out on top.

"Just like old times!" I laughed maniacally, throttling him as if he had a windpipe I could crush. It was mere theater. My hands could never break the thick vertebrae of his neck, but I was gambling it all on the hope that Scramble, in his panic, would react like a man, not like a ghoul. Instead of taking a bite out of me, he did what any person would do when a wild-eyed woman was trying to strangle him. He pushed me away.

His hands slammed into my chest with an audible crack of breaking ribs, and I shot upwards in a parabolic arc, flying halfway across the arena before crashing down on my side. I had goaded the attack, wanted it, but no amount of preparation could save me from the ruinous cost. Even through the henbane, I knew that I had damaged my body at a fundamental level. My breath came in short, ragged gasps, my body instinctively trying to breathe shallow enough to keep the broken ribs from doing more damage. I coughed weakly, and tasted blood.

My vision swam as I pushed myself to my feet, the sight of Scramble racing towards me seeming to double, then stabilize, then double again. I could see the wild haymaker coming a mile away, but my body lagged, and the dodge was more of a controlled fall, barely slipping under his strike as he flew by.

Scramble planted his foot and whirled for another punch. My back was still turned to him. I was wide open for the killing blow.

Then his severed arm thudded to the ground by his feet.

"Thanks for the help," I coughed weakly, brandishing my bloody hand, coalknife clenched in it. When Scramble had pushed me away, the manacles had drawn tight around his neck. In a tug of war between metal, bone, and skin, my skin had lost, and my hand had been ripped free of the manacle, allowing me to finally retrieve my secret weapon and deal the deathblow. Purple flames were already spreading, flaring both at the end of his severed arm and at the stump of his shoulder. Scramble could not scream, but his jaw hung open in wordless pain. He smacked at the flames in a panic, trying to smother them even as the purple fire eagerly leapt to consume the bones of his other hand. As the balefire light flared, I was blindsided by a wave of mental noise. The purple light had connected me to the ghouls, and the influx that struck me was louder and more complex than any I had felt in my life. The brutality, hunger, and determination were familiar to me; those were the deep drum beats that pulsed in every ghoul's mind. But now the green fire had given them life, and the balefire let me feel the full depth of their sentience. There was anger and sadness, frustration and remorse, deafening melodies I had never experienced through the balefire bond before. Scramble's panic, Ramses' fury, a thousand unfamiliar voices shouting in my head.

But above them all, one familiar voice rang out louder, bellowing a single world over the cacophony.

WINONA!

For a moment, Scramble was a walking pyre of balefire, every eye in the arena on him.

Except mine.

I turned and threw the coalknife with all the strength I had left, the exertion taking the last of my gathered concentration as I willed my free hand, skin flayed off by the manacle, to just give me this one last action. Falling to my knees, I watched the glittering blade spin away towards the dais, lit by fire; purple on one side, green on the other. Ramses' shield bearers were already reacting to the threat, piling on top of each other to form a bastion of iron and bone between the knife and their master.

The knife whistled right past them, straight towards King, who plucked it deftly out of the air.

Even as the darkness began to claim me, I still managed a hacking laugh at the poetic justice of it all. If Ramses hadn't given King a meal to bolster his energy, I doubt my ghoul would have had the speed or dexterity necessary to make the catch.

Either way, the shield bearers were out of position now, and even their panicked reaction was just a hair too slow. King dashed forward, slipping inside the protective bastion around Ramses.

In the roiling storm of movement that followed, I did not see the blow that felled Grand Scapula Ramses, The Heart of the Shield Swarm, and owner of a dozen other opulent titles. All I witnessed were single moments, static images between lethargic blinks of tired eyes. Ramses lit from below by purple balefire, sinking as if he were dissolving into the floor. Shield bearers scattering, some leaping onto their master's funeral pyre while others scuttled for cover. King leaping down into the pit, coalknife in one hand and Ramses' green fire brazier clutched in the other.

Then another light flashed from the tree line, accompanied by the sound of thunder. A tiny shooting star leapt from the spot, lancing through the air overhead at an incredible speed. A muted *whoomph* of explosive force reverberated behind me, and I saw the besieging army's grand brazier listing, a huge chunk of its base blasted away. The massive structure tilted further, then began to fall, slamming into the ground in an impact that flattened tents and sent a meteor shower of green coals spraying out over the rest of the camp. One coal landed near me, and I watched in a haze of delirious pain as it lay smoldering in a little divot of earth before going out with a smoky hiss. I looked around at the destruction, managed one last bloody smile of grim contentment at the mayhem I had wrought, then let the darkness come rushing in.

XLII

Recovery from my ordeal had been its own journey, and not a pleasant one. Worse than the pain though, was the boredom, day after day with nothing to do but think in circles. The invasion of the Continuum obviously raised questions. How had such an enemy gone unnoticed until now? Where did that green fire come from? If they were funding bandits, did that mean that they had already infiltrated the Osgil Empire in other ways?

These questions were troubling, but not nearly the worst of it. Now that the threat was known, the full power of the Empire could be directed towards learning the enemy's secrets. No, this journey had shaken the foundation of everything I had ever been taught, of all the facts I had never thought to question, and those whispers of doubt in my head were far more insidious. I remembered Zeb's sculptures, all replicas because the ancient metal had rusted away, but I also had my goggles, and Foss's pistol, pre-cataclysm artifacts that looked almost pristine. I'm sure the elements accounted for much of it, but something about the contrast felt wrong. There was also the outpost battle, where we fed hundreds, if not thousands, of ghouls into the fire. In my years as a courier, I had seen a dozen ghouls consumed by balefire for every one person bitten, so where were the dead bastards coming from? Yes, there was an infinite sprawl of empty wilderness to the east, but the Continuum had me doubting just how empty that space might be.

Suffice it to say, a month in Skyroost's largest hospital hadn't been long enough to mend all my wounds, but it was certainly long enough to start me planning my escape, "bed rest" be damned. First, there had been the necessary recuperation, as the injuries I had sustained proved to be a more effective prison than the guarded doors of the hospital. I'd reopened the wound on my arm, though that had been the easiest to mend, and now a line of scar was all that remained to mark the injury. The violent pull of the manacles being yanked off my wrist had also torn the skin off my hand like peeling a potato, dislocating my thumb, and cracking two of the small bones on the way through. Recovery had been slower than I would have liked, but I was just glad that I would retain full use of the hand. The most grievous damage had been dealt to my ribs, though, which had taken not one, but two direct hits from Scramble's massively powerful fists. Three ribs were broken, another two cracked, and there was nothing the healers could do other than offer cold compresses and various herbal concoctions meant to dull the pain. Some of those tasted so bad I almost would have preferred the dull ache of healing bones. It almost made me miss the henbane, but, true to the healer's warning, the concoction had left me weak as a newborn kitten, and I'd spent the first week of recovery lapsing in and out of consciousness.

It would still take longer for the aches to subside, but I had mended more than enough to get out of this room, doctor's orders be damned. Yes, I was allowed supervised walks around the hospital and the nearby courtyards, but it still felt like I was trapped in a cage.

I feigned sleep as an orderly came in to check on me, sheets pulled up to my neck as I lay on the hospital bed. Her contented humming marked her location as she walked around the room, picking up the platter with the remains of my lunch, then glancing over at me one last time before exiting the room. I gave the receding footsteps a moment to fade, then slid out of bed as quietly as could be managed. My private room in the quiet wing of the building had been a godsend, but you never knew when a healer might poke their head in. With that in mind, I jammed the room's solitary chair under the door handle, buying me a bit of time in case someone came knocking. Then I slid the topmost layers off the bed, revealing the trove of gear that I had secreted away between the mattresses. It had taken a fair bit of doing to collect, but the healers were still busy with the casualties sustained during the Continuum's assault on Skyroost. Thankfully, nobody seemed to be keeping track of where inventory went, or they might have figured out that a sizable portion of the blankets and changes in clothing I had requested had mysteriously disappeared.

Looking at the mass of cloth, I realized in a rush how selfish I'd been. Everything was in short supply in the city, even with the siege broken, and these blankets could have gone to better use. There was nothing that could be done now, but I made a silent vow to correct my oversight and pay back the hospital in some way.

Feeling slightly deflated, I donned the extra layers now, knowing that I would need every scrap of cloth. It was a mild winter day in Skyroost, which just meant that your spit would freeze on the ground instead of in midair. A firm knock rattled the door as I wrapped my feet in leather, the kind of knock that was a warning before entering instead of a query for permission.

"Uh . . . Don't come in. I'm—" I looked around the room, searching for inspiration and noticing the chamber pot peeking out from under the bed. "—I'm shitting . . . " I called halfheartedly, recognizing the force of that knock as belonging to one Captain Calliope Deimos, recently arrived with the bedraggled remnants of the outpost survivors. The reinforcements from the south had made it to the outpost, having never encountered the Fin raiders that had allegedly been sighted in the area. The horde was still pooled around the fortified keep and far too large to destroy, but the rescuers were experienced northern folk and managed to draw enough of the ghouls away to evacuate the survivors. The original force at Outpost 305 had been nearly wiped out. It might have been a total slaughter if not for Calliope's unit, who had run into the church's attaché while retreating to the keep. Between the discipline of her soldiers and the Balefire Church's mastery over the flame, the combined group had been able to fight its way to safety. Thankfully, Rimkus, Dupont, and Blondie were in that group, and had all survived. Calliope's unit hadn't escaped unscathed, though; many had been dragged down in that last desperate sprint for the keep, including Curtis, the plain-spoken but kind leatherworker I'd met.

Calliope had let out a frustrated sigh when she had first seen my wounds and declared herself in charge of my recovery. I couldn't deny that she had been helpful in that regard; upkeep of the body was a cornerstone of Mycenean culture, and she had passed on a variety of useful, if slightly torturous, stretches.

I retrieved a coil of knotted bedsheet, tied one end to the bedframe, then tossed the makeshift rope out the window. We were only on the third floor . . . it would be fine.

Calliope tried to open the door, failed, then threw a shoulder against the wood, causing the door to shake briefly. That felt a bit aggressive, but in her defense, this also wasn't my first escape attempt. Last time I'd nearly made it to the front door before being spotted by Calliope's keen eyes. Credit where it was due, she soon managed to break down the old chair I had used to block the door, thundering in just as I mounted the window frame.

A gust of cold, thin air blew in, sending cloth billowing. I breathed deep of it, letting it chase away the stale scent of sick and soap that permeated the hospital.

"Sorry, captain, but the Balefire Express is long overdue! High time I got back to work!" I laughed, then leaned back, repelling down the makeshift rope towards the ground below. It was smooth sailing until one of the sheets ripped, but hey, I was only about four meters up at that point, and the fluffy snow drifting against the building created the softest landing pad I could have asked for.

Pbbbsttt! I spat, shaking the snow free as I waded out from the drift, brushing myself off and strolling away as if nobody on the street was staring at me. I ducked into an alley for a moment, then leaned heavily against the wall and tried to force down the bands of pain constricting my chest. My ribs were making their protests known, and it felt like I was once again breathing through a vice, but I was confident that I hadn't reinjured anything too permanently.

I must have looked like a half-frozen mummy wrapped in that cloth, but I still reached the wall of Skyroost's Yard without being stopped. There would be guards stationed at the front gate, but I knew of a small crawlspace hidden behind a shed that couriers used to sneak in contraband from time to time. The hatch had frozen shut, of course, so I was gently persuading it with a length of wood I had scavenged when I heard a voice.

"Why are you like this?" a familiar voice chuckled behind me.

"Stein!" I cheered, whirling around to face the grizzled sergeant. I knew he had survived but hadn't seen him since that night. As the flood of wounded ebbed, he had been moved to another building for specialized care, though none of the healers would tell me exactly where. He looked healthy enough, except for the one leg which ended just below the knee, the empty pant leg pinned back to keep it from dragging in the mud. Crutches under each arm helped to keep him upright on the icy ground.

"There's less of you than I remember . . . ," I remarked tactlessly, then slapped my hand over my mouth as I realized what I'd said.

"Heh! Good to see you haven't changed. I'm so tired of everyone glancing away or avoiding the subject as if I don't know my own leg's missing," he laughed.

"I saw you fight in that pit. Even down a leg, I still wouldn't bet against you. How did you make it out?"

"I'll trade my story for yours," he bargained, turning and beckoning me to follow. "But first, let's get you back into real clothes. They'll have my head if I let the Hero of Skyroost freeze to death."

"If I go back, I doubt they'll let me out," I shot back, looking over at the half-open hatch; maybe I could squeeze in before Stein raised the alarm.

"Don't worry about that. I received a promotion for heroism after the battle, though I wonder if they just want to call me Captain Stein so they can give me a pension and stick me behind a desk somewhere. Either way, I have enough pull to take you out on some 'supervised' light exercise. Gods know we could both use the fresh air. Were you really trying to escape the city?"

I was still tempted to bolt, but the icy wind was already biting through my makeshift garments, and making a one-legged man chase after me felt like it was in poor taste after the sacrifice he'd made.

"I just wanted to get a joyride in. I'm not planning on skipping town, especially now that Rimkus and the other outpost survivors are here. But the engineers were finally able to retrieve the *Ridgerunner* with that crane they built, and she's just been sitting in the Yard gathering dust." After a moment, I relented; if Stein wasn't going to let me make good my escape, then getting to catch up with him would be a decent consolation. "Fine, let's take a stroll, but I need to ask, how'd you find me out here?"

"Oh, that was the easy part. The hospital guards keep me in the loop. They sent a runner when you made a break for it. Wouldn't have caught you, except my lodgings are a fair bit closer to the Yard. Anyway, I knew you couldn't get through the front gate, so heading here made sense," he explained.

"And you just happened to know about a secret smuggling entrance in the wall?"

"Ha!" That was a more genuine bark of laughter, and I was heartened to see a bit of humor in a man who had lost so much. "Some couriers used it to sneak contraband in, right? Well . . . who do you think was buying it?"

Instead of making Stein hobble all the way back to the hospital, he led me to a nearby guard post where he commandeered a set of guardsman winter attire that was slightly too big for me, but it kept out the cold far better than my improvised attire. We were soon walking through the Yard gate, and I breathed in the familiar scent of half-frozen corpses as if it were the headiest aroma.

"Smells like home!" I smiled, even as Stein gagged at the scent.

My team and sled were tucked up against the wall in a secluded pen. The *Ridgerunner* looked pristine under its protective awning, all the exterior damage from the trip repaired by the best craftsmen Skyroost could spare. I had made them swear not to touch any of the interior, but I'd still have a look later to confirm that some items, the hidden coalblade chief among them, had remained undisturbed. My team looked equally well cared for. It seemed nobody wanted to be held responsible for neglecting the Hero of Skyroost's prize ghoul team. Still, despite the care that had been taken, my heart still sank as I took in how small our little family had become.

Bonk, gone over the cliffside when we were attacked. Scramble, destroyed in the pit. And good old Grah, not the brightest ghoul, but he had served his purpose well. I hoped that, wherever their spirits were, they had found peace.

The most worrying ghoul was still present, though, sitting at the back of the pen, eyes watching my every movement.

King.

"I heard they found you both in the woods near the camp." Stein began, phrasing it like a question.

"Yup, I was out cold, swaddled in a length of canvas and close to dying, from how they tell it. Scouts saw the green light and thought it was a counterattack. But they just found me bundled up, and King manacled to a tree nearby, no green fire in sight," I sighed heavily.

"Do you remember anything after the arena?" Stein asked.

"Maybe? Darkness, then being carried, men screaming? Hard to parse truth from nightmare. But I do know that I was in no shape to escape on my own. How did you get out?" I changed the subject, retrieving a balefire torch and opening the pen. I beckoned King out, feeling the familiar orchestra of my team's thoughts, now missing a few key instruments.

"I should've died. The enemy healers they left me with seemed content to let me bleed out and turn ghoul, even after I'd 'won' their contest. When the Skyroost forces attacked, I convinced the healers that saving my life was the best way to make sure their own lives were spared upon capture."

"That was lucky timing on that attack, wasn't it? A few minutes later, and we'd both be dead."

Stein led me to a switchback staircase that crisscrossed up to the ramparts, and I politely looked elsewhere as Stein hopped up the steps one at a time. Offering help to the old bear would just wound his pride.

"Not...lucky," Stein exhaled, taking a moment halfway up to catch his breath. "The weapon you brought to destroy the green fire brazier and that secret route gave the Skyroost forces a pair of trump cards, but once we were captured, they were on a timer. Either of us could have given up the secret under torture, losing Skyroost the advantage of a sneak attack. I'm amazed we managed to mobilize that fast, but the one advantage of heavy losses is that it doesn't take too much time to muster your remaining forces," Stein said bitterly.

"I just wish they'd made it in time to save the others," I sighed, thinking of Erika. They had recovered her remains from the arena, along with the others, once the Continuum had been driven from their camp. There were far too many dead to bury; even with ghoul power, excavating the frozen earth would have been nearly impossible. So instead, we constructed huge funeral pyres, and a few soldiers were kind enough to carry me out past the wall to say my last goodbyes.

Erika...

I was used to death coming to those who fought and braved the wilds; it was part of life beyond the edge of civilization. But Erika, she had been such a force of warmth, of comfort, of joy. That girl had burned so bright in the scant few hours that I had known her, and now it all felt darker with her flame extinguished. I hoped that she, and the other dead, found some small bit of comfort in the fact that we tore down the besieging army's camp to feed the flames. Along with the dead were the innumerable missing, Maki chief among them in my mind. With all the destruction, there would be many families in Skyroost left without closure.

I shook myself from the macabre reverie. Something Stein had said was picking at my thoughts, something wrong.

"Wait . . . my weapon?" I asked. "What weapon?"

"Yes, you certainly kept that card close to your chest, didn't you? Thank the gods they opened that crate as soon as it arrived, or they may not have found it in time. But I guess we were due some good luck," Stein shrugged, standing up straighter and reading himself to continue the climb.

I grabbed his arm before he could start moving, and Stein picked up on my change in demeanor. "Stein, I only brought medicine here. I don't know anything about a weapon."

"Winona, it was in the crate with the medicine. I heard it from someone who was there. They opened it up and found the medicine, yes, but there was another flat wooden box packed beneath it, covered in all sorts of elaborate decoration."

I . . . I couldn't have brought a weapon all this way without realizing it . . . could I? I thought back to lecturing Billy about how you should always know what's inside the cargo you're carrying. Then my memory snagged on another detail, even older: Ronny delivering the crate . . . the crate that was larger than the dimensions he'd given me. It had to be larger to hold the battery, but maybe that extra space had also been used to hide something else.

"That rat bastard," I grumbled to myself, then addressed Stein. "But . . . I saw the explosion that took out the enemy's brazier. You would need a black powder cannon to do that sort of damage. I would have noticed THAT, at least!"

He shook his head, realizing that I truly had no idea what he was talking about. "It was a relic, a weapon from the old world. I heard it looked like a small rocket, like a firework, but with the force of a battering ram contained inside. The metal tube it launched from is hanging over the Duke's fireplace in his manor. I'm sure he'd let you see it if you asked."

I was still struggling to wrap my head around the idea that I'd carried this ancient weapon so far without knowing. What if it had gone off? I'd have been blown to bits before I even knew something was wrong. On top of that, how had Ronny obtained something so rare? Trying to exploit the power of old-world relics had led to more than one execution, and the single hoard of such treasures that I knew of was under guard in the capital.

Then I shook my head and stood aside to let Stein continue the climb. Ronny and I would be having a lengthy conversation about that weapon once I made it home to Ozero; hopefully, I could get to him before my new boss Bishop Rimkus found out. I doubted that the bishop's methods of information gathering would be half as gentle as mine. But for the moment, Ronny was safe, as the bishop was now in Skyroost along with Vicar Dupont. Given that I still had that coalblade in my sled, it was fair to say that I had my own reasons to worry about the bishop, but that was a problem for another day. The bishop was a stern figure, but hopefully, my part in saving the city would balance out the heresy of keeping the weapon if he found out. Hopefully . . . .

Stein began to ascend again, thumping his crutches against the old wood with every step. "But to what you were saying before, I don't think the Skyroost forces could have attacked any earlier. The weapon, the path, they evened the fight, but an even fight with ghouls still would have been a bloodbath. They were waiting for the right time to strike, and you killing their leader was just the moment they needed, though I still can't get anyone to tell me how you managed that particular feat," he regarded me speculatively.

"Sorry, Stein, some secrets aren't mine to tell. Suffice it to say it's hush-hush church stuff," I placated him. The bishop would surely be interested in that story as well, and I was not looking forward to the questions that might arise then.

The vista from the top of the wall was breathtaking, awash with the wild beauty of deep winter. The hours of daylight were brief, but for now, the sky was an endless blue, and the blankets of snow made the world appear as if carved from alabaster. The single aspect that marred the scene was the tendrils of campfire smoke drifting lazily up from where the enemy encampment had been. Skirmishes still flared up from time to time, but the army of the Continuum was conducting a measured retreat, pooling their forces at the far end of their trench even as our soldiers pressed in from the other side. The massive defensive trench had been a deadly bastion when they had us corralled in the city, but that advantage flipped the night that our forces had driven them from their main encampment. Now they were the ones surrounded, and our guardsmen were adapting to this new enemy, using their own tactics against them to tear down their green fire torches and revert the ghouls back into mindless beasts. It was an effective strategy, but it also meant that we hadn't captured any of that heretical fire for closer study.

"Do we know where they're pulling back to?" I asked, hunching my shoulders against the icy wind.

"Somewhere west, towards the ocean. We have a few scouts trailing them at a distance, but honestly, we can't spare enough men to keep a tight net on their movements."

A soldier called Stein's name, an old acquaintance apparently, and I excused myself and walked to the top of a nearby bastion to afford them a bit of privacy. I sat there, tapping one foot, letting the tension build until it was unbearable. Then I let out a deep sigh and turned to face King. I found a slot in the stone to hold my torch, then reached up, gently sliding his hood back. Padded leather straps held the mask in place, and I removed those next, slowly easing the covering off his head. Sunlight touched that face for the first time in months, and I bit the inside of my mouth to keep the tears from coming. The ghoul doc had done his work well, but no science or magic known could halt the process of decomposition forever. Still, he looked good, peaceful in a way. His eyes still tracked me, though, the wind and grit frosting the orbs over like old marbles.

"I've thought about it a thousand times," I told him, taking a step back. "What happened that night, how I survived . . . I keep coming back to the same conclusion. After you killed Ramses . . . you saved me."

King stood there impassively, no recognition in those purple-tinged eyes.

"There was always a way out, a way to survive if you were willing to pay the cost. You taught me those words all those years ago. It had been so long that I didn't even recognize the old lesson at first."

I started to pace, glancing at King, then turning away again, unable to look at that face. "But then I remembered that the Skyroost route hadn't been on Ramses' map; you didn't tell him about it. It made no sense. A random ghoul would have every reason to side with the Continuum, to help them in any way possible. But not you. You would never have given those routes to the enemy. So, we both lied to him, but he believed you because he never could have imagined that you had any reason to lie. After I passed out, you must have grabbed a green fire torch and carried me away from the fighting, though how you managed all that is beyond me. Then you drew the attention of those scouts . . . But you had to know they would have destroyed any ghoul infused with that green light."

My pacing stopped, and I forced myself to meet his gaze.

"The scouts said they found you chained to a tree nearby. They figured that you were one of my ghouls, that I tied you up to protect myself before I passed out. That's the only reason they didn't toss you into a brazier."

I shoved him hard. King stumbled back a step, then righted himself, regarding me with that same blank expression. The outburst gave me no relief.

"You did that! You put the torch out, and before that, you chained yourself up to keep from killing me once the light was gone."

I knew he couldn't hear me now. *I knew.* But still, seeing that blank look . . . Gods, it was like a knife to the heart. My gloved finger jabbed him in the chest. It felt like punching stone.

"You could have run! You could have left me for the scouts to find and had another chance at living! Damn, stupid bastard!" I shouted, voice quavering as I held back the tears.

"Even if you left, at least I'd know you were out there, somewhere. Living, existing . . . whatever! I saw that spark, it was you, you were back! Fuck!" I cursed, shaking him by the front of his coat.

That emotional dam I'd reinforced for so long was cracked clean through, and my voice fell to a whisper as if the slightest noise might shatter it, drowning me in the pain it held back.

"I had you back . . . and now I've lost you all over again."

The deep breath I took should have calmed me, but it came out weak and shaky.

"Sorry. I'm just . . . it's a lot. I don't think we've seen the last of those guys. Ramses talked like he was part of something bigger, and if he was a Scapula, there must be a body of the Continuum somewhere else. I don't know what comes next. There are too many unanswered questions, and if they end up being connected, well, it can't bode well for us. I don't know if this is the last leg of this journey or the first leg of a bigger one . . . But, whatever happens . . . we'll face it together. I'm glad you're with me."

I pulled him into a tight hug, giving a soft mental command for him to wrap his own arms around me. It was a poor imitation of the real thing.

The dam broke, and the tears began to fall.

"Thanks Dad."

Acknowledgements

First off, thank you to my parents, Donald, and Jean, who believed in my creative endeavors even when I did not. I also need to thank Arielle V and Adam K, the brave adventures who waded into the swamp of my early drafts and saw what the story could be. A special editing thanks to my brother Brendan; you didn't always tell me what I wanted to hear, but you always told me what I needed to hear.

Thanks to the team at Stillwater River Publications for their invaluable assistance. To Steven and Dawn Porter for being a light of sanity in the madness that is publishing your first book, to Cecil Shrestha for their editing prowess, and to Elisha Gillette for the absolutely stunning cover art.

On a personal note, a special thank you to insomnia, coffee, empathetic English teachers, tabletop games, and the freezing waters of the Atlantic for providing an endless well of inspiration.

Finally, I need to thank you, the reader. Life gets busy, and there never seems to be enough hours in the day, so thank you so much for taking the time to give this book a read!

About the Author

Donovan Lewis was born in Boston, Massachusetts, and stayed just long enough to pick up an accent and a penchant for reading books past bedtime. After a decade as a pilot, Donovan decided to write a short story and finally put all those daydreams on paper. After two years and over one hundred thousand words, Donovan realizes that the situation may have gotten away from him at some point.

Donovan likes to write in the morning, then spend the rest of the day paddleboarding, woodworking, and climbing on things he is not supposed to.

www.ingramcontent.com/pod-product-compliance
Lightning Source LLC
Chambersburg PA
CBHW030548020726
47494CB00005B/1530